AT

Death
of an Anglo

Bilingual Press/Editorial Bilingüe

General Editor
Gary D. Keller

Managing Editor
Karen S. Van Hooft

Senior Editor
Mary M. Keller

Assistant Editor
Linda St. George Thurston

Editorial Board
Juan Goytisolo
Francisco Jiménez
Eduardo Rivera
Severo Sarduy
Mario Vargas Llosa

Address:
Bilingual Review/Press
Hispanic Research Center
Arizona State University
Tempe, Arizona 85287

(602) 965-3867

Death
of an Anglo

Alejandro Morales

Translated from the Spanish
by Judith Ginsberg

Bilingual Press/Editorial Bilingüe
TEMPE, ARIZONA

ISBN: 0-916950-82-4
Printed simultaneously in a softcover edition. ISBN: 0-916950-83-2

Library of Congress Catalog Card Number: 88-70371

PRINTED IN THE UNITED STATES OF AMERICA

Cover design by Christopher J. Bidlack

Back cover photo by Alessandra Pilar Morales

Acknowledgments

This publication is made possible, in part, with public funds from the New York State Council on the Arts and the National Endowment for the Arts, a federal agency.

TRANSLATOR'S INTRODUCTION

Alejandro Morales's second novel, *Death of an Anglo*, originally published in 1979 in Spanish by the Mexican publisher Joaquín Mortiz as *La verdad sin voz*, is a fictionalized account of an idealistic young doctor's attempts to improve the lives of the Chicano residents of Mathis, Texas, in the early 1970s. Morales, a professor of Hispanic literature at the University of California, Irvine, as well as a novelist, told me at a meeting of Chicano writers, critics, and scholars that he had read about the prototype of his hero, named Michael Logan in the novel, in *Time* magazine. From the bare facts of a case reported there, Morales created a compelling tale of heroism and human failings, both of which are exemplified in Logan, a rebellious intern who seeks to cure his patients rather than grow rich from them.

After completing his internship, Logan rejects the possibility of joining a prestigious and lucrative medical group in Oklahoma, deciding instead to set up a solo practice in Texas and serve a Chicano population sorely in need of medical care. Aware that other Anglo doctors had unsuccessfully attempted to establish themselves in Mathis, Logan is undeterred in his noble efforts. However, his continual difficulties with authority diminish his effectiveness. He virtually abandons his wife and two small children to enter an adulterous relationship in Mathis with the young widow who assists him; ultimately, his serious drinking problem is in great measure responsible for his untimely death.

Logan's chronicler, the implied author of the narrative, an ostracized Chicano academic and aspiring writer named Eutemio, shares much with his hero. Also a creative and dedicated idealist, he too is troubled by the self-interest that dominates his profession, and he rebels against a system that requires him to produce arcane theoretical literary criticism disengaged from the context of contemporary reality and concerns for social justice. Although Eutemio and Logan do not spend a great deal of time together, Logan's commitment to what he believes in, despite the weaknesses that undermine his ability to fulfill his ideals in life, becomes, quite literally, Eutemio's literary inspiration. Eutemio had considered himself a coward, but his contact with Logan enables him to take a similarly defiant stand. His writing becomes his way of attacking the irrelevance and hypocrisy of the ivory tower and, more importantly, of condemning the injustice of Logan's death.

Eutemio's narrative, of course, is *Death of an Anglo*. Written in the aftermath of Logan's murder and burial but before those responsible have been brought to justice, it represents Eutemio's attempt — and on another level, Morales's — to create a literature of commitment; it serves as an elegy to Logan as well. Through the creation of *Death of an Anglo*, Eutemio has also found a way of participating in and to some extent continuing Logan's work and his imperfect but real heroism.

Eutemio's anger is apparent in the text he produces. As a writer he has sought to express a vision that has not been widely accepted among his university colleagues. To be more accurate, the novel makes it clear that his work has been ridiculed by them, and they would prefer that he teach at a less exalted institution — a high school or a state teachers' college, where interests such as his would perhaps find a more congenial home. Eutemio defends the legitimacy of his artistic vision through the aggressive language and subject of *Death of an Anglo*. Although capable of writing correct, standard, albeit colorless Spanish, he chooses to use a more expressive, rebellious, even vulgar language that reflects the truth he wishes to convey about a reality that is harsh, aggressive, alienating, and at times offensive. This translation attempts a faithful rendition of Eutemio's language. In this context, I am most grateful to Alejandro Morales for his careful reading of the manuscript, his helpful suggestions about the translation, and the cordial encouragement he provided throughout the project.

But the story told is larger than Logan's experiences in Mathis and Eutemio's struggles with his pretentious and petty colleagues. *Death of an Anglo* presents a broad view, although an intentionally "shattered" or fragmented one, of a series of disparate and even conflicting elements — Anglo, Chicano, Mexican, Aztec, WASP, humanist, scientific, technological, mythological, artistic, medical; the ivory tower and the barrio, the theoretical and the practical. Some reconciliation of these elements begins to emerge at the end of the novel with the hope that Michael Logan and his chronicler have together begun to achieve

6

a synthesis of the tangle of contemporary American life and the recognition that all these elements can be accommodated.

In addition to Alejandro Morales, I would like to thank Thora Girke of Union College and Karen Van Hooft of the Bilingual Review/Press for their kind assistance in the preparation of this manuscript.

JUDITH GINSBERG
FORDHAM UNIVERSITY

For Albert

It happens at times that in a moment of mystery, in an incomprehensible flash, the spirit expresses its most profound word, the spirit, the instinct, or the subconscious. Then the truth without words, gestures or acts is revealed bitterly to us: we perceive the absence of love or loneliness or disdain or irrevocable loathing.

—José Revueltas, *The Stone Knife*, translated from the Spanish (*El luto humano*) by H. R. Hays (Reynal and Hitchcock, 1947).

I

"Doña Gertrudis, buy these pills and take one at night and one in the morning."

"Thank you, Doctor Hales, thank you very much. Ay, God bless you, Doctor."

The heavy body rose slowly and walked toward the noonday light.

"Be careful, don't trip on the books and equipment on the floor."

"Doctor, why did they do this to you? Why don't they want you here? You should report this to the police."

"Don't worry, Doña Gertrudis. I'll see you next week."

"I hope so, Doctor, adiós."

The blue eyes watched as she was swallowed by the heat; the earth rose like brown smoke deforming the heavy woman: . . . Why don't they leave me alone? The sons of bitches have started . . .

The man in the white coat shook his head, he went into the office; he stopped in the middle of the broken glass and torn books; his eyes dragged his hand to the floor; he picked up the picture of his family, his wife's lips, his daughter Allison's blond hair made him cry; his hands began to pick up a whole broken life; broken by them, by people that didn't understand, that just hated. Salt water, bitter: . . . All that work, all those years, humanitarian fool, stupid, jerk . . . His hands began to tear up that life; they knocked down the tables and chairs; his feet went out the door: . . . What the hell am I going to do? They've hurt me, they've broken the windows in my house, they've thrown rocks at me and now my office. My wife's fed up; maybe she's right; it's better for us to get out of here. I don't want them to hurt my wife and daughter. I've given enough, eight months of humanitarianism is enough. I'm leaving, let them go to the curanderos . . . He took off the white coat and threw it on the floor; he started down the old wooden steps. The faces watched him from the other side of the street. Most of them liked him; the dark faces pursued him: . . . Don't let this one go; dear God, don't let this one go . . .

"Won't another one come, Doña Gertrudis?"

"Yes, this one is leaving; it looks like he has gotten scared; I don't think another one will come."

The Anglo faces watched him walk to his car. They watched him with hatred; they wanted to ruin him: . . . Bastard traitor, Mexican-loving bastard. If you don't get out, we'll take care of your house, and if that doesn't convince you, we'll take care of your wife . . .

"Now Doc's beginning to get the message."

"You're right, Henry; the Mexicans have their curanderos; they'll take care of them."

"I know, Rodríguez; you understand; you're a good Mexican."

"Let's see what he does when he gets to his car."

All along the street the stores were made of white wood; their damp cheeks pressed against their jaws, their teeth were grinding to stop from screaming or crying, they watched with eyes wide with shame. He was stunned by the sight of his car—spat on, kicked in, covered with green, white, and red stripes—its tires punctured. The title of this picture was propped on the windshield: "Greaser Ambulance." His eyes burned.

"Leave me alone! Please don't do anything else to me!"

"Hey, Doctor Hales, now you've got a Mexican car."

"How are you doing, Doctor Hales? If you have any trouble I'm here to help you. Isn't that so, Rodríguez? Go on, Rodríguez, tell Doctor Hales that I'm a good friend of the Mexicans."

They laughed with open mouths; the devil went down the street wrapped in the dirty wind; Pistol Man, laughing, moved away, chatting, his arm around his companion. Rodríguez wanted to put his arm around the doctor, ask his forgiveness, at least help him a little.

Alone on the street, his face grimy, he left the car and started down the road that led to his house: . . . But what do these bastards want? I only came to help these poor people. Why do they want to chase me out of town? That little old man is always sitting there; I saw him the first time I came here with Beesley. He's been sitting there every day under that tree, calm, just waiting, waiting for me, in the morning his eyes greet me; in the afternoon his eyes embrace me and wish me a good night . . .

Now he was leaving the center of town; it pained him to see the house where his loved ones lived: . . . I bet Beesley is laughing. Karen talked with him last night and she told him that they were trying to run me out of town; now he's really going to die laughing. Maybe he's right. I don't get it. What am I to them? . . .

Still quite far from the house that very slowly drew closer, he felt terribly heavy-hearted! The car headlights practically kissed him in the ass; his lungs breathed deeply as he shouted.

"Careful, you son of a bitch! Who the hell do you think you are?"

"Calm down, Doctor, please, calm down. Get in. I'll take you home."

"Rodríguez."

"Yes, it's me."

The car wheels spun the two bodies toward the doctor's house.

. . . Poor Doctor Hales. But what are you going to do? Nothing. It's better for him to get out before they do something to his wife . . .

. . . Why, Rodríguez? He hangs around with these bastards too. He helped me . . .

Suddenly the bodies lurched forward and then hit the back of the seat, interrupting his brain's reverie.

"I almost passed it, Doctor."

Many died in those moments.

"Go, Doctor, leave town."

The car violently bit the road's skin, leaving him wondering in the dust.

"Daddy! Daddy!"

The shouts invaded his mind; the lives that he had in his head spoke to him. His body got down on its knees and felt the impact of the child against his chest.

"Allison."

He felt his eyes and arms close. The high heels clicked, bringing Karen.

"What have they done to you now? They hit you! They hit you!"

"No, they didn't do anything."

"What do you mean they didn't do anything? Look at you!"

"Yes, but they didn't hit me. Please leave me alone, I want to shower. Please, we'll talk later."

"OK, but this is it. If you want to stay here with your poor Mexicans, stay, but I'm going, Leroy; Allison and I are leaving. I'll call Beesley tonight."

The powerful female buttocks ran toward the patio where the sun was playing. Hales, tired, went into the bathroom. His fingers contemplated the shirt buttons, they undid his pants; his feet kicked his shoes into the corner; a hand affectionately took hold of it and he urinated.

"Manolo, how do you like it?"

"Oh, how pretty and what pretty girls."

The Mexican bullfighter strolled slowly, enjoying the Newport beaches.

"How do you feel?"

"Fine, but if the damned gringos throw bottles I'll never come back. That blond's a doll. Look at her!"

The arm reached out to get the faucet; the water sang, its stream splashing him with wetness: . . . Maybe Karen is right, screw them, I have to think of my career, my family. What if they kill me? . . . If they kill me? Shit, they really could kill me . . . No way . . . His penis was hard; the water gushed over it; semen flowed from it: . . . Karen, your body, your legs . . . He covered it with soap: . . . Will she suck it tonight? . . . His head white with soap closed its eyes; his hand covered his chest with the white foam: . . . He was frightened, naked, wet, blind, if someone were to come in with a knife. To open his eyes and through the clouded glass see a stranger, standing there . . . How many years of study, and what crazy ideas I have, but who is going to help these poor people? Maybe that's how it's got to be . . . He dried his hair, his neck, his chest, his ass; he wanted to take a shit but he didn't let himself; the clean legs left with the man so that his hands could dress him.

"Leroy, dinner's ready. Allison, go and wash your hands."

"They're clean, Mommy."

"Wash your hands, Allison, please! Sit down, Leroy."

"Are you going to call Beesley?"

"Yes, I told you that I would."

"Good."

"Did you wash your hands, Leonor?"

"Yes, Mamá."

"Good. Sit down. Your father's home and we are going to eat soon. What are you thinking about, Fernando?"

"Nothing, dear, nothing."

"It must be something because you've hardly said a word for the past few days. Look, if you aren't feeling well you should go see Doctor Hales; I hear he's very good."

"That's what they say about all of the ones that have come."

"The ones who've come?"

"Yes, Francisca; look, dear, please pass me the milk. Your glass, Leonor."

14

The stomachs received enough food; the teeth chewed the meat; the cold milk went down the throats and the tongues savored the ice cream. They ate without knowing that they were consuming themselves. The hand lifted the spoon to the mouth.

"Aaaaayyyy! Maammáa!"

In the bus the bodies went flying; they left the road above the bridge; the water received them without complaint. The bus was found the next morning.

"What the hell's the matter with these drivers?"

"Well, Captain, he was going very fast."

"And how do you know, stupid, or were they all drunk like you are now? How many are dead?"

"We've got thirty-two bodies, but I think there are more under the truck."

The hands picked up the telephone, they dialed, it rang twice.

"Good, send her tomorrow to the place where we always meet. And who's going to know? Don't be a fool, just do what I tell you."

"Yes, Señor Presidente."

"Yes, with Doctor Harold Beesley, please, Harold?"

"Karen! It's wonderful to talk to you! How are you? Don't tell me, I bet I know, everything is absolutely TERRIBLE!"

"Harold, stop kidding. You know what things are like here. I think they beat him up today. I'm afraid and I won't stay here another day; Allison and I are leaving here tomorrow."

"Karen, calm down, take it easy. How is he now? Is he coming with you?"

"I don't know what he's going to do. But I won't stay here another day!"

"Karen, is he there? Good. Let me talk to him."

"My wife says that you want to talk to me, Beesley."

"Look, Leroy, this is enough playing at humanitarianism; you can't help those people. If you don't get out of that town, you'll starve or they'll kill you. Don't be stubborn, I need you here; besides, the fourth slot in the corporation is open; the job is yours, so come with me. Look, I'm going to be very frank with you, Leroy, this is the last time I'll make this offer. There are other doctors who want the job. It's very simple, either you come here and become a millionaire or you stay there and let them bury you. Don't be a fool, Leroy, don't waste your talent there. I'll give you a week, after that I can't guarantee you the job."

"Don't worry, I don't think it'll take me that long, just a few days to tie up some loose ends, but I would like a week or two to rest."

"OK, I'll wait for you. My best to Karen and Allison, and we'll see each other soon; goodbye until then."

"Goodbye, Harold."

His body received the weight of the woman who was crying with her hands caressing the back of his neck. The sun between their legs sent sound waves that he hardly heard.

"I don't want to take a bath."

"Leonor, get in the tub and get washed before I come and give you a smack on the backside."

"Why do you have to do that, Fernando?"

"Because that's my job; it would be worse for the old guy, for everyone, if I didn't help Pistol Man."

"They only want to arrest the old guy to scare him and to see if then he'll pay what he owes. He'll just be in jail for a few days."

"And the children?"

"The older girl can take care of them. Thank God I'll be there, because if not, who knows what they would do to the old man."

"Leonor, get into the tub!"

"Let's go, time to get washed!"

"Give Daddy a kiss and then to bed because we're leaving tomorrow."

The sun climbed up on the lap of the little god. The lips kissed the freshly washed hair.

"You see, Allison, what a good time you had in the tub. Good night."

It was eight-thirty when the sun went down to live another reality in another world.

"Leroy, do you think they'll attack us again?"

"No, they've already done enough to me. Now they'll wait and see what effect their medicine produces. You're going tomorrow and I'll go in two or three days. They'll know they've won. . . . Rodríguez, why? . . . Rodríguez."

"What?"

"Nothing, nothing."

"Francisca, should we go to bed?"

"It's just nine-thirty."

"We can talk a little bit."

The hard penis followed the furry target that rested between her legs. He kissed her white buttocks, he licked her clitoris.

16

"Karen, Karen, lift them up, more, more, like that. . ."
He petted her with his finger. She, face against the pillow, lifted her vulva and buttocks to receive him.

"Oh, Fernando, Fernando, give it to me, give it to me . . ."

"Karen, here, all for you . . ."

"Just for you, Francisca . . ."

She clutched the pillow when she felt him come; her body was pressed against the bed but she kept the target in a position to receive the violent and rapid thrusts that sweetly penetrated her. The bodies dropped, exhausted, calm, happy in that moment, to enter another world.

The hours pass in a single night and the hours follow the day and the days the months.
"Emigdio, it's time; I can feel it already!"
"Zoila, I'll get Mamá."
"No, no, there isn't time, stay with mmeeee, aayy, it's coming; bring me some clean rags. Hurry!"
"Zoila, look at it, I can see its little head! Aay, aahh! A little more, more, Zoila, more! Here it is Zoila, a boy, a pretty boy."
"But I still feel something in my belly."
"It's nothing, Zoila, you just have to wash, rest now."

"One of the fifteen hostages that Fred Gómez Carrasco has held for a hundred and fifteen hours escaped shortly before dawn. The authorities announced that Carrasco has declared that today will be the last day of his attempt to gain his liberty. There is no possibility that Carrasco, accused of fifty murders, can escape the five hundred heavily armed police officers who have surrounded the prison."

"Emigdio, I feel something in my belly that wants to come out!"
"Ay, Zoila, what a woman you are, maybe it's another one! Listen, we have to go to the doctor at the hospital. Yes, that's the best thing; you'll have it there."
"I can't, Emigdio."
"Why not? In a few hours we'll be there; it's not far. If you have a few more they'll put it in the newspaper. Come on, before it gets light."

"Henry, where have you been? It's six in the morning!"

"Oh, I had to work late! Leave me alone, why do you complain? You have everything, bitch."

"Don't yell, you'll wake the children. Look at you, you stink of perfume and semen from those whores you run around with. Why don't you go back to your Mexican whores, lice-ridden Mexican sluts. Maybe you're a Mexican; yes, you're a Mexican. You make me sick, Mexican, Mexican, Mexican-lover!"

"Look, Zoila, we're almost there."

"Karen, tell Harold that I'll be there in two days, or maybe I'll leave today; I don't know. If you can get an apartment in the dorms it's better. I want to be near the hospital."

"Take care, Leroy."

"Now that they know that I'm leaving, they aren't doing anything to me. They're even going to help me. Don't worry; we'll see each other soon. Kisses."

"Allison, take good care of Mommy."

His arms carried her toward the bus; his eyes saw his wife's mouth and his lips felt hers again.

"We'll see each other in two days. I'll call you."

He walked away from the bus that raised the dust as it moved through the town's white street. He walked toward his car. He had to wash it and fix the tires that had been punctured. He laughed as he approached the car, because with its flat tires it looked like one of the cars the young men from the barrio had, a real work of art.

"Yes, Doctor. I'll fix it for you. Doctor, please don't go; we need you . . ."

The legs didn't want to hear the rest of the sentence; they took him quickly to the office. The open door gaped like a dead mouth with an alcoholic's breath. His eyes found the broom and he began to sweep and to separate out what he wanted to take with him. The pictures, the diplomas, the books, the instruments and the drugs went into the box. The mind worked quickly, trying to finish soon; he was determined to do what he had to do. His hands felt his wife's breasts as he picked up the children's toys. He saw the feet, the legs, the waist, the breasts, the beautiful face of a young woman. He rubbed his fingers nervously when the lips said:

"My son is sick, Doctor."

"But, Señora, don't you see the condition of my office? Don't you see me?"

"I don't understand; you're a doctor; you have a little bit of God in your head, in your hands; you can help my son. Look at how thin he is."

The glass they were stepping on overcame the worlds rooted in the three heads. The hands, the eyes, the ears, and the nose examined the thin, yellow boy who complained of a pain in the pit of his stomach. His liver hurt him.

"I want the boy to urinate in this little cup."

The inflamed liver sent out a cup full of Coca-Cola.

"Doctor, your car's ready!"

"Señora, your son has hepatitis; he has to stay in bed until his urine clears up; he needs complete rest, without any activity and he has to eat well. If he doesn't get better, take him to the city."

The calves carried the woman's private parts and the thin boy followed the curve of the firm buttocks.

He put two boxes filled with books, instruments, and diplomas in the back seat of the car.

"Thank you, Doctor; it's a shame that you were afraid of us."

Music was playing softly and the hum of the motor opened the doors of a new home: . . . I'll never get myself into a situation like this again. These people can survive, they do in Mexico, infested with hepatitis, typhoid, dysentery, and more; here it must be easier. Now to work the way I should and to live as comfortably as I deserve. What the hell was I doing in this town! It was a crazy idea; I don't belong here. Besides, I deserve a better life. Pistol Man is right, all these people need are the curanderos; they are happy with them. I can't stand that song again! . . .

"Five."

"That old guy isn't so old, is he?"

"No, no, they're his son's. They took him away and he never came back. His wife went to look for him and since then old Bilabí has been taking care of the children alone. That's why I'm telling you, Pistol Man, I don't know why we have to arrest him."

"The old bastard doesn't pay what he owes!"

"Yes, but the children, the young girl can't manage all of them."

"Just shut up."

The police car entered old Bilabí's life. The little hands touched everything, they screamed and played and ran all over. Their total silence fell, a silence of territoriality, that you can feel, that weighs on you. Old Bilabí emerged from this silence. His white head approached and he tried to open the police car.

"Listen, old man!"

The hand found his neck and the old body encircled the girl's feet.

"I want to talk to you first!"

"Calm down, Pistol Man, calm down, don't get so excited!"

"To jail, old man, let's go!"

"Don't do that, you animal."

Pistol Man's eyes kissed the little nipples of the girl that was helping her grandfather.

"Keep quiet, you smart-ass girl or it'll be worse for your grandfather; the captain wants to talk with him. We'll bring him back in a few weeks."

"What are you going to do to me? I'm a citizen. My rights, my children, where are they?"

"Don't be frightened, Señor Bilabí; I'll help you."

The police car closed its mouths, making a sharp turn, and for the first time Pistol Man saw the sex of the little growing nipples under the tee shirt that the girl was wearing.

"Adiós, Grandpa! ¡Adiós, abuelito!"

The little bodies ran behind the police car just to see it disappear quickly into the dust.

"Your house is beautiful, Diane."

"Oh, this is nothing, this one isn't as big as the one we had in California. Allison, how pretty you've gotten."

The three of them entered the large living room decorated with obviously expensive furniture, then to a study, passing through a small library; soon they arrived at the patio where they sat down to have a cold drink: . . . My God I was frightened; those people, you don't know what they are capable of doing . . . Allison was noticing the clean windows; the sun looked into the rich and luxuriously furnished bedroom.

"But you don't have to be in the student apartments; you'll have a higher rank than that; with Leroy's salary you'll have enough to buy a big house outside the city."

"But Leroy wants to be near the hospital."

"Yes, but you'll see that his dedication won't last forever. You'll want your own house soon."

"Hello, dear!"

"Harold! Darling!"

20

"Oh, Karen, thank God you're back! Allison, my only love, how are you?"

"Fine thank you, Doctor Beesley."

"And Leroy, where's Leroy?"

"He'll be here tomorrow. He had to pick up a few things and finish some business that he had. He'll be here tomorrow or the next day. Don't worry, he'll come."

"Good, because I'm going to work him hard; there's an awful lot to do, and I want him to be in the middle of it all. Diane, please get me a drink."

"Karen says that Leroy wants to live in student housing."

"Why? After working in the hospital a couple of days for twelve or more hours, you'll see that he'll want to get as far away as possible. Those crazy idealistic notions will soon be erased from his brain. In this profession there's no time or place for idealists. Well, maybe he's right in wanting to be nearby in the beginning. Listen, we have some fantastic doctors. One named Redacky came from Chicago, a great guy. Dangerous, though, a cardiologist; he invented a pacemaker device, but instead of selling it and making millions, he made the patent so that no one would make money from his invention. Even though he's good, a guy like that could ruin the profession. Diane, could I have another drink, please."

"I'm very happy to be here with you again and I know that Leroy will be happy too. Thank you, Harold; thank you, Diane."

"Don't get sad, here is where you should be, you'll see, he'll be successful here. Yes, well! I'm ready for the third, let's have another round, everyone; give Allison a Coke. Let's all toast Leroy, the Hales family, success!"

The clinking of glasses was repeated in thousands of places all over the world. It was the last noise that some heard, it encouraged the desire for more, for others it turned into blood, the shouts and the music drowned out the sounds of the bar.

"You're going to get a spanking when you get home tonight."

"After a week like this one, I don't care. I called her; she knows where I am. Here, buy another pitcher."

"Bravo, listen everybody, Michael Logan is buying!"

"Now that's news!"

"What a miracle!"

"I didn't say for everybody, you bastard!"

"I'm sorry, Michael, but the twenty's gone!"

21

"Now you're right, Pato, when I get home they're really going to give it to me. OK, let's drink tonight and have a good time because tomorrow they'll screw us."

"Hey, how much do you have left?"

"Almost a year. You know that!"

"What are you going to do? How many hospitals have you applied to for your specialization?"

"To none."

"None! How's that? Didn't you want to specialize in pediatrics, neurology, plastic surgery?"

"Naaah, that's for guys who want to get rich."

"You'll get rich, even if you don't want to."

"Don't tell me that there aren't any poor doctors!"

"Don't be a jerk, Michael, you know what I mean."

"Pato, I don't want to screw anybody!"

"Look, I don't want to fight with you. Hey, Michael, look at Silkfuck. She's mine tonight."

"Hey, Silky, how's your job?"

The hanging breasts made his penis rise.

"Here, my Silky."

"Pato, I'm burning up. This job is making me sick."

"Did you tell the company doctor?"

"That old fart just wants to feel my breasts. And he tells me I don't have anything but the computers always show red."

"Have another beer, Silky, then let's go to my room to talk."

"Hello, Michael, Silky, how did you do today, Pato?"

"Good evening, Doctor Calva, intelligent bastard, ostentatious Chicano sellout. The next time you correct me like that, as brusquely as today, I'm going to punch you out. And I don't give a shit that you're the chief attending physician."

"OK, Michael, excuse me, but the amount of insulin that you prescribed without seeing the patient would have been a fatal error. I don't care how much you've worked, you have to see the patient even if you have to walk a mile through the whole damned hospital. We're the new school of doctors; and we're good, we mustn't make any mistakes; we have to follow the procedures and . . ."

"That's enough, have a beer. Dance. Calva, we understand, thanks."

"OK, OK, Pato, but tell me, what happened when Beesley called you?"

"Nothing, he just introduced me to the new head of emergency; he starts there on Monday. His name is Hales. He seems to be a good guy."

22

"Oh, yes. Well, I'm going. I'll see you. Michael, look. I'll see you Monday. You know you're a good doctor, but you have to take it a little easier. Well, I'll be going. Don't drink too much, it destroys your brain cells and with the few that you have to begin with . . ."

Calva's shining intelligence floated to the bar where he spoke to a colleague and the two brilliant, bald men quickly left.

The two bodies entered by night; he was yearning for her and she felt a power over the man. The cottage with its warm lights glowed in the clear night. The sea entered, rose, and fell, and exited, its song and rhythm pushed them, made them run to the cottage. The guards took care of them; they did not say a word. They saw her and they also wanted her. But every week they were given theirs, the money, the special privileges and a little bit of blond ass, for being one of the Presidente's bodyguards.

"Let's take a shower."

"Oh, yes, I love to with you."

The stream of warm water fell on the two playful bodies. The penis and the vulva spoke to each other and caressed each other; he came like a young boy by just touching himself, and again the Presidente suckled her nipples, her stomach, her hair, he penetrated her recesses with his tongue, he stroked her buttocks; the feminine hands smoothed the Presidente's hair. His tongue went deeper and deeper; her beautiful hands held his head, she lifted herself to meet his tongue: Mama, Mama, dear, Mama: . . . Oh, beautiful . . . His hands spoke, his eyes savored her nipples, his tongue heard the wet kisses.

He heard her soft moans, but the virgin, now exhausted, received Pistol Man opened as wide as possible. Millions of microseconds had passed in this position; for hours she had shed tears and perspired through new experiences; the masculine hands explored all of her; they explained everything to her; her eyes closed to feel his now constant, sharp, tender penetrations again.

"Dried-out meat again? Why don't you give me something decent to eat? I've been here two weeks and nothing has changed. I want to talk to my granddaughter. Where is my Teresa?"

"Shut up, you old bastard! Go to sleep, they're letting you out in a few days."

Pistol Man traced the valleys, the highways, the images created in the room's clear ceiling. The female mounted the male, innocence was now initiated, they had copulated seven times. Her lips, her feminine hands entwined around his organ, loved him.

"Your grandfather is getting out tomorrow. You have to explain this to him and convince him, because I'll be coming to visit. If you don't let me, I'll put him in jail again."

The slender, fetid body rested next to him, unconsciously playing with his penis.

"When is my grandfather coming home?"

"You have to convince him; I want to come often, if not I'll tell everyone what you are, what you've done with me. I'll tell them that you're another . . ."

The hands pulled up the pants. The fluid had stopped, he dried his hair, nakedness saw Pistol Man button his jacket.

"I can't come tomorrow."

The fifteen-year-old heart heard the car start and leave defiantly. It could not explain what it felt.

"I'm so drunk I don't know what's going on."

"You'll get it when you get home, Michael."

He had the waivering voice of a homosexual when he walked in the door. The bright light made his eyes want to flee. The body threw the clothes on the floor; it saw the children. It entered its bed; the weight fell heavily.

"It's five o'clock in the morning; sometimes I hate you, Michael, you drunkard, you don't know how to say no; you don't know when to stop, I hate you."

"I hate you, Henry! I hate you! You've been with those whores again! Don't tell me where you've been, I can tell by your eyes and your stench. Do you think I'm going to wait around here every night like a fool? You're a Mexican, you love them so much! Mexican-lover! Answer me! Why don't you answer?"

"Goodbye, Carol."

"If you come home again like this you won't find me here! Did you hear me, Henry! Henry!"

The house's door spit him into the countryside.

Everyone has felt that sharp pain in their mind, because everyone has assumed some guilt. We all share a fundamental dream of action. The stars violently sped toward their mission; the gods did not sleep at night, they labored over the future, not of man, but of themselves. Millons of dreams were dreamed in this instant; they were not under-

24

stood, not recognized, forgotten. He dreamed about a fantastic man; his eyes, it was strange, asked him what happened. He said nothing. Millions dreamed it, millions cried; he heard his name, but it was not his fault. Ugly, disgusting dreams; his hands full of shit, standing on a plain where phallic keys sprouted from the earth; a woman with bottles inserted in all the natural openings of her body flew across the room.

"I don't care, he's not recommended by one of the fifty best; his articles aren't worth anything."

"I didn't like the way he talked, the way he dressed."

"Weak, theoretically weak. Is the Chicano coming or not?"

. . . Fucking pedants I always come when I feel like it, I come like a river of pure, warm, white fertile semen that flows within me . . .

They move among the shadows; they embrace motivated by dreams, by the masturbation of the unconscious. The croaking ends and the morning song begins it anew.

The living cadavers pass by, eaten away by the years, their hands limp, their eyes hopeless, their mouths soundlessly opened, their dry, tangled locks greeted him again as he entered the room. Only Calva with his feminine strength could constantly put up with this. The smell of rotting flesh lingers in his nostrils; he can't eat; it makes him sick to think what he has left upstairs. He sniffs the aroma of cake as he tries to forget the aged children.

"You've almost finished, it's Wednesday, tomorrow is the last day of the round. Friday is the goodbye party. And I don't give a damn; we finish at seven; let's go to the dorms to celebrate."

"That bastard Calva won't let me out at seven, he gets furious. And your new boss? We'll see if he doesn't screw you for leaving early."

"No, I don't think there is any problem with him. It's like at times, I don't know, he seems pretty strange. He sometimes seems very sad, as if his mind were somewhere else. He's a good administrator and he knows what he's doing; that's for sure."

"Well, lunch hour has flown by; it's time to go up to the above-ground cemetery."

"Hey, can you lend me that magazine, I want to read the article about Redacky; he's a really dedicated guy. You're going to like him."

"We'll see on Monday."

Pato's eyes guided him through the corridors to the emergency room; there everyone trusted him because he had a natural talent and he took over forcefully. His legs took him there when his penis spotted Silky Silkfuck's warm flesh.

"Pato! You've got to help me, I'm burning up! Pato, please help me!"

"Silky, what's the matter with you?"

"I don't feel well, I'm burning up inside, I have stomach pains. I'm afraid. Last night I saw some men, I saw two men who came into my room. They came up to me and suddenly I didn't see them any more. I thought it was a dream but I know they were in my room because they searched it. What do you think they wanted?"

His hand was already around her breast.

"Calm down, calm down, I'm going to give you something to relax you. Come to my room tonight. Stay with me until this thing blows over. Don't worry, everything is OK. These dreams won't bother you any more."

Pato's ear heard his name.

"Come with me and I'll give you the pills and if you want you can go right to my room, OK?"

He saw her breasts vibrating a yes. His body moved away from her and found itself across from Doctor Hales.

"Come with me. I want you to take care of a severely lacerated child. Every laceration is full of glass."

The screams penetrated his ears, his brain, as he entered the room. Pato's mouth kept still, his eyes enjoyed the blood; the confident, artistic machine began to function.

"I'll leave you with him; I'll send you two nurses; you'll be here for a while."

The dark body nearly knocked Hales over, the mother begged him with her hands.

"Sit down outside, outside, Ma'am, please. The doctor will do everything possible to stop the bleeding. Ask God for his help and I think we'll be successful."

That is how old Bilabí said goodbye as he left jail one week later.

"Thank you, boys, but aren't you going to take me to my house? You brought me here in a car; my house is very far away."

"Go on now, old man, maybe someone will give you a lift. Maybe you'll run into Pistol Man."

"Yeah, he's in that neighborhood now. Go on now, old man, before I get angry."

The leaden heart's dry legs walked in the dust; he followed his feet that were taking him home; his head down, his chin against his chest, his nose smelled shit on his body: . . . In that place they didn't even give me paper to wipe myself, not even newspaper. These men are bad. What did I do? What did I do to them? I should get angry, but that, at least for me, never got me anywhere. I still have a lot to get mad about; once I got angry and they hit me with a stick, broke some teeth and some ribs. Today the law isn't worth much; that's right. They take advantage of it everywhere; all over they just do as they please. I wonder where Teresa is. The kids probably drove her crazy; she's a good girl . . .

"Ooohh, Henry!"

"Look how you've learned, sweetheart, you're so pretty, now turn around, give it a kiss, take it in your mouth, don't stop, don't stop, oh, God, yeees."

His lips kissed her long hair. His hands said he loved her. At the door was the sound of little voices and little hands.

"Tere, Teresita. Teresa, Teresita, when are you going to come out of there?"

"Leonor! Come out of the bathroom now! Come out of there, I told you! Doña Gertrudis, you don't think another one will come here?"

"No, there have already been a lot who have come and who have been quickly sent away. I really don't think another one will come."

"Don't be such a pessimist, Doña Gertrudis. I still hope that another one will come that can get along with Pistol Man."

"If he were the only one, we wouldn't have problems. You know that very well, Fernando."

"I know that very well; she's a good girl. This is also a good road, good like she is. I know it well. The earth feels me, it recognizes me and it cares for me, soon I'll be with her. I remember when we were . . . I was never anything; my grandparents, now they really were powerful, they owned the land; I don't know what happened, but we lost it. The fairs we used to have. People came from all over. They would all come; they would come from the other side of town to peer at us and pretend that we were disgusting. But they certainly licked their fingers after they ate the food. They came with their noses stuck up in the air, but they left with them full of the aroma of delicious food. And they pretended not to like us and that we were worthless . . ."

The old man's legs saw the house and they obliged him to sit down and rest a bit. Before him was the land; the world surrounded him. . . . What the hell am I doing here? . . .

"Michael, Michael! We don't have time now to consider the world philosophically; it's your job to give the medicine. That's who's going with you."

"Who?"

"Amy Nelson."

"Oh yes, of course."

"Doctor Calva, they're paging you to room 15."

"It's Mrs. Murray, she's torn out her tubes and oxygen mask; the woman wants to kill herself. Ciao, Michael, don't waste time with the patients; give them the medicine, that's all, don't let them tell you their life stories. Nurse Shulman, let's go."

"Doctor Logan, I'm ready, and you?"

"Yes, of course . . . Amy . . . Now, where should we start?"

"Michael, do you feel all right?"

"Yes, I was just distracted for a minute."

"Michael, you're hung over and you're depressed. And I bet you fought with Cody. I know you too well. Think about her and your two children. When was the last time you took them to the park? A simple thing like that, taking them for a walk. If you're not careful, this place will eat you up and ruin your marriage; if you let it, it'll be that much easier."

"All right, now, tell me, who is the first victim of the monster of medical science?"

"This is Mrs. Burciaga, she has an inflamed liver caused by malnutrition, and, don't laugh, she has a syphilitic infection. She's seventy years old. Calva has asked for a blood test to determine the kind of syphilis and the degree."

"It's obvious that it's terciary."

His hand stroked the syphilitic fingers; he touched the joints, his eyes examined her hair. The crossed eye seemed asleep yet when the doctor opened her mouth he set off a biting attack.

"Michael, help, help! Someone!"

"No, no! I'm OK!"

The clutches of madness drew him near; the alchemist's hand pushed the forehead of the lymphatic head, and it sank into the pillow. The uvula, the tongue, and the molars still struggled, longing to chew his forearm.

Pistol Man managed to get back into the police car without being bitten. The dogs had still not accepted his smell; he was a stranger, an enemy.

"Teresa, please, tie up that dog! The next time I'm going to . . ."

The words were drowned out by the screech of the police car as it found its way toward town. The cigarette was stuck between his lips; the police car moved quickly, straight ahead: . . . Prepare the list of families with Mexican surnames. Damned government, always bugging me with its forms. They should just take my word for it; I know all these greasers around here. Not one of them slips by me. I don't care about the ones that are here; I like them, I really do, but don't let any more come. We've got enough already . . . His eye spotted the old man seated by the side of the road. His foot stepped on the accelerator.

. . . Ay, what a tingling, it's asleep, it's asleep, asleep, asleep. I have to stop, I have to walk; when you get old you want to rest and resting just makes you feel even stiffer. Ay, there goes Pistol Man speeding like a mad man; one of these days he's going to run over a child. Smoke, Teresita must be cooking. Thank God, I've just got a little ways to go . . .

El Señor Presidente appeared before the disgustingly luxurious table, dirty gold cups, place settings of fine silver with ivory knife rests, jewel-studded candlesticks, a gift of the oil men.
"Marimbo, is the meal ready?"
"Yes, Señor Presidente."
"Let's sit down, my pet."
"How did it go in Acapulco, my love?"
"Quite well, I think we have resolved that problem of . . ."

"From the Geriatrics Department."
"Yes, but I know that he'll always be there. Those abandoned old people, forgotten by their families and by everyone else. Their abandonment turns them into monsters that want to destroy themselves and the world that has forgotten them. And they stay there sometimes for months, years. Let them all die; I can't save anyone. What a jerk I am, isn't that so, Cody?"
"No, Michael, you're not."
"Can you forgive me for the other day? Look. I'll try not to drink so much. You're right, I don't know when to stop."
"Michael, I don't care if you go out for a beer with Pato or with Silky or with whoever, but don't overdo it. You don't know when to stop, that's the danger. You don't know how to say no."
"I'm going to stop drinking completely."

"Don't think I'm going to feel sorry for you when you say that. If you can do it, do it for yourself, for you, not for me."

"Cody, don't give me a hard time, don't challenge me!"

"Michael, don't get mad. We should discuss this calmly."

"OK, but I don't like it when you say that I can't do something. I've done a lot and I'm going to do more."

"Doña Gertrudis, thank you for coming, I don't know what to do with the boy."

"Don't tell me that he's still sick! Didn't you take him to the doctor?"

"Yes, but he didn't do anything; he didn't give him anything. He just told me that he had hepatitis and that he had to stay in bed."

"And did he?"

"Yes, he was in bed for, let me see, almost a month. His yellow color went away and his urine cleared up; it seemed like he was all right."

"It seemed like it, and now what's the matter with the little angel?"

"Well, Doña Gertrudis, as I was telling you, he was all right, but the other day . . . Last night he began to scream, to shake and it seemed like he was choking. And now he has an attack like that every so often."

"But give me more details, did he talk to anyone, did he do anything that would have gotten a neighbor angry, has anything unusual happened to him?"

"Oh, of course, now I remember, imagine, I didn't pay any attention to what happened. You know, Doña Gertrudis, I didn't think it was anything."

"Now tell me, don't be embarrassed; it's important that you tell me everything. Did the child see anything?"

"No, it's not what you think it is, nothing like that. I'm not like that. Let me explain. About four days ago, yes, it was the first day that he had gotten up and I let him go outside. I told him to take the basket and to collect the eggs. He took it and left."

. . . What a nice day it is, I'm going to see if my bicycle is next to the corral. If Chafuri took it I'm going to tell his mother; no, I'll just steal his glove; no, I'll steal his trucks, or his marbles; no, I'll hit his . . .

The small thin hand lifted the latch of the door of the wooden corral; the spring and the wire welcomed him; they knew each other very well. The whiteness of the rabbits always overcame the dust: . . . But, how can they stay so clean and I always get dirt all over my clothes and Mamá hits me? . . .

The stone fell on the animal's whiteness making a spot; the small creature declared vengeance. The red cap with its shiny little knife that his father had given him entered the shed. His eyes searched for spiderwebs, checking the corners in case a black one was hiding there ready to jump out; the body advanced cautiously, with hunched shoulders as it continued to survey every nook. He found the hens fluttering in the holes they scratched out for bathing: . . . They take a bath in dirt; Mamá hits me when I get myself covered with dirt; dirty hen . . .

He approached the large boxes where the eggs were; he checked the perches to make sure that no hens or roosters were observing his crime. He made his hand reach into the box; the hen ran out protesting the theft of her maternal egg. He took a step toward another box, two. The kidnapping of the unborn was getting easier; he again reached out his hand, the beak almost reached his eye; he threw over the basket trying to scare him, but he again leaped for his face; the spurs cornered him, the child fell on his seat, his hands tried to protect him from the violent attack, his ear felt the spiders' webs, his hand fought against what he thought was a fat black spider that was walking on his ear; now it was in his hair, the rooster continued jumping and pecking at his face.

". . . Oooowww, ooowww . . ."

"Mamaaá, Maaamaaaá, Maamaaá!"

Bobby's kick sent the rooster running, defeated for not having harmed the knife's shine.

"Hey, what's the matter? The red rooster wanted to eat you up. Come on, let's go to your mother."

The young man's arms lifted him up; he tried to speak, he wanted to cry, he couldn't, he cried tears but there were no screams.

"What happened to you? Just look at you! Oh, what a boy!"

"No, Señora, the red rooster attacked him. He had the poor kid hiding in the corner. That red is very . . ."

"You don't have to tell me, I already know it. Come here my little angel. Sit down, we're going to give you a spoonful of sugar. Thank you, Bobby. We'll give my little man a bath and change his clothes."

"Mamaá, Mamá."

"Don't try to talk; everything is all right now. Get into the tub . . . I gave him a bath, I put him to bed, that was all, Doña Gertrudis, but I didn't realize until today what had happened to him."

"Of course, of course, the poor child had a terrible fright; that damned devil of a rooster even tries to attack you through the wire when you walk by there. Thank God he didn't get his eyes. I'll cure the boy."

"Please, Doña Gertrudis, please."

31

"Bring me a crucifix, a candle, and a sheet."

Her nose remembered the mint leaves that she had to burn; she looked around; when she got to the door she stopped and crossed herself.

"Come in with me; explain to him who I am and that I'm going to cure him and that you will be outside waiting for him."

The two bodies received the sick child's gaze, which devoured his mother.

"My child, this is Doña Gertrudis; she is going to cure you. Do you understand me? She is going to make you better and I'll be in the living room waiting for her to leave and waiting for you. Don't be afraid, Doña Gertrudis is going to cure you."

Her lips kissed the young male's forehead. The mother slipped out of the room with her heart practically in her hands, hoping that the boy would recover.

"Felipe, Felipe, Felipe, it's me. Do you recognize me? You do, don't you? I'm Doña Gertrudis. I've come to cure you, to remove the evil you have in your heart. Let's see now, sit up against these pillows, like that. Good, very good."

The crucifix appeared by one knee, the mint next to the other and the burning candle was placed at his feet. An aluminum cup was filled with hot bitterwood water. She added a little piece of mint. His nose smelled the strange odor, suddenly the sheet covered everything. His lungs choked, but they heard the old woman's resonant encantations. Signs of the cross, prayers, smoke and . . .

"Here, drink this."

His lips, his throat, his stomach, felt the warm, penetrating liquid. They stared at each other with enlarged eyes.

"Felipe, come back, come back, come back, come back to your body, Felipe, come back. Here, have a little more. In the name of the Father, the Son, and the Holy Ghost. Felipe, you are in your body, Felipe, you are cured, Felipe, you are healthy. Jesús, María, and José."

She gathered up everything and the light of his mother entered the room.

"Mamá, Mamá, Mamá?"

"Yes, Jason, everything is all right, your father said that you would be fine and that you have an ear infection. Yes, that's all; here, drink this and then I'm going to put some drops in your ear and tomorrow you'll see that you'll feel fine. And now I want you to go to sleep; I know, I know that it still hurts, but soon it will feel all better; now go to sleep, Jason, go to sleep. Daddy and I will be in the living room. Now go to sleep."

"And the children have already gone to bed. How time flies. Teresita, I just stopped to rest a little. I was coming home very nice and slow, resting from time to time. And I got here late, when my children were in bed."

"Don't worry, Grandpa, you're tired. Sit down and I'll give you your dinner."

"I'm not hungry, Teresita; give me a beer instead, please. No one has bothered you, have they? Tell me the truth. I don't know why I'm asking you since the children would tell me everything and of course you have never lied to me. You look tired, Teresa, the children have tired you out, exhausted again. Go to bed. I'll have my beer in my room; I'll put out the lights. Go on Teresa, go on."

The beer relaxed the body huddled in the soiled mattress; he slept the night heavily. The bedclothes reeked; they reeked of the memory of the woman who was flying; he saw her and he could not believe that two pieces of flesh fell on his arm.

The row of coffins, thirty dead that they found on the train that night. They thought that everything was fine in the man's hands. He was a good man, he had two children. He was good but the company wanted them there before seven o'clock in the morning. His eyes were burning; he saw a light, maybe he heard a noise, a whistle, the tracks were blocked.

. . . I can't stop now, if I don't get there we'll be screwed . . .

"Ay! My wife, my chiiildrenn!"

"Stop, stop the traiinn."

"What was that, dear?"

"Don't worry; it's out there, the guards will take care of it. You keep still, my love, I want to squeeze this pimple you have on your back."

"Ouch! That hurts."

The First Lady's eyes contemplated el Señor Presidente's white buttocks. Every little pimple was a challenge to her.

"Let me squeeze this one; look, you have a lot of them here on your right side."

Listening to the news, naked with an erection. Acapulco, he wanted to roll over.

"Hey, love, make me come."

"Wait, here you have a tough one. Let me clean it for you first."

. . . The world spinning through the universe, and here I am bare-assed listening to the national news hour, and on top of me, the soft breasts of a woman who would rather squeeze my pimples than make love . . .

"What list? Oh, the one from last year?"

"Yes, but we have to add the names of the new ones. There aren't a lot. They're always bugging me for something; well, at least they pay us well."

"But I don't feel right. I'm spying for the government. I'm spying on my own people. I don't know why. No, I'm not going to do it; you do it, Pistol Man."

"Look, don't be a fool, Fernando, you're well taken care of; until now you've cooperated with me like a good Mexican. Besides, it's your duty as an American to help your government. And, as I said, your family can use the money. It's a good deal, don't be an idiot."

"OK, what I'm going to do is use the old list and add the new names. The boys told me that Mister Bilabí got out. I think you overdid it with him. He's too old to be in jail so long. But everything has been worked out, hasn't it?"

"Yes, everything's worked out just fine."

"We won't have to bother the old man again, will we, Pistol Man; you went there several times, didn't you? . . . A cup of coffee? Yes, a cup of coffee, yes I want a . . ."

"Look, I'm going. I'll be at Costa's store if anyone wants me. Send the list, and that's it."

The room opened and the body was lost in the outside world. His eyes observed the sound of wood against wood. Next to him, the file drew Fernando's attention, reaching him through his eyes that remembered the names that his fingers began to search for in the box, first slowly and then as he became accustomed, he was lost in the world of index cards.

. . . Index cards, letters, data, paper and more paper, pure shit, this isn't medicine. What I hate are all these damned forms; I use the medications because I need them; these bastards ask for an explanation for everything . . .

"Michael, are you ready for the action?"

"Hey, Pato, what the hell are you doing here?"

"I'm going to the party; it's going to be really wild. Come on, let's go."

"No, I can't, Calva will blow up. You know what he's like. Look, why don't you go? I only have one more to do; I'll be finished soon; go on, go ahead, Pato."

The elevator doors swallowed the friend who was already thinking about Silky. His hand dropped the pen that signed the language which translated the symbols of responsibility: . . . A cold beer would do me just fine. Damn it, Pato. Shit, do I feel relaxed. If I call Cody to tell her that I'm going to the party, she'll get mad and maybe she's right, I can't stop with just a few; I have to keep drinking until I can't see straight. But the worst is the next day. It's not the physical hangover but the mental one. Pyschologically I feel disgusting, like a pariah. I can't face my wife, my kids. And then I tell her that I can stop. Well, this time I am going to stop; from now on I'm not going to drink. I'll call her right now and tell her to have dinner ready at seven, because I'm going to surprise her and get home at seven on the dot . . .

"Just a period and you're finished with the paperwork. It's easy, isn't it?"

"Amy, you know very well that I hate all this. Don't torture me, Amy, don't be mean to me."

. . . to me, Michael, to me, you don't know what the word "torture" means. Such a handsome guy, intelligent, spontaneous and so dumb. Michael, open your eyes, look at me. You don't even like me enough to go to bed with me. Michael, you can love two women; it's possible and it can be as beautiful as loving one . . .

"Amy, aren't you going to the party?"

"Yes, let's go."

"No, they're waiting for me at home."

The body she loved moved away; the white coat held shoulders that turned to go.

"I'll see you, Amy."

"Michael."

"What?"

"Say hello to Cody and the kids for me."

"Sure thing. And don't be cruel to the menfolk, Amy honey."

The words filled the corridor crammed with lights, white clothing, hygenic odors, noises, the sounds of immaculate machinery, and strangely enough, she was alone. Michael picked up the telephone and dialed.

The white shoes were already soiled, he never polished them.

"Hey, doc, I'll shine your shoes for you."

The spotted white shoes continued on ahead. They passed stores that always offered their furniture, clothing, or groceries at greatly reduced prices. They passed newstands of brutal happenings, of pornographic magazines, of men selling chewing gum and candy and their drug-addicted sisters or healthy, ignorant, hungry young women. The hand approached him, then the Indian woman's skinny body with an infant hanging from her breast.

"Please, Doctor."

The white shoes hurried past the body, almost running: . . . But where the hell am I, pal? Isn't this the land of the rich where they can fix anything? Why am I seeing all this? Rich people, drug addicts, whores, poor people, good ones, bad ones, old ones, young girls, beggars, fags, priests, virgins, young people, saints, and more, it's madness. But we shouldn't think about it; it's a cliché, an old tired topic that no one is interested in anymore. Now you're supposed to think about theoretical issues, not even mention these helpless emotional impressions. Poor shattered hearts, they don't feel any more. Come here, I'll put them together again for you . . .

The mouth in the child's face opened: . . . He looks just like Jason . . .

"Give me a fifty cent piece. Have pity, Doctor, help me, only you can save me, Doctor."

He stopped, a fatal error: . . . now the others are coming, I have to get out of here . . .

"Here."

"For me, Doctor?"

"Ten dollars for me, Doctor."

"Cure me, Doctor."

"Save me, Doctor."

He stopped, he wouldn't run now, he wouldn't make that mistake again. He always came down this street, always. And it takes just as long from the hospital to the apartment: . . . I don't know why I turn down this street . . .

The building he lived in loomed before him. He saw the lights of home; his wife was ready for him, his children were playing, bathed and clean, already in their pajamas and watching television. The doctor went into the little store where the six pack of beer that he usually bought when he got home was waiting for him.

"Good evening, Doctor."

"Good evening. No, you'd better give me a couple of bottles of soda please."

"Yes, yes, of course."

The bag appeared walking in the street in his arms with the finger that pushed the elevator button.

"Hi, Michael."

"James, how are you?"

"Hey, are you starting cardiology on Monday? You'll really be impressed by Doctor Redacky."

The vertical jaws opened on the fourth floor.

"I'm going to have one, two, no about four strong martinis. Ciao."

He was alone in the iron box until the fifth floor. The machine stopped suddenly; it pushed him out as usual. It closed and quickly escaped, telling him it didn't want him.

"I know what you're like you crazy machine! . . . I think I'm tired . . . to my door . . ."

"We were expecting you, Michael."

"Daddy, Daddy, I want to play house."

"Daddy, I want to get out the train, please, Daddy, you promised me we would."

"Wait, Jason, I want to hug and kiss Shane and you. First let me talk to Mommy and rest a little bit and later we'll play, OK?"

"Yes, give Daddy a minute to rest. Jason, you have to clean up your room, and Shane, you have to help him because if the room isn't cleaned Daddy won't play with anyone. So get going. Michael, will you play with me?"

The feminine hands relieved him of the burden he was carrying. Then they took him and caressed and petted his shoulders, his neck, his hair.

"I'm awfully happy that you came home and didn't go to the party."

"But, Cody, you could have gone too, but you didn't want to get anybody to take care of the kids."

"Don't worry; I didn't want to go; I'd rather stay at home with you. We'll go another time, but tonight I want to be alone with you and the children."

"Cody, kiss me."

"Daddy, come and play; Daddy, come here I want to show you our room."

"Wait, don't you see that I'm talking to your mother. Look, I'm going to show you how Mommy and Daddy kiss without breathing."

Their lips joined, making a smacking sound that made the children laugh.

"I want to do it with you, Daddy."

"I want to do it with Mommy."

"OK, but just once and that's all because Mommy and Daddy want to talk a little more. Besides, I have to set the table for dinner."

"Cody, come here."

His hands grasped her buttocks, they pressed her breasts, he slipped a hand into her blouse and his finger circled her nipple; he knew Cody and when she was interested that was the way to win her.

"Go play with the children and let me set the table."

"Will you take a bath with me tonight? Please, Cody; dearest, sweetheart, my darling mmmmm I love you. OK, kids, let's wrestle; come here, Shane; careful, here comes the monster, Jason."

The three children played and tumbled on the rug. The woman observed them as they played and shouted like maniacs; she knew that she controlled them all to a certain extent. It was easy now with the children, and she always had a certain power over him although in some ways he was able to withdraw from her. Sometimes she didn't know him; there was something in him that sometimes made her hate him. She couldn't clarify it in her mind but it frightened her; she was afraid of losing him; she was afraid for him. She wasn't afraid of losing him to another woman: . . . Not another woman, but something else that I can't identify; there's something in him that makes him different from other men; I always see fame and death hovering near him, always wanting to take him by the hand and steal him from me. Fame and death are the women that I'm fighting with, they're my rivals . . .

"Oh, Michael, don't hurt him; sometimes you play too roughly with him."

"Well, it's time he learned to take it."

"No, Michael, don't make him cry."

"OK, OK, come on Jason, let's eat."

"I don't like Daddy."

"Let's go, son, go wash your hands and you too, Shane."

"But they didn't even wash my poor Susan's hands; sit down to dinner. How do you expect me to eat when you tell me that I'll have to pay five thousand dollars for my daughter's body?"

"Callahan, here are all the charges against your daughter."

"But here all it says is that they were going too fast and they were driving recklessly, But, how do you know? You found them a day later."

"From the consequences, sir, from the consequences."

"And I'll bet you they were smoking marijuana; they're all incredible potheads."

"How can you charge me five thousand dollars when they didn't harm anyone? She's the one that was killed; her body is disfigured. For the love of God, we aren't rich; you think that we're all rich."

"Aren't you?"

"And Steve, how is he?"

"We've got him in jail, thank God, because it's going to cost him a pretty penny."

"But, why?"

"Because he's the one that was driving."

"But you told me that they found the bodies out of the car. How do you know that he was driving?"

"He was driving and don't ask any more questions!"

"Please, gentlemen, I don't have that kind of money."

"Borrow it; if you don't comply with the law, your daughter will be buried here and you'll have to bring her flowers here on her birthday."

"Please, don't be cruel to her memory! Don't you realize that I've lost my daughter?"

"Yes, we realize that, but you have to comply with the law of the land, especially because you are a foreigner. Imagine what would happen if everyone who came to visit our country came with the idea that they could do everything their way."

"But the simple fact is that I don't have the money and I can't get it. I have a thousand dollars in checks and that's all. I'll have to ask my wife to send me money to transport the body."

"That will cost you five hundred more, but of course it will be by plane. We haven't prepared the body; that is your responsibility. We've done an autopsy, that's all."

"And what did you find?"

"You'll have to ask the doctor."

"Mr. Callahan, the least we could accept is two thousand dollars. With that you and your daughter would be able to leave the country freely, without any further obligations. I can offer you this as a representative of the Department of Transportation; I will, of course, have to justify lowering the fine to my superiors."

"Thank you!"

"Mr. Callahan, if you are not grateful, or rather if you are not in agreement with this arrangement, you can go to Mexico City and deal directly with the authorities there. The body of the deceased, of course, would remain here."

"No, no, I am very grateful and I agree with the plan and what you have offered me. With two thousand dollars, not a dollar more, we can leave by plane? With no other problem?"

"That's right."

"Good, but as I say I only have a thousand with me; I'll have to call my wife."

"Give me all the information; I'll take care of all the formalities; don't worry about it any more, Mr. Callahan. If you like you can go to the hotel."

"No, I don't want to; I'll stay with her; I'll stay here with her. I don't have much more time with her."

"As you like, but as you know these transactions will take at least a full day. You'll be back in your country in three days. That I can promise you."

"Sir, when you speak to my wife, tell her that I'm OK and that we'll be home soon."

"Very well, Mr. Callahan; my country extends its sympathy to you in this difficult moment. Personally, I am very sorry; I have a daughter too. I hope that this tragedy is not repeated. Goodbye, Mr. Callahan. They'll come for you tomorrow about three to take you to the airport. Try to eat something, Mr. Callahan."

"No, thank you, let the others eat."

The window and the incessant eternal noise of the ancient city beckoned him to contemplate his nation, his beloved nation: . . . Fuck their mother and mine, cowardly bastards, incapable of anything. This city is falling apart and we don't even open our eyes; I'm just as guilty as all my predecessors. But it's not their fault; they have always been conquered in one way or another. We're trapped by a collective consciousness that we have accepted unwillingly and unknowingly. I, who tell them, who practically predict the future for them, I am believed because I am the authority. If I told them that I could transform myself into a bird, would they believe me? Yes! I tell you what is projected for the future but you cannot make it happen. If I were president of a really powerful country, I wouldn't abuse my people. I wouldn't abuse them the way that imbecile over there does. Yes, we're making progress, we're building, but then, what happens? We allow everything to decay, we don't maintain anything properly; we enjoy the act of creating but we soon abandon what we have created in search of other parameters. The university monument is a disaster; the library is an embarrassment; we don't keep up the murals the way we should; if it weren't for the tourists they would have already faded away to nothing. Yes, we're the most developed country of Latin America but you aren't the ones that I want, cowards. Why do you let yourselves? . . .

"Señor Presidente, they're waiting for you."

"Ah, yes, thank you, Marimbo."

The symbol of Mexican greatness appears, the revolution continues.

He approaches his parishioners, Señor Presidente, turned into a destructive reality, hyperbole of the abuse of the little power that Mexico actually has; the San Manuel Bueno Mártir of third world rhetoric. The applause and the shouting beckon him to his show; the sacred act commences, the rite begun and transformed into myth since 1910.

"Mexicans, the time has come for us to initiate a new path that will demonstrate our nation's true capacity!"

"Jason, turn down that noise."

"No, I want to play some more."

"Me too."

"It's ten o'clock, it's past your bed time. It's time for you to wash up. Let's go, wash your hands and brush your teeth and then to sleep. Turn off the television, please."

"Cody, the dinner was wonderful, thank you. Let's have dessert now."

"Daddy, Mommy, we're in bed now!"

"I want a kiss."

"I want a kiss and a big hug."

"Cody, two glasses of water."

"Just a minute, here I come."

"There. Now let's wait until they're asleep; they're tired and soon they'll be safely lost in dreams. Sit down, you brought soft drinks and I bought you a six-pack of beer."

"But why, Cody?"

"Michael, I don't want to take beer away from you. I just don't want you to lose yourself in it. Have one, it's good and cold."

"Cody, you're right. I thought about this and you're right. Bring me a beer and bring one for yourself and we'll have them together."

"How did it go today?"

"OK"

"Are you ready for Monday? Everyone I know who's worked with Redacky says he's fantastic, a good teacher and a good person."

"Look, I'm a little afraid, but that always happens to me when I start something new. I'll get over it and I think I'll be successful. I don't think there'll be any problem, Cody. Go see if the children are asleep."

The feminine body got up; it leaned over to kiss the man; the masculine hand reached for a breast; his lips nibbled at it, he undid the buttons of her blouse.

"Take off your bra."

"Let me see how your children are."

41

"They're asleep, aren't they?"

"Yes."

"Let me help you with the bra."

"I'm cold.'

"Leave your blouse open like that, like that, Cody, beautiful. Kiss me."

He took off his trousers, the long white legs folded over the sofa; he took off the dirty white shoes and he threw the white coat in the corner.

"Let me turn off the light."

"And lock the door."

The bathroom light sheltered her; he gazed at her long, shiny, blond hair; from behind the sofa he bent over to kiss her. His hands caressed his wife's full, firm breasts. He shook his head, his hands reached for her belt and lowered her slacks. He placed his head on her abdomen, his arms, his hands caressed her back; he took down her panties; he touched her head; the blue eyes stared at her man's penis.

"Touch it, Cody."

She leaned over the sofa and took the phallus that seemed to expand with the movements of her hand. She drew it to her mouth; she kissed the tip. Her tongue circled it, moistening it.

"Michael, sit here."

"Take off your blouse and your panties."

They were naked, on their knees in front of the couch, touching each other and embracing. There was nothing else that they wanted at this moment. They kissed and ran their tongues over each other's bodies. They loved each other and each wished to give the other pleasure. He wanted to bring her to the peak of orgasm and play with her. She sucked him and she stroked his testicles to make them fill with the white liquid she wanted to drink. They teased each other and smiled. They got ready; they loved each other completely, they nibbled at each other, each willingly sacrificed for the other because they both gained pleasure from the wonderful union of the man and woman who were sharing their most intimate being.

"Are you ready, Cody?"

"No, touch me some more and help me with the diaphragm, here, Michael. Like that, good."

"Open your legs more. Yes, that's it."

He caressed her clitoris with his hand, he suckled her breasts. She was rigid, at the point of coming. She took his penis and rapidly stroked it."

"Not so hard or I'll come in your hands."

42

"I'm ready, Michael. How do you want to do it? From behind? Do you want me from behind?"

"How do you want it, Cody?"

"Michael, how do you want it?"

The hard member rose in the darkness and found a chair in the kitchen. He placed it in the middle of the living room and sat down.

"Come here, Cody. Come."

She stood in front of him. His hand touched her clitoris.

"Oh, Michael, I'm coming."

She opened her long legs, took the penis and guided the marvelous penetration. She rocked on the organ that she loved, faster, more intensely she moved; she offered her breast to her man to suck; his tongue licked and caressed her.

"Oh, Michael, I'm coming. Michael."

"Cody, faster, squeeze me with it, my love, my lover, my wife, my whore, my friend, my mother, my love, I'm coming, I'm coming, here, here, here . . ."

Joint violence lasted a few beautiful eternal instants. The intertwined, piled up bodies were still for a long time. The noise and light of an insecure outside world penetrated through the window. But they, since they were calm and in each other's arms, were in love. It was eight years and they were still so innocent and crazy. They were calm and secure in these moments, in this earthly paradise called "life" and "the world."

"Teresita, I'll be in the corral. You two come and help me so you learn how to do the work."

"Yes, Grandpa."

The two generations went out to the warm and tender countryside. The red sky announced the beginning of the mythic journey; they would wait for him as they had waited for him for millions of years. The column of dust pursued the approach of the police car: . . . This man has settled in here. But, why doesn't he admit it? He loves her but he's afraid of seeing what he's gotten into. It happens all the time. No, she's young and pretty; even though I'm an old man I haven't lost my eye for that. Dear God, please don't let her be hurt. Take care of her, protect her. Take my life if you want, but protect her, dear God . . . The police car came to an abrupt stop in front of the house.

"Good evening, Mr. Bilabí."

The troubled face tried to smile.

"Good evening, Pistol Man."

The boots stepped onto the porch. They entered the house with the sound of the kitchen door.

"Teresa." The voice was heard in the bedroom. There was a pause as his eyes confessed the truth, gazing at her picture in his heart.

"Pistol Man."

"How are you, Teresa?"

"What do you want?"

"Don't ask me that as if you were afraid of me."

"No, it's just that, sit down, please."

"You won't even offer me a glass of water?"

"There's beer, soda . . ."

"Just some water, please. I'm thirsty. You're not afraid of me any more, are you? I don't frighten you, do I?"

"Not now, Henry. I'm not afraid of you now. I just . . . I don't want you to hurt me."

"I won't hurt you. Don't you see that . . . No, I won't hurt you. Do you believe me?"

"Yes, yes I believe you."

"Look, you're very young. I don't want to make you cry, ever. You've changed so much in the short time that we've known each other."

"A lot, Henry, and you too have changed."

"Not me. I'm still the same. I don't change. I'll never change. And don't think that because you . . . never. Does the old man know?"

"The children have all told him; you can't really hide it, Henry."

"Don't call me Henry. Everyone calls me Pistol Man."

"Does your wife know?"

"She doesn't know anything. Has Fernando come around here?"

"He hasn't been back since the day you took Grandpa away."

"Did the old man get angry? Didn't he tell you that he was going to throw you out of the house for being a . . .?"

"Don't say that Henry! Don't think that!"

"OK, OK, don't get upset, please. I didn't think anything bad, don't cry. I'll never say it again."

"Don't do that again, son; leave the chickens alone. They'll peck out your eyes if you don't let them be. Come on, we've got to go in."

"It's a beautiful night, isn't it, Grandpa?"

"Yes, it is; we love it. But some people are afraid of it because they don't understand it."

"What do you mean, Grandpa?"

"Nothing, children, nothing; the night is beautiful."

"I want to see the monkeys."

"Oh, Grandpa, make the star drawings!"

"Grandpa, show us the people that live in the sky."

"And the animals too."

"And the monsters that live there too, please, Grandpa."

The aged body sat down there on the earth with the world of innocence on his lap. Happily they began to travel through the sky, through the entire universe. How happy the children were: . . . My grandpa is really smart, and good, and he knows all the men and the things in the sky . . .

"Which star is that, Grandpa?"

"The one over there, what's that one called?"

They heard about the mysteries of the stars, about the heros, the nymphs, about wars and infinite love. How happy the children were among the stars!

"But I don't know what kind of list it is. I just don't know. This is the second year that I've prepared it. It has the names and occupations of the men, single and married, and how big a family they have and when they got here. I think that's all."

"And you say that they send it to the government."

"Yes."

"But I never heard of anything like that. Why do they want it?"

"I don't know. I only know that the people on the list are all Chicanos. I don't like what's going on. You know about the riots there; the Chicanos don't want to put up with any more. The young people are rebelling because of everything we've been through. And the business about Dr. Hales, why couldn't he stay? Just because they didn't want him; that's all, because they didn't want him, because they didn't permit us to have him here. I've been working for Pistol Man for some six, seven years? I don't know, maybe I should quit this job and work in the fields, help with the harvest, then I wouldn't have these problems."

"But that would mean starting to travel all over the country again. That's not what I want for my daughter. We've got a house here and we're fine."

"Yes, we're fine, but I don't know what's going on. I'm unhappy, I don't feel well. Sometimes I think the people on the farms hate me because I'm working with him. It's not like before."

"Well, if it bothers you, maybe you're right. Maybe it would be better for us to go somewhere else. Maybe it would be better to go back to working the harvests."

"No, maybe there's another way, I don't know. But they never should have chased Dr. Hales away."

45

The day began with a miraculous burst of blood red light shining on the Lincoln Continental parked at the door of the magnificent castle of the triumphant couple. The modern clock struck five when the two young people left in their cars. The gardener waved when he saw them rapidly pull away, the tires leaving a trail of smoke. The unstoppable hands softly struck nine when they heard the successful Beesleys say goodbye to the black servant.

"Have dinner for the children at exactly three o'clock. Don't forget, Niger."

"No, ma'am."

"Well now, it's getting late. Goodbye, Niger."

"Goodbye, Ma'am."

Quickly the two vulnerable bodies locked themselves in the Lincoln Continental and rapidly pulling away they headed for the highway. Washington closed the gate of the estate. Enjoying the privilege of the MD plates, they parked in the restricted area in front of Doctor Hales's apartment.

"Good morning, Doctor Beesley, Mrs. Beesley."

The couple walked up the steps without responding. His fist wounded the door.

"Don't knock so hard."

"Hello!"

Three voices simultaneously called for Leroy's attention.

"What a surprise! Come in."

"What are you doing this glorious morning, Karen?"

"Reading the newspaper. Diane, coffee?"

"Yes, please. Let me help you."

The student apartment heard everyone at once and it lent itself to easy conversation, letting them cross sentences when their ears caught the most interesting of what the four of them said.

"Things are going well, aren't they, Leroy?"

"Yes, I think I've been accepted by the interns. No one has given me a hard time. I'm happy."

"Don't you see? You're better off here than with all those poor people."

"Yes, and Karen tells me they're going to go out and buy a new car today, Harold."

"That's great, Leroy."

"Well, you know what they did to mine."

"Listen, let's talk about something else. Let's forget that crazy episode."

"What do you mean, 'crazy'?"

Karen's brain immediately grasped the unavoidable.

"Here's the coffee."

Words of salvation were inserted.

"Harold, what do you suggest, should we buy a Volkswagen or a Fiat?"

"A Volkswagen? Listen, you deserve something better. And what's more, I've heard that Bekstrom and Pergmun are very impressed with your performance in the emergency room and that they are going to offer you a partnership in their corporation. You'll get rich. I've heard rumors that they'll offer you fifty thousand to start. There's no doubt that you established a reputation for being exact and that people respect you. Look, buy a car like mine or the one I wanted to buy, except that my wife wanted a Continental. I love Jaguars. And I'm going to buy one. Diane, I'll never listen to you again."

"I bet you hear me now, big ears!"

"Look how this woman treats me."

The laughter quickly disappeared from the room.

"You're lucky not to have had a rebel in your first class, Leroy."

"They still exist?"

"Of course, Calva's had a problem with young Logan. He's a good doctor but he doesn't want to do things according to the rules. The other day Calva made him rewrite all the charts. He was furious. Then Calva threw him out of the room and forbid him to smoke his cigar. Logan was ready to slug Calva. I spoke to the two of them. He calmed down after I threatened him with having to repeat geriatrics. He did everything that Calva told him to do."

"Where's he now?"

"With Redacky. You'll have him in three months."

"I'd like to meet him."

"I think I know who he is. He smokes a crooked cigar, doesn't he? And he's handsome too."

"Hey, be careful with this woman, Leroy, careful."

"Tell me, how is Martínez doing? It was a risk to admit him. You know, he's like the ones you just left down there."

"Pato is one of the best doctors I've ever known. If Bekstrom and Pergmun offer me what you say they will I'm going to insist that Pato comes with me."

"Don't rush, calm down. I don't know if Bekstrom and Pergmun would want a guy like Martínez. They are an exclusive outfit and they only want the best."

"He's the best you can find in emergency medicine. He's a genius, a natural, and above all he knows what he's doing and he's sensitive to the patients. Furthermore, Bekstrom and Pergmun aren't perfect doctors either."

"I know what you're talking about; they were lucky they weren't sued."

"What was it, Harold?"

"Pergmun is careful but Bekstrom is a fool at times. Everyone at the hospital knows it. A man came to his office, a patient of Pergmun's; he had all the symptoms of an embolism and Bekstrom told him it was just a neck spasm and sent him home. That night the man died of a massive embolism. It was really stupid. But Bekstrom was lucky; the guy was of Martínez's and Calva's persuasion. You say that Martínez is good, maybe you're right, but I don't know if your future colleagues will accept him. The only one of his kind that I know is Calva and even though his problem is that he doesn't know if he's a man or a woman, he's one of the best that we have."

"How do you tolerate his homosexuality?"

"Well, it didn't come out for five years; besides, he's a Harvard graduate. My alma mater always turns out the best. Also, I always thought he was a European."

"Stop talking about the hospital, it's a bore."

"You're right, Karen. How much are the houses where you live? Leroy and I have talked about moving. Allison doesn't have any place of her own to play, she doesn't have friends. She's alone and I feel very sorry for her. And when Leroy accepts Bekstrom's offer we'll be able to pay whatever we have to."

"Fine, Karen. I knew that you would accept, Leroy."

His thoughts were delving into the past because of the present; his wife's legs were walking on the broken glass there that day. The woman with the yellow baby had asked him for help, but he didn't stay. She was beautiful: . . . I don't understand, you're a doctor; you have a little bit of God in your mind, in your hands. You can help my son. Look how dried out he is. . . . I wonder where they are, what happened to those poor, unfortunate people? . . .

"Well, the houses. They're gorgeous and they start at one hundred and fifty thousand, but once you sign the contract with Bekstrom and Pergmun you can take it from the corporation and find a way of taking it off your taxes. That would be the easiest. I hope you get a house that has . . ."

"Now circulation is controlled by the heart, which works like a pump. It's a muscle whose interior is divided into two cavities, which in turn are divided into two others, an upper part, the auricle, and a lower part, the ventricle, which communicate through a valve which lets the blood flow from the auricle to the ventricle, but never in the opposite direction. The heart sends the blood to the body through the arteries; the blood returns to the heart through the veins. The passage of the blood from the arteries to the veins is done through extremely fine tubes, the capillaries. The blood leaves the left ventricle of the heart through a wide artery, the aorta, which, after dividing, irrigates all the organs of the body. At this time, the blood is bright red. In the capillaries, where the blood finally flows, the blood transfers the oxygen to the cells and receives the waste products and the carbon dioxide. Now it takes on a dark red color. The capillaries join together to form the vena cava that carries the blood to the heart's right auricle. This is commonly known as the great circulation. From the right auricle, the venous blood is forced to the pulmonary artery which takes it to the lungs, where it yields oxygen. It returns to the heart through the pulmonary veins which take it to the left auricle, from which it goes to the left ventricle, to begin a new cycle. The circulation from the right heart to the left heart through the lungs is the so-called small circulation. That's right, you think I'm an idiot for giving you this superficial review. I'm sure you're asking yourselves, what happened to the great heart specialist Doctor Redacky? Well, I don't think I'm an expert. I'm always learning. Those of you who think that you will become great cardiologists because you have studied a few months with me are plain stupid. It's true that I have many years experience and that I know a little about cardiology, but now I want to see what you know. You'll be the ones to teach me. The development of the pacemaker is the result of the imagination of doctors like you. You know something, you have imagination, use it, apply it. I am here to guide you and to make you doctors with effervescent imaginations, who don't believe in their M.D. degrees, because those that do are stagnant snobs. Get out and learn about the world, be human, don't think yourselves indescribable, untouchable or gods. Make a revolution to charge less. I hope you're here because you want to be good doctors and not because you want to get rich. Make a revolution by being different, rebels and enormously good, the best in every sense of the word. That's all for today."

Arteries, jugular veins, pulmonary veins, femoral arteries, heart after heart, face after face, green, black, blue eyes, the sad smiles of the moribund, the happy ones of those who were saved, every human facade with the hope of salvation passed by.

"Yes, you'll save me. What do you mean, you can't? A transplant, you can do it easily. I don't want to die!"

"The time has come. I don't want you to see me like this, as an invalid. I don't want to live any more; it's unfair to you and my children. Don't be afraid, you'll have to go on without me. You're young. A woman like you shouldn't be alone. Find someone who loves you and who will take care of my children. Don't be afraid and don't cry, please, because you'll make me cry. On Monday I'll let the children come. It will be the last time that I see them. I want you to help me. You have to be strong because if you aren't I won't be brave enough. I depend on you. I know that because you love me, you'll help me die."

"Mommy, Mommy! Daddy, Daddy! Doctor Logan told me that I can go home tomorrow with you and that I'm all better."

The mother took the child in her arms, receiving his healthy heart. Tears ran down the cheeks of the boy-father who said nothing. Two months passed already; the family was having dinner together and smiling, chatting. The father's eyes watched everyone, the fist fell to the table and amid sobs and shouts his mouth cried from the heart.
"I would give my life for my children."
The man's grateful body ran to the master bedroom.
"What's the matter with Daddy?"
"What happened to Daddy?"
"Mommy, Mommy?"
"Your father is very happy that we're all together. It's his way of telling us that he loves us a lot. Don't worry, just thank God that you have a father that loves you so much."

"Pato, I'd like you to come over tonight. We could have a few beers."
"Ah, Doctor Logan is doing his charts carefully and, it appears, with enthusiasm."
"Not with enthusiasm, but to learn something. Redacky asks us to do them in such a way that we do learn. Are you coming over or aren't you?"
"Yes, if you let me bring a friend."
"But don't let Silky get drunk. You know what she's like when she's loaded."
"But who told you I was going to bring Silky?"
"Who else could it be?"
"It's someone I never thought I had a chance with. One day I was

50

talking to her and I asked her to go out with me and she said yes and we've been together ever since."

"Are you already living with her?"

"No, but I think that if Amy asked me to live with her or said we should get married, I would. I don't dare ask her. I'm afraid she would say she didn't love me."

"Amy!"

"Yes, Amy. Imagine, I never thought I had a chance. She's beautiful and I really love her."

"I'll tell you, if I weren't married, she would be the one I'd go after. Physically and psychologically she's a woman. Like I said, if I weren't married I would try and make my nest in her heart and between her legs."

"You're a bastard, Michael Logan, but maybe that's why I like you so much."

"Bring Amy, Cody and I would love to have you over. What you've just told me makes me very happy. But Pato, keep calm, don't go crazy, take everything nice and slow. And Silky, are you still fooling around with her."

"Yes."

"What are you going to do?"

"What? Tell her I can't see her any more. I feel sorry for her, but what can I do? But I'm really going to miss that ass."

"What a bunch of bastard chauvinist pigs we are."

"No, I really feel sorry for her, but I think she'll find somebody else. She's been with a lot of us."

"Is she still saying that they're harassing her?"

"Yes, and she's crazier than I don't know what. They're paging me; I have to go to the emergency room."

"How're you doing there?"

"Fine, Leroy's been like a father to me."

"Leroy?"

"Yes, Doctor Hales, Leroy Hales."

"Oh, yes. OK, I'll see you. Bye."

"Thank you, Señor Presidente, I wish you success on your trip."

The elevator of the Torre Latinoamericana spit out the chief executive and the small group of officials and guards.

"I think you have enough votes to convince the ones who are waivering. However, if we don't convince that black bastard, it will be hard to get the African votes."

"But I think the trip will convince them that we want to cooperate.

Furthermore, the financial assistance will convince them more than anything else."

"I feel strange, uncovered, unprotected, especially after what happened in Guerrero and at the University."

"Don't worry. We have guards everywhere, we're well pro . . ."

The sudden spitting penetrated the minister's legs; the blood spotted his grey suit; a volley of shouting and of hidden muzzles directed the panic; the parked car exploded, breaking the building's windows; the Presidente heard the buzzing of the world when five men threw themselves on top of him protecting him from the little lead balls that tried to kiss him as they fell; they dragged the chief executive inside. He was able to see two wounded men shot on the sidewalk full of scorched blood. Firemen, police, federal guards provided cover and made the civilians flee; under federal law no one in the building could leave until everything was cleaned and orderly. In about two hours the attack was covered up as if nothing had happened. The Presidente found himself awake and alive in his heavily guarded El Bosque residence.

"How many died?"

"Three of ours, two civilians and one of them — a girl who had a machine gun under her skirt. She didn't have any identification and the police, as usual, blew her face away with bullets."

"What a bitch."

"Thank God that no officials died. You, sir, suffered lesions in the shoulder and neck."

"It must not appear in the newspapers; absolutely nothing."

"It's all been taken care of, sir."

"There is only one problem; we have the bodies of the dead civilians. What should we do with them?"

"Put them with the girl's. They just disappeared and that's all. Do the same with ours. Send two agents right away to their homes to find out if they are sick because they didn't show up for work and we want to know why."

"The same procedures we followed in Tla . . ."

"Don't tell me anything further. You know what to do. Now leave me alone. I don't want to see you until tomorrow and pray to God that nothing gets in the papers. Because if it does we're fucked."

"Sir, just one thing more, there is an old, ragged man who . . ."

"That damned bastard, torture him until he tells everything that he saw and everything he knows. Get everything he knows out of him. Torture him until he makes things up! Now get out!"

The Presidente's eyes filled with tears of rage and hatred. He prayed.

He prayed to his God to help him cover up what had happened. He offered holy prayers that his plans not be ruined: . . . God, help me, I beg you not to let anyone find out; if you help me now when I need you more than ever, I promise you that I'll always be a good Christian. Please, help me, please, let me make it, let me be what I want to be, please, dear God, please . . .

"Cody, bring me another beer, OK? Do you like this group, Amy? I think they're terrific."

. . . Saturday in the park, think it was the Fourth of July . . .

"Chicago, I really love them. That's really power, bro', the power of song, of art."

"Pato, you're as crazy as I am."

"You're right, Michael, except that Pato is a little calmer and he doesn't blow up."

"I think you're right, Cody. Michael, you have to realize when you can attack and when you can't. The most important thing is to know when one must be humble. You see, you have to know how to get power and know when to give in. Sure, there is a time when power or no power you have to say what you have to say; defend yourself and not let anyone trample you. For example, I never made trouble for Calva. I did what he said and that was that; I fulfilled my obligations. And he gave me an outstanding report. And what's more, he's not such a bad guy. Redacky gave me a good recommendation too. I went with Hales and it looks like when I finish he'll make me a partner in the Pergmun and Bekstrom corporation."

"Really? You're always full of surprises!"

"I don't believe you. Who would want a greaser Chicano like you in their practice?"

"Congratulations!"

"When will they offer this poor guy something?"

"Don't say that, Michael."

"Pato, why didn't you tell me before?"

"They just told me this afternoon, Amy. I wanted to wait to be with my friends, with Michael, Cody, and you."

"Cody, bring two more beers. Pato and I have to celebrate."

"Michael, how many beers have you had?"

"Cody, this is a special night for my friend Pato; apotheosis, Pato. I drink to your future success."

"And to yours, Michael."

"And maybe to the future marriage of Doctor and Amy Martínez."

"He's getting carried away, Amy."

"Yes, look at how his ears are getting red. What childish men."

"Hey, girls, why don't you make some sandwiches? Please, we're hungry."

"And put on another Chicago record."

"Tell me, Pato, what's Hales like?"

"Like I said, he's a terrific guy. He's serious, but he's a bit crazy too. He's got a mother, a wife and a daughter; he was born and grew up in a town near here. He's had his ups and downs like everyone. When he was young he liked car races. He had his own racing car. He was in jail once for drugs, I think it was for possession. He went to college and then to medical school."

"A humane type of person?"

"Yes, for example, before coming here he was in Mathis, Texas. He tried to help the Chicanos there but the Anglos didn't want any Anglo doctor getting interested in those people and they threw him out. He went through a lot. At first he resisted but in the end, after they broke into his office, and destroyed his car, and I think the next step would have been against his family, he decided to come back to the hospital here."

"Do you mean to tell me, Pato, that they chased him out of town for helping poor people."

"Not just poor people, but poor Chicanos, they all had Mexican blood."

"But, that's ridiculous! He wasn't doing any harm there. Didn't he have any Anglo patients?"

"I don't think so because his office was in the Chicano neighborhood and very few Anglos ever went there. That's how it is, Amy. There are still a lot of people who don't like us. What I find strange though is that Hales told me that if Pergmun and Bekstrom don't accept me, he won't sign on with them."

"Pato, why don't you go to Mathis?"

"Because I don't want to. My revolution is here, doing what I do and getting into that damn racist corporation they've got. I want to be welcomed and honored and I want to become a specialist in emergency medicine and be accepted by those snobs. I want to be accepted for what I know and for my contributions to the art of healing. That will be my contribution. My struggle is here, not there. But listen, this doesn't mean that I am going to forget where I came from. No, sir. I'm still going to help my people; there are still a lot of serious problems that I can help to resolve. I never forget who I am and where I came from. I know that I'll have to take a lot of criticism for my position. And they'll criticize me not only for being a successful man, but also because I'm going to marry an Anglo. Right, Amy?"

"Yes."

The slender attentive girl's answer came. The silence lasted a few intensely happy moments for everyone. They loved each other in this ordinary living room. The sandwiches were passed around; they savored coffee and dessert. It was a beautiful, intimate evening. If love between two couples could be sexually consummated without harming anyone, what a lustful orgy of affection they would have enjoyed.

The silence in the apartment said nothing about the absent mouths. The couple moved about in the interior; the children went about in the worlds that only they knew and in the bathroom he was looking at his penis: . . . Bitch, I have to use you more. Amy, you and your ass, I lost you, I lost you, no, I never had a chance, but that's what Pato thought too . . .

"Michael, are you finished?"

. . . But I have my sweet tail . . .

"I'm coming."

The woman studied him through her eyes.

"What are you doing, Michael?"

"I'm getting ready for you."

"Crazy. What do you think about Pato and Amy?"

"I never would have believed it. But they make a great couple; they seem to be seriously thinking about marriage."

"Pato's been terribly lucky, Michael."

"He deserves it, Cody; he's a good buddy. I hope that everything else goes right for him."

"Don't be such a pessimist, Michael."

"What did I say?"

"It was the way you said it, your tone."

"Well, I'm thinking about Silky. I don't know exactly but I feel that things aren't so good for her in this situation."

"No, I think that Pato will be one of the very few that reach the top and stay there. Very few people have the opportunity and Pato is one of the chosen. There's no reason why it shouldn't be him. Even if there's a problem with Silky, Pato will come out all right."

"Yes, and I'm going to Mathis."

"What? What are you saying? Go where?"

"Nothing. The stuff about Hales was interesting, wasn't it?"

The naked bodies, he erect and she moist, got into bed.

"Yes, but very dangerous."

"No, I don't think so. It's just that Hales didn't know how to get along with the people in Mathis. You have to know how to handle them."

"I see, and you think that you could do it. Don't be crazy, Shane, Jason, you and I have sacrificed too much to let you go to people who don't want you. What have we worked for? So they'll kill you?"

"Calm down. I'm not going right now. Let's not talk any more about it. Look at me and let me see you."

"Michael."

"That's it. It's good like that."

"That's how you do it, Michael."

The parking lights blinked; the cars huddled there were waiting for their owners. The general hospital watched over them, calming their impatience while thousands of humans were nailed in the throes of dying, eating, working, being born, fornicating, fighting, shitting, talking, pissing, shouting, and praying in their insides that gurgled and wriggled in incessant movement. There are some who never leave it; they reside there like vegetables, with dried out green heads. The decrepit trunk is still watered and somehow or other it gets to the internal pump-wound blowing bits of plasma to the skull. There the healthy and the sick are prisoners of scientific hope. An applicable praxis for carnal miracles and disasters. The poor are interned here, dreaming of luxury. This dream allows them to accept their servitude. They never escape, bloodied, erudite, moles, condemned to achieve wealth and glory and nauseating errors. Everything is part of the dream of those who pursue each other in this place. The light jumped from the feminine profile that he already adored: her hair, forehead, nose, mouth, chin, neck, breasts, abdomen, vagina, legs, calves, feet.

"Amy, where are you going? Amy?"

"Not tonight, Pato, not tonight."

"You're not coming to my room?"

"No, I'd like to be alone."

"Something bothered you tonight, didn't it? Something that I said? About us getting married? That was the truth, Amy, I love you and I want you to be my wife."

Her eyes smiled at him, caressing his cheek.

"Do you love me, Pato?"

"Yes."

"And I love you. We'll be man and wife; but tonight I don't want to be with you. Maybe it's because I already know that it's decided.

56

I feel that tonight will be my last as a single woman. I am totally committed to you. It doesn't matter what happens from now on; I'll be yours. I'm not a total innocent. I have loved other men; but I feel that I can't escape what's happening between you and me. Our relationship is good, Pato. Tomorrow I'll be completely, physically and mentally yours. We'll love each other and we'll hate each other and we'll see how much we can take, because that's what it's all about."

"You make me laugh a little, Amy."

"You make me laugh too, Pato. Good night, my love."

"Amy."

"No, Pato. I'll see you tomorrow."

She went into the dormitory; he waited outside for the light from her room. A half hour passed. He left looking back in her direction.

The woman with the sickly child came running and looking back over her shoulder. She went into her friend's kitchen.

"Doña Gertrudis! Doña Gertrudis!"

"What's the matter child? What's the matter! You're shaking. What happened to you? What did you see?"

"Oh, my God, I saw her, I saw her."

"Who? Who did you see?"

"I was in the outhouse and, and . . . Give me something to drink, please."

"Here's some water with sugar."

"Oh, wait, now I can talk, oh God, what a fright!"

"Tell me, calmly, you can tell me."

"Yes, now I can talk. I was in the outhouse, I finished and I left; the night was clear, you could see everything clearly and I wasn't at all afraid. The stars, the moon, the warm breeze made me feel happy. I was walking home when I don't know what I felt, but, suddenly, I got a chill, a shiver. I stopped to look around, the wind, everything was quiet. You could see the lights of the house in the distance, but of course the house isn't far. Well, just then I decided to return home as quickly as possible. The dogs began to bark, then to snarl and to howl. Then I was afraid. I started to run when I looked behind me; I stopped, Doña Gertrudis, I stopped, and I saw that a person was coming along the barn wall. At first I couldn't tell anything. But when it got closer I realized that it was a woman. I started to move to the side a little but I kept seeing her. She was coming faster. Then I realized that she was wearing a long dress that was billowing in the wind; but there wasn't any wind, everything was still, except her and her dress. She was coming toward me as if she were flying, like she was gliding along on the air. I saw that she had long hair that seemed to dance in the wind. Then I looked at the ground and I realized that the woman had no feet and that she was flying across the surface of the land. At that moment, Doña Gertrudis, I felt myself freeze, my hair started to curl, I couldn't move. I saw myself running but I didn't move. I saw myself screaming, but I didn't scream. She was getting closer to me. She was coming toward me with her arms outstretched. I don't know how I did it but I took one step and then another. I began to run faster and faster. I didn't turn to look back and see if she was coming after me or not. I arrived home as you saw me, unable to speak or even to breathe. I was terrified, Doña Gertrudis, just terrified. What was it? What did I see?"

"Poor dear, poor thing; what you just saw is the great messenger. Didn't you notice that the dogs howling turned into a cry, a long, sharp cry?"

"Yes, yes that's what it was like. You mean that I just saw her."

"Yes, you just saw her. Something has happened tonight; someone has just lost a child in one way or another. A Chicano child has died."

As he opened the door of the dark room he was greeted by the shadow of a woman he did not know. Her sobbing voice made him hurry to the lamp, to light.

"Silky! Silky! What are you doing here? What do you want?"

"I came to see you, to talk to you. You know that they are still following me and that they're going to kill me. But that doesn't matter any more, at least not to you."

"Silky, I can't see you any more. I don't want to see you."

"I know. I know about Amy. I'm happy for you, really. She'll make you happy and she can give you more than I can."

"Why did you come, Silky?"

Her face, her breasts were enraged and cried the truth.

"You didn't know it, you didn't know it, but you did know that they are following me and that I'm sick. I've been poisoned and that's why I did it, that's why I did it. And what's more, I'm sick, you know that, and I thought it would be born deformed."

"What are you telling me? What? You were pregnant? And you aborted it? A child of mine, why didn't you tell me?"

"I've been poisoned, it was going to be deformed."

"You didn't tell me!"

Screaming, his arm descended on the woman's face. A black rage threw her to the bed that was bloodied by her screaming, hysterical mouth.

"Take that, you fucking whore, there. Why didn't you tell me?"

"I'm sorry, Pato, but I did it for both of us! I don't care if you hit me, I deserve it, but please, forgive me. I did it because I love you."

His fist replied quickly and strongly, striking the wounded vagina and pounding the teary face. Her wild sobbing enraged him almost until the point of fatal madness. Many have experienced this moment that has ruined their lives. A mere microsecond of black rage that dulls common sense has nipped the glorious career of the chosen ones. It can happen to anyone; you don't know when, how or where this event awaits you. It comes quickly for some, late for others, and never for some. You have to protect yourself against the fever. Some take precautions by thinking. They think about why they think; they think instead of the thought they were thinking; they illuminate the recesses of their thought. Others save themselves and others must be saved. Drenched in confusion he was pummelling her bloody face when the men dragged him away from the female body lying on the floor.

"Leave her alone, Pato, stop!"

"But she didn't tell me!"

"That's enough, Pato, that's enough."

"Take him to my room. This goes no farther. Don't say anything. We all know who she is and who he is. You, call Logan. Jerry, you call Amy. Tell her to come here right away. Let's go, quickly now and don't make such a racket or there'll be trouble."

"Amy, I don't know what happened. We found him on top of Silky beating her. She was unconscious from it. Robert is with her."

"But, why was he hitting her?"

"Like I said, I don't know. You can ask him. What we don't want is for this to get out because it could ruin him. Pato has a future with you and in the profession. He's a great guy. We have to save him."

"But if Silky says something."

"Amy, who's going to believe her? Everyone at the hospital thinks she's nuts. She just lost her job because she's so crazy. She's slept with practically all of us. She's a poor wretch. Who's going to believe her? She herself won't even remember what happened."

"Was she drunk?"

"She's always drunk."

"No, Jerry, it's all of you who keep her drunk all the time."

"Amy."

"Michael."

"What happened to Pato? He beat up Silky?"

"That's what they told me. Let's go upstairs."

"Good evening, doctors. Where's the great future doctor? Now you've screwed yourself."

"Amy! Amy!"

"Here I am, Pato."

"Amy, she didn't tell me. She didn't tell me."

"What didn't she tell you, Pato?"

"Amy, come with me."

"I think I know what you're going to tell me, Michael."

"I had a feeling that something like this was going to happen. You think she was pregnant and aborted the child too."

"Yes."

"And Pato couldn't take what he heard in addition to what she did. And of course, he began to hit her. But what I didn't realize is that he was capable of such brutality."

"Michael, the important thing is to help him get out of this mess. The guys are right that no one will believe Silky. Now we have to convince Pato or make him accept what has happened as one of those things in life. Bah, Pato is going to be all right; this isn't going to stop him. But Silky? What are you going to do with her?"

"She'll stay with the guys. That's how to handle it; as if everything were normal. Robert, how's Silky?"

"Pretty bad, in addition to the beating she did the abortion herself. I don't know what the hell she stuck in herself but she's bleeding, and we have to put her in the hospital right now."

"But, how are we going to explain it?"

"Don't worry about it. Why talk more about it? Take Pato, Amy. We'll clean up the room and have Silky admitted."

"Are you sure about all of this?"

"Yes."

"Have Pato pull himself together. Silky won't say anything, at least not for a while since we gave her a shot to put her out. When she wakes up it will all be like a dream for her."

They looked at each other for a long time; they told each other that they alone were the ones who could protect each other because at that minute like all other human beings they wanted to eat each other in order to advance in the world of competition created by intelligent men. She gazed at the man she had chosen for her life. She was one of the few that could choose. Others in this world fell in love with what they could get. It wasn't their fault; they were ugly, even if they had big breasts, or terrific buttocks. In this reality, at any rate, this is the way it was; intelligence was not a criterion. They were bright; it was easy for them. Therefore the essential took on importance for the brainy doctors, primitive, savage, magicians. He carried his bones with fatigue; she took the bag of confused brains to her room. Their walking bodies entered into the natural darkness; suddenly they were flooded with modern technology's illumination. The magicians looked at each other with the knowledge of the discovery that within them lay the capacity to kill in order to punish, or to save, or to try to change the past, what was already done.

"Drink your coffee. What happened to you, Pato?"

"I don't know. I went crazy for a minute and then I got over it. When I realized that she was carrying a child of mine and that she had killed it for me, I was furious."

"And who are you to judge that what she did wasn't best for everyone?"

"No, Amy, I have the right to say what is to become of a child of mine."

"She does too."

"Yes, but she didn't tell me."

"What do you expect from that poor girl? You've all had her; she's the major sperm depository in the dormitories. How can you be so sure that the child was yours? Are you absolutely sure? Answer me."

"No."

"Good. What matters now is to finish the internship and become a partner in Bekstrom and Pergmun. Pato, I don't want to lose you."

"Why, Amy?"

"I love you . . . Pato."

How many times are these words repeated in a single night, in thousands of languages, they've lost their meaning and each time someone says them they have a different connotation.

"Yes, we like you, but you have to fulfill the requirements."

"What are they?"

"You, like the rest of us, have to produce. However, we know that you are weak, theoretically weak. You're the only weak one that we have hired. I emphasize this because we have produced works of quality and originality. It won't be easy. In fact, it will be quite difficult for you, but we do want you here with us."

"Professor, what have you published?"

"It's better not to talk about that now."

"Professor, why do you leave the country at every opportunity?"

"Well, you see I have . . . well, actually, I am from a very well-known family, upper class as they say there; they need me there, they want me there."

"Professor, you are famous as the outstanding genius of the department; the high priest of Marxism. Everyone loves you. But neither your philosophy nor your intelligence can save you now, only you can help yourself. But of course you don't want to sell out or compromise yourself. And what is it that your great intelligence has created?"

"I am the weak one, theoretically speaking, help me, master, help me."

"Yes, of course we want you and we're going to help you."

"Professor, you too are struggling for security here. But you are somewhat different than the rest. You live with a homosexual and you rub asses diachronically and synchronically. Tell me, you who are so clever and highly respected, to be perfectly frank, what have you published?"

"Articles, scientific, computer articles."

. . . Here the smart ones are really bastards, tough mothers and I, who know nothing, am an expert in nothing. What am I doing in this situation? . . . But they say that they want me and I hope I can stay . . .

"Pato, I love you, oh, I love you!"

The moist, mounted, penetrated vagina copulated with the rich future doctor's organ.

"Adorable, your ass is adorable, Cody, Cody, I love you, I love you, I love you, here, here, my dearest, I love you!"

"Do I want one? Of course I want another patient. What difference does one more wretched patient make. Leave her in room nine."

Silky arrived at the white room that had been hers for several days. They both agreed and the rash intern grabbed angelical Silky's nipples. The orgasm left his pants wet.

"The sheets are wet, Henry, should I change them?"

"No, Teresa, don't change them. We'll sleep in what's ours."

"For months now you've been almost living with us."

"Your grandad seems to have accepted it, the children talk to me and play with me, even the dog doesn't bark at me. Teresa, you know that what we do means more now; for me it's something sacred."

"Henry, you're a good man, really good, and I lo . . . "

"Teresa, I have never told you this, and maybe I'll never tell you again. Teresa, I think I love you."

The little stand had chairs for the hungry. Heads turned and eyes stared at the blondes that were strolling through the market. The smoke, the odors, the glances whetted the appetite. The sound of the tortillas caressed by the hands that were making them was mouth-watering.

"Two chicken tacos and a Peñafiel."

"Six pork and sausage and a Victoria."

"No, sir, why would I pass the meat to you if it's worse than yours? I don't care if it's your cousin."

"Here, buy yourself a few beers and we'll talk tomorrow."

"No, not with that. Beer's gone up a lot more; that's hardly enough to buy a Victoria. I'm better off throwing you to the boys in blue."

"That would be stupid. Later you'd have to buy them drinks for a year. No, let the meat rot, that would be better. You're not a buddy."

"Look, I think we can make a deal. Let me have some lunch and I'll see you there this afternoon."

"OK, see you then."

Her red lips approached the policeman and attracted the attention of the inspector who touched her breasts with his eyes and his mouth. The small, skinny woman drew near, stopping behind the other cop. At this moment the hawkers' cries reached a crescendo.

"Buy these, Miss. What can I give you, sweetheart? Two for five; melons, six for ten pesos. Tell me how many you want, young lady."

They weren't even able to lower their hands. Their chests were filled with something so heavy that their legs were unable to support it. Three more opened fire. The inspectors fell, sightless. The onomatopoeia of the machine guns splashed the chests and heads of the instant cadavers. Technology made it easy to turn faces into strawberry malts whose glasses would break into little pieces with more gunshots. Shouts of children, wounded women and other policemen who tried to catch up with the assassins were added to the scene. The butchers in the market covered the cadavers with meat cloths stained with pig's blood. The people learned about the attack when they heard the Presidente.

"Mexicans, these attacks against our people will no longer be permitted. We, the government, will find these rebels, these revolutionaries who are intent on destruction and who have no respect for the rights of others. You will help us by allowing your homes to be searched."

He dried his hands, his arms, and his almost full beard: . . . What a handsome guy you are, Michael! . . .

The mirror of personal reality sang to him: . . . Oh, what a looker! . . .

The hair was straightened as he went from the bathroom to the corridor. He went to the desk, his pen and his brain were not cooperating. His mind was distracted by a nurse's body, he looked up: . . .EXIT. . .

The stairs heading down were cold, slippery, anti-hygenic, people had spit on them. One damn foot slipped on the other. What kind of an athlete was the heavy man who turned into the corridor and headed for the cafeteria with a crooked cigar in his mouth? His brain-eye intensified his slight smile when he saw Redacky's face.

"Sit down, Michael. What would you like? It's my treat. Just coffee? Are you sure?"

"Yes, Doctor."

"Absolutely sure?"

"That's what I said, Dr. Redacky."

"All right, don't get mad."

"No, of course not. Look, even if I wanted to I don't think I could get angry with you."

"Oh, really. You know you seem a bit down the last few days. Are you tired?"

"Yes, I am pretty much. And sometimes I think about quitting all this. It's not that I don't like the profession, but I don't like what I see down the road—an office, my patients, a pretty house, living with my family, getting old and dying of a heart attack. How boring! It's not a good life. For doctors, life should be full of adventures, of exceptional cases; it shouldn't become routine, a job like any other."

"Michael, you really are crazy. But I like your kind of crazinesss, it's like mine. The decision is yours. Don't let yourself become something run of the mill, like most of your colleagues. Don't get swept along by the current of mediocrity."

"But how can I avoid it? I feel that I'm headed in that direction. I'm afraid I'm going to get bored and give it all up. I must be a strange guy. Who ever heard of a doctor who loved his profession but who was also fed up with it?"

"Michael, you're not the only one. I think that we fuck over interns like you with so much work that we turn you into stagnant doctors, so overworked that you're bored with what should be inspiring. The program is overwhelming; it strains a young intern so much that we kill his idealism, we kill his compassion, and his humanity. When they leave here they only think about getting even for what we've done to them, for how we've made them suffer. The easiest way of doing that is by getting rich, with the excuse that they deserve it because they've worked so hard and studied so many years. Here, as I say, we kill them, we make them technical doctors, scientific monsters. Some completely lose their capacity to feel, even for themselves, their wives, and children. They don't even get hard when they see a pretty young thing. They are so set on becoming specialists that nothing else exists for them. And so the patient becomes an example, a specimen upon which one will carry out an experiment. The patient becomes a guinea pig and a source of wealth. We dehumanize you poor guys. But some of you manage to salvage some idealism. You are one of those and I hope you never lose that sacred gift. You're tired and bored now, but prepare yourself, dedicate yourself to learning everything you can because you will be called upon. Maybe you think I'm an old nut who thinks he can see the future; maybe you're right. I'll admit to you quite frankly that men like you and I are crazy. But the outside world interprets our madness as a source of proud artistic creativity, when actually, the fact is, we're crazy, Michael. And it's proven in our very creations."

"Yes, of course, you're right, Doctor. We're all crazy."

"No, Michael, that's not what I said. I said that people like you and me are crazy. The others are sick. They aren't psychologically equipped to resolve the obstacles that reality has put before them. Look at this old newspaper, Michael. Here, this article about a peasant who walked from Mathis to the hospital. His name's Emigdio, that's right, Emigdio and his wife Zoila. She had had a baby there in their hut, but they decided to walk the whole way to get to civilization, to the hospital and to be in the newspapers. She had two more children, and so what? Well, that was their contribution to our world, yours and mine. That's to say he knew it was crazy to make his wife walk here, but they knew that it would be the best for them and for their children. They tried to do the impossible, what people in the outside world call craziness, ignorance, and stupidity. They achieved their goal, they were successful, they took a risk, of course, a very dangerous risk for themselves, for her and the children, but once they had started, there was no turning back, it was a personal challenge."

"Where did they come from? From Mathis?"

"Yes, Mathis is a town of, well, the majority of the population is Chicano. But the Anglos control them and exploit them, another example of a flaw in our paradise."

"It's the second time that I've heard about that town."

"Have you talked to Hales? He was there. Not for long though, they got rid of him."

"No, I haven't talked to him. But why did they throw him out? I've heard something about it, but I'd like to know what explanation they gave you."

"Michael, talk to Hales. You'll be with him in two weeks. He'll tell you everything. Someday, Michael, you will find something, somewhere where you can make a revolution. I'll see you upstairs."

The miraculous, crazy phenomenon drew away from the potential one: . . . Fucking genius, I really think he is crazy . . .

Now in his brain, the newspaper, Emigdio, Zoila and the children, Pato, Redacky had engraved the word that he was going to pursue for the rest of his life. The coffee was cold; the smock and the dirty shoes left the chair and the table where the odor of Doctor Michael Logan hung in the air.

Deadened by boredom he saw the girl that had been left with them. A strange body scarred by the scientists' miracles. The thin little hands motioned him to stop by the sick girl's bed. A heart, the vital eye or defect, a person's psychological defect. She had had various operations, but they were always encouraged by the illusion that one more would correct her congenital abnormality. Her heart was like a sieve for blood. As soon as one hole was sewn up, another one would open. Now she had little machines, tiny computers that allowed her a few more years, months, days, hours, minutes, seconds. That is what they told her parents. The doctors enjoyed the experiment. The girl no longer had a name; she was identified by the operation of the piece of machine implanted in her. The interns came in to see her, not to talk to her, but to study her and to give praise, to marvel at all they had done for humanity. The child, her parents, they're the real heroes. She and her parents have made the sacrifice without even knowing it. They represent this century's martyrs. The beard with the tired eyes drew closer to the girl. Her hand wanted him to come even closer. She touched the ear that bent over to hear her whisper.

"You're my friend because you look like my saint. My mother told me that he would save me. You look like my saint and my mother told me that if I prayed to him everyday, he would help me. My saint sent you, you have to help me because he's the saint of lost causes. You have the power to save me because you look like him. Please, Doctor, cure me, please. If you are my saint you will."

"Michael! Michael! Michael! Where are you going? Don't follow him. Michael is a man who feels too much. He still hasn't learned to repress, to control it. Leave him alone."

"Hey, Michael, how are you doing? Did you leave early today?"

"Yes, I left because I was fed up with this damned place, this fucking holy concentration camp. And if they get mad, screw 'em. Bring me a pitcher of beer, I'm physically and psychologically ready to get drunk."

"By no means would it be a loss of prestige, it would be an advantage to have a good doctor with a Latino name. I've told you my position, if Martínez doesn't come in with me, I won't sign on."

"I think I see your reasons for wanting Martínez as a partner. And that way no one can accuse us of racism. What's your opinion, Beesley?"

"Well, Martínez is an outstanding doctor, you can't deny it. But accepting a Chicano, one of them, would be like an invitation to the blacks. Do you want a black partner?"

"I don't think we'll have that problem."

"Why not, Bekstrom?"

"Because there's no black who'd want to join us. We have to admit it, we aren't very popluar with the minorities."

"That's enough talk, we have to decide. Pergmun, what do you say?"

"Yes, I'm for him."

"Bekstrom?"

"Fine, we'll give him a chance to prove himself."

"I'm glad. Leroy, you'll start when you finish your last rotation at the hospital and Martínez can start whenever he likes. He finishes tomorrow in the Emergency Room so he'll be free. If he wants he can take a week's break."

"Doctor Beesley, Martínez is going to get married so I think he'll take that week."

"OK, gentlemen, we all agree then. The salary and all the rest is decided. I prepared the contracts ahead of time, thinking that it would all be worked out. I propose a toast to the partners Pergmun, Bekstrom, Hales and Martínez."

"But we're certainly not going to put Martínez's name on our business cards."

"Don't be stupid, Bekstrom. Beesley, I think the name Martínez sounds good."

"Bring me another beer, you bastard, another beer! I want another pitcher of beer. I want to toast to the lucky ones of the profession, especially my friend Pato, a very fortunate man."

"Shut up, Logan, you're making a racket. If you don't calm down, I'm going to send you home."

"No, please, don't send me home. My wife will be furious. She's told me that I don't know how to drink. I think she's right."

"Logan, you have to start work early tomorrow."

"Fuck 'em, I'll be there early, earlier than any of you."

"Michael, you're going to get sick. If Redacky realizes it he's going to . . . "

"I'll take a few pills. I'll be OK . . . ."

"Yes, but Michael, you had a problem with Calva, and I'm just telling you not to get into trouble with Redacky."

"Thank you, James. Thanks, pal, buddy."

"Let's go, Michael. If you don't come with me I'll call Cody."

"No, don't do that. I don't want her to see me like this."

"All right, have a cup of coffee and let's go home. It's still early. It's not ten yet. I don't want to leave you, I know you. You'll get home at four or five in the morning. Here, here's the coffee, drink it up."

"James, I think that I know what I'm going to do when I finish here."

"Yes, what's that?"

"I'm going to be the doctor for all the drug addicts in this great city . . . no, I'm going to be a parachute doctor; the only doctor to drop from the sky to make his house calls. Do you know why, James? Because I'm a saint and they come from heaven, don't they? No, I think I'd rather become a whore doctor, or maybe the medical consultant for directors of pornographic movies so that they can justifiy them as a contribution to science."

"Keep quiet, you're talking nonsense. Let's get going. Get up, there's the door."

The white ketchup and beer stained smock and the dirty white shoes were guided by James who helped Michael, not because he was a friend but because he imagined Cody waiting for him at home, worried. Cody was always on James's mind. The white lights went out into the night hardly lighting themselves and the road before them.

He slept heavily that night, snoring and passing foul-smelling gas. Cody hated him when he came home like this. She didn't know him and she didn't want to. Her feminine rancor couldn't take it and her body changed places to the living room where she slept until dawn. He woke up with raw, swollen eyes. He vomited the green beer that he couldn't digest. His brain was reeling, his nose caught a whiff of the bacon that made him vomit more, and the shouts of the children wounded his sodden brain. The mirror shot him looks of death: . . . what kind of a doctor is this one? The sacred medical saint, naked over the toilet bowl, vomiting and passing wind? What miracle of science is this? . . .

The feminine body looked for her partner: . . . How disgusting, what a man! . . .

"Michael, do you want scrambled eggs with bacon, milk, pancakes? What would you like, my love?"

The red wet face could not believe that a human being could be so cruel.

"Get going, Doctor, you have to be at the hospital in half an hour. Your clothes are on the bed. The coffee, if you can stand it, is on the table. Hurry up, before Redacky calls. Let's go, Doctor Logan." . . . Cruel animal, damned bitch! You're going to kiss me. Another vomit and everything's out, I have to shit . . . a little cup of coffee, two miracle pills and I think I can make it until my shift is over: . . . I'll never do this again, never, I'll drink a little, but not like last night . . . My damned head is wiped out with pain and my eyes won't open . . . It's like they turned my mouth into a garbage dump.

He tried to spit the green slippery slime that dripped down to his stomach. He showered with cold water and then hot. He was almost asleep, his penis limp: . . . Cody, how long will she take to forgive me for this spree? . . . The doctor avoided the children and he timidly left his wife.

The pimply face timidly approached his lips, tenderly kissing them. The poor student had had a terrible reaction to some vitamins and her face, which should have shown her natural beauty, was horrible. Her neck, her little breasts, her firm abdomen and the buttocks crowned her beautiful legs. They went to the bedroom and there the young woman crouched down and showed her delicious, odorous ass which pointed the way to her pubic hair. First the tip of the penis, then the head, all the way in until the erudite organ penetrated, until the professor felt he had reached the poor girl's insides. The hours passed until eight o'clock at night; the lecherous professor quickly dressed and went down the stairs, physically and morally exhausted: . . . If they realized what a bastard I am. How we take advantage of this poor homely girl, urging her on with impossible dreams. We just use her for sex and to keep our jobs. What a rotten mentality we have. We're society's parasites, they need us as a measure of culture, to create false necessities, to cure them. . . . but we're just as miserable as any other creature . . . poor girl, I hurt her. I don't know if she likes it or if she does it to be part of the action. Sleeping with a professor is part of the graduate school whoreshow. We're intoxicated with ourselves, a damn bunch of rotten decadent symbols. Well, I'll undoubtedly be here when she comes on to me again. I feel sorry for her face but I have a real affection for her legs, an affection that only a hard prick can really express. If they only realized what I think, they'd really screw me. . .

The tired, red eyes arrived at the door of the apartment, the modern cave that was called a human dwelling. The doctor came in, sat in front of the TV and laughed with the children: . . . Thank God for the pills I took, at least they helped my stomach so that I could work the rest of the day . . . but my poor eyes look like street lamps in the red light district . . .

"Michael, could you go to the store and buy more meat? Pato just called and he and Amy are coming for dinner; they'll be here in an hour."

"No, I'm not going to the store. Why didn't you tell me they were going to come tonight? I'm really tired, exhausted. I'm going to shower and go to bed."

"That's your own fault. You should have thought about it when you were wandering around like a drunken bum in all the bars in town. Last night you came home reeking of beer. You told me that you weren't going to get drunk any more. You'll never be able to stop. Michael, the bottle for you is like a mother's breast, you're like a child, once you start to suckle, you can't stop until you've fallen asleep."

"Don't start, Cody. Don't start to fuck me over."

"Don't talk that way in front of the children."

"Don't yell at me, Cody, please, don't yell. I'm not a child that you can scream at."

"But can't you see how angry I am at you and that I have to scream to keep myself from going crazy?"

"Cody, can't we talk about something without screaming. The only thing I'm asking you is to please not scream at me."

"Mommy, here come Uncle Pato and Amy; Daddy, Mommy, here comes Uncle Pato."

"Michael, are you going to the store or should I tell our friends to come another day?"

"Shit."

"What?"

"Nothing. Give me the money. Give me some extra money because I'm going to buy a six pack. Don't get mad. Pato likes beer and I want to at least be able to offer our friends a drink. Sweetheart . . . you know, you really like to fight. You seem as soft as butter, but you're a champ. Like butter, but let's go a few rounds."

"Be serious, Michael. I'm in a bad mood and I'm angry with you, so don't kid around."

The doctor lightly punched her buttocks, shadow boxed, touched her breasts.

"Don't fool around, Michael."

He tapped her head and stroked her breasts, he looked at her with affection. She couldn't stay mad at him for very long. She gave in. She wanted to, but she also wanted to hear the false promise that he always made her. She wanted to hear the excuses that he always gave her. Her ears caught the sound of the doorbell.

"Daddy, Mommy, here they are. Uncle Pato is here."

The girl's little hands opened the door.

"Hi, folks, how are you? What are you up to?"

"We were fighting. My wife is furious because I got drunk last night. I was hung over this morning. But I went to work. My work comes first; alcohol hasn't yet affected my profession."

"I don't want to butt in, but since I'm a friend, I'll tell you that Cody is right, you drink too much beer."

"You do too, don't pretend to be so innocent."

"I am innocent, innocent of having five or six pitchers of beer; and to prove it I brought you two six packs. We have to celebrate the good news. Amy and I are going to have our first heir."

"Amy, congratulations."

"Thank you, Cody. Maybe you can give me some advice. Of course I'm not totally ignorant, but I've never had the experience."

"Will you nurse the baby?"

"I think so."

"Pato, let's go to the store."

"OK"

"Jason, Shane, you want to come with us?"

"OK, everybody, let's go to the store, let's buy snow cones."

"Where are you going, Fernando?"

"Francisca, how about going to Costa's for snow cones?"

"Fine, let's go."

All was quiet in the neighborhood controlled by Pistol Man. People said he had changed a lot. For the first time he felt loved and accepted by someone who loved him. Little Teresa had brought a change to the town. She had a certain power over Pistol Man; a power that came from the mythic right of the beautiful woman to rule the beast.

The people commented on this among themselves. It was really marvelous news. Pistol Man was in love with Teresita. Old Bilabí just accepted it. He didn't complain. Maybe if he had been younger he would have killed the man who had taken his granddaughter's virginity. The people had also commented on the list of names, but, of course, that was one of the federal government's requirements. Don Costa, behind the enormous counter, was the judge, the wise man of the neighborhood. Everyone gathered there to have a beer, a soda, ice cream, snow cones and to buy provisions. Costa, an Hispanic type, with a squared face and a steely jaw, didn't say much but when he did, people listened. He liked oratory and he liked the long view of things that started with the past and flowed through the present and ended with his grandchildren's future. There in this native Spaniard, Mexican, Chicano's little store, there were not only Chicanos, but a few Anglos like Pistol Man who also liked to visit the knowing old man. The Rodríguezes arrived, happy to see their friends, happy to be together, happy to experience life and the world in a healthy body. They arrived greeting those already there when the police car braked violently in front of the porch steps.

"Hello, what's new? How is everyone?"

"Hey, Pistol Man, how are things going?"

"Everything's fine, nice and quiet. Fernando, ma'am, how are you?"

"Very well, Pistol Man. And your wife? How is she doing? I heard that she was ill, that she's had a serious attack of nerves. Yes, that's what was explained to me."

"Yes, ma'am. Yes, it was her nerves. But I think she is better now. Oh, Fernando, haven't they spoken to you?"

"Who?"

"Some government men; haven't they visited you?"

"But what do these men want? What does the government want? What do you think, Don Costa?"

"It's really very simple, the Chicanos are making a lot of progress and they are really getting ahead. Politically they are united and they have gotten a lot of high state government positions. That makes the ruling political family in this country nervous. In addition, there's what happened in East Los Angeles. A lot of people died and they had to bring in the National Guard to calm things down. The intellectuals have put forth their programs, a new conquest of the Southwest by the Chicanos: a political, economic, educational and intellectual conquest. Now they're struggling to free themselves and gain control of the area. We are always receiving more immigrants who are incorporated into Chicano culture. We're now dangerous for both sides, even if we don't want to be. They're afraid of us."

"Keep quiet, Mr. Costa. Everything you've said is a madman's dream. The president has said that it is idealists like you who make problems between the races. I'm happy because I know my place and you should recognize yours in this system."

"You aren't afraid, Pistol Man?"

"No, not at all. I'm not afraid of any person or any group. The government controls and conquers everything. I have faith and rather than a group or an individual, I'm afraid of the government. They keep watch over us and dominate us. The government kills whoever it wants."

"It glorifies and murders, doesn't it, Pistol Man?"

"That's how it seems, Mr. Costa. It glorifies and murders. First it creates its heroes, it gives them everything, fame, prestige, money to carry out their projects. That's how the government does it. Then, suddenly, without it being clear who did it, it kills. But how can we blame the government? Because it was the government that gave them everything."

"It's illogical but at the same time very logical. It's better not to aspire to be a hero, a leader of the people; only death awaits you."

"Señor Costa, this whole conversation frightens me and makes me uneasy."

"I'm sorry ma'am, but people want to know about these things, the phenomena that allow governments to function, that are necessary to keep them going."

"It's almost as if they chose us to do what you said, Pistol Man."

"I'm leaving now."

"Listen, Pistol Man, before you go. Can you tell me how the Bilabís are?"

"Of course, ma'am, Fernando can also tell you. I think they are all well."

"I'm glad to hear that. Please send them my regards."

"Let's not play pretend. Everyone knows what my relationship is to that family. If you like you can ask how Teresa is and her grandfather and the children and the animals, if you're interested. I can tell you that they are all well and what is most important, they're happy. They respect me and I respect them. So let's just quit this phony hypocrisy. Even if all of you hate me, there they love me. Teresa tells me that I'm a good man and I believe it because she says so. And may God help any of you bastards who dares to stain her honor. I'll see you tomorrow, Fernando."

"Thank you very much, boys. Yes, Doctor Logan, until tomorrow."

"As I was saying, Michael, we're going to get married and we'd like Cody and you and the children to be the witnesses. What do you say, Michael?"

"I don't think there's any problem. But, are you sure?"

"I'm sure."

"Let me tell you what it means to be married. It's not all in the bedroom enjoying glorious moments of love. And since you're going to have children that makes life more complicated, and then when they fight . . ."

"Yes, I can imagine. I've seen you and I've given it a lot of thought, Michael. We've made our decision. You'll be the witness, won't you?"

"You know very well that I will. Congratulations, pal, I'm very happy for you."

There in the middle of the street the insignificant men embraced. The world observed them from all angles and elevations. Some saw them as rare birds, crazy, others understood it in a different way, and some really understood. They were alone in the immensity of that city, far from their destinies, far from those places that they wanted to know. They strolled, chatting, laughing and spinning the bags they were carrying. At that moment they did not exist for anybody but themselves. The buildings continued spying on them, choosing one of them. If one were to die there would be more to replace him. Doctors were not important, they were only indispensable at the necessary moment. Only those who give something lasting, those who bring to light greater knowledge will continue in spirit. But those who exist as sponges of already existing knowledge, they can be easily replaced. The creators; praise for the creators, praise for the rebels and the creative geniuses.

"Tell me, have you signed the contract with Pergmun and Bekstrom?"

"That was going to be my second surprise. Hales called me today. Tomorrow after we get married, I'll go sign the contract and then he's invited us all to his house for dinner."

"But the children, what will we do with the children?"

"Bring them. Leroy told me that you could bring them. Look, you're starting in his section on Monday; tomorrow you'll meet him. He's really a great guy. I finish tomorrow and I'm going on my honeymoon. You and Hales will finish together. You'll be in his last class."

"Pato, how are we going to get to Hales's house? We'll have to ask James if we can borrow his car."

"No, tomorow they'll give me a company car. You know, this is really like a dream. Sometimes I have to stop and ask myself if this is all really happening to me."

"Yes, it's happening to you. You're right, you've been lucky, but what's more important is that you're one of the best doctors. That's what counts with those dried up old guys."

They arrived at the dry wood of the hall desk. They went up in the machine that lifted bodies and things. They went into the living room with the children."

"Has Amy told you what's happening to these two marvels?"

"Yes, Michael."

"We have to celebrate. First, let's have dinner and then we can have a few drinks. Help me with the grill and bring two beers, Pato. Amy, come here with us. Cody, is the meat ready?"

"Yes, I'm coming. Children, go to your room and play. Mommy will call you when dinner is ready."

"Cody, bring a beer for yourself."

"I'll be there in just a minute."

From the balcony the four could be heard chatting and could be seen embracing, relatively happy. Their appetites were stimulated by the aroma of roast meat. Sometimes people looked up and gazed at the two young couples. Jason was crying and Shane was the innocent one, the little angel was scolded by Daddy who was finishing his third beer. They opened a bottle of red wine for dinner. They ate happily while around them men, women, and children were killed, boys and girls were raped. The city's monsters watched the lights of the buildings. There are so many, one must be chosen, which one will it be?

The implacable city noise whirled about the central park of the hospital complex. From time to time the chirp of a bird was heard, looking for its mate. Meanwhile, in Switzerland the human swine were licking their asses, green with money. Saylor and Aurton were reconciliating, maybe they would get married again in Israel. But what a damned waste of paper to report the shit about these beings prostituted for alcohol, fornication, money and diamonds. How many millions did the male prostitute pay to the female. He gave her his holy diamond. There are a lot of pigs like these. The little bird, among all the noise, all the city's misery, alights on the newspaper tossed by the bench. A dog passes and urinates on his face and her face; he might well have defecated. On the right was a photograph of the greatest whore of all. She buried her husband, the chosen martyr. There they have him with his unfortunate brother still buried beneath the torch. The little bird contemplates these photographs, images of the odious, urinated upon. These photographs make him hate the concentration of millions and millions in these parasites' dirty hands. How many times had the poor insignificant bird cried. It is unjust that he does not have enough to build a nest, to give his offspring food. The newspapers are thrown away after one reads about the mythical creatures of contemporary society. Where are the ones we only see in the movies, through electronic tubes, and photographs? Are they really alive or are they the creations of those in power to distract us from the truth? The more the bird thinks the more he hates. They deserve to die, death to these mythic untouchable bastards who lose ten thousand dollars in Las Vegas and laugh about how little it cost them. What kind of justice is that? What does the chief executive say about these swine?

"Mexicans, in Cuba all the children drink milk and milk is our country's greatest problem. Of course in the North, in that country, milk doesn't matter to them. That, Mexicans, is why we are the leaders of the third . . ."

And the great whore married, for at least nine million dollars; her damned ass, cunt, and tits are undoubtedly lined with gold. But it is necessary to hate, a simple rule, in order to love. The great lovers of the world are the evangelists who prostitute God in order to turn him into a merchant in the temple. The little bird is maddened by rancor when he hears the songs and prayers of the Villy Brahams, millionaire apostles of gold. Dogmatic Jehovah's Witnesses, they and only they will be the ones to enter paradise. The little bird lowered his beak. His eyes saw the formally dressed couple accompanied by another couple and two children. The little bird knows everything. The four and the two waited under the tree. The priest arrived in fifteen minutes of the most commonly accepted time.

"Should we start now, Pato?"

"Yes, Mario, make it a short ceremony."

"OK, short it will be. All join hands, please. Close your eyes and think about everything that's good in our lives, everything that's bad, in your God, in everything that being married and in peace means, in love and happiness and everything that these connote. Now, look at me and listen to me with love. I, Mario Saldaña Sánchez, priest of one of the religions of the universal God, declare Ignacio Pato Martínez and Amy Nelson married until their love ends or death parts them. May God bless you."

"Bravo, congratulations, Pato, Amy."

"Thanks, Michael, thanks, Cody."

"Mario, that was very well said. And thank you Jason and Shane. Where are they?"

"Look at them, Pato. The children want to celebrate your wedding with an ice cream."

"Great idea. That's what we'll celebrate our marriage with."

The little bird stretched his wings, let him leave his droppings on the white veil, on the ugly children; let him leave his droppings on everything that they are and do. Chirp, chirp, chirp, the bird flew away.

"Mommy, look what a pretty bird, Mommy, look, Mommy, it's flying away."

"Yes, Shane, it is very pretty. It flew away."

"Michael, Amy and I are going to sign the contract and pick up the car. We'll come by for you about three."

"Fine, see you then."

The six bodies separated in opposite directions; they did not turn around.

She was seated with her head down on the lower staircase at the entrance. Her fingers played with the heels of her shoes. She picked up a twig. She studied it, she broke it into little pieces, she threw them trying to reach the edge of the sidewalk. Her head hurt; she was suffering from an internal headache that had invaded her brain. It was not her fault that she liked it. Sometimes her mind wandered as she looked and listened in another world, and they saw her sitting on the lower staircase. She had entered in so many houses, apartments, rooms. Those places had entered her; in her body she had large chairs, large pricks, many beds, bottles, boxes, and other large objects that came to the minds of those that slept with her. Silky Silkfuck had a vagina that merited the medal of honor for services rendered beyond the call of duty. Silky Silkfuck, glorious bloody whore, sanctified by the priests that sniffed her ass and licked her with their tongues and their lips, sanctified by the madness granted to her. The only guilt she has to bear is that she never knew how to say "No!" Thus they found her with all that she was, waiting for the faces that she recognized as if in a dream, the faces that had what she desired.

"Look who's there, Michael. What do you think she wants?"

"I don't know but we'll find out in a minute."

"Hello, Doctor Logan, Mrs. Logan, oh, and the children, how pretty they are. I had one but it died. I think it happened a long time ago.

Maybe it was better that way. Do you know that they are still pursuing me. It's true, Michael, you know it's true."

"Yes, Silky, I know . . . Silky, what do you want?"

"What pretty children you have . . . I had one but I don't remember its name. Do you remember your name, Mrs. Logan?"

"Silky, what is it that . . ."

"I came to congratulate Pato and Amy. I accompanied them when they got married. I was with them at that moment. I will always be with them; me and mine, what was his, will always be with them."

"I don't think he'll be by here; they've already gone. Talk to him when he comes back."

"I came to congratulate him, I don't hate him or Amy. I wish them all the best. Everyone thinks I hate him, but I don't. I still love him; of all the men I've known he's the only one I think I've loved. Well, I'm going. Tell him that I don't have any ill feelings toward him and that I wish them all the happiness that's possible. But, Michael, they're still pursuing me; they want to kill me. I swear to you, they're going to kill me."

"OK, Silky, bye now. We'll be seeing you."

"Please, tell Pato what I told you, promise me. Do you promise?"

"Yes, Silky, Michael will tell him, I promise you."

"Good, well, goodbye. See you soon."

The rapid phenomenon disappeared. The wooden splinters marked where she had been; they formed a circle of sharp points and in the middle was an abyss of nothing.

He followed the line with his pen. At the end he had written his name, *Dr. Ignacio Pato Martínez.*

"Good, then we agree on everything. You'll start when you get back from your vacation."

"Thank you very much, Doctor Bekstrom, Doctor Pergmun."

"I congratulate you, you will certainly be successful with us. Please send my regards this evening to Hales and his wife."

"Thank you."

"Don't mention it. I hope that you'll do well with us."

. . . Well, if the only thing they require is writing, I don't think I'll have a problem. But it seems to me that they think that I've come like some sort of a hero; there is only one direction for those that are heroes and that's down. I'm busting my ass for a few thousand mythical little green pieces of paper. The ones everyone hates are the ones who haven't written anything but they're tenured because they were the first ones hired in the department. Educational institutions used to be in caves, now they are in the tombs built by the first graduates. And the graduates of the tombs constructed the impersonal monoliths we know today . . .

"You have signed on with a full understanding of your responsibilty. You have to publish something of quality this year, or you're out."

. . . Don't worry, Great Theoretical Roman of Glorious Criticism; you, like the rest, need the insignificant creators in order to survive. Of course you're right, even the madmen of imagination need the sharp observers like . . .

They got into the car, one just like the one that Pato knew he would have. For Pato it was a delicious triumph; he had done the impossible. He had been accepted into a medical corporation not because of who he was or what he represented, but for his credentials as a doctor and an expert in his field, or for his capacity to become an expert. The happy, peaceful six went through the streets of the city. The glances that they saw were quite familiar; they had seen them somewhere else, at another time: . . . I've seen them before; it's as if the exact same person had already lived this and it's happened to me; maybe I'm the one; I've existed in another time, in another place, in another novel; that's it, I am memory, more and more is added and is transmitted from century to century . . .

"Pato, how's it going? How do you like your new car?"

"I'm very happy, Michael. But it's almost like a dream. I'm happy but at the same time I'm afraid that it's all going to be over just as suddenly as it started."

"Don't think that, Pato, we're off to a good start. Don't you think, Cody?"

"I have to say that I don't see any problems or anyone who is going to ruin what you earned through your own efforts."

"What's more, your friend came to tell us that she had no ill feelings for you and that she wishes you both all the happiness in the world."

"She came to see you?"

"Yes, she's still the same; she thinks they are persecuting her."

"Where's she living now?"

"In the dorms, as usual, two new interns are taking care of her, according to what the guys say."

At the moment they were passing the tenements where the new or constantly renovated interns of the barrios lived. They were passing those little ugly white houses, dirtied by the memory of the Chicanos.

The neighborhood was getting ready for dinner; Dad would soon be home from work. The children at home were watching television; others on the street corners were talking about the quetzal feathers they would win in the gang wars. A lot of them would die; young lives lost for nothing, lost because they knew no other reality; a violent death is part of the code of conduct described in the argot of the warriors. The pig car passed through the exciting hellish streets; their eyes looked with distrust, understanding, hatred; their eyes always saw with something on their minds.

"Pato, you know I feel pretty uncomfortable riding on these streets in this, don't get mad at what I'm going to say, pigcar."

"Michael, I feel uncomfortable too. I feel as if the person driving is, or should be, someone else. I'm going to return this car and get a smaller one, not a really small one, no, I'm going to get myself a sports car."

"And what are you going to do with the baby?"

"Amy says that we'll be three for a long time and we could certainly all fit in the Jaguar that I'm thinking of buying, or in the Mercedes or the Porsche."

"Watch out for the light, Pato."

"Be careful, if we hit a child here it would really ruin things."

"I don't think so, Michael, it could all be fixed. I have confidence in my people; I know that they could understand the reason for any accident that might happen."

"I think that there is precisely where their problem is. What I mean is that maybe they have too much confidence in their leaders; they leave it all to them."

They were passing by places that the politicians did not see, didn't know, didn't even imagine, because when one doesn't live in those places, they remain invisible, they don't exist.

"Mexicans, we have to salvage our indigenous past; we are the inheritors of our ancestors' glory. Although we live in poverty, we have the strength to achieve greatness for Mexico because the ancient tears of suffering and intelligence course through us. Mexicans, we know how to suffer; we know that we must suffer in order to progress; we know that in order to conquer we must suffer. We, therefore, are the supreme examples, the leaders that the nations of the third world will follow willingly and proudly. Mexicans, we are . . ."

The car was climbing the hill to where the rich people lived; society's filthy bastards always raise themselves up, they always want to be above in order to have a view of those below, to be looking at the professional sufferers. The heights here, the heights there, the turf of the nouveau riche. Once they make it you can see them in the elegant neigborhoods disdaining the poor beggars.

"Oh, these damned beggars, why don't they get a job? If I can they can too. Let them work. I won't give anything to this dark, lazy Indian woman. What would the fucking gringos say?"

It's awful to hear the swarthy mestizos talk about their own people. How quickly and easily they forget who they are and where they came from. Who the hell says there is no racial prejudice in Mexico? El Señor Presidente, the ambassador to France, the classless, the cabbies, the middle class, the upper class, those who find metaphors where there used to be blood, without a doubt the political family. You can see the rich putting on a show in the jewelry stores buying original necklaces for five hundred dollars while outside an Indian woman is selling the same necklace for fifty pesos. Of course they work at what they can, but the Mexican is not disposed to help his fellow Mexican, but to screw him. Someone said that in Mexico everyone drinks milk, in the United States they don't, but the Mexican doesn't want to help the beggar because he knows that the stupid rich gringo will. Let them go north, there's a lot of work there, here there's nothing we can do for them, there are a lot of hungry mouths. If they went, so what? It doesn't matter if they go.

"We're almost there, you can see Leroy's house up there. It's a ranch house, he's got four acres, stables, a swimming pool and a lot of forest. It's really a beautiful place. Leroy said that he didn't want anything so big but the corporation insisted that he buy the place, so he did. It's Mexican style, see the tile roof, Michael. You like it, don't you, Cody?"

"Now look, Raime Ezodner, don't be a fool, no one will pay any attention to you. Don't you see that you're a failure? You should accept it. Don't act as if you were someone important when you aren't. Don't come to me with secrets that everybody knows. Don't come around with gossip; it's a terrible thing for a man to be a gossip."

"But, Professor, I want to help you."

"That's fine, but I'm not interested in gossip, don't make my life difficult. I don't want to know what they think of me or what you tell me that they think of me."

"But, Professor, I want to help you."

"How can I believe you? Especially when you've lied about your education, saying that you had degrees. And what happened? Where are the damned degrees?"

"Keep quiet, Professor, keep quiet."

"If you really want to help me, don't show me the daggers you're putting in your dear friends' backs. If you do to them what you've just mentioned, you'll be doing the same thing to me."

"Yes, I like it a lot. If Michael and I have a house some day I'd have a tile roof."

"We'll have it, Cody, we will."

The car pulled up the long private drive to the Hales'; there was a beautiful lawn, trees, grass everything carefully manicured, like a dream house. He parked the car at the front door, a young woman with green eyes and a lovely face returned their greetings. They went into the living room where the tanned leather chairs were happy to receive so many bodies. Everywhere plants added their creative presence to the atmosphere created by the lady of the house. Zapotecan rugs on the wall testified that the couple knew something about the country to the south. The carpet was hidden beneath red shawls from Guadalajara. The heavy, coarsely elegant Mexican furniture, the antique objects from both cultures, added to the creation of an exquisitely primitive dwelling.

"You're right, Pato, the house is beautiful; it's different. Do you like it, Michael?"

"Yes, this is my style, a house that has its own personality."

"Leroy, how are you?"

"Fine, thank you, Pato. Amy, congratulations. Do you always enter into all these important contracts on the same day?"

The informal introductions were made only to fulfill the old ritual. They all saw each other, listened to each other and liked each other. They enlived the discussion with drinks. Michael drank beer from the can and the others had cocktails.

"Oh, yes, the young woman who let you in is Adela. She's very pretty; but don't think anything bad, she's part of the family. Of course she works for us; she cleans, takes care of the children, does the shopping, she does a lot, but here we treat her with respect. She eats with us and has fun with us; she's a part of the family."

"Doctor Hales, I noticed that you said part, as if you were speaking of a thing, an object. You said 'part' instead of 'person,' or 'relative.' I can't believe that a maid, a servant, can ever be more than a maid in this country. Pardon my pessimism, but that's reality. The servant is either the maid or the concubine for whom she works."

"Michael, I've heard that you're a rebel, a maverick, and I believe it, however, we don't treat Adela in the manner you describe. Perhaps we are an exception, I don't know, but we treat her well, as if she were someone, a person. Listen, if you knew anything about me you would realize that I'm not a hypocrite, and that I don't think I'm better than everybody else. Maybe I did use the wrong word, but you shouldn't condemn me for that. I'm not a capitalist pig; I have respect for labor and for the laborer."

"I see that you've already met."

"Yes. Pato, it's a pity that I couldn't get your friend into the corporation."

"That would give your idiot partners a thrombosis that would kill half of them."

"Karen, some more beer and cocktails, please."

"Fine, but you'll have to take them into the dining room because everything is ready."

"Let's go then."

From the living room with its clear personality they stepped down three steps to a dining room in the middle of a jungle of plants captured in pots of mixed blood; intertwined branches sprouted from each one. The exotic, rare, and peculiar greenery seemed to be spitting at the invaders. The room did not belong to the humans but to the plants that lived, ate and reproduced there, in the world of red forms, branches and trunks that were the catalysts for the creation, for the rebellion that only one body there would be capable of achieving. Only one would be capable of communing with them. On him fell the droplets, the spittle of the succulents, the cacti, the ferns, of all the plants that felt him there among them. On him, only on him, the eternal roots that have always dug into the earth for survival, the roots that were there before their oppressors, the roots of memory that only a few will be capable of perceiving, of knowing. Logan was one of them, a man who understood plants, the sacred green of the region. . . . To conquer death one only has to die . . . The plates of steak and lobsters were placed before the desirous brains. . . . Suddenly the room was filled with men in white coats, they were in my group and I told them it was not their fault; it was a legitimate sacrifice . . .

"Our efforts to uncover the riches of our natural resources have been fruitful, especially in the strengthening of our oil industry. I am pleased, my fellow Mexicans, to announce to you that we have discovered a new deposit of oil. Now the great state of Campeche joins the great state of Chiapas and the inexhaustible well of Veracruz as one of the major oil producers of our nation. Now we have the capacity to assert our leadership of the third world; we will begin programs that will demonstrate to the world at large that our nation, our people, comprehend the variety of human society."

The pulque was already beginning to disentangle the rhetorical net that el Señor Presidente cast over the nation's radios and televisions. The square in that distant spot, distant from the capital, distant from the perceptions of the metropolis, where the mustachioed one had died and where Don Casimiro's son had died, where they had assassinated many miserable creatures, was choked with the voice of the chief executive, of the authority, of the one who declared himself the peasant's true reality, the one who must be obeyed. The pulque sharpened the dust-covered man's wit, his understanding. The pulque was downed in one gulp; the glass shattered against the wall and his heart understood: . . . Fucking bastard, fuck your mother with your pretty words! How are you going to help me? I'm drunk but I see the situation that you educated guys have us in. I know who I am, you bastards, and I want my rights; I have the right to benefit from the wealth you're talking about. Oh, my dear little virgin, help me pull out the tongues of these liars who make promises and don't keep them! I'm dying to live a decent life, for my children to have new toys from time to time. I'm a slave of hunger and work. I live in Porfirio Díaz's time. This is the legacy of the Revolution, a new dictatorship. I'm a peasant who can't read or write, I'm an ignorant brute, a dumb ox, that's the way these bastards' promises have kept me. I'm fed up. But the day is going to come again when . . .

"Our oil production will reach eight hundred thirty thousand barrels a day. This wealth with give us the means to develop agricultural programs, better to support that sector of the population, a small sector, that has not received the most sumptuous food."

"The dinner was delicious, Leroy."

"Wonderful, thank you, Karen."

"Michael, did you like the lobster?"

"Thank you, I've had enough."

"Shall we go out on the patio and talk?"

"Sure."

"Would you like a brandy or a liquor, or anything else?"

Their voices gave an affirmative answer almost simultaneously. Thousands of lights below affirmed that they were shining, denying the night a small piece of its immensity: . . . What an enormous space, I can't understand what it is. Space and my decision, my future, the lights from those little houses, in each one there is a family, a whole world, a history, politics, but what nonsense am I thinking about? But maybe someone sees our lights and is trying to understand who we are, what we are doing, what we think, what every light, every house means; we are like satellites spying on each other, we see each other, but we don't understand each other, it's fear, the fear that we have . . .

"Oh, thank you, Leroy, thank you."

The flutter of the clear, intense star, the diamond that the woman with the sick baby had: . . . Was it a diamond? . . . but how could her husband buy her a diamond if they hardly had enough money for food. I wonder what she's doing now. What happened to the child? I always remember that lovely woman, I didn't know her name. Maybe if I'd been more aggressive, if I'd fought fire with fire maybe they wouldn't have chased me out. Maybe I would have won. No, the psychology of Mathis is one of suspicion, like all small, isolated towns, they don't trust outsiders. They didn't kick me out because I was a gringo. No, they got rid of me because I wasn't one of them, because I didn't fit into their old fashioned society, because I changed the long established system, and finally, because I helped the Chicanos . . . I should have stayed, I know that I would have won! How surprised they were to see the lights in my office . . . I was doing a good job there . . . And why did Rodríguez help me? . . . he felt sorry for me, of course he did . . . I'm so stupid! Rodríguez, Rodríguez is the key to everything. He was just about to come out against Pistol Man . . . he was vacilating, he was always on the edge of declaring the revolution . . . he's the key . . . he wanted to help me but he didn't realize it . . .

"Leroy, Leroy, Leroy, please come here, sit down with us, and you too, Michael, You were both lost in thought, you'll have to tell us what you were daydreaming about."

"No, Francisca, I wasn't thinking about anything."

"What do you mean you weren't thinking about anything? I saw you, it was as if you were in another world. Please, Fernando, tell me what it is. Maybe we were thinking about the same thing."

"You know the stars make men think, they encourage contemplation, they make me remember the past, people who've been in my life, in our life and times, the situations of the past. I have a strange thought. I believe that memories, the act of remembering, occurs when the person you are remembering is also thinking about you. At this moment that man is remembering me and our city."

"Who are you thinking about, Fernando?"

"I'm remembering Doctor Hales. How badly they treated him. I wonder what he thinks of me. I wanted to help him but I didn't know how."

"Fernando, do you think his wife is thinking about me, because I saw her in my thoughts, too."

"I don't know, but if another one like him comes . . . I think that everything is going to change, Francisca, I really do."

"Leroy, I bet you can't guess who I was thinking about?"

"You, my dear wife, were reflecting on our stay in Mathis, the city of Mathis and its people, that's what you were thinking about. Aren't I right, Karen?"

"Yes, I don't know what it is but I feel very close to that place, especially right now, at this moment."

"Excuse me, but I've heard so much about that town that I'm dying to hear what happened to you there. It seems that everybody knows but me; please, Leroy, would you tell me?"

"If you're interested, but it's an experience I really don't like to talk about; it's one that could have ended in disaster. But as Karen says, I feel troubled by the memory of Mathis. Maybe it's due to the fact that for the first time, and precisely on a night that is so important for Pato and Amy, for me and Karen, and maybe for you too, Michael, it's time to take stock of everything that we've accomplished. It's true that Karen and I have achieved all the dreams that we had, but I'll confess to you that Mathis is a memory that still bothers me and Karen and I think it always will."

"But what went on there, what happened to you?"

"OK, Michael, I'll tell you how it was. It's very simple; I arrived in Mathis with the ambition of establishing a medical practice in the middle of the Chicano community. I had ideas of being a great humanitarian and saving people, curing their bodies. It was an egotistical and false idea, because if I had really believed in it I would still be there struggling for what's right. In the beginning everything went fine. I had my office, the patients came every day to see me; I took care of everything. As I said, the first few months were very pleasant. Then, suddenly, everything changed. I was paid a visit by a doctor from the other side of town, this guy was a doctor, a politician and a policeman; he was into everything. He told me that I had to leave because my presence in town disturbed the normal processes of daily life and I was a bad influence on their Chicanos. I told him that I had no intention of leaving. The doctor left, telling me that he had warned me and that he was not responsible for what might happen to me or my family. I immediately lost myself in work, I forgot every-

86

thing and I continued there. That night I left my office late and as I went down the stairs of the porch I was showered with stones and bottles. It was a fast attack, I didn't even see who it was. I dragged myself inside the office and called the police. A man they call Pistol Man told me that I was drunk and that the citizens of the town did not attack outsiders. And if I didn't stop accusing his people, he would throw me in jail. Well, the attacks became more and more dangerous. Once they circled my car with gasoline and set it on fire; another time they smashed it and punctured the tires. And then they went into my office and destroyed all my equipment. Why? I don't know why. Maybe it was because I was an outsider and even worse, someone from the city with a modern education. Or, perhaps it was because they were afraid that I would become too influential in the Chicano community and that I would encourage them to rebel against the Anglo system, a system that had been established many years ago. Everyone had their place in this little town and this could have destroyed some niches. But that wasn't what I was interested in, I couldn't have cared less about the social situation, politics, the status quo, none of that mattered to me. But, nonetheless, in the position that I was in, working with these people, I couldn't avoid getting involved in those issues. Sometimes I found myself giving advice about how to deal with the boss, how to defend yourself against the authorities, the police, etc. I think that I would have gotten involved in politics; it was, as I said, inevitable. My presence there was a challenge to the power structure, to the power of the Anglos who manipulated the sellout Chicano politicians, who controlled everything and everyone. But now, as I look back at everything from here, I realize that if I had made an ally of, or had gotten to know better, a Mr. Rodríguez, maybe he would have helped me. Of course, Rodríguez was the key. Rodríquez was the one who could have saved me."

"Why did you give up, Leroy?"

"Look, Michael, when you have a family that might be harmed, it's impossible to fight. I wasn't afraid for what might have happened to me. I was afraid for Karen and Allison."

"You were afraid for yourself."

"Of course I was. I don't want to be a martyr and die for nothing. Once I'm dead, what can I do? The martyrs are the idiots of the world, they shed their blood so that others come out ahead, to make the sacrifices easier. You're right, I was afraid and that's why I left. I came here and thank God I have a friend like Beesley who could help me after a crazy adventure like that one. I don't know how I could have risked my family. But, in the end we're here, safe and sound."

"You gave up too easily. You should have sent your family here and gone back to fight; then if you asked for your good friend Beesley's help, I wonder if he would have helped you, what do you think? He wouldn't have helped you at all. You should have fought until . . ."

"Michael, if you think you can win against that environment, against the old ideas, I invite you to Mathis. You won't be successful, it will be impossible, you'll come back the same way that I did. You can't do it, Michael, and you won't do it, because if you do, you're a crazy . . ."

"Look, Leroy, don't say that to me, because I'll do it and you'll see that with balls and brains even that place can be won over. And I'll show you that I'll be the kind of doctor that you wanted to be before your interests shifted away from medicine and you turned to the accumulation of money."

"Gentlemen, please, we have to change the subject, let's talk about something else. Anyhow, I don't want to remember those times, please, Leroy!"

"Yes, Karen, I agree, Pato, why don't you help me with the hors d'oeuvres in the kitchen."

"I'm going with you."

The lights below twinkled and carried the thoughts of the two men that stayed there to other places they both knew. The two doctors felt themselves to be in Mathis.

"Michael, you're going to work in my specialty. I think that you can learn something from me and I can learn something from you. I think we can cooperate, don't you?"

"Yes, Leroy, but don't tell me that I can't do what you couldn't do; please, don't say it again."

"I don't agree with your opinion of me, but forget it, it's not worth the time; it's absurd to talk about the past."

"You think so?"

"Don't you want another beer?"

"No, I think we're leaving."

"All right, I'll see what Pato says."

"Yes, of course, see what Pato says. Pato will do whatever you tell him."

"Michael, don't have such a negative attitude, please! Pato makes his own decisions. I don't manipulate anyone. And I hope you remember that."

"OK, let's see what Pato says."

"Now we've come to the beginning of the ass-kissing, a game in which we must participate in order to survive here. I wish that I could tell them to fuck off but I can't because I haven't reached that position yet, nor gotten the power that we all want. In this country too, as in the other one, you notice the abuse, the abuse of a little power. We're an oppressed people and when we get a little bit of power we abuse it. You can see it at all levels of the hierarchy. A secretary can screw you if she doesn't feel well, if she's in a bad mood; a beggar always wants to bug you, even the religious pigs, of course it's an old theme but it's enormously important, especially today."

"Hey, Marxist Pinnacle, what are you offering as a solution to the problem? You're a pure, damned critic, pure talk and nothingness. Look, Marxist Pinnacle, you are committed to inaction, to cheating the students with your production of nothing. You are truly an intellectual impressionist, because only from the impression you give in class you can be judged. It's truly a shame."

"No, because I don't believe in what I do. The difference between my inaction and the action of the rest is that they construct books because the system obliges them to. I hate the system and I won't participate in maintaining it with my lying efforts."

"Liar, you've been living with that whore for I don't know how many months. You don't love me any more, Henry. You prefer that slut, that filthy pig . . ."

"Shut your mouth or I'll break it for you. Yes, I don't love you anymore; I'm leaving you. You make me sick. You're always ill, drenched in medicines that don't do anything for you. Don't you see that they don't help? You don't matter at all to me; I hate you. Look at you, a stinking skeleton, a victim of your faith, not in me, but in those bastard doctors who lie to you to get money. Don't you realize it's all in your head? Idiot, fool!"

"Get out of here, Henry, you Mexican whore-lover, go to your concubine. I hope your children are deformed and retarded, and that you bleed for twelve years in the witch's bed. You're under a spell, get out, you're the devil's thing. Leave before I die of rage, of fright, you're the devil. Help, the devil. Help. Ayyy, help . . . !"

"What's the matter, Amy?"

"I don't know, I saw something that scared me so much I dropped the tray. Oh, I'm awfully sorry, Karen, look what I did to the plates and glasses."

"What you saw was a coyote. Look, the poor thing is more scared than you."

"Coyote! Are there coyotes around here? I thought that there weren't any in this area any more."

"The coyotes have survived the plague of mankind. I take care of them; they aren't bad animals. However, they have to eat, it's their right. All that's left for them to do is to come down at night and steal what they can. It's not their fault; they're forced to behave that way. It's our fault."

"I agree, Leroy."

"I'm glad, Michael."

"I'm glad, Fernando, that you've killed it. That coyote has killed about four of our hens."

"It's not their fault, it's that there are so many up there that they don't all have enough to eat. Then they have to come down and steal what little we have. It's because of the curse of man who has modernized everything to the point that an animal in his native surroundings no longer knows how to cope with them."

"That coyote has frightened me so many times. When I went out at night, I knew that he was afraid of me, and even when I saw his little ears, I couldn't get used to him."

The houses in the night are filled with yellow lights. The great noise, the great leveler, the police car pulls away. The Chicano race is moving, looking, contemplating, meditating from an objective distance. Man's artificial light, yellow intellectuality, that manifests its morality, its virtues, the totality of its being, inspires the synthesis of it all by bestowing the creative spirit which emanates from the triumphant cosmic force. Everyone sees themselves in the darkness by means of their senses, by touching, tasting, smelling. But by day, hurling its luminous pangs toward this reality, they fall asleep, entwined physically and psychologically, within themselves and with each other. Every image is to be found in the memory of the race which is not differentiated by being dissimilar because in the very dissimilarities are to be found human similarities. And asleep within us is the beautiful anima, the ancestral images that lie in the unconscious waiting for the kiss that will arouse them to action. Asleep in palaces with memories and intuitions of the depths of being, they are beyond the world of action. Only the poets, the creators, will be blessed with the kiss that will awaken them from the dream of passive power.

"My little girl, please, don't take her away! Where is she, my little girl? Don't steal my child! Doctor, help me, I'm afraid that they'll take

90

her away and I'll lose her forever. I don't want to lose her! I've always been afraid that in this country they would steal her from me . . . my precious child. Where is she? Please, tell me!"

"Give her some morphine, she's in shock, look at her leg. Call Doctor Goodman, tell him to come right away. She's lost a lot of blood. Give me two pints of blood and twenty centimeters of tirobecyn and get her ready to be operated on immediately."

"My baby! They stole her. Greedy things, they steal everything from us! My child! I'll kill them! I'll kill them! Where is my little girl?"

"Doctor Logan, Doctor Goodman is here now."

"Logan, I was sleeping. If it turns out that you could have taken care of this case I'll break your balls."

"Look at this broken leg. It's a vascular surgeon's dream."

"Shit, we'll need a miracle for this one."

"You can do it."

"Doctor Logan, paging Doctor Logan to room three. Doctor Logan, paging Doctor Logan to room three."

"Doctor Logan, paging Doctor Logan to room three, room three, room three, four, five, six, what will be waiting there? A lacerated child, a broken arm, an abortion, a knifing, a rape, a heart attack, what will the good people send me next? It doesn't matter what it is, I'll cure them all. I'm the miracle man, the little god that will save all the sick."

The doctor's hand pulled back the curtains. The odor of the half naked body on the table suddenly made him nauseous. His mind turned to the Chicana nurse.

"Get me alcohol."

He splashed the hygenic potion on his hands and forearms; he took a deep breath and the nausea disappeared.

"He must be about fifteen. They found him in the park, lying there like this. The police think that they were at a party, he got sick, and his friends took everything that they could either sell or use and then left him. Heroin, he has the marks between the toes of his right foot and his tongue is terribly swollen and infected from the injections. His blood pressure is low."

. . . Why do they send me these wretches? It's a waste of time to try to help these animals. I cure them today and tomorrow they'll be here for the same thing again. The time they take up would be better spent on a legitimate patient. How I hate these poor creatures, slaves to that shit. They should sentence all pushers to death. Hang them as soon as possible for destroying our young . . .

"Doctor Logan, Doctor Logan!"

"Yes, yes, what's his pulse?"

"Hardly anything, Doctor."

"Don't tell me this pariah is dead. Don't tell me he's dead! No, he isn't. Bring me the electrodes, this cadaver has to live, he has to live. Give him another one, more, give him more, he has to live!"

"Yes, his heart is beating."

"Check his pulse again."

"Yes, Doctor it's OK now."

"This pariah can't die; he's our trophy of industrial, scientific, cultural victory. Let him live so that the world realizes that we save the living dead from death so that they can live death! Isn't that so, Chicana nurse? But what tits you have, my love, the better to suckle, obscene tits."

"Doctor Logan! Hales, Doctor Hales!"

The white dress left the room screaming with fright of what she saw and felt from the eyes of the little medical god.

"Logan, what's going on here!"

"Nothing, Leroy! Nothing that you could understand! Nothing."

"Michael, I want you to go home, or go have a beer, it doesn't matter where you go, just get out of here. I think you've been inside too long. Go home, please."

"No, I want to stay. I want to perform more miracles."

"Michael, don't be stubborn. Go home."

"But, Leroy, I can perform miracles, I just did one for that poor thing on the table. Ask the Chicana. Oh, what mammaries!"

"That's enough, Michael. Go home. Do what I tell you. Now get lost."

"I'm going, I'm going, you hypocrite cop-out. You and your little friend Pato have prostituted yourselves for money. You don't understand anything, you don't know what a real doctor is. You're a damned mechanical technician of human bodies, or rather a butcher of human bodies. I'm going, I'm going to hell; I'll leave! I'll show you what a doctor is, a doctor who's really dedicated to his profession, you'll see. I'm going to show you all, the whole damned world. Fuck the world!"

Hour after hour leaves its mark on the spent cells of the hands that stroke penises and vaginas in the human cages. The hand took the cup filled with wine, blood, and the sacrifice of the eternal little medicine god. The divine intoxication raises the miserable creator, poet, scientist, into a creature who for an instant possesses the power of the gods.

"Gentleman, I almost feel like a god because our efforts to cover up the attack have been an administrative apotheosis. Let us celebrate with the ambrosia of the gods, the best wine that Europe can offer for this joyous occasion. Now one of two things will have to happen — either they'll change the constitution so that I can remain in power for another six years, or they'll elect me secretary general. They are all, as our predecessors used to say, receiving their well deserved payments in advance. The revolution continues for the betterment of our nation, doesn't it?"

"Yes, yes, Señor Presidente."

"Long live Señor Presidente!"

"Long live the Revolution!"

"Logan, shut up, calm down!"

"All right, all right, don't get angry with a poor crazy drunk. But I've decided. I'm going to continue the Revolution. I'll go to Mathis and I'll win. I'm going to show them that you can win."

"Señor Presidente, a young woman would like an audience."

"Yes, tell her to come in, please, Marimbo. Gentlemen, please enjoy everything that is here. If you will excuse me, someone is waiting for me."

"Doctor Michael Logan, Doctor Michael Logan, a lady would like to see you; your wife is here."

"It doesn't matter what she says, I'm going to Mathis. I'm celebrating my victory over myself. I've just got one week left and then I'm going to Mathis."

"Michael, you're drunk."

"Yes, Cody, I am, but it has nothing to do with my decision."

"Michael, Leroy called me and told me what happened at the hospital, come with me and let's go home. I'll buy you a bottle of wine and you'll have it there and you'll talk to me about Mathis."

"A bottle of wine, what a good idea!"

The Theoretical Roman, the powerful wiseman of the land of the caudillos, was looking at the slender girl with long black hair. He uncorked the bottle of his country's red wine.

"A bottle of wine, what a good idea."

"Yes, my brilliant professor, you're the one I like. I'm glad you work at the university in the evening. It's easier for both of us that way."

"Here, have a little of this."

The kiss came suddenly, the glass fell, smashing, staining the rug that reminded him of his home town. He sat in the chair, she reached for the light, the clock said eleven thirty when they took off their clothes. There was silence in the outer courtyard; in the chairman's office the telephone's beacons blazed with the not unexpected call. Mounted on top of him she rocked to and fro singing like a little sparrow. The telephone's harsh ring broke their rhythm.

"Yes, everything's fine, about two hours more. I want to finish this article."

He took off her blouse. She, calm and satisfied, knew that she was the better of the two; his wife couldn't give him what she could. Their hearts beat rapidly with fear and excitement, their frenetic pace caused the penis to slip out and it painfully bumped the female hip.

"Oh, my poor professor, you hurt yourself, poor thing! Let me kiss it and make it better."

"Michael, don't be crazy. What are you going to do there? It's not your place."

"You're right, Pato. Michael, don't play the hero. Stay here and establish a practice and relax. I was there, Michael, and it wasn't easy."

"I don't care, I don't want to do what everybody else does. It would bore me and in a few months I wouldn't be good for anything or any one. I'm sure about my decision."

"And what does Cody say?"

"She's not going with you. I suggest that you don't take her, or the children. Don't be a fool, Michael. Pato and I will help you. Maybe we can get you in our group."

"No way, that would be the worst thing that could happen to me. I'd rather be in private practice than join that conspiracy against the citizens of the third world."

"Don't talk nonsense."

"Well, I'm going; thanks for everything, Pato. Thanks very much Leroy for not reporting what happened on Monday."

"Give me your address there please. I'll call you from time to time to see how you're doing."

"Pato, give me a hug."

"No, Amy and I will be there when you leave."

"I plan to put Cody and the children in Corpus Christi, about twenty miles from Mathis. There they'll be safe."

"Thinking it over again, maybe this experience is just what you need to get rid of your impatience and your overbearing personality."

"Goodbye, Doctors."

He left the building. The pride he felt was shown in the smile he offered to his friends as he passed by. He walked to the used Volkswagen that he had just bought from a friend. It was loud, but the motor justified the variety of colors, the holes and dents that adorned the car: . . . Cody is going to like it. At least she'll have a car to get around with when I'm not home and she won't have to depend on friends. Those days are over. We have our own car . . . He flew through the steets that he usually walked home on, but he didn't recognize anyone from the new perspective of ownership, of being the owner of a car: . . . I've advanced, I've joined the capitalist system; if I don't watch out, soon I'll want a Cadillac . . . No one knew him, no one expected him in such a messy car, all doctors should buy themselves big fancy cars.

"Michael, is that you?"

"Yes, who do you think it is?"

"But, what's that?"

"It's my new car, James."

"Oh, it looks like a half-wrecked freak."

"How funny, it's mine and I like it. Don't ask me to give you a push."

"Michael, who were you talking with outside?"

"With James. Come here, I want to tell you something. We're leaving Friday."

"Michael, you know perfectly well that I don't want to go. I'm only going because I don't want to break up the family. I haven't felt well these last three days. I've had trouble sleeping. I dream that you're far away from me, in a boat in the middle of an immense lake and I can only see your shadow; you're like a memory."

"They're just dreams, Cody, let's go downstairs. I have something I want to show you."

"Michael, I can't be angry with you. The other day when I told you that I was going to leave you and that I didn't love you and that I was going to take the children, Michael, now I realize that you are going to need me more than ever. Michael, I ask you one more time, don't go to Mathis, please."

"No, I know what I have to do. Look, I can't explain it to you, but there's something I feel inside myself, something that draws me to that place. I don't want to discuss it, but I know I have to go. Come on, let's go, Shane, Jason, downstairs! Let's see our new car, our Volkswagen."

"Michael, did you buy a car?"

"Yes, I bought it for you; it's yours. I'll use it the first few days and then I'll buy a motorcycle. You'll be independent in Corpus, you won't have to depend on anybody."

"A motorcycle, you're going to buy a motorcycle?"

"That's right, maybe I'll be the first doctor in Mathis to visit his patients on a motorcycle. What do you think? With my crooked cigar and my motorcycle I'll look like a modern-day Satan, the primitive scientific magician."

"Come on, let's take a ride."

"Yes, Daddy, let's go, Mommy, I like all the colors. But it's hurt; fix it, Daddy, please, Daddy, fix the holes that it has."

"Don't worry, Shane, the holes don't hurt it at all."

The family traveled through the city. They happily stopped to have dinner; they chattered like parrots, shouting. Michael got angry with the children, he yelled at them, they cried, he listened to music by a group called Chicago, everything was forgotten, the children laughed at their amusing father. The police car went by with its screaming mouth, it stopped in front of a bar. Michael saw the man on the ground with a white shirt, gushing blood. He was a Chicano: ... Those bastards, how they like to kill each other. Why don't they pick on Blacks, or Anglos or the Chinese? Why do they kill themselves? These idiotic humans like to kill themselves, they have no brains, they don't think ... A hysterical woman's shouts swung on the children's ears and they watched the policeman beat up a man who fell beneath his blows.

"Here, you bastard, take that, and that, and that, and that, uuuh, uuuh, here's a kick, take that, you bastard, I've got thousands for you, here, here, here!"

"Leave him alone, Pistol Man. That's enough Pistol Man! Enough!"

"Here, you bastard, you think you're a fucking big deal with a pistol, but by yourself you're nothing. Here, take that, don't show me your puss again or I'll bust it some more, you son of a bitch, here, take that uhhh!"

"Help me because if you don't he's going to kill him. Help me get him off of him. Pistol Man, that's enough, leave the bastard alone. You've already beaten him up. Now you've killed him!"

"No, absolutely not, I don't want him dead, I want him to live. I want him to live because that bastard's going to pay me for it. Any son of a bitch who shoots at one of my men is going to answer to me for it! How is he? Tell me, how is he, Rodríguez?"

"He's got two punctures in the stomach but it looks like he'll pull through, with luck he'll make it. The bullets went through the sides of his stomach."

"As I said, for any of my men I would kill the idiot who harmed them. And I'd do more for Rodríguez; I'd kill and kill him again. Rodríguez is my friend, my buddy."

The wounded man's body told him of mysteries he didn't understand; struggles, thousands of years of struggles were personified, encarnated in the bloody fiber of his being. All the battles and dances of death express the rite that had been carried out and expected of men like him. His art was chosen for conflict, for the violent resolution of winter and summer, of the moon and the sun, of death and life, of the blond and the swarthy. Thus he corresponded to the primordial cosmic sacrifice of the martyr who observed him, who felt him from far away, witnessed by his wife and children, his blood stained and sealed the contract made by thousands of creators before him. Pistol Man approached the man he had to hate, but he felt sorrow for the blood and the pain that the other displayed. He did not know what to say to him, he did not know why he felt that way: . . . Me, worrying about this man? Me, who was always in control. I'm frightened by what is happening to me. I care for him, I feel compassion for him; I don't know how or why I care for him; I don't know how to . . .

"Pistol Man, the ambulance is here, Pistol . . ."

"Yes, take Rodríguez with you."

"Rodríguez, a Chicano!"

"Yes, you fucking idiot, Rodríguez, or do you want me to grab you by the balls like that son of a bitch, that cow poke lying there? Do you see him? Yes, Rodríguez first!"

The woman was praying in the room. She asked the saints and the Virgin Mary to intercede with the Son for the salvation of the wounded man. The women's murmuring helped to establish a safe and comfortable feeling: . . . The candles, because their odor suffocates the healthy . . . that will be good for him, with the smoke and holy water he'll get better more quickly . . .

"What do you think, Doctor? What's his condition?"

"He's all right, Pistol Man, he's OK. I don't know why you're so interested in this Mexican's well-being. He's like the rest, strong and healthy. They seem like lower forms of life, one-celled animals. When one organ is harmed they regenerate it; that's how underdeveloped life forms are. My presence here was unnecessary; the curanderas took

97

care of everything that was needed. And furthermore, you know that I don't like to come to this part of town. These people don't need me. I'll be seeing you, Pistol Man. I don't owe you anything any more, goodbye. Oh, listen, watch out for yourself, people are beginning to talk, first Teresa, Bilabí's little girl, you're just screwing her, aren't you? That's your only interest in her, isn't it? And now Rodríguez. Be very careful, Pistol Man, don't turn romantic on us."

"No, of course not."

"Don't turn romantic on us, take care of yourself."

"Yes, yes, of course."

"And don't call me again, do you understand?"

"You don't understand, sir? You can't put a trailer hitch on it."

"Now look, you do what I say, I'm paying you for what you can rent me and not for your advice which I haven't asked you for."

"All right, it will be your funeral. I'll give it to you but please, be careful. What you are going to do is almost impossible and I warn you that they'll give you a ticket."

The Volkswagen parked by the entrance to the apartment, with the trailer loaded to the gills with furniture, books, clothes, bicycles, dolls, flowers and other technological and modern artifacts of the aborigenes of the time, declaimed the move with an absurd profile observed by the friends that had helped them.

"I think this is the last box."

"Cody, we're ready. Let's go."

The carriage, a traditional analogy in relation to man, there his life awaited him, everything he owned was represented there, immobile in time, its reality quivering toward the past, the centuries of his memory. He had done it once before, many times before, he was the charioteer of this mythical car. It was funny to realize that it made no difference, his car was made of fire, his soul consumed the physical charioteer in order to conquer its service. He knew what he had to do; nothing could distract him.

"Michael, I want to give you this, a medal, look, it's in the shape of a lamb's head, on the back it has a picture of Saint Jude."

"It's gold. I really liked it when I saw it . . ."

"Yes, I like it, I'll put it on right now. OK, everyone in the car. Come visit whenever you like, you know where I am."

The eyes bid farewell to the hearts that loved each other so; you are so handsome, you are so beautiful; you're everything that I had hoped for; you're everything that I need. You are so handsome to me, but now I can clearly see, now there are no clouds to darken the sky.

The musicians sang and played. These people did not hear them but they listened somewhere else, in Chicago they said goodbye, in Merida they cried over the separation, in New Brunswick their hands touched for the last time. They were not the only ones that had accepted the right to move on; the right was granted thousands, maybe millions of times every hour, for innumerable situations, here in this world and in the distant one that they had known on their oneiric journey. The car started, they headed for the highway.

He was given permission where the sun rises to be there. It was sad for him, but he did it because it was required of him. He returned to the battle. He passed through Pittsburgh, then Dallas and suddenly the door opened. The Marxist Pinnacle greeted him, the glorified martyr of inaction, two of Santa Ana's pigs were with him. The most hateful and deceitful of the two was the notorious Mr. Gart, a man who has violated everything he has ever said, a man who directs a school which has suffered from his idiocy. This bastard thinks he's a big deal, even his own wife is afraid of him, damned swollen-bellied bastard; if someone has to die, let it be this pseudointellectual. This faggot from New Mexico abused the Chicanos there. He and his brother killed several of them for the pleasure of eliminating the downtrodden; this man must die, he and the two old women who control the district. The beautiful words must be prayed; the holy prayer over the tomb of the three is necessary and good. The other pig was Elores, but he can only be handled by the Chicanos, cut him a bit, slash his belly, puncture a buttock, destroy a lip, do a Van Gogh on his ear, give him a trophy so that he doesn't forget who he is, so that the bastard doesn't lie. The official document was presented. Now the situation will have to change, the attack against him would now come from other quarters. But he's ready and willing to fight against all the glorified pigs. The young men went out into the night. He was starting out in a new direction. He followed him with slightly slanted eyes.

He was careful with all his friends and he respected his enemies because he knew who they were. But, from among his friends, who would be the enemy? He continued his journey, at times glimpsed through oblique windows and paradise, the island where he wanted to be. He followed the path, his mind created a gargoyle that revealed the rot of his soul. The imprisoned screaming madman also appeared in the picture: they wanted to turn him into a company trademark — they wanted to observe his madness — and everyone was at least listening. They just found the Gearst woman, another pig of the capitalist world. She sells a lot of newspapers. Undoubtedly they will save her, just like the senator. They'll save her because she's got money; if she were some-one else she wouldn't even make the back page of the newspaper. That's why they use it to wipe their asses in Copilco.

"But what the fuck, of course he does, el Señor Presidente also wipes his ass. Do you think he walks around with his legs spread like a mule who's just peed? No sir, the President has to wipe himself because he's full of shit, the bastard."

"Yes, you're right, they're a pack of liars. They were going to pay us for our land. What's this piece of paper worth?"

"They say that if they find oil we'll be rich but they won't give us anything until they find it . . . and we're still waiting. And those mechanical horses that are digging up the land?"

"They say there's nothing there, just air."

"The earth also farts."

"It's been a whole year of farting."

"Yes, and we don't have anything for it."

"What are we waiting for? If those lawyers don't reply, we'll have to arm a few farts of our own."

"Yeah, we'll even show them that we eat beans also."

"Not even the highway they built has been of any use to us. Look at the cars fly by, a hello and a goodbye with a blinking of lights. We've just got rotten luck, not even the highway has helped us."

"Thank God we've left that behind, Michael."

"What, Cody, what?"

"All those horrible wells, those mechanical horses taking oil out of the earth. It was as if we were in a field of maniacs bobbing up and down and stretching their arms trying to grab us, trying to smash us against the earth, smash us into pieces, little bits of flesh."

"Stop thinking about it, we'll be there in a few minutes. Look for the address of the apartment."

The apartment, arranged by him through a contact, was near the Corpus Christi hospital. The friend had said that it wasn't very nice but that the price was right and that the hospital was right there . . . maybe Michael would consider a position at the hospital instead of going to Mathis . . . The car stopped in front of an old building, a Victorian house. How did this curiosity get here? The wooden house was white, man's psychic house, his mask of external appearance. The floors gave the vertical and the spatial. It was an old house, the roof and the upper floor maintained the tension of superego control; the lower part, the basement, was the dirty part, the doctor's instinctual drives. In the kitchen the magician produces the psychic transmutation, the rooms that intercommunicate murmur to each other, the barely perceptible noises, the stairway that connects it all went up and down, full of life. It seemed to welcome them, giving off multilayered resonances that the family immediately understood. The house cared for them, it wanted them to be together and it identified with her and with the children.

"OK. Here we are. Give me the key. They told me that everything is ready. I'm going to put the furniture in the garage and park the VW in front."

The key penetrated the eye that was gently pushed with the door toward the interior. The family found itself inside the wooden body. She felt good, the little ones, although tired, added affection to the rooms. The stairway invited them to race up and down it. From above the voices chose the rooms they wanted. She laughed at something and the man's smile answered, drawing near her, his lips kissed her cheek.

"Michael, this isn't bad. I haven't gone upstairs but this floor is big; it has seven big rooms and for what they are charging us, I'm very happy. A fireplace, Michael, an enormous fireplace!"

"Yes, and it has a big back yard, and five more rooms upstairs, and a basement . . ."

"The attic, it also has an attic. The man at the agency told me that they used it as an artist's studio; he said that it has a row of big windows and that . . . But I thought it was an apartment."

"Well, Cody, it's a whole house, a lot bigger than an apartment."

"I think we've come home, Michael. And were you expecting an apartment? The house is beautiful; I'd even like to buy it. We've achieved our dream. Let's put the children in their sleeping bags; put them on top of the beds. We'll fix everything up tomorrow. And put our sleeping bags upstairs, too, we'll sleep upstairs. Let me go and choose our bedroom. Thank God, Michael, we've finished and we've arrived here safely . . ."

"We've finished and we've arrived at another beginning. The house is pretty; I like it. Cody, I think I'm going to make this room my study. Look at all the bookcases it has."

"Go get sleeping bags, the children are exhausted. We'll talk later. Go quickly."

"Yes, I agree, we've arrived home . . . but . . ."

"But go, hurry up! The sleeping bags!"

"I'm going."

"I'm going! But the Cinco de mayo was really something for the students . . ."

"I hope we never have one again because they don't know how to behave themselves. These Chicanos are like a plague of animals that fight like cats and dogs . . ."

"Hey, Lapointe, what's with you? The liquor is going to your head. Look, all the students aren't like the few outsiders that crashed the party. It wasn't the fault of the four hundred and fifty of them who came because they were really interested. Lapointe, we're not all savages. Anyway, you have one of them in your own department . . ."

"Ugh, he's disgusting. He's there because he has to be there, the bastard. He's not worth a damn. Raime tells me that he never prepares for his classes and that all he does is go to bed with the students. His résumé is nothing; Raime and I could teach what that filthy bastard teaches."

"So why don't you? What are you still doing here? After five or six years you still haven't got the degree. Raime, you say that you've finished all the requirements for the doctorate, but what happened when you took your master's exam? What? Oh, you're going now. Yes, of course, I'll see you: . . . Opportunist, you hate us but it's only with us that you can get a job. Raime is an opportunist who exploits being a Chicano. We pity him because he's a man, no, not a man, a whore who has sold his own pride and self-respect in order to take revenge on those he feels have hurt him. Raime and Lapointe are a pair who are ready to fuck their mothers to take revenge on them, and yet actually they are innocent; they had nothing to do with the decisions that were made and which cost the two of them so dearly. It's tragic; Raime thinks he's a very important, powerful guy who knows a lot of inside stuff, but all the Chicanos know what he's really like and who he really is, but he insists on living a lie. The two of them, Raime, the failed expert, and Lapointe, the protegé of the unproductive Marxist Pinnacle, don't have the balls to confront the Professor with what they really think of him. The only thing that they can do, like old whores, is lie, fabricate myths, and stab him in the back. And the worst thing is that when they see him on campus they greet him very cordially, smiling . . . Today, in a meeting of Chicanos, Raime said very sarcastically, "and he is a doctor." How Raime wishes he could use that title . . .

"Quiet everyone, telephone for Pistol Man."
"What do you want? It's me, Pistol Man, Evans, what's new?"
"They told me that one of your men was wounded."

"He's getting better. Were the men who did it on the list that you sent me?"

"No, no, it wasn't a rancher, it was one of our own who was in a fight and they shot at Rodríguez because he was trying to do his job."

"Look, Pistol Man, watch out for those Chicanos, don't let them get close to you."

"Listen, don't tell me how to live my life, you're not the first one to give me advice."

"What, what are you saying to me?"

"Nothing, what do you want?"

"Nothing, I just wanted to know what happened."

"Well, now you know . . ."

"All right, report to me if anything unusual occurs, we want to avoid what happened in California, Arizona and New Mexico. We don't want them to win here, that would be too much. We won't be able to hold our people back. So long, Pistol Man."

"Yes, of course, see you soon, but don't leave angry because I've just told you the truth. OK, if that's how you want it. Raime, Lapointe, don't be like that, don't act like idiots. All right, if that's how you want it . . .

"Manuel, go to . . ."

"What, what did you say to me . . . ?"

Dear Amy,

We're here. The house is magnificent. I was expecting an apartment and it turns out that the man from the agency gave Michael a Victorian house. I think it's the only one in Corpus. Michael and I have fixed up all the rooms and we're pretty well settled. We have the absolute necessities but after Michael is better established, I'll buy the things we still need, like a bed for each of the children, a washing machine, and a vacuum cleaner. The fireplace is gorgeous, it's big and it's made of black stone. I'm not going to describe the rooms for you, I'll just tell you that we have lots of them and we hope that you both will be able to come visit soon.

Yesterday I registered Shane in school. I'm not sure if I like the elementary school that she'll be attending; I don't like the atmosphere that the buildings evoke. But Shane seems to love it and her teacher is very nice and bright. Jason will be at day care very nearby. He's already made friends with the boy next door. The neighbors seem very nice even though most of them are older people, except for the ones on our right. He's a professor at the University, he teaches literature in the Spanish department. His wife is an elementary school teacher and they have two children, a girl four and a boy six. The husband is very interested in what Michael is doing.

Well, I'll call you soon; they just installed the phone today. It's late and I have to go and pick up Shane and Jason. We're alone; Michael left for Mathis three days ago.

Here's our address and telephone:

1409 Custard Rd.
Corpus Christi, Texas 78501
(512) 778-5071

Say hello to everyone for me and a hug for Pato, with affection, thinking of you all the time.

Love and peace,

Cody, Michael,
Shane and Jason

II

Reaching the grey, cloudy sky, with a smile of blue pleasure, he bathes his arms with the fresh sun. Next to the moon, his eye now resting against the hills jumps to the spot where for the first time he saw her enter his mind. He loves the field through which he is walking; he can't accept the cocktail they have offered him. He wants to stay here; he doesn't want his profession's palaces: . . . Understand, I want to save myself from what they want. She had already accepted him; she was the first one to come and talk: . . . But she's not sick; she'll live to bury us all. She likes to talk, gossip and medicine are her profession. Quite a few have come to see me; the only thing some need is more food . . . that night, the first one, well, now . . . the first night was really bad. I had to sleep in the VW. Then I went to Mr. Costa's little store . . . he told me what I wanted to know . . . Doctor Hales's office . . . I had a sweet roll . . . no, I had a sweet roll and a cup of coffee . . . he didn't ask me why I wanted to know . . . he didn't say anything to me about Hales . . . they didn't say anything to me at all . . . they looked at me strangely . . . I bet they thought, "Here comes another crazy doctor, another one who is going to try and stay" . . . the house isn't very nice but the rooms are big . . . it was clean, as if someone were taking care of it . . . and someone must be cleaning it in hopes of another one like the first one coming to town . . . How many were there before me? Then I slept in Hales's bed . . . there's enough furniture . . . I went in and I took it . . . no one asked me for rent, nor wanted to know who I am or how long I plan on staying . . . nothing . . . nothing. So, up goes the shingle and I start working . . . Doctor Logan has come to stay . . . Here she comes, she's a good woman, but she isn't sick . . . I'm afraid because I feel that now I've begun . . . I think about my parents, my aunts and uncles, my grandparents with their hands crossed over their stomachs, yellowed, with long stiff hair, the mummies of Carmen, they still have the odor of rotting meat. I don't want to turn into that. I'm afraid of getting old, afraid of dying, nothing is going to save me, not even what I am doing now . . . afraid of getting old, of dying, and when I think about old people who are so close, they have one foot in the grave, the grave where we have to wait for all eternity, wait, we wait for death in life and in death we wait for . . . Here comes the wise woman, the street greets her, the houses, all the objects of this dusty, white hot cold town that has already made me feel alienated . . . not just the town . . . but I myself feel that they know me better . . . they know something that I don't know, who will tell me? . . . who will do me this favor? . . . if I were there with the gringos of my profession, what would I be doing now? Not enjoying this sun, this sky, the clouds, this morning, this feeling . . . I have to write to Cody . . . No, I'll call her . . . Now she's seen me . . . the watery flesh of her body, who would have enjoyed it? Who has slept with her, old, ugly, mother of someone or mother of no one? What were our mothers like? Our fathers? I bet no one wants to think about that . . . you shouldn't be afraid . . . we're all the same . . . we're all heading toward the same end . . . But why the hell am I thinking about this depressing stuff? . . . Here she comes . . . oh, this hurts, ah, her leg, ah, her shoulder, her neck. I always see an ancient tear in her . . . His smile greeted the wise sack of strong, pitted, Chicano flesh.

"Doctor, Doctor . . . Doctor Logan, stop daydreaming and pay attention to me, please. Look, this morning I woke up with a pain in all my joints; I can't take any more! Oh, Doctor what do you suggest?"

"I suggest that you come in and have a cup of coffee and you'll see how quickly the pain passes."

"Do you think so, Doctor?"

"Yes, come in, please."

"Thank you very much, Doctor. You are really a gentleman. But look, my side hurts me . . ."

"Doña Gertrudis, I think the warmth of this cup of coffee will take it all away. The last time you were here you told me about a man who had been wounded who wanted to see me but who couldn't leave his house . . . I didn't understand. Why can't he leave his house?"

"Oh yes, it's my friend Rodríguez. He works for Pistol Man and he was shot in a quarrel in a bar. The doctors don't want to take care of him because he's a Chicano and also because he lives out there with us."

"But where you live isn't very far away."

"That doesn't matter, the learned doctors of this town don't want anything to do with us. After so many years you get used to it. And, well, that's the way life is."

"No, not at all . . . that's not how life should be."

"Doctor, you can't change anything. I hope you didn't come with impractical ideas . . . I've seen a lot like you. The last doctor who came ran away after they ruined his office . . . They didn't touch him or his wife physically the way they did to the others. You know, Doctor, this coffee is really delicious . . . don't tell me, Doctor, that you are interested in fighting against them. You can't, it's impossible."

"I'm going to have another, would you like some more?"

"Yes, I think I already feel the effects of your prescription, Doctor, just imagine. I'm better! But, as for what we were saying; it can't be done, can't be changed . . ."

"Doña Gertrudis, I want to go see Rodríguez. I think I know him. Yes, I do know who he is."

"Yes, of course, dear God, there are so many people who need help. Look, Doctor, I know a widow, very nice and pretty, and the other day when I was talking to her she told me that she was interested in a job. Of course, I realized that when you start to have more patients you're going to need some help. And I thought, with all due respect, that this young woman could help you and you could help her. She has fine gentle hands to massage the sick and she has a heart full of compassion for the world. If anyone approaches her, she is responsive to them; she's a good girl, Doctor."

"Yes, Doña Gertrudis, I need help but I'll have to teach her a lot . . . Does she learn fast, is she bright?"

"Oh, she's sharp, Doctor. I'll bring her tomorrow."

"Good. But I can't promise anything, I'll have to talk with her. Doña Gertrudis, I want to talk to Rodríguez. You say he's wounded. I want to see him."

"OK, let's go, Doctor Logan, let's go right now."

"I can't. I have to be here for the patients. We'll go to his house tonight, what do you think?"

"I think that will be fine. We could even pass by my friend's house."

"No, we'll go see her tomorrow."

"OK, I'll come by for you about six o'clock. I'm going now, thank you very much for the coffee. Your medicine is very, very good."

The fat old woman with her matchmaker mentality went down the stairs which groaned with the weight of the world covered with clothing, filled with affection, and copulation that was achieved only through the young people that she joined: . . . Oh, what a cute doctor; he's just right for my Margarita, a precious flower who has hardly been opened by the sickly child . . . Don Costa's store was closer with every step that the burned, thick and hard skin of old age, took: . . . Let's see if Pistol Man is there; let's see if he knows about the presence of the new magician. The magician will relive the episodes of the previous magicians, of the many who in other towns of common reality tried . . .

. . . This damned toilet isn't worth your mother, the fucking thing doesn't get rid of the shit, I have to . . . This bastard toilet . . . The damned shit . . . maybe someone around here can help me, a plumber, that's it, a plumber. But where's the paper? I forgot to buy it . . . I have a roll in the car . . . But what am I going to do now? . . . The towel, the towel . . . The black water, coffee, yellow, clear, fell in the tub where he rinsed the dirty towel; the smell was fetid, as if the shit were floating outside of dead flesh: . . . I must be rotten inside. It's my genius and my intelligence that makes the shit stink.

"Hello, Professor. Have you voted on your colleagues? Marty O'Leigh's case is a tough one. He has no theoretical base; his field requires a solid position because dialectically one cannot judge by any diachronic or synchronic interpretation. Don't you see it that way?"
"I don't see it that way. But I'll tell you this, Marxist Pinnacle, giant of oral criticism, I'm opposed to your judging us; I'm equally opposed to having anyone else who hasn't published or who only knows how to play the guitar or publish their works themselves, by their private publisher, to judge the rest of us. I don't want to make you angry but it's clear that you've fucked up. But don't say anything to the Aristocrat, the high society intellectual over yonder, because I might have to use his publishing company to save myself. Adiós, Marxist Pinnacle, genius of great renown, committed to nothing. You should return to your own country to make the revolution, there's more opportunity there and it's more likely that it will happen."

While waiting for a patient he sat down to write a letter to the woman with whom he had two children. Her legs, her arms, her breasts, her body was there with him . . . How nice it would be to have her here, how nice it would be to screw and to stay together for hours . . . Oh, I can't write anything . . . when I start my mind goes to other things. There goes the police . . . they're going very slowly . . . they're coming in . . . it was about time someone came to collect the rent . . . But, what's he doing? He's going? Bah, he came in, looked at me and left.

This place is really full of nuts. Leroy was right the people here . . . I don't know how to explain it . . . I'll give it time . . . I have to get to know the Chicanos better . . . The sound of a hand knocking on the back door filled his head; the message was strong and sharp. Someone was knocking at the back door. His body hurried praying that it was a sick patient, someone who needed him, a true patient. His eyes saw no one through the window curtain; the space was empty the way his heart was.

He turned his head toward the examining room. The knuckles of the old hand knocked again on the door. He quickly dashed outdoors, almost trampling the little old man who was resting on the bottom step.

"Whew, when you come out you really come out flying." The old man's affectionate smile sunk into Michael, annoyed by the pain in his leg.

"Hey, what are you doing, playing hide and seek, or what?"

"I came to look for the doctor, do you know where he is?"

"It's me, come inside to my consulting room. What's the matter with you?"

"I don't think it's anything, bags of fat, from old age."

"Sit down, there on the table. I'm going to examine you."

"I don't have anything, my head just hurts a little."

"Examine him, but he's already condemned. He killed six innocent people. Even though he's crazy, he's condemned."

"But it's not his fault; he's an idiot, a retard who watched a lot of television and believed everything he saw and heard. This damned government's to blame for letting in those bastard pornographic, violent gringo movies."

"There's nothing the matter with me; I'm not crazy. You're crazy; I did what they asked me to do. My friends on the television told me to kill my neighbors. It was nothing; talk to my friends on the television."

"Yes, yes, your friends on the television. They tell us that you just saw that picture with the maniac who killed sixteen people in Texas."

"He went up to the tower and he shot at the students on the campus. This guy has had it. If we don't sentence him the people outside will lynch him."

"That's not our concern. Declare him insane so that they'll send him to Camarillo. He'll stay there forever. Put a note on the recommendation; he'll never leave."

"No, Doctor Logan, don't you believe he'll leave, he's very happy there. Why would he want to move when he has everything? He's got his house, his children, there are three now, his wife, a fine, good woman. My son's name is Eduardo, he takes good care of me . . ."

"Mr. Guzmán, I want you to take off your clothing and lie face down on the table. Excuse me, someone is calling."

The little office's mouth received a pregnant woman with four runny-nosed and dirty children; they came in—ages two, three, four and five. Some sat on the floor, others hung about their mother's feet.

"Good afternoon, Señora. I'll be with you in about twenty minutes."

"Yes."

"Señora, if the children would like to go outside, there is a place behind the office where they can play. I have two children myself."

"Thank you, Doctor."

His hands covered, explored the old man's body; there were a lot of lumps; it was frightening to feel several in one place.

"Thank you, Mr. Guzmán, you can get dressed now. I want you to come back tomorrow with your son, please. I want to talk with him."

"Well, now you see that it's the balls of fat, if there's anything wrong with me that's what it is."

"Be sure and eat. When you feel weak, be sure to eat something."

"Yes, I do feel weak, I only want to sleep. I really feel weak."

"Don't forget, tomorrow with your son."

The old body left. The notebook was on the desk devouring the doctor's notes: . . . Gustavo Guzmán, 70 years old, diagnosis: possible lymphatic cancer . . . His ears heard the sound of the man as he left the office. The pencil fell from the notebook; he closed it. He went into the waiting room to see the woman with the four children: . . . I have to examine them . . . suddenly he felt thirty eyes silently waiting for him.

The minutes during which the hens, sheep, cats and dogs copulated were counted by the 110-year-old lady ever since the moment when she was noticed by the famous Cruz who raped her when she was bent over the river washing her husband's clothes. He slapped her hard, to make her more accommodating: . . . Well, the bitch didn't want to cooperate, she didn't realize who she was screwing with; the bitch learned, though, and I thank God for letting me do it to the girl . . . yes, God is good . . . at least the young girl had a man in her life . . . But what kind of life can the boy have . . . these bastard butchers sliced off his whole dick . . . circumcision, rot, castration, those mothers . . . I have to sue them . . . bastard doctors, butchers . . . they know everything . . . now they tell me that I have to make my boy a little girl

110

. . . that I have to get him an operation to change his sex . . . it would be a famous experiment . . . that we'd be famous because of my son . . . we were counting the minutes after the fifth operation; on account of that change, because of that experiment, the poor thing died . . . I had to kill the doctor whose hand slipped . . . they blame me? Who in this room blames me? . . . Who? . . .

"Who is it?"

"It's me, Doctor, Gertrudis."

"Come in, I was expecting you earlier, you said at six."

"Yes, but I knew you wouldn't be ready. I knew they were going to come. You see; now, tell me you don't need help. More will come, Doctor, many more."

"I'm very happy to have them come. I want to help them. Now, let's go see Rodríguez; I hope that he can help me."

"Don't ask him for anything, I don't think he'll want to help at all. In the end he's controlled by Pistol Man. What I mean is he doesn't want anything to interfere with his life the way it is now because he knows that it could hurt his family and he doesn't want that. He doesn't want to endanger his family."

"But listen, what do you think I'm going to ask him, to attack the mayor's office? No, I want him to help me to get to know the Chicanos. How can I help them if they have no trust in me? Of course, you say that they will come, but a lot of them come unwillingly, because they have to, not because they trust me. I want them to get to know me."

The two bodies closed the office; he left a light on. Maybe it was a bad habit but he always left a light on for the thieves. The Volkswagen was waiting for them. The car devoured the highway, passing trees that helped to prevent bugs; it passed an old man surrounded by children who waved when they saw them flash by their eyes and ears. The doctor suddenly caught sight of the vibrating fat that grew from the old woman's stomach. The tumor shook with every bump in the road. She was sitting at that moment as though she were afraid to be imprisoned in the cheap German capsule. Logan's beard caressed his neck which received the gentle pull of the fingers of his right hand.

"This place is pretty; some say it's horrible but I like it. But I've noticed that even though on the surface things appear calm, there is something bad underneath. Today the people who were waiting to see me were talking about a list, a government list. I was interested in the list and I asked one of the men about it. I don't remember his name, I never remember names, I asked him what this list was about. But he didn't tell me anything, just that he thought that it was a list of Chicanos, of the men who had arms and those who knew how to use arms."

"Did you bring the list, Marcelo?"

"Everyone is willing to follow you, even to hell, Casimiro. We only need about fifteen more rifles and we'll be set. And let's see who denies us what is ours. Casimiro, just tell us when, we're fed up with waiting."

"The whole nation is waiting for you to speak, Casimiro."

"Casimiro, we won't go back on our word, we're determined."

"Keep calm boys, the connection from the North will arrive soon with what we need. Bear up, bear up! We'll burn this list now; we know who is with us and who isn't. We'll burn the enemies of justice. We'll start burning tonight, we will!"

"Oh, Doctor, I feel a burning in my chest. What do you think it is? Ay, I'm dying, Doctor, what is it?"

"Doña Gertrudis, it's just that you shouldn't eat so many chile peppers; at your age you can't eat as if you were a girl of twenty."

"No, it's something more serious."

"No, it's nothing. Will we be there soon?"

"The house is just ahead; look, the little girl is playing outside. Pull the car all the way in."

The dust kissed the cheeks of the pretty Rodríguez girl. The cheerful little body ran to the door from which the beloved old lady's body emerged into the world.

"Aunt Gertrudis, hello!"

"Yes, yes, child. Where is your father? We want to speak to him. You have to come inside; it's getting late, and you know how your mother is; let's go inside and you go to sleep."

"No, Aunt Gertrudis, I want to play . . ."

She got out of the car with her eyes filled with the house, Rodríguez's little homestead, everything in its place, just as it should be, everything in order. She turned and a woman was coming holding a bag, garbage falling into a barrel by the side of the car. She passed so close Logan could almost touch her. She didn't say anything and she didn't look at anybody; she wiped her hands on her apron. She stopped in front of them with her hands still holding the cloth. Their eyes met.

"Francisca, Francisca, look, come here, I want to introduce you to the new doctor, Doctor Logan. He's come to help us, he knew Doctor Hales . . ."

"How long will you be with us, Doctor Logan?"

112

"I don't know, ma'am."

"Stay as long as they let you, Doctor, maybe a month, three months, ten, a year, who knows."

"Someone knows, Mrs. Rodríguez; but I've come to stay, to work, to practice my profession here in Mathis and no one is going to drive me out. If you'll allow me, Mrs. Rodríguez, I'd like to see your husband."

"Yes, of course."

"Francisca, Doctor Logan tells me he's going to give Margarita the job. You see, he's a good man, and I think that if he stays with us, he'll be the first one who does, won't he?"

The doctor's mind contemplated the buttocks of the two who were walking in front of him; the sounds of female joints took him to a bed with open legs flaunting themselves and offering the place of penetration that he desired: . . . Cody, I have to write to Cody; no, I'll call her tonight, I'll be there this weekend, I have to buy what I need, the bathroom, where's the bathroom? No, why should I bother them, I can hold it . . . From the outside they were talking very close to him. Their reiterations made him realize that he was before a man lying on a sofa. The medical hand touched his forehead, the thumb lifted his eyelid. He opened his black bag, he listened to the lungs with the stethoscope, the fever was quite high.

"Let me see his abdomen . . . it looks as though they change the dressings frequently, the wounds are clean, but there is an infection in both of them. It's strange, the bullets went through on either side of your stomach, you're lucky my friend, very lucky. I'm going to give you a shot of penicillin. Do you know if they've given you penicillin? Yes? Good, very good. Also, I don't want them to put all these bandages on you. We'll clean the wounds and we'll put on these patches and that's it. I want you to eat well, and when the fever goes down you have to start walking. I'll leave you some pills with your wife and in two or three days I promise you'll be all right. As for the pain, you'll have to put up with it. I'll be seeing you, Señor Rodríguez, and thank you."

The eyes of the man on the sofa saw him without saying anything; they did not know how to respond. They looked toward the ceiling. . . . You're going to help me survive here; you don't know it, Rodríguez, but I know you, I already know who you are, you're the key, Rodríguez, you will save me . . .

"See you soon, Señor."

In the kitchen Francisca offered him coffee which he refused; Doña

Gertrudis said she would be staying there. He went out into the night, contemplated the stars, the beautiful evening, that millions of people did not appreciate. At this moment he was a giant, in front of the world he was God, a magician, alone, sad, separated, dead for those who knew him, a memory for his wife and children, not to be with them was to be dead, lost on the earth, in memory. He loved them, but he loved all humanity; he didn't know how to tell them that, only through his actions, doing, not talking, doing. He breathed the air: . . . I thank God for giving me this moment, these are things that I don't want to give up . . . The stars penetrated his brain, he arrived home, opened the refrigerator and took out a beer, then another, the third was the easiest, he drank more . . . everything became just a memory when he fell asleep.

"They only wanted the land that was promised them, the land that the Revolution promised them, that was all. It wasn't necessary to kill sixteen of them to demonstrate the army's strength. Señor Presidente, please take the troops out before there's another outbreak of violence!"

"We don't deal with traitors, with communist revolutionaries who obtain arms with the marijuana they grow."

"But, Señor Presidente, that's not true. They pay with money and not with drugs. Even though it would be easy to get rifles for drugs; several times the gringos have . . . they got them from the ones in the North . . ."

"Did they kill the leader?"

"Casimiro is alive, his son was killed. Now they're burning the big houses. I don't like the atmosphere that's developing in the North, even on the other side of the border, they're expecting something . . ."

"Señor Presidente, a 'colleague' is waiting for you in the bedroom."

"Thank you, tell her to wait for me for a minute. Look, I don't want any of this being made public."

"But it already has. The American press has discussed the subject, reducing it to an exchange of gunfire between rebellious marijuana growers and the army. At any rate it's difficult to cover up the death of sixteen people and the five hundred peasants who want land."

"All right, let the army stay there with observer status; and tell the landowner that he'll have to sacrifice a few acres, tell him that his cooperation is needed, and that if he doesn't want to help us, we will be forced to take severe measures against him, his family and his belongings."

"Señor Presidente, the young lady is waiting for you."

"Yes, yes, goodbye, Señor Ministro."

"Good night, Señor Presidente."

"Good night, Teresa, and let me repeat that I don't want you to go to that new doctor, I don't want you to. I'll take you to one of ours."

"No, I don't want to go to one of yours! They say that this one is very good. I'm going to go early tomorrow. My little sister is sick and we can't waste any more time. Now I'm tired and want to go to sleep. You know that I love you Pistol Man, but please, let me go to this doctor. I feel more comfortable going to him."

"He'll be like all the others that have come, he'll only last a few months. But all right, go if you want to."

"Thank you, Pistol Man, you see, you're very kind. Good night, my love."

The button breasts of the incipient woman offered their back, their buttocks, the penis full of blood slipped itself between them, the two spoons in love were quiet, peaceful, he fell asleep, tired . . . Thank God the little girl is asleep. Grandpa said that he would get up with her . . . I have to take her early tomorrow . . . he doesn't want to take me . . . we'll have to walk, it's not far, poor little girl, the fever is very high, but it's worse at night, during the day she plays and eats fine, she's growing . . . that's what mother used to say, that she's growing. He has to be good, everyone says that he is. God help the doctor so that he can stay with us . . . Don't let Pistol Man get angry with him . . . let him stay with us . . . The tick tock of the clock marked all of her body, of her vision, of her dark world, shadows, suddenly the light will come, that's how it happens. Darkness and nothing and in an instant the light appears on her forehead, the light of another day to live.

The Professor entered his office at six in the morning, his right hand held the door, the other guided the portable table with the typewriter. He left the office door open. . . . Coffee . . . put on the coffee . . . yesterday's mail . . . He picked up the flyer. . . . Nice and early, I like to be here early . . . I work well in these three hours . . . the Aristocrat got a grant to finish his book of essays . . . what bastards! . . . the ones with power are always first in line . . . maybe the next time I'll get one . . . I don't push myself enough, maybe I should walk around here like a great scholar, like the powerful intellectual pedants, like the Marxist Pinnacle or the Theoretical Roman, but what the hell have they done, written or . . . The Theoretical Roman has created an atmosphere of fear, of insecurity, he's screwed me . . . instead of feeling more comfortable, having more self-confidence, I feel diminished, belittled . . . Baldy Foureyes, he's my salvation, now we have to vote; I'll vote to give everyone tenure. In reality our vote doesn't count . . . it's just a way of making us feel important . . . because the decisions, at least under this regime, are already made when they talk to us. And to get ahead, to accelerate a bit, everything has to be perfect; they want us to be superhuman. Who's perfect? Why am I here? Well, I like literature, literature has inspired me in what I really want to do . . . just like Michael, there in Mathis doing what's important . . . although I'm envious of him . . . well, I'm crazy too . . . we both suffer from the same madness, we want to be modern day heroes . . . but he doesn't realize this . . . or maybe he does . . . maybe everything he does is to become famous, because he's selfish, a drunk and crazy like me . . . but he hasn't called . . .

"Good morning, Professor."

. . . Ah, the secretary who is always busy and gets nothing done has arrived, but she's always up on the gossip; she's always complaining that she's got a lot of work, and the other one too. That one, the model, spends the day talking on the phone with her friends, about the clothes they bought, make-up, nail polish, what airheads . . . another cup of coffee . . . I'll have another cup of coffee and I'll sit down and write . . . and fuck them all, and win the battle . . . the war waged in the universities of our country, in the places where they give more credit to the people who talk about books than to the people who actually write them, the true artists . . . let's go to war on this glorious morning . . .

The female voice filled the office; he saw her for the second time; the girl's body penetrated into his safe territory; he felt uncomfortable with her, their eyes met: . . . This young woman says that she's all right, that she wants to touch me, that she wants to kiss me, she asks me to touch her, to embrace her. How many times has she offered me the opportunity? But I'm a fool for not taking advantage of the offer; I can't and I don't want to . . . anyway, these last days with the fear, the pressure of work, I haven't felt like it, I haven't even thought about it . . . but now, now it's big . . . I have to move my leg, cross it so that the growing protuberance doesn't show . . .

He woke up feeling naked, his leg moved to the edge of the bed, searching for the floor; the other leg and foot followed, the torso with arms and hands grabbed the sheets to support his neck and head: . . . Damned head, I can't take it, the bathroom, the toilet . . . ay, again . . . no, never again . . . aaaah . . . ay, I want to shit . . . vomit . . . A half hour passed without any corporal movement, he was breathing better, more easily. . . . Coffee . . . a cup of coffee . . . I'll pull myself together . . . Cold water ran over his head, splashed on his face, his half dead brain came out of its drunken stupor, emerged into the real world, the new world of his that he had begun to construct; he had planned it, he had created the characters, he would have to manipu-

116

late them. He had brought forth a new world with new objects, with a new language. The water fell on his body . . . The lump he had in his throat became lighter, he felt better. . . . The time . . . the woman . . . Margarita . . . my patients . . . Fuck! it's six-thirty . . . I can't drink, I have to set up a schedule . . . a discipline of creativity, creative medicine, my patients, my work is the most important thing . . . I have to stop drinking until I've accomplished something really positive . . . my cup of coffee . . . oh fuck! I don't have any clean clothes . . . I'll put on this filthy underwear . . . a little powder and I'm all set . . . that's enough perfume . . . it's a nice day . . . the weather's been gorgeous . . . I'll try and have breakfast . . . damned fucking head, it really hurts . . . I could give myself a shot but no, I'd better . . . when will this widow Margarita show up? . . . I hope she's bright . . . I'll try and convince her to stay here in the house so that she can do the cleaning, and whatever else . . . I have to call Cody . . . but how, if I don't know the number, she must have had the phone put in, she doesn't have my number either . . . yes, tomorrow I'll be with them . . . she must be really mad . . . Leroy, this place isn't so bad . . . well, I still haven't been here long, things are revealed slowly . . . we'll see . . . I don't have anything to eat . . . an egg, some tortillas . . . and two beers . . . ahhh, I don't even want to think about them . . . coffee and that's it . . . the full cup was carefully taken by the body outside to the porch where he sat down. The cup was tilted towards his lips. . . . Here she comes . . . it's her . . . with the child . . . I thought she was older . . . she's young . . . a girl . . . pretty . . . the boy looks sick, withered, anemic; he seems happy, he's playing . . . throwing stones, she sees me . . . the child aims at where I am . . . little withered kid . . . he's at the fence . . . The two faces gazed on each other for the first time; she inclined her head without losing eye contact; his smile wasn't like the other one's . . . The other one wasn't like this one . . . this doctor seems very human . . . there's no distance between him and me . . . I already feel comfortable . . . The doctor's smile wished her a good morning.

"Good morning. You're Doctor Logan?"

"Yes, and you are Señora Margarita?"

"Yes, Doña Gertrudis sent me; I've come to ask for a job for myself and for my son Felipe. We are at your service, Doctor."

"Thank you very much, come in and we can talk . . ."

The crows perched on the roof of the animals' corral. They cawed and cawed from the beginning of the journey until the place that only the birds know, that only the birds see and feel with their eyes and their wings. They spy on men; they are never felt; they are only seen, but there they are more secretive. The butterfly is the same way; how many times has a butterfly been next to a man without his knowing it? Butterflies know everything. The hummingbird is the ideal fighter, the supreme hero who keeps vigil over everything. The crows cawed above the hens pecking at the ground in search of a seed to put in their insides. The butterfly saw her leave with the boy, and its blue, white, red wings followed the two of them. At the same time the humming-bird lifted its wings and set its powerful transparent grey feathers vibrating in order to accompany the innocent sick girl. The crows were seen by old Bilabí in the other direction; they cawed as if they were angry at a fruitless delay. Bilabí was carried by his brain and his legs. He approached the police car parked in the middle of the yard and he touched one of the windows that reflected his pensive image. His head, his eyes, his mouth and his hand said goodbye to Teresa and the child.

"Grandpa, I'm going to the doctor's and I'm taking the girl. I didn't want to wake you! Go inside and have breakfast, goodbye, see you later."

"Yes, child, yes . . ."

The old shoes climbed up on the porch, his hand opened as he listened to Pistol Man talking on the telephone; the old man sat down and served himself a cup of coffee, bacon and a sweet roll that his kind granddaughter had left for him. He picked up the sweet roll, showing it to Pistol Man as if it were an invitation to the breakfast that he found quite tasty. "No" and "stop" said the sheriff's large, uniformed hand. The old man began to chew noisily, he sipped his coffee, and he tasted the bacon with the tip of his tongue. . . . He doesn't eat? Well I'll eat it all . . . what a shame that he doesn't enjoy what he buys us . . . all the children are eating well, his presence here has changed them . . . he's not as bad a guy as I thought . . . but he didn't have to throw me in jail so that he could sleep with Teresita . . . that was bad . . . she told me that they were going to get married as soon as his crazy wife gives him a divorce . . . I don't really care any more . . . I'm very old; I feel that every day things get harder for me, sometimes I forget where I am, what time it is, sometimes I think that when I go into the house I'll find my wife there . . . and I'm sure that she'll be there and I go in, but I don't find her, instead it's one of the children or Teresa making something in the kitchen; she talks to me and I wake up, I come back from my memories, from where I was . . .

"I don't know where they are and I'm not going to ask for them; if I do I'm crazy. I won't take any weapons away from anybody, I won't do it. Now look, if you want to start a war all you have to do is ask them for their weapons, not only will the Chicanos send you

118

to hell but so will we. First them and then us, that's probably how they think. They haven't smuggled arms from here across the border, Evans. The only things that get through are what you tell me should get through; two Red Cross trucks with a thousand automatic rifles. See here, I really don't care if they sell them arms, let the bastards kill themselves. They'll start another miserable revolution in order to end up just the same; that country doesn't change; it never will. Of course I understand what would happen if those trucks fell into Casimiro's hands. You're afraid of him, aren't you? I hope he's successful, I like rebels. No, nothing new. Oh, yes, there is something new, a doctor from Corpus came to set up an office in the Chicano neighborhood, but like with the others, if he becomes very popular we'll get rid of him. Up until now we haven't had any problem with him. I don't know how many have seen him. Yes, I understand. Yes, now with this business with Casimiro and the arms smuggling. Yes, we don't want anybody getting ideas. I know! You don't have to remind me! Yes, I'll talk to him this afternoon. Yes, goodbye!"

His eyes looked at Don Bilabí eating his sweet roll.

"Thank God you're deaf, old man. Isn't it true that you're deaf?"

"Excuse me, Doctor, I didn't hear you . . ."

"I said that I hope that you can live here; I want you to help me with the housework as well as the work in the office. Look, before you decide . . . I want to show you the house, the bedroom for you and your son. Margarita, may I call you that?"

"All right, that's fine. Call me Margarita and my son Felipe" . . . Ever since he died, since he left us, no one has called me Margarita . . . No man has called me Margarita . . . This man can do it innocently . . . but I know who I am, I know that my body is desirable . . . careful, Margarita . . . don't get carried away . . . the good doctor can certainly help you but don't let it go any farther than that . . . don't let it go any farther . . . even if that's what you would like, you mustn't let it . . .

"Here is your room, it has its own bath. I stay in the little room and in the laboratory. I need someone to help me and you can. I can also teach you, Margarita, I'll train you to be a nurse. Think it over, you would earn a salary, you wouldn't have to buy food, or pay rent. What do you say, Felipe, you and I and this town, right, Felipe?"

"Yes, sir, yes . . ."

"What do you say, Margarita? Say yes."

"Doctor Logan, I don't know. It's so . . ."

"First, call me Michael, we're partners, we're a team and you'll call me Michael."

"All right, Michael. I don't know. When would I be able to move?"

"I have to go to Corpus this afternoon; I'll be back Sunday night. You'll have the whole weekend. I'm sorry that I can't stay and help you but I need medicines and I have to see my wife and children. You'll do it, Margarita, you'll do it, won't you?"

"Yes."

"Bravo, let's celebrate. I don't have any champagne, but with these two beers we can consecrate our agreement and celebrate our new medical association. Have a little more, Margarita . . . to us."

"To us, Michael."

"Mommy, a lady wants to talk to the gentleman!"

"With the doctor, Felipe! With the doctor!"

"Our first patient has arrived. There's a smock over there on the bed; put it on and talk to the woman, ask her where she lives, her age, if she's married, if she has children, what's the matter with her, I mean, what symptoms she has. Tell her to wait and I'll be right out. Monday I'll tell you everything that you have to do when a new patient comes, or we'll do it Sunday when I get back. Good luck, go and say hello to her."

Raquel looked at the new nurse and fell, faint, next to the table that struck up a painful and rabidly delirious dialog with her. The monsters were coming to eat her nipples, she looked at the naked man on the bed. . . . He's looking at me, he wants to say something to me, facing the invalid again, his hands full of shit, clean him again, the illness came very quickly, in a few years it had eaten away his brain, destroying the capillaries, leaving him like a child. My son used to bathe him every two or three days because he had very intense pain; my brother used to say that he was working very hard to make death come more quickly; I remember one time we were outside and his dog ran into the street, a truck crushed him; my daughter went out and stood in front of him . . . my poor husband cried very easily . . . . . . "I dog, I dog, I want like . . . to die . . ." He told us he wanted to die . . . Oh, my poor husband. All this happened when he could talk, move; now he can't do anything, he's just in bed. At times I don't know if he's dreaming; at night he screams, a full throated scream, for a minute. I don't know where the poor skeleton gets the strength, he is a skeleton now, my man is a corpse; I remember him when we were recently married, he was beautiful, a big, tall man; we've taken him to all the doctors and they say that they can't do anything. They also told me that the illness comes from him and that he could give it to one of the children; I pray to God that won't happen, let my children live long and happy lives, don't let them suffer with their father's illness . . .

"Michael, she's waking up."

"Bring me a glass of brandy; I'll use the local medicine."

"Doctor, you heard me, didn't you? Yes, you understand me, I am very tired and came to speak to you. He screams a lot in the night, I don't sleep at all, I can't sleep, and the children, they aren't children any more, they're adults, they're big, they can't take him any more either and they tell me to put him in a nursing home. Please, can you help me? He doesn't do anything any more, he just screams at night, as if he were trying to separate his soul from his poor body, as if he wanted to frighten his own soul so that it would leave once and for all and end it. I need you to give me an address, a nursing home where I can take him."

"Please calm down, Señora, take these pills and we'll talk in an hour, please, just rest here a little bit . . ."

"He's alone at home but he doesn't do anything, there's no danger that he'll hurt himself. Yes, rest, sleep a little bit . . . yes, I'm coming . . . I'm coming . . ."

"I'm coming, Teresa, I'm coming."

"Good, if you want to get there soon then you have to walk faster; yes, I know that you don't feel well but we have to get there before there are a lot of people. Let's go, there's the house, we're close. No, it's the one he uses for a house, before it was a shop and a house, both, house, shop and house-shop, but now it's his office; don't ask me so many questions."

She knew the widow, Felipe, Doña Gertrudis, Fernando, Francisca, she knew them all. That's the way relations are in Texan towns, they're either very intimate or they're very superficial, superficial as if one could only touch their skin, not their blood, nor a person's warmth; rarely does a friend know another person's blood. The Chicano people are rarely known, even husbands and wives, even lovers, lesbians, homosexuals; we only share one thing, a part of ourselves, even when we make love; we delight in the vagina and the penis and that's all; we manipulate each other to get a better position, to grab all that we can, always screwing each other, never understanding each other. Her hand pulled at her dress, pulling her to the arm chair.

"Sit here with me, Teresita, I'm afraid."

"Hello, Teresa, how are you? And your grandfather, how's he doing?"

. . . Silly thing, they're talking to you, the little girl wants you to sit down . . . sometimes I feel sick . . . I'm embarrassed when they ask me about my grandpa . . . they must think he lives out in the corral because Pistol Man kicked him out of the house . . . and I sleep with Pistol Man . . . and so what? If I love him and he loves me . . . I'm sure about that . . . but letting him do the things he does to me, makes me ashamed . . . but I love him . . . it's natural . . . I'm not shy . . . maybe I was, but when it's time to make love, I do it for him, I'm open for him, I do everything for him, at that moment I would do it with a whole army; but just at that moment, if an army were there I'd let them all; two by two or three or however they wanted . . . Oh, this child won't keep still . . .

"Teresa, how is your grandfather?"

"Fine, yes, thank you. I came because the girl is sick and I want the doctor to see her. Please."

"Of course, I'll talk to Michael right away . . . Doctor Logan will be out in a moment . . ."

"Margarita, you can call me Michael; I prefer to be called Michael, I don't like titles. You can call me Michael, or if you prefer, Mr. Logan, however you like. OK? Now, what is bothering you?"

"It's not me, I came with the girl."

"Oh, the girl. What's your name?"

"I'm Gloria, sir."

"You have a fever don't you? Does she sleep all right at night?"

"No, Doctor, she wakes up as if she were going to choke. She wakes up screaming as if the devil were chasing her."

"Don't think that, the devil has no reason to be interested in this innocent creature . . . Open your mouth. More. Stick out your tongue. Very good. Yes, I'm sure you wake up choking. You have two big problems, two giant, infected tonsils. Poor thing, I'm surprised you've lasted until now. I'll give you a prescription; when the infection is cleared up and the swelling goes down we'll have to operate. With this medicine, in a few days the fever will be gone and you'll feel better, you'll even be able to go out and play with your little friends, but until then I want you to stay inside and rest. Do you understand me? I don't want you to run, and I don't want you to get excited. Here, Señorita . . ."

"My sister is not a señorita, she's married to Pistol Man, Doctor. Isn't that so, Teresa?"

"Excuse me, Señora, I didn't know that you were married."

"That's all right, Doctor. When do you want me to bring her back?"

"I think she'll be ready for the operation next Friday."

"OK, and thank you very much, Doctor. How much do I owe you?"

"Oh . . . well, we'll talk about that the next time you're here."

"I can pay you right now."

"No, I prefer to fill out all the forms first and then we'll take care of it. Give all the information to Margarita. Do you know each other?"

"Yes."

"Yes. We know each other."

"Margarita, do you work here?"

"Yes. I started today, I think I can help him and he can help Felipe and me."

"I think about getting a job sometimes, but I can't because of my age."

"Why don't you talk to him? Maybe he'll give you a job helping me."

"No, not now, next time, goodbye, see you . . . Margarita, there are people waiting outside."

Her hand opened the door, passing it to Margarita who held it to allow in the bodies that were waiting to see the doctor. The years had accumulated for some, others were harmed by a wild youth, others had been squeezed and drained by their own desires, others had incomprehensible visions caused by their fear of life; the authorities had condemned others as mental aberrations or uncultured Hispanic products. The Chicanos were waiting, they needed to be treated with Western medicine, they asked for attention to be paid to their state of health. The female eyes counted them as they passed through the door, more than thirty who made him work until he shouted, shouted with joy. People who really needed him came to him, he was doing something really important; not only did he cure them but he guided them, he showed them better ways to maintain their health, so that they themselves could keep themselves well; he talked to them about healthier food, but they said that food was very expensive, that only the rich ate steak, that when the cost of gasoline went up so did everything else, that since they were poor they could hardly buy what was absolutely necessary for mere subsistence. He was told all this by the infections, the malnutrition, the lacerated stomachs, the bulging eyes, the dry skin, the yellow eyes, the tired women, the uneven knees, the twisted feet, the drunken minds, the mouths reeking of alcohol, the dripping ears, the chewed earlobes, the abused children, the swollen vaginas, the inflamed penises; hunger was the cause of all in a society that permitted it.

The man was talking to him about the formerly heavy whip of oppression. The Professor thought about it as he sat next to Baldy

Foureyes. The president of the university would arrive in a few seconds; the Professor took in all the gringos that filled the room, there was just one dark-skinned one, no, there were two Chicanos present. Weren't there any more? And those two don't exist in that world because they're not accepted.

"Distinguished colleagues, let me introduce to you the president of the University system, Doctor Alfred Taxon."

The doctor's mouth moved for a few minutes, then he asked if his distinguished colleagues had any questions. The questions and the answers indicated a great perfection was being steadily fulfilled and within ten years we would have the most famous, prestigious and wealthy university in the United States. The intellectuals practically had orgasms hearing about the possibilities, the possibilities for research, for grants, for travel, in order to keep their world separate from the outside world, the little gringo professors went wild with the news, the elite searching for perfection, they wanted supermen, scholars who knew everything about theory and science. . . . We ask for the supreme theoretical prick, the cunt that can explain in Goichian terms, fornicate in a Goldmanian vocabulary. We will defend the Aristocrat, his reality of creating a bibliography of everything in print in order to receive more grants and to engender more aristocrats and construct more essays . . . The Marxist Pinnacle thought about the tip of his penis imparting a complete world view to a graduate student whose ass broke into a glorious Kochian smile.

"What's your name?"

"Professor Morenito of the Foreign Department."

"Your answer, Doctor Taxon?"

"Very well, my answer is the following: These themes will not be treated at the university, they have no place here, and they must be relegated to a lower form of education that is found in another system, of lower quality than our university, that is the state system of schools and colleges; we must give the problem to them, that is their purpose; we are here to develop theory. Only theory."

"Bravo, bravo, excellent!"

"Theory!"

The intellectual bodies, the theoreticians, the Chnidermen of science, Baldy Foureyes, the eclectic, the doctor hired by the university and the county, concerned only about his private patients, applauded with enthusiasm; the ivory tower's powerful eyes rejected Professor Morenito of the Foreign Department and forced him to sit down.

"Distinguished colleagues, many thanks."

124

"Thank you, Doctor Taxon, for your assurances that our system will continue."

"It is my duty to maintain this university's commitment to the highest quality and the perfection that you yourselves reflect. And to prevent the entrance of elements that will cause the deterioration and degradation of our creation. Thank you, distinguished colleagues."

The Professor's head bobbed up at the same time as Baldy Foureyes's.

"Well, now you see, Professor, in order to stay here you have to be the best, perfect, and your publications have to be of the highest quality, as the Theoretical Roman says, 'You must search for the structuring axis' or as the Marxist Pinnacle says, 'The tale's relativity is shaped by the oxymoronic quality of the declaration,' or as the Aristocrat says, 'It's to be found in the research or creation that's in press,' or as the Little Koala Bear says, 'Tenure is to be found with song and the guitar,' or as the Oneiric Bicyclist would say, 'One must search for the way through the oneiric.' These are the opinions of the wise, so you see, Professor Morenito, you have to be excellent, superhuman, in order to be able to stay here. Do you understand me, Professor Morenito?"

"They've all gone."

"Yes, all our perfect ones have gone. Make yourself perfect and you will become one of us; that's all you have to do. Good day, Professor Morenito."

"Good day, thank you."

"Thank you, but I don't have time; it's already late and I want to get to Corpus as soon as possible . . ."

"But you should eat something, Michael."

"Here's the key, lock the doors. Bring all your things tomorrow and I'll see you Monday, or maybe Sunday. Goodbye . . ."

"Yes, goodbye, Doctor."

The child watched the Volkswagen leave for the highway, he followed it until it disappeared into the night; the child contemplated the situation thinking about his mother: . . . My mother is pretty and I love her . . . I love her a lot . . . we're going to stay here . . . I like this place . . . I like the doctor's storehouse . . .

"Mommy, Mommy, I'm hungry! Mommy, where did the doctor go?"

He ran looking for his mother who has all the answers in some place in her body.

"Calm down, Felipe; just a minute, please."

The bearded man got out of the Volkswagen, the strange face drew up to the window; he saw a man eating a sandwich wrapped in a napkin, the fat man didn't get out of his chair, with his hands he motioned for him to leave. The doctor returned to his car: . . . "But where can I get gas?" . . . The police car suddenly arrived, with squeeking tires. It stopped in front of the bearded doctor. The policeman's hat observed him.

"Aha, you're the little doctor that's come to town to help the Chicanos."

The hat got out of the police car.

"I'm Pistol Man . . . you don't know that between six and seven you can't buy gas at Henly's station; it's his dinner time; you were lucky that he didn't get tough with you; Henly's quite coarse, he doesn't like his dinner to be interrupted. You don't talk much, Doctor. Well, that's all right. But it seems to me that if you're leaving tonight you shouldn't come back. We don't want you here, I'm a very frank man and I'm telling you the truth. You're better off going back with the others who came and were run out of town. Don't come back, Doctor, because it will be dangerous; the townsfolk don't want you here, our Chicanos don't need you. Here comes Henly; now I've told you; fill your tank with gas and don't come back. I hope he doesn't kick your ass."

Pistol Man violently started up the police car.

"For your own good, don't come back!"

"Hey, you, how much do you want? The next time you land here between six and seven you'll be in real trouble, you bastard. How much did you say?"

"Fill it up . . . Henly . . ."

. . . Fill those bastards full of lead, fill them with lead is what they want, those Indians will never realize that we are the ones who run things in this miserable country; I told the owner to give up a few acres but the idiot refused . . . now he's arming up against the savages and the army, now all the big landowners have their own armies . . . to keep watch over their land, that's the pretext . . . and the gringos' companies have asked for federal protection; if I don't give it to them they've indicated that they'll arm men . . . what a mess! These damned poor people, no one wants to help anyone else; everyone wants to protect whatever they have, whether it's a lot or a little . . . and the savages, what do they want the land for? They don't know how to work it, they don't have the equipment or the intelligence to make it produce . . .

126

they should pump them full of lead . . . let them kill them . . . that's what the army wants to do, well all right then, let them do it . . . this country is incapable of ever doing anything because everybody is the boss, everybody abuses power . . ."

"Señor Presidente, Robert Evans of the United States State Department is here, the members are waiting for you and him . . ."

"Have him come in: . . . They're running arms across the border, the Chicanos up there are supplying weapons to the Mexican rebels . . . Casimiro is getting a lot, now we know that the majority of arms come through Texas, not the Chicanos; the gringos are the ones who are making the revolution here but it will start up there too, and they know it . . . and here comes Mr. Evans . . . bastards, it's going to cost them a lot to calm down the Chicanos and the rebels, it's going to be very expensive . . .

"Good evening, Mr. Evans, yes, of course we'll speak your language, fortunately I speak it perfectly: . . . fucking gringos will never learn, they don't learn foreign languages, not even Spanish . . . but once this thing blows up, they'll have to learn quickly . . . the Chicanos are in the right up there, but they shouldn't come and be a pain in the ass here . . .

"Señor Presidente, the ministers have gone to the reception room and they are waiting for you."

He parked the Volkswagen in front of the Victorian house, his artist's mind looked at it and agreed with his wife's opinion: . . . Yes, the house is pretty . . . The warm lights invited him in; but fear, for not having written or called, spoke to him, saying that Cody would be angry with him: All right, but she can't stay angry forever . . . His thumb pressed the bell; the children's voices ran toward the door. The door opened as three shouts rang out.

"Daddy! Daddy!"

"Who is it? Michael?"

"Yes, it's me."

The children jumped up and down, their arms demanding his neck, their lips moistening his beard, Jason stepped on his feet, Shane coated his ear with saliva, he felt his wife's body sink into his chest, their mouths wanted each other, their pupils filled with love, the children between their legs separated their genitals; they wanted to talk to Daddy who had returned.

"Daddy, when can we go with you?"

"Daddy, I want to go see your office. Mommy said that it was very pretty."

"Yes, Daddy, I want to go too."

"OK, let's sit down and we'll talk."

"Michael, how are you? Are you all right?"

"Yes, Cody, I'm fine."

"Thank God, but why didn't you write or call me on the phone? I was about to go to Mathis to look for you."

"I really had a lot to do; but now I have a telephone and you can call me whenever you like."

"What's your office like, Daddy?"

"My office isn't at all fancy, it's an abandoned house that used to be a store, it's the same place that Leroy had. The very same place. No one has called, have they?"

"No one . . ."

"Let me make you a sandwich."

"Yes, thanks. No, let's wait 'til after the children are in bed."

"Children, in a few minutes you're going to be in bed and asleep, it's late . . ."

"But we want to talk more with Daddy . . ."

"You can talk to him tomorrow. You got up very early this morning and you've been playing all day . . . in just a minute you're going to get into bed."

"And the neighbors, Cody, what are they like?"

"Very kind; the young man who lives on this side is a professor at the university; very nice, him, his wife, the whole family. He's interested in what you're doing in Mathis; all the rest are older people."

"What's his name?"

"Eutemio."

"What?"

"E-u-t-e-m-i-o, like that, that's how Leticia, his wife says it."

"Eutemio, that's an interesting name, I'd like to meet him."

"Let's go, Shane and Jason, to bed."

"Yes, children it's time, let's go. I'm the horsey, climb up."

"Me first, Shane."

"No, I'm the biggest."

"Don't fight, Jason, you get on Daddy's shoulder and Shane can sit on his back."

"Everybody ready? . . . let's go."

"Faster, Daddy, faster, ride 'em cowboy, yahooo!"

They heard the insects that were flying to save their lives, the lizards froze, protecting themselves from the monstrous sound that pounded their primitive ears, the stones jumped with every horse and human step, the mountain allowed the weight of the weapons, on the backs of beasts, to plod along the unknown path. All human, moving creatures breathed the air, the broad sky embraced him completely, while the stars blazed across the sky, establishing their own existence in the universe. The tranquility of the muleteer and the guide inspired confidence in their performance; he wasn't afraid, he was sure about the risk, it was something positive that he was doing, he was prepared to die. The earth's nipple disturbed the warm place where Casimiro's men were waiting for him. Some stones tumbled down from above indicating the movement of something higher up; the young man's instincts looked up, the horses became excited, he couldn't breathe, the horses were stopped dead by something up above; it was a man, about fifteen feet away. His mouth did not allow him to articulate words, so poisoned was it by what he saw, there was no face in the skull, how could he hear, talk, see: . . . He's going to fall on me, but walk . . . shout . . . the words won't come out . . . I'm moving my mouth but I don't hear anything . . . the straight black hair retreated blending into the silent rocks. For a perpetual instant the animals sniffed at the nothingness: . . . It must be one of Casimiro's men . . . but he doesn't have a face . . . there is nothing where his face is . . . The horses sniffed, the stars were recording it in the history of the cosmos.

"Hey, can't you see? What's the matter with you? Listen to me, Rodríguez!"

"Oh . . . it's you, it was you, the one who was up there keeping watch."

"What are you talking about . . . are you drunk?"

"No, I swear to you; there was a man up there, there, look, up there, he didn't have a face . . ."

"What, he didn't have a face?"

"Yes, I saw him Casimiro, I saw him, the horses didn't move, I couldn't shout out, time stood still, it was an eternity, the whole earth was sweating, I swear to you. He was there!"

Casimiro's men heard and believed in the event. Sometimes he appears only to remind men that he exists, that his power and spirit walk the face of the earth, through the cosmos of our minds; he appears in unexpected places; in sacred moments of certainty, he allows himself to be seen and he leaves his mark.

"What did you find up there, Marcelo?"

"There can be no doubt, Casimiro . . . It was him . . . We found a little damp place, soaked and stinking of cat piss. Let's get out of here fast. The men want to go . . . We'll unload the weapons at the campsite. Look at Rodríguez's horses, they're done for, exhausted. There's no doubt, it was him . . . Let's go soon, Casimiro."

The men's dreams were invaded by nightmares sung by the stars in all their beauty, in part of the system of unreality. The grotesque acts in every man slept in his body and in his mind, while they fulfilled the oneiric reality. They were killing children, decapitating their fathers and taking their mothers, they were fornicating with their brothers and sisters; daughters were sucking the paternal penis, priests were licking the virgin's thing, sadistic deaths, disgusting sacrifices, were carried out before the evil god of God, the grotesque orgy of man danced to a lustful beat; some were screaming, some cried, they struggled in their dreams trying to save themselves, the hermaphroditic angle of the rainbow was swelling up inside them.

"Aaayyy!"
"Michael, what's the matter with you? Michael, Michael! Wake up, Michael! Michael, it's a nightmare!"
"Yes, now I'm OK, yes, I'm fine. Cody, I'm all right, go to sleep."
"But what happened to you Michael? Something happened in Mathis."
"No, nothing happened there. It was just a nightmare."
"What did you dream?"
"Nothing, nothing, I'll tell you tomorrow. Now please, go to sleep."

That morning the hospital walls where months before he had practiced, seemed to be resting in the rays of light thrown off the barrel cactus which pierced his eyes with their morning brightness. He entered confidently, he knew where and with whom he would speak in the pharmacy. The bearded man with the cigar opened his eyes in the hallway flooded with artificial light. He went down to the basement, stopping in front of the door of the department of medicines, drugs and surgical equipment. They were waiting for him at eight-fifteen sharp. It was time, the elevator doors rang open.
"Hey, George, how're you doing? You look really smooth; really, Jorge, you're looking good."
"Michael, what are you doing here? They told me you were getting rich exploiting a tribe of Indians in Arizona."
"You've almost got it, George; and I'm almost getting rich. But, look, I came to ask you a favor."
"If you're going to make problems for me I don't want anything to do with it."

"No, of course not, it'll be very easy for you; if anyone has to take the shit, it'll be me. Listen, I need medicine, drugs, equipment, everything to set up a good office. Drugs and medicines that'll last me at least three months, that'll give you enough time to send me monthly refills of what I've used and I'll have at least a two-month supply in reserve."

"But that takes time, I need time to get all of that; I don't even have it here; but it can be done, of course it can. I need at least a week."

"Can't be, George. Look, I have patients who are desperate; I need the medicines and the drugs as soon as possible."

"Medicines, drugs and bandages for three months?"

"Yes, and I have to have it by Monday morning early, because they're expecting me there. Please, George, please, please."

"All right, it'll be difficult, but I think I can do it."

"Thank you, George; I'll see you Monday morning."

"Hey, Michael, wait a minute. You'll pay me for everything on Monday?"

"But how do you think I can pay you on Monday; that's impossible, I don't have that kind of money. Listen, send me the bill in Mathis."

"Where? If you don't have money, I can't do it."

"Don't be a bastard; charge it to those damned millionaires who exploit the people here; charge it to Beesley, to Hales, to all those bastards who only think about getting money out of sick people; all those sons of bitches who never really cure anybody, just half way, so that the patients have to come back."

"Yes, I know. Send the bill to Pato, to Doctor Ignacio Martínez, we'll see if he'll help me."

"Look, it's going to be more than two thousand, easily, maybe twice that. The more I think about it I'm almost sure, around four thousand. Do you want me to send it to Pato?"

"Yes."

"OK, but I'll tell you now; I'm going to watch out for myself; when they come after me I'll tell them that you insisted, that you showed me a document that gave you permission for what you're asking me, that's the only way I'll get you what you want. I'm sorry, Michael, but that's the only way that I can do it."

"I understand, don't worry about it. I accept your conditions. I'll be here Monday. Another favor, don't say anything to Pato until two hours after I've left . . ."

"OK, I was going to send him the bill in the mail so you'll have at least a day. Are you sure about what you're going to do?"

"Yes, I don't have any alternative; I would have asked for a loan but I don't have time. I hope that Pato helps me."

"I think he will, the first time anyway, to help you get set up, but don't ask him for any more."

"Why do you say that?"

"I don't know, Michael, just because I think that's the way it'll be."

. . . You notice it, you realize that the students get angry with you just because you make them see the truth; students are that way; they give so much importance to grades, they cry if they don't get an "A," but it's also the fault of the ones who give easy "A's," because then everybody expects to get an "A" and to give a "B" is to tell the student you think he's worthless; it's shitty, really shitty, but you have to give them; of course you have to give them and be able to defend them. We mustn't lie to the students; some professors do, they give an "A" to all the students with a little note saying their papers aren't worth shit; the students play the game of contrite disciple in front of the Marxist Pinnacle; of course he tells them that he doesn't want to compromise himself. . . . However, he's lying to them because after writing three rotten papers and getting an "A" they go into somebody else's class and the professor gives them a "C" and they shit in their pants. . . . No sir, even the Theoretical Roman has passed some students with this lie . . . he got Lapointe, who was here five years without ever taking his exams, a job in a high school, you have to help your friends, he tells me . . . Jesus, if he knew what his friend whom he so greatly esteems says about him . . . especially when he's drunk . . . the knife carefully placed in the middle of his back . . . Yes, Theoretical Roman, he's your friend, help him . . . once you told me that you hated him . . . no, sir . . . things change, after licking one's wounds, they heal, well, for them it's that way . . . for me, it would be another story . . . I'm like an elephant, I don't forget anything . . . Damn, it's already four-thirty . . . what a pisser to correct these damn papers, I'm going home . . .

As he got out of the car, the aroma of grilled chicken piqued his appetite; his body entered his home, laughter from the backyard drew him there. It was the new neighbors, the one with the long beard must be Michael, his wife had said that he let his beard grow.

"Hi, Eutemio, we've decided to have dinner together."

"Fine with me, whatever you like. I'm at your service."

"Good, in that case, please have a beer."

"Great."

The two men saw each other with great affection; they knew they cared for each other; their smile joined the two bottles of beer and they got into a very comfortable chat. They went from "where are you from?" and "where did you study?" — from the commonplace — to the personal about each of them.

"Look, Eutemio, I do what I believe in. A lot of people think I'm crazy, a fanatic and I tell you, after what I did today everyone will be sure that I am. Would you like another beer?"

"Please."

"As I was saying, I believe in what I'm doing and that's all."

"Michael, I envy you because you're really living your ideals. I'm not so brave."

"What?"

"I believe that my work is killing me artistically; at least so far. Playing the role of the intellectual in the university system chokes the artist's creative spirit. They want me to write criticism. I do, but it's just so I can eat, and support my family; in this country the artist is screwed, he's not respected for what he is, especially in the university. But, it's the artists who provide them with the raw material so that they can make their living. I don't know how I got into this labyrinth, I don't see any way out, I'm trapped, or actually I don't have the balls to chuck it all; in that sense, Michael, I'm a coward. I got my degree, not to be a critic but to become a writer."

"Eutemio, you and I are equals, the very same men, maybe we were born of the same mythic mother."

"Hey, I should talk like that, you're the scientist and I'm the humanist."

"But we should have a bit of both cultures, don't you think?"

"Of course, but the two are so isolated, so lost in themselves."

"Eutemio, I think the same thing, you know, we're twins, don't you think it's a little frightening? Don't you think the relation is a little weird?"

"I realize that it's different; you know something . . . you're going to think I'm crazy when I tell you this, but I have to tell you, you know that I know that I love you; I've known you a few hours, but I love you, you, your wife, your children and your whole struggle to survive in Mathis . . . Can you understand that?"

"Sure, Eutemio, sure . . . I feel the same way, we're brothers, we're fighting for the same thing."

"Ay, Dios, encantado de la vida y que se acabe algún día . . ."

"Oh, God, life is so beautiful and so short . . ."

The two bodies remained immobile among the stars of the immortal egg, the moments passed, the minutes, the professor was alone, the newspaper was watching him, his eyes began to read . . .

"Look, they did it again, how can they be so stubborn; the same thing happened to these people that happened to us, I can't believe it, it's horrible . . ."

"Oh, my God, they fell! The three of them fell into the Bufadora Gorge! Help! Help!"

"Where are the bastards? They never learn, they come here for Christmas holidays and they go where they don't belong. I don't see them. Where do you say? Over there, yes, no, it looks as if the three of them had their skulls cracked."

"Do you think they're dead, Captain?"

"Of course, look at the blood, even the Bufadora is running red. They're dead, damned hippies who never learn."

"How will we get them up, Captain?"

"However you can, and take them to the gringo priest."

"And the man who told us?"

"Put that bastard in jail for smoking marijuana and causing a disturbance. I'll see you at headquarters. Goodbye, boys."

"OK, oxes, take the reins and go down there. Tie their feet and I'll pull them with the truck. Let's go, get down there, bastards."

The slippery rocks received the delicate feet upon descending the face of the precipice. The sea made love to the Bufadora making it sing like a happy faggot. The Bufadora, like an assliking whore, doesn't know who's doing it to her, but she's enjoying herself between the two of them. She kills the humans, both the boys and the girls.

The stale-smelling workers descended into the lesbian's anus.

"Tie that bastard's feet."

"He's already stiff."

"So what, you idiot! That's the way dead people are."

"Lift 'em up!"

The rigid body was struck by the rocks as it was quickly pulled by the pickup truck.

"Now the woman, the stupid bitch, look at those breasts she was carrying around."

"She's still warm. Is she alive?"

"Hey! She's still warm! She's alive!!"

"No, the captain said they were dead! Tie her feet and let's get this bitch moving. And don't rub her tits, you bastards! Can't you wait!"

The naked breasts of the still warm female moved like gelatin, the rocks gouged her naked back. Her ears caught the young world's laughter; his head felt the moribund woman's shiver as she fell face down into the back of the truck . . .

"Eutemio, Eutemio. Do you need another beer?"

"Oh, yes. I was just reading the newspaper and I realized that those idiots have done it again . . ."

"Show me. What are you talking about?"

"You're right; no one ever hears about this kind of thing, very few people are aware of these physical and psychological atrocities. Every once in a while they print something in a newspaper or magazine but nothing is done, everything is forgotten . . ."

"There has to be a My Lai . . ."

"Even that's not enough, people forget, that's what's tragic. Everybody forgets."

"Not me, especially not those who've hurt me."

"You should forget that."

"No, I can't. They've insulted me because they think they themselves are perfect. They refused to give me a small promotion because they're afraid; the whole university laughs at them and they got scared and because I wasn't perfect, they didn't promote me. They told me I wasn't a good teacher, that I didn't know how to teach and that the department was going to suffer because of my teaching method. The Little Koala Bear gave me advice in the morning and in the afternoon he stabbed me in the back. And then he accuses me of letting him down. He's the letdown, no one has any respect for him. Even Marty O'Leigh, the linguist, tells me that he doesn't know anything and that if he were up for tenure now, he wouldn't get it. All the junior faculty kiss the asses of the guys with power, the ones with tenure. That's how they can screw you, because nobody stands up to them. Don Quixote Tenorio and the breasty Midget Turtle, a Frenchwoman from the chilly climes of the Tierra del Fuego, smiled and told me to get out. The Midget Turtle told me that I didn't know anything and that I had to go."

. . . He spit the words and then laughter from his deformed, grotesquely opened mouth.

"Don't worry little runt, you can get work wherever you want."

"This, too, shall pass . . ."

"Yes, and the Theoretical Roman did it all legally so as to protect the department's reputation, which, according to him and the Little Koala Bear, is the best in the university . . ."

135

Bastards, everyone knows that it's one of the worst, that they have a terrible reputation, that no other department respects them; they sacrificed me to look as if they were strong, demanding, careful, and that if a professor didn't meet the criteria established by them and the Theoretical Roman, they would kick him out. What they do is change the rules of the game when it suits them . . .

"But Eutemio, what do you want to do?"

"What?"

"What do you want to do, what's the most important thing to you?"

"For me, for myself . . . ?"

"Daddy, Daddy, everything's ready . . . It's all ready!"

The shouts of realities, responsibilities, that they refused to acknowledge, imposed themselves by the tugs of the little hands that dirtied his trousers.

"Leave me alone, Jason!"

The silence of the scream shocked everyone; his grimace of hurt was formed by tears that dissolved the good part of his daddy.

"Mommy! Mommy!"

His voice was heard outside when he was offered the bottle of beer.

"Eutemio, if this business at the university is so bad, it's not worth it."

The sciences and the humanities went outside where the salvation they did not see was to be found.

Human history patiently awaits the triumph of the man who has been insulted; but this moment doesn't arrive. It is awaited in the shacks, in the little huts of mud, cardboard, ice, palm trees. In the death houses, in the houses of prostitution, in the orphan asylums, in the prisons, they wish for this triumph. They want to savor it in their hungry bowels, in their wounds festering from a lack of food, a lack of basic nutrition; they want to smell this triumph in the dirty air, in the rivers polluted by the clever ones. What stinks, though, is that it doesn't appear that this moment will emerge just where it should. The lower classes are fucked everywhere in the world, the Chicanos are still defeated because they believed the revolution's false promises.

His heart beat more rapidly, his decision came instantly, without thinking, it arrested the trust of the powerful man who asked him the question.

"I'm very sorry, but I can't help you with that. Do it yourself, but don't count on me."

"You're my officer, Rodríguez, you have to do it. I order you to do it!"

"I won't do it. That man hasn't done anything wrong, nothing against the law. And he's beginning to help my people and we need his services. I say that he can stay here. He hasn't done anything wrong."

"Look, let me explain that his presence here causes trouble, a lot of trouble. I know this because a lot of important men have told me so."

"What men? What are you afraid of? This guy hasn't even been here a week and you already want to kick him out. None of the ones who have come here have done anything bad, they've come to help, that's all. Why don't they let us have a doctor, a teacher, a priest, someone who wants to help us. What the hell are you afraid of?"

"I have orders."

"From who?"

"That's none of your business. Who are you to interrogate me?"

"Aren't I your friend? Why did you help me when they hurt me? Why did you insist that they take me to the hospital first. Aren't I your friend? Answer me, Pistol Man."

"You're talking nonsense, Rodríguez, think it over. I want you to help me in this matter. And you're going to, because if you don't, you'll be sorry . . ."

"What? My job? Don't be so sure that I care about this job, a job that makes me takes sides against my own people. I realize a lot of things now . . . I've been stupid and I've let myself be manipulated, manipulated by you and all the sellouts in this town."

"Don't say anything else, Rodríguez, please, don't say any more . . . I'll expect you at the office. That's all."

The cloth door slammed shut. The family heard the night enter through it.

"I wouldn't have said those things to him, Fernando. You're going to lose your job."

"I can't take it any more, Francisca. Something's happening. I don't know what it is, but we shouldn't give up. Logan has to stay, at whatever cost, he has to stay in Mathis."

They were hidden there, crouched behind the brush, the desert cacti. They had spent two hours dragging themselves closer through the sand, and then through the soil. When they were very close they let out yells from human mouths and from the mouths of the rifle, songs near death, gunshots of paz-paz-paz-paz-paz-paz-paz-paz, ironic sounds of the new attack. They counted fifteen, one per minute, when the sky's aggression ceased. With great pain the tall man went to his son.

"Do whatever you like to me, but leave my son alone. He isn't responsible for anything."

"You speak Spanish so at least you'll understand why I'm going to kill him for you. It's a pity you didn't die with the other wretches, so you wouldn't have to see this. It's logical that you've survived until now, they protected you very well. If you were one of them, one of us, maybe we would pardon you. But you're one of those others, one of those that steals our land, our money, our food and our children, and what's worse, our right to be human beings. That's why I'm going to kill him for you. And also because I think you have to pay for one child with another. That way we're even. Don't you think? What's the matter with you, can't you talk any more? You people always have an answer. All right, say goodbye to your boy."

"Fucking bastard! If you're going to kill us, kill us together. We want to die together."

"No, I want you to see him afterward, after his life has left him, after the chill of death has taken him. I want you to take him in your arms and cry for him. Like I did, like me, like a poor person, like me. Marcelo, take the boy away! Move him, I tell you!"

Casimiro felt the man's eyes, weighted with hatred, strike his face. His hands could almost reach him, the men held him back. He saw the boy's body trembling with cold fear. The modern spittle stained his forehead with paz-paz. They searched, looking for weapons, ammunition, and food. They were leaving, heading toward the openings in the sky.

"And what about him?"

"I really don't want to kill him, but we have to."

The flames licked upward, making a circle of heat around his eyes. The sparks crackled, bits of wood fell, he poked the chips with the iron to make the fire hotter. He leaned back in his chair; he was calm, his hands didn't tremble, but . . . it's so nice to be alone, but we're always alone. Now that an election year is coming, who should I give power to? There are three people that the Party will undoubtedly support, but the people are restless. It will have to be a candidate that favors the people. The tower incident . . . was horrible . . . it must be an election year . . . they're organizing in the north . . . but they say that those times are over . . . no, I don't think so . . . there's hunger . . . the classes are becoming more and more separated. . . . The facade . . . leaders of the third world . . . if they know there are people who are worse off they calm down . . . propaganda . . . How foolish we are . . . How docile my people are now . . . the capitalists are half asleep . . . the middle class is only interested in acquiring things, the house in Satellite City, the Mustang . . . the poor don't have time for anything but eating tortillas and tacos, drinking a few beers . . . and having children . . . children for the homeland . . . the leaders of the third world . . . it's so nice to be alone . . . nice and warm next to the fireplace. Who would have believed me?. . . leaders of the third world . . . someone in the north is organizing the transport of weapons . . . someone respected . . . above suspicion . . .

"Excuse me, Señor Presidente, but an urgent message has just arrived from the north."

He took the brown envelope with a tired sigh, his fingers broke the seal and withrdrew the official paper. His eyes hardened his jaw, the irritation in his brain made his hand clench into a fist. As he rose, he threw the paper into the fire.

"I remember the first time I met him. I think it was a Monday, about nine o'clock, he was returning from Corpus, and when he arrived there was a whole crowd waiting for him. I remember he came loaded down with instruments, drugs and all sorts of other things that he had brought in the car."

"Oh, yes, Doña Eulalia, and how he made us all work, the boys and the girls. He didn't charge us for the visit, but we paid him with our sweat."

"And after we finished he sent the boys to buy sweetbread and chocolate and we had a wonderful lunch."

"Yes, and with those trousers that he always wore without a shirt, that hat, and smoking his smelly cigar. And we would ask him what type of doctor he was and what would he answer? He would look at us for a bit and he'd say 'a good one.' "

"Yes, a very good one. But what can we do . . . time heals everything."

The naked anuses among the dark buttocks almost kissed the earth, squatting, their eyes jumped from place to place, waiting for the modern world to arrive in the jungle of the Amazon. They investigated every noise, verifying that it was an animal, or the ancient wind. The man with the pots, the spoons, and the axes had said he would return with more gifts, with more aguardiente, in order to convince them that it was a good thing to allow their land to be used for the new road that carried the animals with round feet, dead animals and live ones, fast and hard animals that spoke with only one sound. When they drank the modern men's aguardiente they saw different things, new things; it was good, change was good, good for them. They were going to receive civilization, the naked men spent days, weeks, waiting. They were sure the men would return. They had seen a modern bird cross the skies. A bird whose droppings were useful, mirrors, marbles, necklaces, cases of aguardiente. What kind of miraculous animal was this? Was it a god? They had to pray to it so that it would bring more good fortune, so that it would return to bless the naked men. They built platforms to the sky, toward the edges of the damp jungle clouds. They asked the god to return soon, so that they could praise him and give him thanks. The bird of the miraculous droppings reappeared. They built more platforms; weeks passed; the belief in the new religion grew; the news spread; other naked tribes came to pray at the altars of the god who defecated modern utensils. They came from afar to see him; they came from afar to witness his miracles; they came from afar to be cured by the modern magic . . .

"Where did they come from? I don't believe it, that's twenty miles on foot."

"That's what the lady told me. But now we're done. Let me sit down and rest a while. How my feet hurt!"

The naked feet, the legs showed their skin's softness in front of the doctor for the first time.

"Yes, I'm a little tired too. Hey, Margarita, wouldn't you like a beer?"

She was massaging her foot propped on the chair; her firm hip caught his eye.

"Margarita, wouldn't you like one?"

"No, Michael, that's not what I want."

The doctor studied all the strength in that leg shaped to attract his brain.

"What, Margarita?. . . What is it that you do want?"

The two legs were placed quite naturally on the chair; the skirt rose almost to the desired spot.

"Oh, God, I'm really tired!"

"Here's to your health!"

"Thank you, Michael."

The woman realized that his eyes weren't talking to her: . . . My legs, what am I doing . . . excuse me, Michael . . . Michael . . . no, don't excuse me . . . I too want to . . . but how?. . . I can't do it . . . I will do it . . . I have to be a woman and live the way I truly want to . . . I should enjoy myself when I want to . . . I deserve it . . . I'm human . . . yes, Michael, look . . . look hard . . . you'll be mine, Michael . . . you'll be . . .

"I'm going to have another. You really don't want one?"

"OK. Why don't you give me a little wine? All right?"

"Here. Margarita, you know that you and Felipe have been here, how long? I think it must be two or three months, and this is the first time we've had time to talk."

"We've worked a lot. I've learned so much, I'm glad about that."

"And you know you've also changed a lot."

"How?"

"You're not the same woman who came here three months ago. See how you look in that white dress, look how you stand, how you wear your hair, the way you talk. Haven't you noticed? Look how the patients see you. Even for them you aren't the same Margarita that you used to be."

"Do you think so?"

"Yes, in the way I treat you, in the way that I should treat you, you demand something new, and you know what you want . . ."

"Yes, Michael, I know what I want, but sometimes I'm ashamed to think about it. Sometimes I have doubts about what I'm doing; this new person is really me, sometimes it frightens me; I look at myself and I realize that I have changed. I have changed a lot, Michael, I know it and it scares me. But I also see myself now and I'm happy. Felipe is happy too. It's as if he were proud of me, and I of him."

"I'm glad, at least something good has come from my craziness."

"You're right, you're a marvelous madman."

"Margarita, don't be afraid now, please, don't be afraid."

"Now, I'm sure now, I know what I want, come sit here, here with me . . ."

The wind outside blew harder, warm, it brought the rain that made the mountains run with mud. From the corner he saw the palms falling on the little windswept houses around the prison: . . . All for a damned weed, all this for a fucking cigarette. The worst thing is that it wasn't mine, and they've screwed me, given me a real beating.

The wind toppled the trees, overturned the shacks, the cows, the pigs, the hens fluttered, the men, huddled against the walls, supported them with their families. They had to hold them up, not let them fall . . . Oooh, the walls are dancing, crumbling. They're like bread, crumbs of bread . . . The young man was eating dirt when they pulled him out. He couldn't move his leg because of the pain; the truck arrived at the hospital. First they slapped him around a little to remind him that he was still a prisoner; they gave him a cold bath before the doctor examined him.

141

"The gringos come here full of vermin; I won't get near him until they give him a bath."

"But his leg is broken."

"It doesn't much matter to me, I didn't tell him to be a pothead."

He arrived at eleven o'clock at night, his face showing the treatment they had given him. His leg was covered with plaster; he couldn't sleep. He was tired, but fear kept him awake.

"What will they do to me now? They told my mother what happened to me. She shouldn't give the lawyer any more money. She sold the house to get the first five thousand and then she gave him another seven. No, Mom, we have to do something else, these damned lawyers and government bureaucrats are stealing from us, they're taking money from us that we don't have and they're robbing us. These bastard Mexicans are thieves, parasites living off the suffering, not only of foreigners, but of their own people as well. This is enough, we have to try something else, another plan . . . ooh, I have to pee . . ."

The urine wet the dirty mattress in the hospital cell. In the early morning, the federal employee with a prophylactic face and a rubber mouth, his nose covered with a perfume-soaked handkerchief, came into the room.

"Mr. Miller, you are in very unpleasant surroundings. Of course you realize that it is not the room that stinks, but yourself. I'm very sorry, but since you are a prisoner, we can't offer you any better accommodations. It's your third day here with us, your mother is here and she has given us money so that we can put you in a decent room, more like what you are accustomed to. The gring . . . ah, *American* Consul has also requested that we do this for you. He has spoken to us on your behalf. You'll be leaving here today; there will be a guard at the door of your room, of course, but your mother and your friends will be able to talk to you. Now we'll also be able to calculate the cost of the damage you have done to your cell. Someone will have to be responsible for that. Don't worry, though, it won't be you, your mother, undoubtedly, will donate something to fix what her son has done, and also to reestablish good relations for you in prison when you return there prior to your appearance before the municipal judge. I have a surprise for you . . . your mother and a friend are here to see you. With your permission, Mr. Miller, I will show them in. Good day."

The broken leg's rage watched the thin, tobacco-stained body, crusher of thousands of miserable people, leave.

"My poor little boy, now look what they've done to you. I'm just furious. I've reached the conclusion that no one is going to help us. The U.S. government isn't doing a thing. I showed them photographs of how you were living, but they don't even react to that. We're determined to do something else, we have to come up with a plan to get you out of here."

"Yes, I've already thought of it, and I think we can pull off an escape."

He often strolled along in the corridors talking to the doctors, the nurses, and the patients who knew him. The guard was always watching him. A nice man, he chatted with him about his family, his home, his fortunes; he was from Michoacán, where life was very hard. Here in Mexico he was rich, rich because he had a house, food, a job; he was a cop dedicated to making his money in the accepted way. He watched him travel the hallways sitting down. He knew he couldn't walk, he couldn't go anywhere without the wheelchair; it wouldn't be possible for him to escape, he was quite sure about that, that's why he let him get near the back door and the exit. That day he told him they were going to change his assignment; he was waiting for his replacement.

"Mr. Miller, where are you going?"

"I'm going to talk to the man in room 103."

"All right, but don't be long because there's going to be a change of guards."

"OK."

"I'm tired of sitting here; I'm going to take a walk."

"Fine, you know where I'll be."

"OK."

The wheels of the man greeting the doctors and the nurses slid away; he entered the American's room; the door was closed and very happily they discussed Mexican reality. The guard was calmly waiting when the new, friendly man in the blue uniform arrived.

"Hey, it's as if you were tired, at least get up to say hello."

"Look, buddy, I don't have time for that. I'm up to here with this place. I'm bored with all these white uniforms around here."

"No, but look at the pretty little things in those little white dresses. Hey, man, I'm going to like this."

"All right, I'm going."

"Where's the gringo hippy?"

"He's in room 103. He's talking to another Yankee. Don't worry, he stays there for hours talking. What else can he do?"

"Good. I'll take care of him here."

"Adiós."

The new policeman sat in the armchair enjoying the nurses' breasts and buttocks; he got up to talk to one that struck his fancy, that he felt comfortable with. He sat down again. His mind made him plan for their meeting. How would he do it? He saw a man go by in a wheel-chair. How the hell am I going to make her?. . . I think the bitch wants it . . . No, I don't think so, she told me she was seeing someone . . . I'll invite her to have a few beers . . . aha, that's what I'll do . . . The man passed by again, he waved to him.

The new guard doesn't know me, let's head for the door . . . I hope he's there; they've been waiting for me for two days . . . there's no one there . . . fucking heavy door . . . they see me now, quick . . . let's go . . . let's go . . . fast . . .

"Thank God you're there."

"Let's take off, to Guadalajara."

The building performed operations, killed, cured, fornicated, shrieked. The cop was lost in impossible dreams, time passed quietly, thirty minutes went by and he got up to go to room 103.

"Hey, where's the gringo?" . . . Damn it, that bastard doesn't understand . . . these gringo hippies are pretty stupid . . . a bunch of idiots . . . they don't know how to communicate with people."

The highway almost let them fly. After half an hour they took off the cast and he was dressed in a new suit when his mother hugged him and began to cry.

"Yes, we've got the papers, the passports, plane tickets, I.D.'s, everything we need."

"What time do we get there?"

"If everything goes well, and I think it will, we'll be in Los Angeles tonight at seven."

"Margarita, what time is it?"

"It's seven o'clock, why?"

"Nothing, it's just that we've finished early, haven't we?"

"Yes, but I think we have to get someone to help us. And I think that Teresa would be very interested in the job. Every time she comes she stays and asks me questions and helps me with the patients. She can do the work."

"Do you really think it's a good idea, Margarita?"

"Yes, we see at least forty patients every day. We need help, Michael. And we should also consider moving to a bigger place, or making this one bigger, or something, Michael, because this is too small."

"I haven't thought about it . . . but maybe you're right, I don't know."

"What's the matter? You're thinking about her and the children, aren't you?"

"Yes. It's been about six months since I've seen them. Cody's mad at me because I didn't give her back the Volkswagen. I haven't sent her any money, just enough for the necessities."

"You should go back; I've told you that you must go to see the children. You should go this weekend."

"But I don't have time."

"Don't be silly, nothing is more important than your children, than your family."

"I don't know if I can go, there are a lot of people who need us here. She doesn't understand, she got furious when she called and she asked me to send her two hundred dollars. I told her I didn't have it. She asked me if I was charging the patients, I told her I hadn't set up the system yet. She couldn't understand, she just wanted the money. I don't blame her, she needs it to buy things for the house, clothes for herself, and for the children. I don't blame her. It's my fault. I haven't given her and the children what they deserve . . . especially the children . . ."

"Michael, I think there's someone at the door."

"I didn't hear anything."

"But didn't you see, something came to the door and then disappeared. No, Michael, someone was there."

"All right, someone was there. Isn't there any more beer?"

"Michael, you shouldn't drink so much."

"Margarita, please don't start on me about that, please, I know what I'm doing."

"OK, I won't say any more about it, but pardon me for telling you that your beard is too long and you should trim it."

"I agree with that."

"Michael, look it's there again!"

"What's the matter with you?. . . Oh, yes . . . there is . . ."

The eyes red from beer drew up to the screen door, they saw, but they didn't believe it, it couldn't be. How did she get here? Why? It's not. . . .

"It's Silky!"

The two people gazed at each other through the screen that turned their faces into rectangular, quadrangular, triangular pieces of memories, each miniscule piece part of a system that gave the other an almost forgotten portrait. . . . The bar, the child, what you did with what you were carrying in your womb . . . Your wife, how you used to get drunk, you never really saw me, you always thought I was crazy . . . but here I am sick, dying, I've come to tell you, to save you; they're going to kill me . . . What does this madwoman want? Be careful with her, do everything possible to get her to go, be careful, do whatever's necessary to get her to leave . . .

"Silky, what are you doing here? Come in, please, come in."

The tangled hair, the full, almost obscene breasts, entered, hanging like buckets beneath the dirty white tee shirt. Her formerly desirable waist and her ass accepted the edge of the sofa's invitation.

"Where are Cody and the children?"

"They're in Corpus."

"In Corpus, yes, in Corpus. I was in front of your house, but I didn't go in, I only wanted to see your house, your family; I stood there for a long time, but nobody came out. I walked and walked until a boy picked me up, he took me to the bus station, there I saw, I don't remember, I don't remember what happened there. Just that I saw myself walking on an unknown road, some men picked me up, and then I turned into a monkey. I was in the trees. I came out on a road and I knew that I would find you on that road."

"Silky, who gave you my address? Who, Silky?"

"The men who are pursuing me in order to kill me gave it to me; they sent me here to tell you."

The woman with the living boy went to the modern magician and rested her hand on his shoulder.

"What did you come to say?"

"Who are you? A spy? Don't trust anyone, Michael, everyone here is evil, this town is condemned to serve as an example of the new policy."

"Of the newly powerful, the invisible politicians who rule the obvious ones."

"What are you talking about?"

"Yes, tell me, Miss, what are you talking about? Explain it to Michael again, please."

"There's nothing to explain, only those who are condemned know about the new policy. They've already beaten me; I tried to fight against them, but they poisoned me with radioactivity in their diabolical laboratories. I took a chemical that let me remember everything that I saw; everything. I knew it all! But they condemned me to be glorified as a madwoman."

"What's she talking about, Michael?"

"I don't know . . ."

"And the assassination of the hero . . ."

"What? What are you saying? She scares me, Michael."

"I don't have much time left, Michael, my life doesn't matter any more. I'm dead already because of what's going through my veins.

146

I came to save you, Michael. Get out of here . . . go back to Corpus, set up a practice and stay with your family. They're going to kill me."

"Now, Silky, don't start with your stories . . . that's the story you told all the interns in the hospital. Look, Silky, if you want to stay here tonight you can, but you'll have to leave early tomorrow."

"No, Michael, I'm telling you the truth. I'm not crazy like everybody thinks."

"Yes, Silky, I know, I believe you, but you should have called me to tell me this, don't you see that you're frightening Margarita and . . ."

"Michael, the telephone, I'll get it."

Moments passed in the mental world of the doctor seated next to the woman with a mental fracture: . . . All the poor thing's screws are loose. . . . oh, why did she come to bother me, why didn't she go to Pato, or Hales, or Beesley?. . . why did she come here to bother us?. . .

"Michael, it's Cody . . . Michael!"

"You don't have to yell at me, I'm coming."

The tired man approached the technological miracle, he swallowed the voice of his beloved woman.

"Michael, Michael, when are you coming, it's been so long, I understand that you have a lot of work, but the children ask for you, you have to come, Michael."

"Yes, yes, I know."

"What, I can't hear you?"

"Nothing, nothing, what do you say about what happened there?"

"I can tell you that they killed a lot of peasants for rebelling against the government and for hiding Casimiro's bandits. They say that someone here is giving them weapons. Michael, something's not right, people are very nervous and uneasy here. They're afraid, Michael, please come back as soon as possible."

"Don't get nervous, I'll be there this weekend."

"Michael, are you all right? You don't sound good."

"I'm a little tired, that's all. How are the kids?"

"They ask for you, they miss you an awful lot."

"Cody, tell them that I'm coming this weekend; I'm tired now and I want to go to sleep. What do you want?"

"How is Margarita?"

"Working hard. Do you want to talk to her?"

"No, just say hello for me."

"Yes. Goodbye, Cody."

The airplanes came down toward the beach where they found a ring of sand long and wide enough to land. The pilot guided the plane to kiss the earth with the promised weapons. The silence heard the murmur of the plane that approached where the new chiefs of social criticism were. Suddenly, the two modern animals were together waiting for the cargo to be moved. The stars spied on the dialogue of the two leaders, of the two friends for the same cause, for necessary violence, necessary because those in power fail to understand anything else. The two men were right and they had the right to change the situation of their people, they were the only two who were united, equal because they suffered the injustice of the powerful, they were the same in their rootlessness and in their desire to find their roots, to learn their history, for wanting to be accepted as human beings, with a face, with a name, and with pride. They unloaded the cases of weapons, the boxes, long coffins, contained automatic rifles that affirmed the new life they were searching for.

"Manuel, are all the rifles carefully packed?"

"Check them yourself. Everything is in order. The only thing you need is to start using them right away."

"Oh, yes, compadre. We'll do what you want very soon. They've already killed many of us; what's worse is that they've killed families and relatives. We're all determined to win or to die."

"We're with you."

"Our compañeros in the North have to keep sending us weapons, food, everything we need."

"The weapons are easier to get because those are private arrangements, food is something else, I don't think I can get that for you; you'll have to get that for yourself. But you can count on the rockets, I can certainly bring them to you. Give me my receipt, I have to leave before dawn. See you next time, Casimiro."

"Goodbye, Manuel."

"Adiós."

The world and the living are funny, at those moments when they do something amusing the monkeys see them in their technological cage that they've built surrounding the open zoo. The monkeys give thanks to something for saving them from advancing to being the scientific clinicians that study them from the outside in order to understand themselves . . . But, how stupid are the ones in the modern cage who study us! It's we who observe them . . .

"Oh, Michael, you're not so stupid. I'm glad that you realize that science alone won't solve man's problems."

148

"Don't boast, Eutemio, not even the humanists can change the world. We're screwed, aren't we?"

"Listen, Professor, bring us more beer, please. Let's see, boys, what is the problem you're putting forth for me to solve?"

"There's no problem, Manuel. I was just commenting that the scientists and the humanists, being lost in their theories and research, only indirectly see people. In other words, the bastards couldn't care less. They're above it all in their ivory tower."

"Good for you, Eutemio, you're right, the scientists and the humanists aren't going to change anything if they don't commit themselves to a truly revolutionary movement. Revolutionary in the sense of doing, doing things in a different way that will make changes within their respective systems. Michael, you're a revolutionary because of what you're doing, not what you say. Eutemio, you're a revolutionary too, because of what you write."

"No, I'm a coward, a cowardly writer."

"You're a writer with a future; you're committed to literature, to a literature of the common person, of humanity, of life."

"And you, Manuel, are you a revolutionary?"

"Yes, I'm a revolutionary because of what I do, not because of what I say."

"But what do you do, brother, you have a good time in the university."

"Well, I do something."

"Hey, Michael, do you know that Manuel is going to Bolivia?"

"Another mug, friend? To Bolivia, for a vacation?"

"That's right, for a vacation."

"Be very careful because the rebels can make trouble for you, they'll mix you up in a revolution without you even wanting it."

"That's the way the Latin American countries are."

"What is it that's happened in Mexico? They say a lot of people were killed, peasants."

"That country's going to blow up again, Michael. How do you see it, Eutemio?"

"Let the country blow up, free the poor masses, let the proletariat march forward."

"What time is it?"

"It's almost two."

"Damn it, we have to go because if we don't they'll be after us with the brooms, let's go, Michael."

"All right, Manuel, I hope we see each other again, thanks for the beers."

"Continue the revolution, Michael. See you Monday, Eutemio."

The neighbors climbed into the doctor's Volkswagen. The doors closed as they spit the two drunks out in front of their houses.

"Hey, Eutemio, what are you doing tomorrow?"

"Prepare my classes, go for a ride, I don't know, whatever Leticia wants to do. Why?"

"I need someone to go with me tomorrow. I'm going to buy a motorcycle. Will you come with me?"

"Sure, why not?"

"But don't tell Cody; she'll get mad; I'd rather she get angry after I've bought the bike."

"However you like, Michael. But listen, don't call me very early; I think my head's going to feel like a watermelon."

"Here, take these pills; they'll help you sleep and tomorrow you won't wake up feeling so bad; I take them and they help me a lot. Good night, Eutemio."

"Oh, how my head's going to hurt me tomorrow."

The street lights saw them enter the families' houses; the humanitarians' dreams of grandeur, of fame, were rolled up against the bodies of the women who waited for them and loved them. They slept, snoring, with open mouths, reeking of beer, lost in the corners of their minds. They were living in another world, with other people, in another time, in another life, there were the other beings of life. There are many people who sometimes communicate that they are there. They speak through superficial dreams that should be talked about in the morning, but they aren't remembered.

"Do you like this one or that one?"

"I like the red one better."

"Listen, do you know how to drive a motorcycle? This 750 isn't for children. Here, take this one and see how you like it."

"OK, Eutemio, do you want to take a little ride?"

"No, sir, I won't get on one of those motorized horses."

The deep, pure, sound spread its power through the open air. His hand turned the animal's horns and when he gave it a little gas, the wheels lurched forward, the conquistadors advanced, entering the jungles of the unknown. From the height of the mountain he saw the mythic people with all their mystery and wonder, the wind blew through his hair, his beard, he cried with the pleasure of becoming one with nature, the beauty, the danger, that drew them closer to the desired spot, to win riches to become famous: . . . I'm an egotistical bastard, I could stay here, set up a clinic here, in this place. They

150

need one here too. I could convince the locals. I'm a phony, I'm doing what I'm doing to make myself famous, to feel important, but . . . but why am I doing it? What am I doing there with them, with those people when my wife, my children need me here? Why am I going to buy this damned machine? I like it . . . that's all, I like what I do; I've gotten this far, I've embarked on this adventure because I like it, I'm lucky to be able to choose what I want to do, I can choose, others can't. I'm free, others aren't. And I don't really care what happens; yes, I love my family, but if I die, what then? They'll keep on living, no one is indispensable. How pretty this place is . . . the conquistadors descended, discovering with every step the beauty of the exotic place, the place that just a few men would be able to know, a few, chosen men, chosen because they chose themselves, or circumstances chose them, but they will always be chosen for the glorification of others. They knew they had the advantage of weapons but not even with them could they conquer the insecurity of the eternal moment marked by their steps toward the secret that time revealed before their eyes.

He signed, accepting the responsibility and with it the absurdity of the piece of paper that obliged him to a certain behavior that the common man always accepted. It meant nothing to him, he played the game only because he wanted to. At the moment this decision was advantageous to him in his circumstances. He alone chose, he made the decision. He handed over the little green pieces of paper which in themselves had no value. The manager received the little pieces of paper with confidence; they guaranteed him the power to acquire another object. It was absurd to exchange seven pieces of paper for a powerful motorcycle. How absurd it was to have faith in those little papers. The two men arrived, both worried about what Cody would say.

"Cody, here come the men. Look, what a pretty motorcycle. You didn't tell us they were going to buy one."

"No?"

The two female bodies arose from the stairs and surrounded the new conquistador who had arrived at the heart of the city with his mechanical horse.

"Michael, why didn't you tell me?"

"Because I knew you'd be against it. You'd told me that there was no way you'd let me buy a bike. But I decided to buy it anyway. I think it's the best thing, now you can have the car and I'll have the motorcycle. What's more, it's cheaper and I'll be able to come home more often without worrying about gas."

"But you might have an accident . . ."

"I'll be careful, don't worry, Cody, I'll be careful. Tell her, Eutemio, don't I drive it well? Tell her, please."

"Michael, please, I don't want to . . ."

"Don't ask him to defend you, Michael."

"Cody, please don't get mad . . ."

"Well, it's done. If you kill yourself you kill yourself. And what about your family? Don't we matter?"

Anger united the glances of the three of them. The wind played with the hair gathered around the motorcycle that tranquilly made its way, with its driver somewhere else, in another world, calm, free, without worry, at peace, as the three of them at that moment wished to be, enjoying the peace that should belong to mankind.

"Michael, we're going."

"OK, OK, but when are you coming to Mathis?"

"I don't know, one of these days. I really want to go, to see if being there with you inspires me. So long, Michael."

"When are you leaving?"

"Tomorrow, early."

"Be careful, Michael. We love you."

He was suddenly alone, solitary, unique, he was one, one in all the world, no one existed, but he knew that he could enter in their homes, he could go and talk to them, see them, touch them, they were there, but what if he died, or if they died; it is so easy to go and talk to them, but how could it be done if they were not in this world, if they were dead: . . . I don't know what that would be like, I cannot imagine it, if they were gone from me I would not be able to understand it, their loss would be . . . I can't believe that we all have to go. I feel, there's something in me that's called life, my son, my daughter, they're going to have to go through this process too, as pretty as they are, time will make them old, they will change, they are changing, every instant they're changing, we aren't what we are at this moment another moment later, how absurd, what foolishness, what idiocies I'm thinking, oh, it's all shit . . . it's on the inside where you have to struggle with reality . . . damn, I have to take a shit . . .

The house accepted him as usual, the doctor's eyes passed through to the back where the children were playing. She observed them through the tunnel that had been their entrance to this whirlwind. The doctor sat next to his wife.

"Cody, don't be angry, please don't. I'm going tomorrow . . ."

"And so you want to leave here with a clean conscience? I'm tired of purifying you every time you do something that affects us. That motorcycle . . . Don't you realize that you could kill yourself with that thing? Don't you see that you're torturing me? I'm always worried about you, always! Why don't you come back? Come to work here with us."

"Don't start, you know that I have to be there."

"Why?"

"I bought the bike so that you could have the VW. And that's all."

"No, that's not all. Why did you invite Eutemio to visit you? Why don't you take me? Why don't you invite your own family?"

"It's dangerous, and I don't want you there."

"But why, Michael? I don't think it's as dangerous as you say. It's one thing or another . . ."

"Or another, what? What are you thinking, Cody? That I'm sleeping with another woman there? With Margarita? I won't do anything that would harm our marriage. Look, I'm not like that. I've had opportunities, but I've never wanted to, because I think about you, I think about my children, and I don't want to harm our family. Don't you believe me? You really don't believe me, do you? And you?"

"Who me? What could I do with two children always with me? You know very well that I wouldn't be capable of it. I simply don't see myself, I couldn't possibly imagine myself with another man. I couldn't."

"What do you mean, you couldn't? If you let yourself . . ."

"But I don't want to let myself! Now shut up!"

"Don't cry, please, forgive me."

"Play with Jason and Shane; they always want to play with you. But it seems like there's no time. There's no time for simple things, for things that are really worthwhile. Dinner, I have to make dinner. Don't worry, Michael, one way or another, things will work out, but I'm afraid, I'm really afraid."

"No, Cody, don't be afraid; you'll see, you'll see. If you want to come with me tomorrow, come with me. Don't be afraid, everything'll be all right."

"Yes, Michael, I know . . ."

"I remember, oh yes, I remember when he showed up on that thing. Oh, what a noise it made. He really made us laugh. I had to hold it in, really hold it in, because if I didn't, just imagine."

"The way he came into town was what the people over there didn't like. They complained about the noise he made, the way he dressed. They say that the Anglos didn't like the way he wore those overalls, like a gringo rancher, and with his fuming cigar he looked like Groucho. Oh, he used to do very amusing things."

"And they got angry because he didn't wear a shirt, and they thought his fisherman's cap was a joke. Pistol Man wanted to get him but Fernando Rodríguez wouldn't let him. Pistol Man was furious, and they almost came to blows."

"The Anglo doctors complained to some organization and they called him a dishonor to the profession, and I don't know what else. But with us, there was never any problem, and wasn't he funny?"

"And he was a good man, a really good man. How he loved parties. He was the first to come and eat, dance, and drink. They say that that night he went out drinking with Rodríguez and some of the others."

"Yes, they used to go out together. When he went drinking with the boys, that red beard of his would get full of foam. Of course he was a good man."

"And what about Margarita? Did they live together?"

"Don't pretend to be so innocent. They lived together, they ate together, and they did everything together. That's these modern times for you. Don't make like you didn't know it."

"Well, the important thing is that he helped us; he was almost one of us. He was a fine man, with his feet on the ground. He never charged me, until I began to have pangs of conscience. I went to ask him what had happened, I didn't want to accept charity."

"And what did he say to you?"

"He said that the bills would come in the mail."

"Which means they were never going to come."

"My old man and I would bring him eggs, chickens, fruit, vegetables, and that's how we used to pay him."

"Yes, we did too. But later he began to charge."

"And so? If he charged, it was the minimum."

"But he did collect quite a bit."

"And they say that Margarita was the one who started to organize the whole thing."

In the early hours of a day of the third month since the motorcycle arrived in Mathis a boy came running from the heart of the settlement shouting out to the world the arrival of another mouth in his family. The unshod feet, the bare legs, the chest pounded the air that blew away the snot dripping from his nose. And time and effort brought him near to the little house of help in which the doctor and the quasi-nurse licked each other's skin, when the shouts interrupted what had just barely, spontaneously and with pleasure, been initiated.

"Michael, someone's at the door."

"No, it can't be; it's too early, stay here, don't move."

"Michael, listen to the shouts. It's a child. Get dressed. I'll go out and see what's happening."

The bathrobe covered her breasts and the damp pubic hair. He stayed sprawled on the bed, as if he were a crucifix.

"Get up, quickly."

"Mamá!"

"Yes, Felipe. I'm coming, answer the door."

The four young eyes on top of bare feet turned as they heard the bathrobe enter. He had clambered over the leaves, over the roses until he got to the lips from which his ears hoped to hear "I understand, let's go." His eyes were glued to her lips, a fearful, intense, quiet young boy.

"What do you want, little boy?"

"My mother . . . my mother is dyyiingg . . . she's dying."

"Where do you live?"

"In the Hoyo, in the Hoyo. Please have the doctor come; the baby is stuck."

"Who is that?"

"My father says that the baby is rolled up in a ball and he doesn't want to leave her stomach."

"Michael, quick, the boy says that . . ."

"I heard. Prepare me a kit for a caesarean, antibiotics and coagulants, and get dressed."

"But the patients who're coming; I have to stay here."

"And who is going to help me if I have to operate?"

"Well, that's a challenge for you; somehow or other you'll have to manage, I'm not going. I've told you that we need a bigger office and that you have to hire another doctor."

"Don't start."

"My mommy is dying, let's go soon!"

"Who should I take, Felipe?"

"Very good idea; at least he can help you dry the equipment, he should learn."

"Quick, Felipe, get dressed. We'll wait for you outside."

The woman thrashed in the earth of El Hoyo; her husband's hand wiped her forehead with a damp rag; he made her open her eyes, and with a sudden cry of spontaneous hatred, she caused the children, huddled in fear and watching from the straw mat near the door of the hut, to burst into tears.

"Get out of here you idiot! Look how you've made me again, bastard!

Get away from me you ugly old man, I hate you! I never want to see you again! Away! My God, help me!"

"Get on, you behind me, you here in front."

"No, I won't get on this thing."

"Come on, this way we can get there fast to help your mother, come on, let's go. You have to sit in front so you can tell me where to go."

"This way, Mr. Evans. Señor Presidente is expecting you. Yes, now you can see the helicopter."

"Who is with him?"

"Several members of his cabinet, General Armón and General Pacheco. They tell me that the situation is serious in this area. Casimiro's band attacked again; they killed seventy soldiers, but the worst thing was they killed the whole family on the hacienda."

"And five Americans. Thanks . . ."

His foot touched the dusty earth, sand of the northern desert in which blood was turned to water which blossomed into beautiful thorns.

"Oh, Mr. Evans! With your permission, gentlemen, we'll speak our neighbor's language."

"Good morning, Señor Presidente."

"Look in all directions; what a marvelous morning. Yet today, Mr. Evans, we have a serious problem. Casimiro has attacked and killed many soldiers. He's getting more and more weapons and his group, or groups, are growing. Mr. Evans, someone is trafficking in arms and ammunition. It's urgent that we find this person or persons. As I have said, the situation is most serious for your country and mine. What have you discovered since the last time we talked?"

"Señor Presidente, I think we've found the city where the organization that supports Casimiro is located."

"Where is it? El Paso?"

"No, Senor Presidente. We're almost certain that the weapons come from Corpus. We know that the main link is there. It appears to be someone connected to the university."

"Are they Americans?"

"No, sir, as we discussed last time, we believe that it's a group of Chicanos. They're preparing themselves here and over there to launch a guerrilla attack in the universities and the towns."

"But why do they come here to make trouble?"

"I think it's fairly obvious that they want to link themselves with Casimiro's revolutionaries in order to organize a simultaneous uprising."

156

"Are you keeping a watch on them?"

"Yes, Doctor, my father is taking care of her. But my mother gets angry with him. That's the way my mother is. It happens every time a little brother or sister comes."

"Are we getting to your house?"

"Yes, Doctor. You can see it there. There's my mother."

There with a skirt of serpents, with a necklace of human hearts, there she is, the mother of those who live in heaven. Don't you see her with her head like a skeleton, the face of a serpent and feet with eagle's claws?

He heard the shouts and the resounding of the words of the boy who did not move his lips to communicate with the modern magician whose brain let drop words that were like seeds that someone far away in time gave to him.

"Oh, Doctor, thank God you've come, Doctor, come in quickly. She's very sick. The baby won't come out!"

The darkest corner attempted to hide the swollen uterus, the skinny spread legs drew together, the head rolled from side to side. Her long black damp hair, filled with the smell of sweat and mucus, hung about her face, red with effort, lighted for the doctor by the rays of the sun that entered through the roof of the hut. The woman of ancient centuries was sleeping when he came to see her.

"We have to wake her; tell her I'm a doctor and I've come to help her."

"Yes, Doctor, yes, of course, we have to wake her. Tonantita, wake up, Tonantita."

"Iaaaayiiiyyaaa . . . aaa . . . aaa! Go away, old man! Bastard! Rotten animal! Ay . . . ay . . . ayy . . . oh, God, help me, look what he's done to me! Aaayyii!"

"We're going to help you, Señora, don't move and don't scream, calm down . . . Hold her, I'm going to give her an injection in her arm, hold her!"

"There it is, now . . ."

"In just a while she'll be calmed down, but she'll be able to hear us and help us with what we have to do. I'd like to speak to you outside."

"Yes, Doctor, let's go out."

The two men walked beneath the northern sun; surrounded by the children, they talked.

"How long has she been this way?"

"About two days, Doctor, yes, two days."

"But, why didn't you call me sooner?"

"Tonantita has always done her work alone; she's never needed any help."

"Your wife is very sick. We have to do a caesarean."

"A what?"

"An operation."

"But why? Tonantita can do it alone; I don't think she needs that operation."

"Look, if we don't operate on her she could die. We can save her. I don't know about the baby. If we don't operate they both could die."

"Tonantita can't die, we need her very much, she's our mother, she can't leave us, she can't."

"Good, in that case I want you to boil water to bathe her in, to get her ready."

"Are you sure we have to do this?"

"Yes, and when I begin to operate I don't want the children to come in. If you want to be there, you can help me."

"How can I help you?"

"I like to talk when I operate; you can watch while Felipe helps me."

"Thank you, Doctor, let me see, will she be asleep?"

"Yes, of course. Felipe, come with me. Bring me the water right now, please."

The doctor was among the shadows of the cihuatitas, seeds of maternal heroism, pregnant females, white of face, body, and dress, waiting in case they would have to accompany Tonantita to the western heavens, to fly with the sun from its zenith to the horizon. The cihuatitas scurried all over in and out of the hut. They cleaned a mat, they covered it with a wedding blanket, the finest and the cleanest that Tonantita owned; and they put her on top of it, her body centered in the whiteness and next to the wonderous vademecum which held the blade that would make the incision that would bring forth the first drop of red blood that would sing the praises of the toci that guided his hand. He was not one of the modern folk when he cut the first millimeter of the abdominal skin, full of white pearls that sprang out almost from the navel running down the length of the slippery fat along the sides of the bloody opening. He nibbled the ear of corn, chewing the sacred kernels, his eyes requested the wisdom of Teteoinnan who took the sharpened stone with whose point he explored the spot where he would open the white womb.

"Dry it, Felipe, dry it. Now we'll cut down here, dry it, careful with your hands."

His fingers moved rapidly inside the warm uterus, the palm of

158

Teteoinnan withdrew the head of the strange newcomer, his shoulders easily followed.

"It's a little boy, Felipe."

His legs, his feet, everything was all right.

"He won't cry, Doctor; he won't cry."

The seeds seemed to dance with the chilly wind that blew through the hut. It was the cihuatitas who were running about, shouting out that the boy's soul had gone because it knew that it was going to enter the world through a scientific opening.

"Now I'll cut the cord."

"But the child doesn't cry; his soul stayed in the other world."

"I have to remove the placenta."

The cihuatitas observed the black and purple ball, wired with veins, globules, and little pockets of blood. They snatched the secret ball from the bloodied whiteness with their mouths. The soul was not there. The cihuatitas saw the tender body turning them into sharp flints that crossed the barrier of centuries, repeating the rite with the Chicano race's knives. One ran off with a little arm, another with a leg, one took the genitals, one the pretty little head, another left with the heart, one of them had the spine. The cihuatitas, seeds of beginnings, spread out upon the waters of the earth that whispered to Tonantita as she returned from her distant journey.

"Dry it up, Felipe, I just have to suture a little more. It's almost over."

"My son didn't cry, Doctor. My son, Doctor."

"There he is. Look at him, he's there. Take him away, please."

"We have to have a wake for him; we have to dress him, like a pure angel. My son is a tiny angel, an innocent, his soul remained in the other world."

The man lifted up the child; he went out surrounded by the cihuatitas who delighted in his tender flesh. Rays of light fell on the sweating doctor, a modern magician whom death had beaten. At that moment he was worthless; all he could do was wash his hands. Exhausted, he cried with all his heart, his eyes, and his mind through which passed the heavy feeling of his profession.

That night he heard the sharp cries of those who kept watch over the little angel, placed with his smile, in his wooden casket. His perfect round face would stay forever in the mental world of the brain that mounted the motorcycle with Felipe, who clung to his back; he quickly rode home to Margarita. Tonantita would live and her husband would again stroke her, seeking to open her legs, to see the hair covered object hidden there, the endless opening of the world . . . I

159

had no right to do a hysterectomy, but she'll have another, she'll be pregnant in three months; but I told her that it would be very dangerous, that she could die. I could have taken it out, she wouldn't have realized it, but what right do I have? I won't be like other doctors who take out poor women's uteruses. I can't do it, I won't do it. It's better for her to have her tribe of children, that's how they affirm their reality, that's how they know that someone needs them, that someone depends on them, that they are important; everyone wants to feel loved, everyone needs to feel important ...

"Do you want to feel important or what? I don't want you to work; you don't need to work; you have everything here. You want for nothing!"

"Don't be silly, it's not because I want to feel important. Look, Henry, Margarita told me that I could learn a lot and that it would be good for me to start with them and then maybe in the future I could go to nursing school, or medical school. Henry, I just want to see if I can do the work. Don't be foolish, Henry, there's no danger of anything. Let me learn."

"Learning is bullshit. If you think that learning is going to solve your problems you're crazy. Education isn't worth a thing in this country."

"I don't care about that. Margarita told me that they need help and I want to help them. And anyway, I don't want to stay at home any more."

"You're just a girl, you should be at home ..."

"Don't tell me that, I know I'm only sixteen years old but with what I already know about life I feel like a woman! I am a woman!"

"Bah, you're crazy!"

"OK. If that's what you think, but I'll tell you one thing. I'm going to work with Doctor Logan and nobody, not you or anybody else, is going to stop me. I'm sorry, Henry, but that's how it has to be."

"If you work with him and with Margarita everyone will think you're like her. Everyone knows she's sleeping with him and by association they'll think the same about you. You'll ruin your reputation, you'll get a bad name."

"You should have thought about that when you took me. What's the difference now? Doesn't everybody know that I sleep with you? I don't know what you're afraid of, nothing's going to happen."

"I have no confidence in that man; I don't like you to be around him. He's a bad influence, not only for you, but for all the Chicanos in town. That man is causing more problems, and, I'm telling you because I don't want to see you get hurt, it's going to cost him dearly."

"Explain that, Henry, what do you mean? Are they going to chase him out the way they did the others? If you try to do that you'll have to hurt me, because I'll stand by him. He hasn't done anything bad. They have no right; me, Rodríguez, Margarita, Doña Gertrudis and many others are going to defend him."

"That won't prevent us from getting him out of Mathis. I repeat, I don't want you to be associated with him! I don't want you to work with him!"

"You can't tell me what I can do! I'm telling you that I'll work for him and I will!"

His teeth, soldered with a rage that drove his hands to strike the table, implored the beautiful, sensual girl who had now realized the power she had over Pistol Man.

"Teresa, please don't go with him, stay here with us . . ."

"But I'm not going to live with him, silly; I'll always be with you. And do you know why? Because I know that you love me. Don't get mad, I'll always be yours."

The female body on tiptoes reached up to kiss his cheek. Her stomach felt the erect penis of the man who knew that he would lose himself in her. His hands stroked her firm buttocks, her moist lips no longer spoke; she guided him to her bed, his wet lips melted over her breasts, letting themselves be kissed. His breathing became agitated when the skirt rose and flew through the air. His face was tender, tense with his love for her. The naked bodies, alone, on the bed, touched each other. She felt herself grow damp, his finger affectionately stroked her clitoris, slowly; she gently squeezed his testicles full of fluid. They sat like Indians, constantly touching each other, making themselves almost climax, exploring the inexplicable sensation; they wanted this moment to be eternal, he leaned over her, she offered him her warm vagina to eat, he ate, and ate, and ate. He reclined with his organ stretched out toward God's heaven as she sucked and sucked and caressed his hairy balls as his penis plunged deeply down her throat. The masculine tongue penetrated the opening between the damp legs of his future little mother.

"I'm coming, aayy I'm coming . . ."

"Me too, Mommy Teresita. Take it all, ay my virgin . . . my whore . . . my beloved . . ."

"Suck, eat, Henry, give it to me, yes, yes!"

On the beautiful girl's pure bed they rested, without moving their naked bodies, sleeping together that night without anger, alone, tranquil, isolated from the problems they lived with when they were awake.

The Marxist Pinnacle entered with all his knowledge and with his underarms covered with capitalist fabric. The Little Koala Bear, now presuming a certain grandeur due to his ascent to the departmental throne and as a result of being the king of an organization that would send him to places he desired, entered with the words of a manuscript that he would never sell. The Aristocrat just arrived from the hacienda where he had created the supreme essays of the land devastated by manipulative men who published his reviews; the Oneiric Bicyclist entered oneiricizing himself with the others. Baldy Four Eyes pushed ahead, eating his lunch in such noisy bites that the hogs were embarrassed to hear the porcine music of this revolutionary, still faithful to conservative techniques. The thick lower lip of the Midget Turtle, a blue dress covering her football-sized breasts, entered with an air of superiority, her open yawning mouth proclaiming the theoretical structures which shaped the intrinsic elements of the meeting.

"Good morning, runts."

The trumpets imagined by the Theoretical Roman sounded. King of the theoretical empire of the small nation, presuming with his Hitlerian dictator's mustache, glorious phallic symbol that penetrated the pines of the luxuriant forest, only God knew how many insertions the student perched in the Theoretical Roman's cave received. The superiors waited for the one whom they were going to destroy and condemn. Five minutes passed and they brought in the Professor, the thorn of pain in the sides of the Theoretical Roman and the Midget Turtle.

"Well, it's about time, runt. Look, Professor Morenito, you are harmful to the department and you have no right to be here, only those with a theoretical background should teach in the university; I know that I am completely correct, you cannot compete with our standards, established by the Theoretical Roman, and planned by the group from that small country that has always met at his home. Get out of here, we don't want you, runt. I tell you as a friend."

"I agree. I, the Theoretical Roman, brought you here because the university gave me the position for nothing, if it weren't for that, I never would have made the effort to bring a Chicano."

"That is so, Theoretical Roman, the Chicanos shouldn't be here because they lower the university's standards. Only those who are perfect should ponder life and art here. Look, Professor, I'm telling you as a friend, your people are still too primitive, those of us from the extreme South and especially we who are from the cradle of the common lament are those who deserve these positions. What right do you have?"

The executive committee's heads smiled in the approbation of the extreme drivel that the Midget Turtle and the Theoretical Roman spit from their tobacco-stained mouths.

"Therefore, your race has no place here; now that the politics have changed, we're going to kick you all out; I wanted to get rid of you from the beginning. What we'll do is change the rules of the game so that you can't win."

"But you can't do that."

"Why not? Everything has changed. We'll get rid of you and all the Chicanos. And we'll establish a theoretical department in a theoretical university and we'll bring the sons of the place where there is no forgetfulness; finally we'll enjoy the kingdom untouched by the Chicanos. That's how it will be, because it just so happens that I'm tired of being a man, now I'll be a little God, the renowned Theoretical Roman with the Hitlerian mustache fucking that glorious cunt who comes to suckle my balls when I'm talking on the telephone with my dear little wife."

"Very well said, almost, almost like a poet, Theoretical Roman."

"Thank you, Midget Turtle, you really understand what I wish to do. These minds cannot understand our system."

"Yes, I know, Theoretical Roman."

"Well then, Professor, you have to keep working hard because your future depends on us. Remember that we will have to write your letters of recommendation. Goodbye, son of the Chicano race."

"Thank God we won't have them for long."

Professor Morenito's jacket left the conference room; the laughter of triumph was heard until suddenly the door was shut and it was cut off, as if a tomb had been closed . . . I have to survive . . . I have to stay . . . I hate them and I know they hate me and that's why, just because of that, I'll stay, and I'll put up with all their insults . . . but I'll stay and I'm going to win because I deserve my tenured professorship. Bastards, they don't know that I'm capable of killing them all. I've killed before and it's easy. They're lucky that my head isn't still living in those times, but I'll beat them, I will . . .

Time never changes in these regions of agony, of the human condition lost in search of its search; the eyes don't change, they're the same, the bodies are the same, born between urine and feces, filled and covered with centuries of seminal mud, with time they slowly progress until they stand up in order to grab with their hands what they think belongs to them, to think, to plan their own triumph or the defeat of others. They are born between urine and feces and very few escape the excrement left by their neighbor, by other human beings in general, their brother, their sister. They are born between urine and feces and the first thing they do is open their mouths and rub their genitals trying to stretch their opening or swell their organ. As they grow up in their bedrooms, these naked animals sniff each other, lick each other, and nuzzle their asses, their vaginas, their penises, the birth opening, taking pleasure in each other without knowing each other, like dogs on the streets outside houses made of boxes, human caves. That's what she was doing when she had a heart attack; she'd been famous, a black bitch, it wasn't her fault, she was the victim of Diana, the glorious millionaire goddess who had manipulated Florentina who lived in Harlem, whoring, getting assistance from the state government whose dollars she used to shoot up with to stardom, a stardom snatched from her by the Glorious Diana who robbed the fame of the Holiday. The black pig declares life "good" in the country where chained and naked African women sucked the white balls with forced affection, where African women grasped their ankles with their hands writhing for the organ's penetration because if they didn't cooperate they got their punishments, a son killed, a husband lynched, a father, a brother, a sister, their life wasn't worth shit, and now glorious, black Diana was burying one of her many victims. The television was speaking to glorious Diana when he made her turn her shining face.

"Teresa, the telephone please."

"Yes, who's speaking?"

"Thanks, Teresa. Very well, Cody. How are the children?"

"They're fine, they miss you a lot and they want to see you."

"OK, look, I'll be home this weekend without fail."

"No, Michael, we're coming there."

"No, Cody, it's dangerous and . . ."

"That doesn't matter, it's been more than a year and I want to see what you're doing. I have a right to. You can expect me Friday afternoon."

"All right, I'll expect you."

"Michael, I'm going to tell you something that is really bothering me; Michael, you don't need us any more. You don't send us enough to live on; I'm working. I don't know what's happened; I think your work is more important than we are; I can't go on like this. I don't want us to continue to be separated, I need a man, and don't think that I'm just waiting here for when you show up. Michael, I'm not a fool, I know what's going on there with Margarita, don't insult me by denying it. Michael, I am so angry with you that I just can't live like this any more. I'll be there Friday, so that you can see the chil-

dren. Think it over, Michael. Also, Pato called and he wants you to
go back to a place that they have in the corporation. He told me he'd
wait for your answer. Michael, it's a good job; we could go back there,
buy a house, rest, and enjoy a little bit of what we deserve."

"Cody, Cody, please, don't start, no."

"No, Michael, I can't stand it! We'll see you Friday. Goodbye."

He hung up the telephone. He stood motionless looking at her and
the children, he hardly remembered what they were like, they ceased
to exist when they weren't at her side, they ceased to exist when he
couldn't touch them: . . . They're there, I know that they're there with
her. I wonder what they're doing, Shane, my beautiful little girl, Jason,
my handsome little man? Don't they exist for me? Don't I love them?
I'm afraid for them, but I have to live. I do love them very much,
but I want my freedom, I love them, I would give my life for them,
I really think I would, but when they're not here, I don't remember
them, they don't exist. Is it because it has been so many months since
I've seen them? I have neglected them, I don't blame Cody. Maybe
it would be best for her to leave me, I'm not worth it, I'm crazy, an
idiot, someone who has abandoned everything that he has worked for.
I'm a fool, but I can't escape it, I've started with this business and I
have to finish it, even if I don't know when . . .

"Michael, Michael, wouldn't you like a cup of coffee?"

"No, give me a beer. What time is it?"

"It's ten-thirty."

"A good time to start on a binge. Bring the beer . . ."

"Michael, what's happened to you?"

"Nothing, Margarita, it's just that Cody is going to leave me. She'll
be here on Friday to bid me farewell. My children are also coming
to see their crazy father."

"Michael, don't think like that. Tell her she can stay with us."

"But how can I do that? You would have to leave the house."

"That won't be a problem, tell her to stay, Michael."

"No."

"All right then, what are you going to do?"

"What I'm going to do is go out and get drunk; I'm going to invite
Fernando to come with me, and then tomorrow afternoon I'm going
to sign the papers for the construction of the new clinic. I'll show Cody
the plans, to see if she likes them."

"And maybe she'll stay, Michael. She could help you, she could handle the books, don't be so stubborn, Michael. Please, don't let her
leave."

"Margarita, you're a real woman, a woman in every positive sense that you can imagine; you'll do the right thing for them, you're a woman. I'm going to Fernando's house and then to Cisco's for a while."

"Don't you want to eat something?"

"No."

"Take care of yourself, Michael. Please be careful with that motorcycle!"

The night slowly progressed with the sad sound of the crickets and frogs who were happily singing outside the Professor's home; the children and Leticia were dreaming the dreams of another world. He couldn't sleep, what his superiors had said to him, he couldn't believe what they had told him in the meeting. But what could he do?. . . How can I defend myself? How can I struggle against their prejudice and racism? I have to write, but I need something, a theme that will grow, and into which I can incorporate those pedants with faith in their Ph.D.'s. I'm going to attack them, kill them with literature, kill them with my creative force, with the creative energy that those parasites feed on, they live off of us who write, but they want to put themselves above writers. Don't they realize that criticism is to serve literature and its creators? But no, they don't acknowledge this because they don't want to, because the Theoretical Roman and the Midget Turtle think they are superior to the creators, they call themselves "scientists." The Midget Turtle says that she studies literature scientifically; in her office she has graphs and charts, graphs that trace the world view of every work worthy of her attention, graphs of fables, of mythology; she also has test tubes, experimental breeding grounds in which she tries to prove scientifically if the atmosphere of the novel was contaminated by a synchronic diachronic invasion of the creole space of the country abandoned to military justice. She's in her office, converted into a cerebral laboratory, adapting scientific methods to literature. There she is among mountains of books, clouds of smoke, a scientific pen creating books of criticism citation by citation. There the glory of the Theoretical Roman is related to her graph of the intrinsic system tied to the extrinsic globule of society: . . . How should I do it? Do I write about them? If I do it they'll get rid of me, they'll throw me out; there's no doubt that if I attack their illusory world they'll screw me, they'll screw me with the system; I don't care, if they screw me, they screw me; and if they do it it's because everything that I say about them is the truth, the plain truth. . . .

"Who is it, Francisca?"

"It's Doctor Logan."

"Hey, Michael, how're you doing? Come in, please, come in."

"Thank you, Fernando, thanks."

"Why do you look so down?"

"I've come to invite you to have a few beers; you're right, I'd like to talk about some things that are bothering me right now."

"Michael, this is the first time you've invited me for a drink; I'd love to. I owe it to you and I really want to go out with you."

"Let's go then, I'm feeling depressed but I also want to celebrate a decision that I've just made, a decision that's going to affect us all."

"Francisca, where are the keys?"

"Here, take them, and please be careful. Things are bad, especially now after Casimiro's new attack so close to the border."

"What happened, Francisca?"

"Casimiro, the bandit in the north of Mexico, has killed a lot of the Mexican regime's supporters; they say he has almost a thousand soldiers with him and that more are joining from up here."

"But the worst thing is they think they are getting weapons here, from this side, and that the Chicanos are supplying them."

"I heard something about him when I was in Corpus."

"That's why things are going to get pretty bad for us throughout this region; they're watching us carefully in every state, as if we were a powder keg. Pistol Man even keeps watch over me and now he takes care of compiling the information for the lists that the government requests."

"Lists? What for?"

"At first I didn't know, but I think they are lists with our names. . . . Poor Pistol Man."

"Poor? Why poor?"

"I don't know, but I feel sorry for him. Now that Teresa is working with you he's in a foul mood. You know that he didn't want her to work in the office with you."

"I had that impression; she works well, she's a bright girl. She'll be successful."

"That's exactly what he's most afraid of. He's afraid you'll brainwash her, he's afraid that will make her leave Mathis. Be careful with him, Michael. He's very jealous, if anyone tells him that you've tried to have an intimate relation with her, he's capable of going after you. Take care, man . . ."

"But I haven't done anything; I just gave her a job. It was her idea."

"He's a very weak man, spiritually and psychologically weak."

"Hey, Fernando, since when have you become a psychologist?"

"From the day I woke up. Let's go, Michael."

"Here's the newspaper, if you want to read about Casimiro."

"Thanks, Francisca."

His eye caught the name Silky Silkfuck dead in a car accident on the highway to Houston. His mind read that she was on her way to a state hearing in Houston; she was going to make a declaration against the Nucplo company, a manufacturer of nuclear chemicals. The authorities claim she was under the influence of drugs. Nonetheless, the specific drug revealed in the autopsy was not reported. Officials refused to give more details about the matter.

"Is it something interesting, Michael? Are you all right?"

"Ah . . . yes, yes, let's go."

The bodies left the warm home's mouth. They approached the police car that was now Rodríguez's; the wings opened and then closed over the two travelers; two travelers from a disgusting world who were flying to the place where catharsis, the doctor's purification, awaited its turn. The police car's open eyes observed the road that it ate with its round paws; whispering secrets to the stunned doctor, the shiny reflections against the car's windows as it rushed ahead following the broken line of the roadway, the eyes of the cars that were flying toward them crossed the tunnels of his brain, the memories sped by, the past flashed by before the windows of memory. He saw her, saw the breasts they all desired, he saw the crazy woman's face: . . . But why? Why did they kill her? What did that silly woman know? No, it can't be . . . of course it was an accident like any other; but she was sure they were going to kill her, it was almost as if she had to die, as if it was beyond her control . . . her destiny was decided by others . . . others that she knew existed but whom she did not know . . . where were they? . . . she couldn't see the enemy but she was sure that they were watching her, that they were harassing her . . . but in what way? What new way do these men have? How can they condemn a person without anyone knowing it? . . . it's a living monster that kills, that sucks the blood of an existing man, a visible person, but what is it? . . . where is it? . . . in what form does it exist? . . . this monster created by . . . by whom? . . . who created it? . . . did she imagine it? . . . She used to tell me that they wanted to kill her . . . She was absurd . . . it was a coincidence . . . she warned me to watch out for myself . . . that I was in danger . . . but that's ridiculous, I didn't do anything to anybody . . . I've only helped . . . I've helped others . . .

. . . Michael, you're in danger . . . Michael, your chest is bare . . . Michael, they're going to rip you open . . . you, who were born to be sacrificed . . . they'll make you a god . . . a legend . . . a myth . . . Michael, they're going to cut your balls off . . . Cody will cry . . . your

children will bury you . . . Michael, their eyes spy on you through
the dirty cracks of humanity . . . No, it can't be. It's stupid to even
imagine it, or believe it . . . Yes, she used drugs, of course, that's how
she died, she really was crazy Silky Silkfuck . . . The lights of the cars
crazed with speed formed a yellow spot of pain.

"Damn it, those bastards are really flying."

"Yes, they're driving too fast."

"Here we are, Michael. You've never been here? To Mathis's
Borlote? I come here from time to time with my friends to have a few
drinks."

"Do they have music?"

"They have everything, Michael. Everything."

The parking lot was covered with gravel that announced the two
men walking up to the door that opened to the dark, smokey, inebriated and merry world of the bar filled with voices rising from the masculine and feminine bodies that were seated in an almost aromatic
rhythm of raising their hands and opening their mouths. Three blond
women observed the new arrivals. The blue eyes drew them closer;
Rodríguez's hidden pistol holder respectfully said no; the anonymous
doctor's blood rushed as he felt the slender girl's hand stoke his neck.

"Not now, sweetheart."

"Why don't you have a few drinks to see if you get in the mood?"

"We'll talk later, sweetheart."

"I'll wait for you, touch me, here, do you like it?"

"Come on, Michael, let's sit over here; we'll call you later, girls.
Hey, Maromita, a pitcher, please!"

"What a miracle; they tell me you've gotten very tough on Pistol
Man. It was about time you woke up, man."

"The pitcher, Maromita."

"Here it comes."

The benches received the men whose heads turned to listen to the
singer whom only two people heard.

"Thanks. Well, Michael, here's to you."

"To you, Fernando. What did Maromita mean when she told you
it was time you woke up?"

"We came here to discuss some matters pertaining to you, not to me."

"But I'm interested in what she said. Don't be . . . explain it to me.
What did she mean by that?"

"All right, it's, well, you know that I'm the only Chicano that works
for Pistol Man. I've always been a real ass-kisser; I would do everything he said even when it went against the rules. I even did things
that harmed my own people. Out of fear of losing my job, I did it

all thinking it was the best thing for me and my family. And like Maromita said, I woke up, I realized what I was doing. I was sacrificing them to save myself. My people are good, they can take a lot and they have, but now we're tired of putting up with so much; I'm tired of kissing so and so's ass. For example, take your situation; Pistol Man wanted to get you out of Mathis, the way he got rid of the others, the way he chased out Hales; he made his life so miserable that he had to go. But I didn't do anything to defend him or the Chicanos. Now I've come to my senses, I don't do everything he tells me; he's threatened me with taking away my job; but he knows that no one would work with him; I mean no Chicano would. There have been several cases in which I've opposed him, various cases dealing with Chicanos. Your case is one of them. You know he wants to get you out, you know that he hates you because Teresa is working with you. That situation, when we arrested old man Bilabí, I had no idea what Pistol Man was going to do, I was a fool, or maybe I blinded myself so as not to see what I was allowing, now the bastard loves her even though he doesn't admit it; he lives with her. And what's curious is that she, too, has come to love the man who violated her. Well, that's all, I've woken up, Michael; I think I've woken up. And that's why I defended you, that's why I told him that I wouldn't kick you out of town. But watch out for yourself, because I think things are going to get bad."

"I wanted to talk to you about that and some other things related to it. Why are you laughing?"

"Never in my life would I have believed that I would be sitting here talking to you, a doctor who wants my friendship and my advice. I had always thought that I'd have nothing to talk about to a doctor, with a person as educated as you."

"Don't belittle yourself, I'm no different than you, I'm like you, the only difference is that I studied a little more than you. I'm a doctor, a glorified technician, don't be impressed by titles, like I said I'm the same as you, I feel like you do, I hate, love, have vices, I eat and shit, we're the same, that's the problem: we still haven't realized that we're all equal, that we're all one."

"But I still feel strange, I don't know how to explain it to you, there's something in us. There's something in our friendship, if it's happened to others, why not to us?"

"But why not, Marcelo? Why can't we be the spark that sets the fire that will burn the whole country? It already happened once, why can't it happen again to us? We already have two thousand men. Why can't we be the Villa or the Zapata of our times?"

"Don't be foolish, Casimiro; we have to play it very carefully. We have the weapons, and now with what we've won, enough to keep us going for a few months, but we won't be able to win, we won't be able to change everything, we won't be able to change the government, they are looking for us everywhere, some day they'll kill us. Here in Mexico, a revolution like our fathers' is no longer possible."

"Don't tell me that, you bastard, you're a coward, don't make me angry, compadre! Don't make me mad!"

They had been camped there for thirteen days, but in that instant, at that moment, the area changed. It was their land, their country, but it became apostatized into a strange territory that was unknown to them. The picture showed the pink skeleton moving a reaper's scythe toward the left side of land sown with human remains that appeared to live, their faces had a vital expression, their hands emerging from the earth were full of energy and strength; from beneath the earth, from the darkness, the organs searched for light to enslave themselves again, to escape from the supreme liberation, everything was transformed in this place, everything was decomposing, entangled in the net of the damp, black and green countryside whose vapors rose to be inhaled by the men.

"Exactly where are we, Marcelo? What zone are we moving in, Marcelo? The smell, don't you like it? It's like . . ."

"It's the manure, the earth's fertilizer."

"Yes, it seems as if we've camped in the middle of a field of manure, I think I'm in the very center of it, look at my feet, they're covered with it."

"Mine too, all the troops are perfumed. The next time we attack the enemy will go running when they get a few whiffs of the odor."

"Oh, compadre Marcelo, don't make me laugh, don't you see you've made me angry."

"That's what friends are for, Casimiro, to remind you where you are."

"Yes, in this place, in Mathis, I feel like a stranger too; what I am doing here is going to cost me, Fernando, and that's precisely what I want to talk to you about."

"Tell me, Michael, go ahead. It's already too late to stop what you're thinking about, you've already compromised me with Pistol Man, and I've done the same to you. Tell me everything, Michael."

"I have to reach a decision. Cody will be here Friday; she wants to come and stay but I don't want her to stay. I won't be able to work with them here; I'll always be worried about them. Cody in the same house with Margarita — it can't be. I can't tell Margarita and Felipe to leave."

"What's happened is that you've fallen in love with Margarita."

"No, yes, but I love my wife and children; I just don't want them here, they mustn't be here with me, they'll be in danger. I know that I love them when I'm with them, I would give my life for them. When they're far away from me I know that they're safe at their mother's side, and I can devote myself to this adventure, to this madness I've begun. When they're with their mother they're a memory, she's a memory, a dream whose barriers I can break by picking up the telephone and talking to them, telling them I'm all right. Or if I want to I can go on my motorcycle and I'm there, home, in less than an hour and I love them and I know that I am loved; but not here, I don't want them to come and live here, it would be impossible."

"Michael, I think you've made a decision, if you don't want them to stay, tell them they have to go; you're completely right about the danger, they will be in danger."

"But it's not so easy, don't you see that once they're here maybe I won't be able to say no; when they are here, I'll see my kids, my Cody and I'll want them to stay, I may not be able to tell them to go."

"I don't know what to tell you, perhaps she'll make the decision."

"Yes, she told me that I would have to choose, either she stays here or she goes to her mother, or we go back together to the hospital and I'll work with a friend."

"Michael, what do I know about these things? The only thing I can tell you is to wait and have the decision make itself, right then. Does she know about Margarita?"

"I think so, and perhaps that will convince her that I don't love her and she'll go away, believing a lie, because the truth is that I do love her, but I want to finish this business, I want to be done with this."

"And what does Margarita say?"

"She's told me that she'll continue working and she'll return to her house."

"And what's bad about that, if you don't love her?"

"I don't know, Fernando, I don't know, but I do know that she has to stay in that office, because if she doesn't, everything will be ruined. She's essential to the practice, to the town, to the patients, to the future and whatever's going to happen in the future."

"Do you love her or not, Michael?"

"I think I love her too."

"As much as Cody and your children?"

"I don't know, I just don't know."

"Michael, you're really mixed up. Hey, Maromitas, another pitcher! I'll tell you one thing, I couldn't do to my family what you've done with yours, or what you're going to do, I simply couldn't."

"I agree with you, I'm a fucked up mess and that's why I'm going to have another beer."

"I'll go for that."

"Here's something else I'd like your opinion on. I've already decided what I'm going to spring on you, but I want you to tell me what you think Pistol Man and the others' reaction will be."

"But what is it? We have to get to the point because if we don't, we'll get plastered and I won't be able to give you a logical answer."

"OK, then, I've decided to build a clinic."

"And you want to know what the others are going to do? They'll make your life miserable until you leave Mathis. I've already told you, you've been lucky, very lucky, but when you start to build a clinic, all hell's going to break loose. Understand that they don't want you here. They almost destroyed Hales's car and his office, they're capable of beating you up, really getting rough and nasty. Don't do it, don't do it."

"But you're going to help me, you said you'd help me, didn't you?"

"That's why I'm telling you not to do it because it's a move that will affect me and everyone else."

"And that's why I need to know if you're committing yourself or not, but you have to commit yourself completely."

"If you start this project, I'll help you, I already committed myself the first time that I defended you. Listen, Michael, let's have a few more beers, we'll dance a little with the ladies and we'll enjoy the music."

"That guy sings very well."

"Yes, he's a poor manipulated poet, frustrated by his friends, friends who used all his music to make themselves famous and then forgot all about him. But he had a part in his problems, too, because of his habit."

"What's his name?"

"I think he's called Lira, I'm not sure, I don't know."

Those few days passed as if they were pictures of his life that he, from below, watched fade away; he would enter one, and then leave it to enter another. He was not sure in any of them, sometimes he would stare at the wall as if he were a somnambulist, he would stare at Margarita, at the horizon, at a patient's wound. He would become lost in one picture only to find himself in another, he would fall asleep in one and wake up in yet another, but he saw them all, he would see all the images of his life, it was like witnessing several films in which he was the principal author, actor and spectator. He could not believe what he saw, the beer he drank, the shouting, the words that he said sounded absurd to the people who knew him. He would begin to work and suddenly they would find him in the kitchen drinking beer as fast as he could, they could not stop him until he got drunk and slept, dreaming, entering into the happy pictures that he desired. Physically, his body walked, but his mind slept in those pictures that he watched from below. He awoke when one of the characters in a picture came to life and spoke to him.

"I remember that I was sitting, chatting with Don Costa, the poor man, he's been very troubled by his varicose veins, thank God at least I don't have that affliction, I was sitting down, as I was saying, when she came in, very pretty, not because she was a gringa no, but don't misunderstand me, it's just that the gringas think they're so beautiful and all I see is tons of make-up to hide their ugliness, but she was very natural, you could tell. Well, she came in with the two children, and how adorable they were, really beautiful. His family was standing there and he came into the room, when he saw them his mouth dropped open and he didn't know how to respond. The children went to him right away and hugged their daddy's legs. I remember he got down on his knees, crying, he kissed the children. He couldn't say anything, he had it all hidden here, in his heart, here in his throat. He got up and with a cry of love, anguish, and, I think, sinfulness and resentment, he called his wife. Everyone who was waiting saw him, but then they saw him in a different way, not as a doctor but as a man, just a man."

"Yes, Doña Paquita, you're right about all those details, that's how I heard it described, but nonetheless she didn't stay with him, perhaps because he didn't love her any more; you know he was living with Margarita."

"No, as I was telling you, he loved his family very much, that's what I don't understand, why did he let her go?"

"She just stayed that day, she left in the evening, didn't she?"

"That's how it was, but they embraced, hard, you could hear her shouting all the way to my house. She yelled at him that he didn't love them any more, that he only thought of his career, she screamed that she had put up with so many years of misery so that he could finish his studies and now he repaid her by abandoning them, sleeping with another woman, oh, she hollered so many things at him, she told him that he was a slave to a dream that would only bring him failure, that he should go to the city and set up a practice, that his friends were willing to help him. The children began to cry, she got them in the car and they went, I don't know where, Doña Paquita, I think to Corpus . . . It was very early, around seven, they didn't even have time to eat dinner. Maybe she did what was best, maybe she was right, she was tired of living alone, of the children not having a father, apparently he no longer responded to her as he should have, as a husband, as a man. He saw her as removed, as if they were on the outside, as if they no longer belonged together, as if they had become lost, he had become distant; but still, there was an intense love between them, you could tell by the way they looked at each other."

"Oh, my God, how these young people complicate life! In our day we accepted reality without complaining; it's so sad to see people suffer."

The Midget Turtle's scales arched with the shiver of French rage that moved up her spine, reaching her brain with the accusation of liar, the turtle-like eyes studied the primitive Professor: . . . How I would like to destroy him, completely erase him, forever, they're all so short, repugnant, stupid. What do they know? They don't know anything, we, the Theoretical Roman and I, are right, our system, our education is the true one, the only one, and we must impose it here in this individualistic Anglo-Saxon world, in this university system; the theory, the study of literature is the new science, what do those savages know, fools. In my laboratory, I construct technically more than all the rest. I'd really like to erase them all, make them disappear, I listened to him, I heard the hateful words, he was right, I have to transform him into a monster, destroy his character, as a scholar and a professor, destroy him . . .

"You're lying, you liar. I already told you."

"You mustn't deny it, I'll tell the Theoretical Roman everything, because he and I are one, one voice, one ear: . . . Why don't they like me? Why am I here? I should go back to where they understand me. Yes, I'll claim my own country. I'll tell them that I'm not an American, or a Chicana, but I hate them both, ay! . . . my situation is worse than theirs; what should I do? . . . my children . . . my husband ay! Why did I marry that man? A dreamer, he talks a lot but he never comes through with anything . . . he's *always stuck at home*, like a mole, afraid to come out into the wind . . . Why do I feel anxious in the world?. . . . They say that I, his wife, have drowned his creative capacities. But I have my career, I don't know what I'm going to do, I have my family, I love my husband, I should have stayed there where it would not have been so difficult but I let myself be convinced by the Theoretical Roman's promises, and his plans. I was so stupid, I didn't think about myself, that's what the Professor always says, that we don't think for ourselves, we let them think for us . . . These primitive Chicanos shouldn't make my life so difficult. What did I hear? That the Theoretical Roman has eliminated the special group!. . ."

"No, Theoretical Roman, no!"

"You shouldn't have done that, Theoretical Roman."

"That's what the Professor wanted."

"No, Midget Turtle, no."

. . . You say no, but I'm going to hurt him, one way or another I'm going to get Professor Morenito.

The lumber to build the clinic was damp from the rain where they had bought it. The clinic was located in the middle of the barrio so that everyone could get there without bothering with a car, those in the barrio would use it with ease; in three weeks they had almost finished half of the building, only the flesh and the amenities were missing. Now it was a naked skeleton whose bones were used as stairs by the workmen who donated their time, the carpenters, four of them, the electrician and the plumber, everyone was working for the promise of free treatment for their families. The skeleton had a large waiting room, seven consulting rooms, an operating room, a laboratory, and a small office for Logan. The neighborhood was excited to see the clinic grow; at least it promised them a permanent doctor, who promised them help at prices they could pay; they came to chat to the rhythm of the hammers, the saws, the rhythm of tangible manual creation, that they could feel, measure, that made them happy to see everyone together, working for something that they had chosen. But their eyes were prepared to keep vigil at nightfall, to protect the wood, the windows, the wiring, the tools, everything that was theirs, to protect it all from the men who swooped down in the night to steal or burn the material. Who are they? Sometimes it's Pistol Man's men who come to destroy what they hate and fear, sometimes it's Chicanos who work for the system, who have been granted power by those in control. Logan's men kept watch at night over the advances of the outsiders, they waited with fear, with hatred they kept vigil over the basic necessity of affirming their existence, and sometimes they realized that they all were struggling to impose what they were afraid of losing. Dawn would come and they would rest a little bit, and Pistol Man would innocently arrive to see that they had not suffered any damage and he would leave, amazed by his men's cowardice, by the failure of his side. From a distance could be heard the mixture of sounds from the police car and the modern horse that almost always met on the rise in the highway; for a few minutes the noise of the police car was drowned in the deep sounds of the iron horse that was entering the area of fragile security.

"Good morning, boys. Hey, Gabriel, what did Pistol Man want?"

"Nothing, Doctor, that cop always comes by to see if his men have done any damage. He comes to see if they've burned more of our lumber, or broken windows, but today he left very angry."

"Yes, the bastard went away pretty ticked off, his damned boys haven't been by but when they come, we'll be ready, just let those damned bastards show up!"

"Let those mother-fucker sellouts come here, I'll remind them who they are!"

"Keep calm boys, I don't want you to use those rifles, that would be the worst thing that could happen, that would give them the excuse they need to prohibit us from finishing the clinic; let's not be fools; if they attack us we have the right to protect ourselves and to protect what is ours but don't make trouble; let them start and we'll answer."

"That's it, that's what we wanted to hear, OK, Doctor, we'll do what you say, if they come to get us, we'll answer them."

"Gabriel, how's the work going?"

"Fine, very well."

"Yes, but when will it be ready? We have to finish soon because the longer it takes, the more dangerous the situation gets."

"Of course, I understand, Doctor. Look at what we've done; we'll be finished in three more weeks."

"No, Gabriel, you've already told me that."

"You take care of the patients, I'll worry about the construction, but if you want a good building, you have to be patient."

"All right, all right, I'm going. It's almost eight o'clock, goodbye."

He felt like a mute as he quickly made his way to his office, mounted on his cold horse; he didn't say anything to the natural elements that he felt, saw, heard; the wind spoke to him in its sonorous language, it urged him to go more quickly, to catch it, his hand gave more food to the horse that roared along the road with his friend, and that almost became one with all of reality. He was mute as if he had returned to the beginning of creation, he could not shout, it was as if they were punishing him for a sin, for a crime that implied a return to a primitive state. He passed near the field that produced corn. The sunlight became more intense as he turned onto the big curve that brought him closer to his office. All the ears of corn bathed in the heat pursued him together, watched by the eagle that patrolled the zone in which the doctor moved. The eagle arrived before him making a mark in the sky that affirmed his greatness as a hunter and a guardian of his young. The doctor parked his motorcycle in front of the stairs to his office where Rodríguez's police car and the bodies of the fifty patients that he was in the habit of seeing every day were already waiting for him. The voices from the television, of Margarita, Teresa, laughing with Fernando, the children crying, the mothers shouting gave the impression of an insane asylum: . . . And I'm the craziest of the crazies in it. Fuck it, another damn day is starting, fourteen fucking hours of old, dry, smutty, ugly, painful, hurt, lying, affectionate, beaten faces. Sometimes I don't know if I can take it, maybe Cody was right, what the fuck am I doing here? Because they need you, Logan, because they need you. There's the door, inside, Logan, inside, now they've seen me, OK, here I go, get in there with the lepers, perform miracles for them, let them touch me and be cured, I'm going; I'm going, stop screaming, children, the magical doctor has arrived on his powerful, miraculous horse. Margarita says that I should try to get another doctor. I'll call Pato and see what he says. Inside, Doctor Logan, there are miracles to perform.

"But I've been here since six."

"And I have too."

"Me first, my children and I are very sick, look at them, Doctor, look how they are."

"No, I was here before all of you."

"Look, you all know that the office opens at seven-thirty so that you can call and make appointments for the next day. You have to call to avoid waiting for an hour and a half. Remember, the next time you have to call first. If you can't call, send a child or relative the day before to make the appointment. The people who are arriving now have appointments starting at eight o'clock. Those who don't have an appointment have to give their names to the nurse and then fill out forms; if it's difficult for you, the nurse can help you; I'm very sorry but Doctor Logan can only see those persons without an appointment when there's time; in case of an emergency, the nurse will talk with you first; thank you very much. Oh, good morning, Doctor Logan."

"Good morning, Margarita. Good morning."

"Doctor Logan, how are you?"

178

"Doctor, when are they going to finish the new clinic?"

"There's still a bit to do."

"Doctor, tell the workers to hurry, we want our clinic in our neighborhood."

"Yes, Doctor, we don't like to go into town."

"The gringos give us nasty looks."

"And they yell nasty things at us."

"Gabriel told me he would finish in another month."

"Michael, Fernando is waiting for you in the kitchen."

"Good, excuse me."

The doctor entered, his body changing from a shirt into a white coat. His brain's nose smelled the coffee that invited him to have a sweet roll and a hot cup of it before starting his work. The other man's eyes looked at his back, his buttocks, the legs of the man standing in front of the stove, they heard the delicious black stream land in the cup; the smoke rose in the house's soft air; the standing body turned, the other man saw his feet, his knees, his penis, stomach, chest, beard, and eyes. Two smiles declared "good morning."

"Did you go to the clinic this morning?"

"Yes, it looks like everything is coming along very well, at least they haven't burned anything."

"I'm surprised that Pistol Man hasn't kicked you the hell out."

"Do you two talk to each other?"

"Of course, we've known each other for so long that we can't live without talking to each other. His own interests prohibit him from not talking to me. He's got to, I tell you. I, I'm almost sure, am his only direct connection with the barrio, except for Teresa."

"Do you think he'll keep trying to get me out of Mathis?"

"Yes, he'll get you out, if you let him, he will."

"What can he do to me? Make my life miserable, punch me out? Whatever he does, I'm not going."

"Look, Michael, watch out for yourself, maybe you shouldn't ride the motorcycle by yourself; ask someone to take you where you want to go."

"I'm not afraid. What can they do to me? Beat me up? The worst would be for them to kill me, but I don't think Pistol Man is capable of it. He's too fond of himself to risk prison. No, he won't kill me."

"But you do realize that you're in danger."

"When won't I be?"

"People like you who come to upset the balance of things are always a good target."

"Oh, don't be such an alarmist, Fernando."

"The other day I was in Costa's store, two Chicano Uncle Toms were there talking to their bosses. They were saying that if they got permission to build the clinic in the Chicano neighborhood it would attract more Chicanos and that Mathis couldn't handle any more. They said they were willing to kill a few to let them know that they don't want any more greasers in their community."

"Those kinds of things don't happen any more, we're living in a time with laws and civil rights."

"You don't understand the red neck mentality, what will it take for you to grasp it?"

"Yes, I believe you, Fernando, I really do, but I'm not afraid of them. Why can't we just be ourselves?"

"With these new weapons we'll be like new, compadre."

"What beautiful machine guns, just look at them, compadre."

"Compadre Marcelo, we'll have to have a few drinks to celebrate our good fortune."

"And to thank God for friends like Manuel."

"That's right, to our friend Manuel."

"OK, boys, come get these boxes, bring the mules, hurry up."

"Because if we don't move fast we'll have the government on top of us."

"Casimiro, give me what you owe me."

"Don't get mad, Manuel, because I only have three quarters of what I owe."

"If you want me to keep bringing ammunition and weapons you have to keep your promises. I'm one of you, we're fighting against the same enemy, but if you don't come through next time, I won't bring any more."

"We almost have it all, if you like we can pay you with something else, but you've said that you don't want that."

"I don't want some rotten piece of ass."

"What rotten piece of ass? We've got a beautiful girl that we took in the last attack. She's a gringa who was working with some wealthy ranchers, you've got to see her; she's got a great ass and really firm breasts. Casimiro has had her a couple of times but . . ."

"For an old guy of forty-seven I came in her three times, in, out, turn her about, over and up and drink a cup!"

The men's laughter echoed through the canyon, the birds flew, the snakes froze when they heard the steps of the scouting detail that came across them, from above they prepared for the ambush of the ten men that they had discovered.

180

"Casimiro, you've whetted my appetite for the girl, where is she? I want you to pay me everything you owe."

"It's a deal then?"

"No, you can't pay the five thousand you owe me with a tight cunt. But I still want to try her."

"What a bastard you are!"

"You're taking advantage!"

"No, Marcelo, think about the risk we take to get you rockets; if it weren't for us you wouldn't have anything, not even the poor gringa to offer me. You have to keep up your end; you owe me five thousand. Now, I want a piece of the gringa's ass, let's see how you left her. OK, Casimiro, Marcelo, let's g . . ."

Paz, paz, paz, burning breeeaast unndderarmm, ay, it flew. Manuel's body doubled over and fell, his mouth full of dirt, his hands clutching the flesh hanging in knots of blood, screaming with sharp pain as he felt himself choking and faint in a black abyss.

"They're up there, shoot, bastards! Go on, up there, I want the balls of every one of those sons of bitches!"

Paz, paz, pazzz, they watched the men climb up toward them, fear, sweat from the error that they had discovered too late . . . There are a lot of them, but we just saw a few, about ten . . .

"Let's go, there are a lot of them, they were behind the rocks!"

"Lieutenant, they're coming from above!"

"We're fucked! Shithead, why didn't you see the rest of them? Ay, they've ripped me!"

"Well, boys, this is it!"

"Just give it to us!"

"I'm afraid, I, I want to go to my farm, with my family!"

"Shut up, shut up, don't run, don't run away!"

Paz, paz, pazzz . . . Mama, they're going to kill us, we're fucked, they're coming from all sides, they're like me, young, yes, I'm going to talk to them, I'll give up, I won't shoot, they'll understand that I have a family, two little children and they need their daddy; it's not my fault that I'm here, I was called up, like everybody else, I came to serve my country, but never, I never thought that this would happen, it's a mistake, we made a mistake, it's not fair, we didn't realize that there were more men. I'll explain it to them and they'll let me go, we're brothers, I have two children . . .

Paz, paz, pazzz.

"Up there, kill them all, stupid, insolent bastards, bring the balls of every last one of those mother fuckers, bring them to me and I'll eat them!"

His companions' faces wore another expression, of rage, of intense hatred that deformed eyes, nose, mouth into something that was not human, their words were incomprehensible, their language was an ancient one that affirmed the monsters that from all sides were dragging themselves toward them."

"Kill them, kill themmm!"

Paz, paz, pazzz.

The last one's hands went up begging with terrified eyes full of tears for his life, sleeves, shirt, green trousers, a young body soiled with excrement, he dropped his rifle from fear, his trembling smile was unable to speak; five of them reached him, ten monsters more got closer to him, twenty surrounded the circle of stunned silence; he could not breathe the words, he did not know the ancient language at that moment, he knew it before, before he had seen the deformed monster, before his eyes had suppressed the weight of the victims, how absurd it was that he could not remember the language. Casimiro entered into the eternal center, the filthy navel of all of them, the repetition of the eternal sacrifice of the fouled, pissed on, sweat-soaked, agonizing, insulted man, two hundred eyes stared at him.

"I have . . . have . . . tttwoo . . . chilll . . . drenn . . . I have two children!"

"I had one!"

Paz. paz. paz. paz. paz. paz.

> pazpazpazpazaz.pazpazpaz.
> pazpazpazpazaz.pazpazpaz

pazpaz . . . paz.paz.pazpazpaz.

The green uniform, the white sand, and the red blood formed the picture of the new revolution, a contribution of the young man who was marching down the hill.

The night had been the dead man's wake and had covered the entire landing field five miles from Mathis. Burning pain kept the wounded man half-conscious and complaining that no one loved him when the wheels touched the dusty ground. The binoculars had followed the plane since it came out from the white moon, which regarded the scene impassively. His finger wiped the grime from his eyes which again became a way to spy on the crew. Two men got off; his right arm motioned for the other one to run; they spoke and took out a man who could not walk; they seated him beneath the plane, his body fell forward on his face, the other two talked with their hands and then the taller one ran off. The scientific eyes sat down to wait.

The wind went through his hair, his legs rose and fell like pistons that made his heart throb, his arms, with his fists clenched, struck the empty space that shattered before his running body as it headed for the barrio. He passed the first of the neighborhood's houses, the clinic's skeleton, he ran and ran, he almost reached the Anglo district; he stopped and wiped away the sweat with his sleeve, he cleaned up his face as best he could, he ran. He started to walk as calmly as possible. He now saw the house from where he was. He shattered more space, he arrived falling on the stairs, he got up, knocked on the door with his knuckles. The feminine body came at the sound.

"Is Doctor Logan there, please? My friend is seriously hurt, please, Doctor Logan."

"He's not here."

"Where is he? He has to come. My friend is dying."

"He's at Fernando Rodríguez's. Do you know where he lives?"

"No, take me there, help me please."

"All right . . . it's that . . . OK. Wait for me."

The vultures kept watch over the cadaver; they contemplated it, hungrily, with their strong beaks they ripped the green uniform, tossing aside bits and shreds; the birds penetrated the naked chest exposed to the air, snatching pieces of flesh, they pushed the smooth, almost beardless face from side to side, as if wanting to tell it that he no longer mattered; they began to eat it, in an hour and a half they had devoured the eyes, they had opened an amusing round hole in the nose that looked like a tunnel of cartilage, and they had separated the cheeks, the lips, the mouth was opened and they pulled on the tongue that stretched to the right elbow. A noise made them take off like a black cloud only to descend again upon the body.

Pistol Man awoke when he heard the police car approaching; the magnificent eyes saw five men lift the body that struggled against them; four got in with the one who could not walk, they got into Rodríguez's police car; the tallest one stayed with the airplane: . . . Rodríguez and Logan, with these bastards; they certainly won't be forgiven for that . . . After the car left, he waited fifteen minutes and went down the other side to where his police car was parked. He didn't go to Logan's office because he had already seen all he needed to know to be convinced about the whole matter.

When they ask for permission and kiss the hand of the great father on the sun's currency, they come to the pyramid that is believed to have existed in the valley of the ancient empire, the valley that is be-

coming a monolithic block of wretched and unfortunate starving creatures that drag themselves along the highways of the ancient nation;
the peak has snapped; it has been broken off by the interests of capital, it floats above the foul-smelling block, watered with the flesh
sacrificed by the rhetoric of the god chosen by the holy family. Tlatoani,
excreter and divulger of authority, lives there, no savage questions
his right to stroll through the national palace with his testicles in view;
this year he had a special auditorium built on the roof of that place
that is said to belong to the people, all the old leaders have come to
this new place to offer homage to the nation's political god; they have
all come except one.

"Señor Presidente, an urgent message has just arrived from the
North."

"Read it, please."

"Yes, Señor Presidente. 'To the President of the Republic and sacred
and honorable tlatoani of the glorious homeland.' "

"Get to the point! Get to the point!"

"Yes, Señor Presidente. It says: 'Casimiro has received more
weapons. He attacked a small exploratory party. He killed them all
brutally, I await your orders. General Pacheco.' "

"That's enough, it doesn't matter who it is; they're worthless . . ."

"Señor Presidente, I have more urgent news, in Copilco and in Tlal-
pan . . . there have been several demonstrations . . . several people have
died . . . they say that the police relied too heavily on force and that . . ."

"First call General Pacheco and then tell Pedro to come here . . .
leave me alone now . . . These bastard animals, fucking animals, why
don't they just calm down? . . . What can I do to better their lives?
If they don't stop coming to the capital, what do they think? That we
can solve all their problems here? What miserable creatures, they still
expect a miracle, don't they see that there won't be one because we're
a pack of condemned beings, we can't change, we and ours, two dis-
tinct worlds born of the same mother and cohabitating in an incestu-
ous relationship. I hate them and I hate myself for being one of them
and for making them believe that I am theirs, bastards; this time they're
really going to pay for it; Casimiro, I wonder if you know who your
father is, and you bastard Indians who don't belong in this advanced
city of the future, I'll give you a licking; like children crowding around
their father you come to find protection, now, for believing that you're
more than you are, you're going to pay me. Poor things, they tell me
they're born deformed, with two feet on one leg, with too many fingers,
without ears, without noses, without jaws, that many of them crawl
through the mud and the shit, they eat dogs, snakes, dead people,

184

they're animals that lend each other their wives, their daughters and their sons, but there are millions of them, they're starting to invade places where they shouldn't be, in Chapultepec on Sunday millions of them, disgusting, diseased, ugly, stinking, come to fornicate in the woods, they roll in the dust, of course, and they're fornicating while the children are playing on the ground, runny-nosed children, the children live off the snot from their noses, that's why they walk around with their noses overrun with green snot, that's what they have to eat, they keep it to eat, in the woods I saw many males talking, sometimes they barked, I went up to them, they had a naked female there, on her hands and knees she was swaying the dark wet hair of her inflated parameter; there were ten dogs circling around her, she licked their nipples, shoulders, legs, neck, head, she sucked on the one who was in front of her until he exploded in her mouth, the one that was behind her sent a jerking massage to the semen-covered target, the other naked ones licked the virgin's body waiting their turn with the sensual goddess; more males arrived, they were talking with the ones who were waiting and they joined the line, I saw all of this, I don't know how long I stayed there . . . I walked, I walked until I came to another group, but now it was men and women of all ages, they were laughing uproariously as they watched the males fornicating with the females, as they watched the men jerk off, the girls put sticks in their vaginas, as the women kissed each other, as the young boys fornicated with old women, as the girls licked the testicles of men with grotesque bellies, everyone was running about, others were dancing, some were stretched out on the straw mats, others were piled up in the mud. They weren't completely naked, some wore ties, another a fine hat, another a belt stuffed with money, one woman had on a fur, another one wore a diamond necklace, a woman was urinating and she put one-peso coins in her vagina, a man had a golden wand in his anus, a woman had a gold watch hanging between her volcanic breasts, another man wore the keys to a Continental hanging in his pubic hair; they saw me, they called to me and came up, they offered me what they had, I felt my feet take a step back, they moved quickly, my body turned and flew with the air . . . I don't remember how I got home that night . . . but that proves that they're animals, a bunch of primitive ruffians. It's been many years now . . . I don't remember how I got . . . ."

"Señor Presidente . . . Señor Presidente, they're burning the neighborhoods in the north of the capital, the poor people are marching toward the center of the city. They say they're coming to the main square to visit their president, that they're going to build a village here."

"Burn their damn shacks, they won't get here. Where's Pacheco? Burn them. . . !"

"I remember, oh yes, comadre, it was horrible, don't you remember how you could see the light of the fire from here?"

"Poor man, that night it was Pistol Man's men that threw gasoline, they say they left a can full of gas under the motorcycle, and that's why there was such a terrible explosion."

"Not only did they burn his motorcycle but they broke the office windows too, they almost burned his consulting room; it was just lucky that he was there."

"He called the firemen but they refused to come, they didn't say why, just that they couldn't get there. The front yard was like a battle zone. Don't you remember, comadre?"

"Oh, God, it's as if everyone connected to us is damned; like that nice doctor, with his long red beard, he didn't hurt anyone. I was surprised by the way he spoke Spanish, like a little parrot, really, they say he was born in one of the barrios in California, that his mother was Mexican or part Mexican, it doesn't really matter, but how it used to make me laugh when I saw that red beard moving up and down when he talked, he spoke like a little parrot, he loved our ways."

"He was more of a Chicano than some who are born Chicanos. I was there when Pistol Man came in the morning, he came very innocently as if he didn't know anything; he told him that people didn't like him, that the Chicanos wanted to get him out of town, that we had burned his motorcycle. I got furious. I was so angry that I started to scream, you can't imagine how I was, comadre, you just can't imagine. Fernando Rodríguez had to calm me down because I was about to start slapping him."

"Fernando's really doing a good job, even though Pistol Man hates him because Fernando points out to him all the injustice he's done, he still respects him. And Fernando is right that we shouldn't be so easy going, we have to get tough, comadre, don't you think?"

"No, Fernando. Why would I want a pistol?"

"Don't be a fool, they burned your motorcycle; you think that they're going to stop there? If the motorcycle doesn't convince you, then it'll be the office, and I think they're even capable of setting you on fire."

"Don't be such an alarmist."

"Take the gun."

"I've never used a gun in my life. I don't know how to use it!"

"Outside, I'll show you how."

186

"Where are you going?"

"Margarita, he wants to give me a pistol."

"What for?"

"If they know you have a gun at least they'll think it over before they come to burn down your house. Don't be fools! There are times when we have to get tough."

The backyard remembered the wars between the two eagles; then it had packed thousands of bullets that sometimes came packaged in a cadaver. The pile of dirt lost its shape with the impact of every synthetic pellet that bored in with its purple casing. His two hands fired in unison, fearlessly, simply guided by the armed doctor; he felt comfortable with the handle in his sensual hands, his arm around the neck of his mind gave him the sensation of a strange power, to snuff out a life with the finger of an intelligent hand that had never felt stirred by that force.

"How does it feel?"

"It's heavy."

"You'll get used to it."

"Yes?"

"Michael, I'm going. You keep the gun, practice with it; I'll tell them not to come looking for trouble because they'll find it."

"OK . . . goodbye."

Alone, with the sharp wind, he stayed with Tloni. His new companion made his fingers feel strong wrapped around its torso. . . . How heavy you are, you cold thing, instrument for perforating objects . . . But what am I thinking? . . . silliness . . . Fernando is right, I need the pistol to protect myself . . . but I can't believe that they want to kill me . . . of course they want me out of town . . . but to kill me . . . I'm a fool, those bastards . . . gringos. They're gringos in every sense of the word, they're gringos . . . and if they are capable of killing me? . . . But why? What the hell have I done to them? I have nothing to do with them, I'm even willing to help them, is it worth it? . . . maybe it would be better to get out of here . . . let some other idiot come and put up with the abuse . . . fuck . . . Why? I'm walking, the blackened white shoes stepped up, how long had passed: . . . I need new shoes . . . the man went through the kitchen, into the bathroom; his hand put the pistol on the back of the toilet; he lifted the lid, opened his fly, the foaming sound of the piss hitting the water erased him from existence. The man who did not exist for himself wandered through his own house unseen by anyone, invisible, the objects saw him; the window softly closed its lids as the night brushed against the house's eyes. He peered into the boy's room. He had fallen asleep sprawled on the little rug, he covered him. . . . Jason . . . Shane . . . He quickly went to the kitchen, his eyes saw the brandy, his hands opened the bottle, he drank the stream of liquid, choked, then he caught his breath, he swallowed again, he waited two minutes, five, he drank some more, calmly, unseen, he went to the living room . . . he stopped, drank gulps of alcohol, he left the bottle on the table with the magazines, he watched Margarita asleep on the sofa in soft blankets, he knelt down beside her and watched her.

"Margarita, Margarita."

His hand caressed her between her legs.

"Michael, what? . . . what? . . . oh, no . . . no . . . I don't want to now, no."

"Margarita, I love you. I want to eat you, Margarita, let me eat you, Margarita."

His mouth kissed her; she didn't move, their lips came together again. His hands removed her dress; it fell to the ground on her shoes; her bra and panties were added to the pile of clothing. His penis's wildness in his brain made him suddenly take off his clothes. He kissed her, trembling with feeling, her breasts against his chest; she didn't respond, he lowered her to the cold floor, he took down the blankets and put her warm body on top of them, his tongue licked her whole body; she said nothing.

"Margarita, you're teasing me, if you didn't want to, I know you would have stopped me before now, I know you, sweetheart, sexy, my lover, you're driving me crazy!"

A faint smile escaped from the feminine mouth. The masculine finger rubbed her damp, warm, full clitoris, now they had both given in; she said nothing. He put himself in front of her beautiful face, her mouth saw his penis, intensifying the wetness of her vagina. She looked up at his erect penis, she opened her mouth. The feminine hand brought it down between her lips, she sucked it as she stroked the skin of his testicles. He licked between her legs that rose and kicked toward the ceiling.

"I'm almost there Michael, please, Michael, I'm almost there, now, now, Michael, I'm coming."

He got in front of the hair-covered thing he loved so much, his hands buried between the cushion and her buttocks, he put his tongue in; he licked her, he tickled her with his tongue, she raised her legs until she grasped her ankles with her hands, she remained that way, tense and calm, she came hard and sharp, she rocked on the arch of her back.

"Now Michael, now noww, noww!"

His head withdrew from the beautiful woman who was rocking on

188

the soft blanket in the middle of the floor in an old house, between the Chicano neighborhood and the town of Mathis, Texas.

He was caught between several worlds, trying to give something to every one of them; that night he got home mentally exhausted, on the verge of giving up. Three people had come to his office. They came in without knocking, and sat on the desk. The one who started to speak remained standing. He didn't believe what he had heard, he was tired of all the shit that they wanted to make him do. . . . I can't please everyone, I'll do my work and participate in everything I can, but I'm not going to prostitute myself in the image they've created for me. I won't do it; I don't give a damn, I won't do it. First these pseudo-erudite bastards tell me I'm not worth shit as a professor and then my own people come and start in on me that I'm not Chicano enough. What the hell do they want me to do? Walk around campus wearing a sign that says "I'm a Chicano"; what a pain in the ass they are; I am too, but in my own way, I can't make myself what they want. . . . His hand opened the door not wanting to make noise, but the children came to greet the father who did not want to be a father at that moment; he took it as best he could. He went to the kitchen where Leticia was fixing two drinks.

"Here, you look like you need this."

"Thanks. Go to sleep now! I'm tired, we'll play tomorrow."

"Oh, Daddy, I wanted to show you the book I bought today. Please!"

"All right, but then you go to sleep."

"I'll make you another one."

The three voices began to laugh, they fought, laughed, grew calm, the sound of the light announced a fearless darkness as the children asked to kiss their mother.

"I'm coming, I'm coming!"

The two sat down on the sofa in the living room. She looked at him to tell him that the children were in bed. Eutemio knew it, but the night's importance was that he could write; it had been a while since he had been able to sit down calmly to write, but he was bothered by what he had heard: . . . Damned students, if you don't give them what they want they fuck you . . . I can't satisfy everyone, that's all . . . Maybe I should give it all up . . . no . . . that would be the easiest thing . . . I couldn't do it . . . I have to write . . . but I don't have anything . . . anything that really says anything . . . it doesn't matter, I'll try and see what comes out . . .

"Eutemio, what's the matter?"

"Nothing. I'm just in a bad mood; I'm tired; it seems as if I'm getting nowhere. I feel useless, I have no self-confidence, everyone at the university has taken it from me, even the Chicanos."

"What? What did they say to you?"

"Nothing. I don't want to talk about it. I'm going to my room, I want to write and no one lets me, that's what gets me furious, no one lets me and no one takes me seriously, I want to write, that's all, let me, Leticia, please, let me. Excuse me, I was thinking about what I told Michael; I'm a coward; I told him that I was a coward because I wasn't doing what I truly want to do, I was thinking about him when I came home, he's courageous . . ."

"But it's cost him a lot. Do you want that to happen to us?"

"No! It's just that he's done what he wants to do. I want to write and you don't take me seriously. Now don't get mad, just let me alone, I told you I was in a bad mood, I think, I don't know . . . Ohh! Let me alonnne!!"

"I just want to be with her. Leeet meee! Didn't you hear? She's mine, the girl is mine. Take all the horses, burn everything, and kill all the rich privileged ones, their time has come, now leave me."

"Casimiro, I don't agree with what you've done; think it over, what did we want? Not this, Casimiro, think it over."

"No, Marcelo, we can't stop now, now we have to get everything we can, principles can't stop us now, not now."

"The army will see the smoke, they're very close, Casimiro. Casimiro, listen to me."

"No, under no circumstances. I've been very patient with that thief and murderer. You know what I want you to do, go into the town and take out all the inhabitants and set fire to everything, all the houses, the shacks, everything that the poor people have. Tell them that if they don't turn in Casimiro it will be worse for them, and it won't be our fault, but Casimiro's."

"With all due respect, Señor Presidente, but the people will react violently against this order, we have to consider all the possible consequences. I think that once we locate Casimiro it will be easy to take him. Please, Señor Presidente, reconsider your orders."

"No, as I've said, I've already waited too long, now Casimiro has more weapons, he's killed many people, the lower class protects him, and now they will have to suffer the consequences that I warned them about. Don't ask me any more questions, go do what I've ordered. Don't kill anyone; just get everyone out of town and burn it. That's all, that is what is required at this time."

"Yes, Señor Presidente."

The army trucks announced their presence in the narrow streets of the village where Casimiro was born. One thousand soldiers surrounded the place. People began to leave when they heard the presidential proclamation. Panic swiftly spread; several windows and bottles were accidently broken, one was thrown near the only tank stationed in the square where everyone was passing by; the tiny bullet flew through three bodies which then displayed holes from which sprang blood that the men, in their panic, stepped in. The shots came more frequently, more accurately, the soldiers on the outskirts of the town aimed toward its center, the bullets crossed, hitting more civilians and the soldiers on the other side; the volley lasted half an hour, the bodies would not be buried because they would all be burned.

"General Pacheco, everything is ready. We await your orders."

"Shoot the prisoners, there must be no survivors in this case. No one could cross the lines. How many men have we lost?"

"Twenty of ours have died. The enemy shot from within; they didn't give us a chance to protect ourselves."

"Burn everything; let nothing remain. I don't want there to be any cadavers; clean everything, make it all disappear. Casimiro will know we're not fooling around, it's all over for him and for everyone with him."

They had not found him in two days. The little girl was playing in the garage near the clothes and the old newspapers, looking for clothes for the doll that her father had given her. Her little body sat on a pile of newspapers, pulling on the rags, she was looking at the doll; her daddy, she loved her daddy, why doesn't he come to kiss me at night? . . . Daddy doesn't come to play with me any more, or to tell me pretty things, a lot of people have come to visit Mommy, a friend of Daddy's hit her, I wasn't afraid, Mommy hit him too, he said bad things, I don't like that man; my baby is cold and I'm going to make her a dress, there's a lot of clothes here, I like this for my baby . . . The girl was playing in the pile of clothes, she pushed aside the papers, the cockroaches ran underneath the damp rags, she wasn't afraid of them, a shoe was sticking out, it had a foot, a leg, a strong smell reached her nose . . . doodoo, someone made doodoo; I'll tell Mommy; poopy, someone is asleep in my clothes, clothes for my baby, poopy, someone made doodoo . . .

"Mommy, someone made doodoo in my clothes! Mommy a shoe, a leg is sleeping, it made doodoo, Mommy!

She ran crying to tell her; she told her mother that someone was sleeping under the newspapers and the clothes in the garage. Her mother got up, the idea suddenly struck her, he used to stay in that corner when he was sick, when he was crying, when he didn't want to see his wife, his child, when he was afraid of what he was, when he was ashamed of what he'd done, when he didn't want to see Mommy, when, like a child he needed help. . . . It was the second time that he'd been sick when we'd found him there in the garage, I remember that he wouldn't go into the house because he was ashamed, he begged my forgiveness, he was like a child. He told me that I should leave him, that he was worthless. Why did this happen to us? We never expected it, I never expected it, he didn't either, he thought he was very strong, as if nothing could beat him, as if he could conquer everything. But now I know that under those old newspapers, there underneath those cheap old clothes is where he is, but now he's not hiding, now he can't hide, I know he's dead, I know that the shoe, the leg that made doodoo is his . . .

"All right, then where's the cadaver? These damned druggies are a waste of my time."

In time Pistol Man went through the living room, the kitchen, and the garage.

"Did you call Logan?"

"Is he coming here?"

"This poor guy has been dead for several days. How come no one looked here?"

"No one thought he could be in the garage, under all this junk."

"Who found him?"

"The little girl."

"How nice, what a damn shame for the girl to have a father like this stupid idiot, he didn't even show enough thoughtfulness to leave his daughter a pleasant memory."

"Shit, it really stinks!"

"Hello, Pistol Man, how are you?"

"Fine, Logan, fine. I want you to sign this certificate first, if you want to see the cadaver, it's over there, dead from heroin."

"But why did you call me? He was already dead. I've told you not to call me."

The body, relieved of the newspapers and old clothing, gazed at the blackness of infinite space that reformed in another place, in another time, in search of another opportunity; the extension of the doctor's ear was implanted in the naked, yellowed chest.

"Dead. But why didn't you call another doctor? Doctor Brown is the one in charge of these cases, isn't he?"

"No, his type doesn't come to places like this, even for a dead person. They know that you're here."

"Look, Pistol Man, the next time there's a case like this one, I'm not coming. Your assistant told me that a boy was dying, that means that he's alive, not dead for two days. If you call me, Pistol Man, I won't come. Be careful, Pistol Man! Be careful!"

"You're the one who should be careful, you know what you're doing, you know that you're walking on thin ice."

"Don't threaten me, Pistol Man. I'm not afraid, so don't threaten me!"

Pistol Man smiled as he watched the furious doctor head for the street where Rodríguez's police car was waiting for him. He ran quickly to get to an emergency operation, a boy was being poisoned by a stomach full of the green bile of an acute peritonitis. He was furious because the dead man had stolen the minutes necessary to open up the boy. He was led quickly as Margarita wiped away the sweat of his rage.

"Michael, calm down, please!"

"That dead bastard, it's Pistol Man's fault. If this boy dies it's because of Pistol Man! I don't have enough time. I can't be in two places at once. I'm so stupid, no one listens to me, no one cares about this little boy's life, look, he looks just like my boy. Look, Margarita, don't you see, he's got fine hair just like my son! Margarita, it's my son! My son can't die! Help me, Margarita! Someone help me!"

"Michael, Michael, what's the matter? The boy, you have to help the boy!"

"He's ready, now, let's go."

"Are you all right?"

"Yes, let's go, they're waiting for me."

In what spontaneously became an operating room, the doctor, masking with anger and with veins the blood that made his heart beat, that filled his lungs and gushed to his brain, approached the child, who had become an objective case for saving; that was all the modern magician was thinking. His hands did what was necessary, with their own strength they quickly opened the side; the ocean was yellow and green, to be shipwrecked now was death, he was afraid of losing him, but he kept penetrating the infected fat, they sucked up the puss, the bile, the poison that spilled out over the intestines, the boat was in serious condition; the ocean was rising and covering the surface of what he saw, the boy was breathing shallowly as he finished closing the purple leak, the minutes marked the end of the struggle; the cihuatitas were waiting, not with as much desire this time, they were even rather sad and tired of the meal's repetition, bored with the permanent struggle, with the closed cycle, open to the infinite, until the disappearance of man known as man, the cihuatitas were watching the last sigh which was now unnecessary but that the doctor in vain, wanted to register; to believe that he would play again; death was too real, how many who are alive have seen a human being die, how many have discovered a dead person, how many have had their hands full of the blood of a dead person who is still warm? What is it that previously made him move, that gave him his smile, and his voice for speaking? Why does it have to be this way? The white mask went outside, it walked to the little hill full of lead, the piece of whiteness sat on top, the night birds were singing, the toads inflated their croaking into space; the doctor was alone again, an invalid, and alone.

He was alone, outside on the street, the sky was dark, the moon and the stars were there too, he was looking into space, to the unknown, the novel was in the garbage, the garbage men would throw it out tomorrow: ... Black René is right, the literate are idiots and ill-mannered, he was joking but nonetheless that's how I feel sometimes; but I'm staying, I'm not leaving, I've decided, I'll stay and fight back, I'll take on my supposed superiors. Jokes hurt, when they're true. But it can't be true; these bastards at the university are doing the same thing that they did to me in high school; it's just the same, they make me feel inferior, all their theories, but I realize that I know everything that they know but I express it differently, in other words. They have humiliated me, I feel stupid, they almost made me believe that I wasn't smart, they made me feel weak, like an invalid among them. I have to play their damned game, but we have ours too, actually we can't even talk to each other seriously, there is no real dialogue, maybe it's better, because maybe if there were we would verbally destroy each other. We all play the game, but maybe Black René is right, but this man who wrote the novel is also right you don't have to be afraid of words, you have to understand them; his first novel, maybe the bastard was crazy but he also tells the truth, he's that way too, eschatological, but hell, we've all got a prick or a cunt. Maybe Black René hasn't used his? Or maybe he's used it too much? Black René is a real professor but he's more like a capitalist for denying it. Damn it and me because I feel like I'm stupid, like I'm not intelligent, that I'm worthless, but he certainly isn't stupid, and he's intelligent, and he's really worthwhile. How lucky that guy is, Black René is lucky. But I'm a stupid jerk, a man who's not worth anything, at least I hate, and love, and I admit it . . .

"Eutemio, Eutemio, where are you?"

The professor stuck his hand in the garbage and took out the novel. "I'm here, Leti."

The mail comes and goes, through it, in it, run good words and bad of the system in crisis. Our letters travel in it, letters of news in the town where Mommy and Daddy live, the brief news of friendships, of forgotten friends, opened letters make them live, they interrupt our life for a moment, for an instant they live in our memories, in our minds: . . . I have to write to _____ , to _____ . Today I got a letter from _____ , he says that everyone is fine . . . Letters from the past come to break the daily routine. The mail goes toward the future, with its confirmation or negation of plans, with the outline that we want to impose on the trajectory of our life. Sometimes we feel happy or angry when we open the envelope; but then at some other time we forget it only to remember it later. The mail brings endless junk, advertisements that insult us, that threaten us, that try to incite us, that insist that we buy, contribute, remember, join, call, write to someone or something. Lost time, lost energy, but we always open the envelopes, forcing ourselves to discover the secret of what is hidden in the white, the brown, the blue of the information's overcoat. Nonetheless, like Pavlov's dogs we wait for the mailman. . . . Wasn't there any mail today? . . . It bothers us to hear that there was none. Opening the mail she was waiting for him with a letter separated from the past.

"Michael, you have a letter here from Pato. Don't you want to know what he says?"

"No, I don't care what he says. I'm not like you, always spying to see if the mailman has come."

"Look, it's important. He doesn't want to send us any more medicine because Hales no longer wants to OK it."

"We'll look for someplace else then."

"He wants you to call him. I think you should talk to him. Tell him to send us another doctor."

"You talk to him. I don't want to talk to anyone."

"Stop mourning for the boy, it wasn't your fault."

"Of course not, it was that bastard's fault."

"Look, if we had another doctor that would never happen. You could always stay in the office and the other one could make house calls or go wherever they needed him. I've done the books and for the first time we're ahead. We could pay a doctor to come and help us."

"But who's going to come here? Do you think we can find another crazy like me?"

"Talk to Pato, maybe he knows someone. What's more, the clinic is opening in two weeks and you're not going to be able to take care of everyone, it's impossible, don't make us coax you. Please, talk to him."

"OK, I'll talk to him, but first I'll have a drink."

"Don't drink so much, Michael."

"Now you're going to start with that."

"Talk to him; that's all."

"Did Teresa leave already?"

"Yes, and that's something else that's bothering me. Teresa isn't in good shape. Pistol Man is making her life miserable."

"OK, tell her that if she can't come, fine. We can find somebody else."

"But we have to keep her, don't be so cynical."

"The girl is having a very hard time because she's working here, she's just making problems for herself and for us too. Pistol Man is furious because sometimes she stays quite late."

"Michael, call Pato, OK?"

"Señor Presidente, a telephone call."

"I told you I don't want to be interrupted when I am with the young lady."

"It seems to be urgent, sir."

"Bring me the telephone. Yes, who? What? When did this happen? How many gringos escaped? Send me the prison director. That man had told me that they were ready for them if the gringos tried to free those pot heads. No, not the police. I want the army to surround Lecumberri. And if any Yankee gets near the place, they should grab him and let him have it. They shouldn't shoot, unless it's absolutely necessary. How is the jail? Did they kill a lot of our men? All right, as I've said, if any Yankee gets near the place, take him and give him a beating and then interrogate him . . . We'll have to let them go, but it will cost them . . ."

"Hello, Henry, Manuel Lemus and five men are prisoners; they're being interrogated but they refuse to say anything about Logan. Just that he helped them when Manuel was wounded; they don't want to implicate him."

"But Mr. Evans, I saw him with them, he went to get the one who was wounded and they took him to the office. I saw it. Logan is mixed up in this business. I know, Teresa, my wife, told me that he has a gun and undoubtedly he has a lot more of them."

"Watch him carefully. We'll make a decision soon and I'll let you know. Goodbye."

"Michael, what's new? How are things going?"

"You know very well how things are here. Why don't you send us more supplies? Why doesn't Hales want to authorize it, Pato? You're not the Pato I used to know; you've become one of them. Here the Chicanos need medicine and you sit comfortably in your big house, very well dressed and sticking it wherever you can. Remember where you came from, Pato."

"Hey, calm down, what the hell's the matter with you? I know how you're doing, I spoke to Cody."

"How are they?"

"Michael, why don't you come back? Come work here. You can continue your work here. There are thousands of Chicanos here too. Don't be a fool, come with us."

"How are they?"

"Cody is working, the children are fine. They always ask for you. They want to know when you're going to come back from this job. Cody told them that you had to stay there until you finished. The three of them are waiting for you, they pray for you every night. They need you, Michael; you should go back. Cody seems to have become very religious. She and her mother go to see the evangelists. They pray a lot."

"I think those women will turn my children into religious fanatics."

"Well, why don't you go back?"

"I can't now, I'm doing something that you all thought was impossible. I can't go back until I finish what I started. Listen, you say that you can't send me more medicines, but what if I sent you the money with every order?"

"That would be perfect; there wouldn't be any problem."

"OK, then, Doctor Martínez, that's what I'll do. One other thing, I have too much work, I can't do it all; I can't handle everything that has to be done. I simply need someone to come and help me, send me a doctor. You don't have to even answer, there's no one as crazy as I am who would come to this place."

"No, wait, I think I know someone who would be willing to help you for a while. I'm not sure, but I can explain your situation to her. She's a very adventurous girl, just like you, Doctor."

"Don't start joking. Seriously, do you know someone?"

"Like I said, I'm not sure if she'd be willing to go there, but I'll talk to her. It doesn't bother you that she's a woman?"

"I don't care what she is, as long as she's a doctor. If you can convince this doctor tell her to come in two weeks, at the latest. We're going to open the new clinic. If I don't have someone by then, I'll have to tell people that I can't take care of everyone and that some of them have to go find another doctor in the nearest town."

"What, can't the other doctors there help you?"

"Those bastard gringo doctors don't want anything to do with poor people. Only if they can pay in advance. If not, they don't treat them. And even when they do see them, they mistreat them. It's almost impossible to explain the atmosphere of this place; you'd have to come here to feel the mistrust, the silent discrimination that exists. In this town nothing is said but everything is done and everything is felt. It's something that I didn't think could still exist in this country. I thought it had been all taken care of in the 60's, but it wasn't, nothing has changed, nothing has changed for anyone."

"Michael, I'll do everything I can to convince this girl to go there. Look, Michael, I have to go, some friends have just come. But send me the medicine order with a bank check and I'll send you the stuff as soon as possible. Don't worry, I'll talk to the girl. Goodbye, Michael."

The click of silence shattered the space and the buzz confirmed that no one was listening to him.

"Thank you very much, my doctor friend. Of course, I'll expect the new doctor in a few days, won't I?"

The angry disillusionment was controlled sufficiently to put the telephone in its cradle. The doctor drank another beer.

The pulque ran down the cliff following the two young men who were abandoning their position, being unable to obey the frustrated orders of the drunken commanders. The mestizos were returning to the dry lands that no one wanted, they were returning to struggle for their survival. The rifles had achieved nothing, they had no ammunition, they couldn't kill, they had no strength or power with which to negotiate, they were deserting what had, at first, seemed glorious. The road smelled of manure, they followed it, disappearing into the red sunset for which so much blood had been spilled. His hand scared the flies from his lips, the furious sprawled body reached for the rifle, he tried to get up, falling down he realized that they were leaving him.

"Let them go, leave them alone, Marcelo."

"Cowardly bastards, traitors, we can still fight, don't go you Indian bastard cowards!"

The echo repeated through the ravines, it was repeated through the cliffs. The legs were dragged through the stones, they tumbled down, they rolled until they stuck in the branches of the thicket.

"Go on you sons of bitches! We don't need you, you mother fuckers! Don't come back or I'll kill you myself!"

"Compadre, calm down, no one can hear you."

"They're all going, compadre, just a few are staying. They're all afraid."

"They're going in search of their families, Marcelo."

"They burned our houses, the fucking government burned our houses. But, why don't they get angry? Why aren't they crazed with rage? They're going off with their tail between their legs. Why don't they get angry?"

"They're afraid of power; it's not like it was before. Marcelo, we're fucked; we've lost. We have no weapons; we can't get weapons. Lemus has been in jail for two weeks; he'll never get out and we'll never be able to get weapons."

"Compadre Casimiro, don't talk like that. We can still fight, we can still win."

"It's not like before; the only thing we can do is to run and try and save our necks. Here, compadre, have another glass of pulque to chase away your anger and to help you sleep."

"No, I can't sleep now; I'm always awake; I feel as if I had been awake forever. It's almost as if I couldn't die because I'm always awake. I don't know what sleep is like anymore. When I close my eyes I rest but I don't sleep. I hear everything, compadre, I hear it all very clearly."

"Yes, I'm like that too. I hear everything, but I don't hear anything."

"It seems that we're always waiting."

"How sweet the earth smells, compadre. What a wonderful aroma the manure has, as if it wanted to shelter us."

The white coat sheltered the doctor, numbed by the long night; Fernando's eyes explored the new building. He did not believe that they had finished it without an incident more serious than the destruction of a few windows and the loss of the motorcycle; the policeman walked through the rooms that would soon welcome the sick multitudes. Here the modern magician would perform his cures, practice his magic. Here too the cihuatitas would reside, helping the toci magician. Here a new advance would begin, here the ultimate plan would be consecrated. The stupified doctor, lost in the rooms with his mouth open, could not, at this early hour of the morning, believe in his own brain, that the place was ready.

"Well, here it is, Doctor Logan. How do you like it? I told you it would be worth it to wait a little longer. This office is solidly built, well constructed."

"Thank you very much, Gabriel."

"But, Doctor Logan, instead of being happy you seem very sad. Come on, Doctor, cheer up, have a little drink of tequila to celebrate the end of the job. Cheer up, Doctor, try not to look so sad."

"Michael, do you want to go?"

"No, Fernando, I don't want to go. I haven't slept well, last night I couldn't sleep. A strange odor was bothering me. What's more, it seemed as if I could hear everything so clearly, so exactly. I heard everything, Fernando, but I don't think I heard anything. It frightened me, Fernando. I got up and went to sit in the kitchen with the light on. Have you ever felt that way, Fernando?"

"Look, Doctor, come here, I want to show you your office. Cheer up, Doctor, try and be happy."

"I am happy, Gabriel; I'm just a little tired. Let me have that drink."

"That's it, hey, guys, come drink a toast to the clinic and Doctor Logan! The town wants to have a party to celebrate the new clinic. Are you willing, Doctor?

Tall, slender, dark, she entered the luxurious office of the doctor in charge of the emergency medicine section. A man whose reputation was made on the accumulation of money, a modern office, a rich guarantee of a cure, someone who charges enough to make you mortgage your house guarantees the defeat of the illness. An appearance to deceive, to defraud the patient, to make him believe that he is in competent hands. She always regarded this display with mistrust, the ostentatious ones did not like her, she knew that the corporation had earned thousands for the four of them; now he wanted to talk to her, she knew that this one was an exploited and manipulated Chicano, whose name got them thousands for the supposed programs that the corporation promised. She knew that they had bought a jet that they claimed to use to go to Mexico to help the poor. She heard that they used it to fly to emergencies. The plane was equipped to save the sick and to abort the illegitimate children of the rich. The corporation had contracts for one hundred doctors to provide service in the company's hospitals, or in hospitals with economic problems, hospitals that were on the edge of bankruptcy. Once they had a foothold there it was easy to convince the owners, through blackmail, bribery, and other of the profession's silent methods, to sell the hospital. She knew that the corporation was growing, she knew that Hales was a man whose goal was to become a millionaire in ten years, a man who was willing to do whatever was necessary to fulfill his dream. She had heard it said that he truly did want to help the poor but that right now he could not because he had to make the money necessary to permit him to dedicate himself to the unfortunate of the world. Hales and Doctor Martínez were the same; they talked about the latest toy they had bought, they talked about their wives' Mercedes Benz or Jaguar, about the diamond necklace that their wives wanted. They talked about the nurses they had laid, the hotels where the best prostitutes were to be found; they talked about the beach houses they had bought, the sailboats that they had sold in order to buy a bigger yacht for trips to the Bahamas. From time to time, in an irritated tone, they spoke about a patient they had to see because one of their staff of doctors was unavailable. The faithful patient waited for the doctor's call or visit; but when these doctors called or visited the frightened patient, they would put on their show and afterward leave the hospital to enjoy the good life, they went out to eat, to drink, to dance, to fornicate, laughing, they returned to their beach homes, or their country place or their apartment near the hospital, laughing, they remembered that they had to save lives the next day and therefore they should not drink too much because it would be unjust to vomit upon those they were going to save. She knew about all this; she knew what these gods of medicine really were; she saw Dr. Martínez's spotless suit, custom made for his body; the doctor's smiling self-confidence greeted her as she sat in the leather chair. The male eyes undressed her.

"Are you interested, Doctor?"

"From the way you describe it, it seems as if everyone who graduates must want to go to Mathis. However, you don't have to tell me about that area because I'm already familiar with it; it's redneck country. What you've told me about Logan makes him sound like the most popular man in town, but, as I said, I know the place. You say that he needs help, I think you're right, but haven't you also said that what Logan is doing is difficult. Do you want to sacrifice me, Doctor Martínez? Why? Because I'm a woman? Because I don't meet your requirements? Why are you offering me the position in Mathis?"

"Doctor Kastura, I think that you're the right person, with the physical and psychological characteristics to be successful there. Look, Doctor Kastura, Logan needs help, he's going to open a new clinic, nothing fancy, it's a clinic in which there'll be many patients to see every day and he can't do it all. You're like him; in one way he's a rebel and that's very important for where Logan is. In addition, I believe you have demonstrated a social conscience, what Logan prac-

201

tices is social medicine. I think that's a mistake but that's what he does."

"Is that why you don't send him medicine?"

"I don't have anything to do with that; it's the organization that makes it difficult for him to obtain what he needs. Excuse my frankness, but who are you to doubt my commitment to the struggle? I serve as an example for Chicanos; the young people who see me will want to be like me. I'm one of the best doctors in my field and everyone respects me. I fight for the cause in my own way and you shouldn't insinuate that I don't."

"Look, Professor Morenito, we're not insinuating anything; we just tell the truth as we see it. You identify more with the gringos than with the raza. If you don't change, we'll screw you."

"That's how it is, Professor Morenito, you have to be totally committed, or you're out."

"Just a minute, I've been at this university for two years, and ever since I arrived everyone in the department has tried to stomp on me, and from the beginning you also have tried to control me. But I'm telling you that I'm not going to prostitute myself for those pedants or for you. I'm not going to deform myself to conform to the image of the professor that you want me to be. I won't do it for anyone or anything. And as for my commitment, you know quite well that they've tried to crush me precisely for my ideas, precisely for my commitment to the struggle, and not just the Chicanos' struggle but the struggle of all those who are oppressed, manipulated, and exploited. Don't come here to tell me tall stories, come to the point. Don't try to scare me, that tactic doesn't work with me."

"We think the grades you gave us are very low and that you aren't taking into account our social status."

"I take everything into account; those grades reflect what you deserve after I have studied each case objectively and subjectively. I told you from the beginning how you were doing in class, some paid attention and came to talk to me and I helped them, others waited until it was very late. And that's how it is, now it's very late. If you're not satisfied go talk to the Theoretical Roman or the Dean of the college."

"We won't talk to those bastards."

"That's right, one of them thinks he's still in his own country and the other one makes us wait three hours."

"Listen, Professor Morenito, we're not satisfied with your answers."

"Be careful, Professor Morenito."

"Of course I will, and you pay attention."

The five left banging the door against the wall. . . . Son of a bitch, how they fuck everyone; my damned head really hurts. I don't feel well; I'm weak; it's high blood pressure. It's because I ... they've all got me scared, I don't feel well, I feel tired, I just want to sleep ... Let me see if I can write something about this blasted foreign world, about the world of the Anglos, the Chicanos, the blacks, yellows, reds, women. We all want to be one, but we don't realize who the real enemy is, I've said it before. How my eyes hurt. Come here little typewriter, I want to make you talk. But how will you talk? In perfect Spanish, acceptable to all, so that they will say that everything is properly expressed, well written, or will you talk the way I want you to, you'll show my hatred and rebellion against the standard, the norm, the acceptable. If you don't do it their way they'll fuck you. How are we going to do it, little typewriter? How are we going to do it?

The large mouth, hanging open with fatigue, entered the bedroom; she stood in front of the mirror and began to take off the clothing that covered the Midget Turtle's monolithic mammaries.

The Almost Artist was nauseated contemplating the ball of fat, his tobacco legs took him out of the room.

"Where are you going? I want to talk to you."

"I have to finish this picture and I'm going to be up very late; I don't want to bother you."

"Wait, I want to talk to you about your attitude to Professor Morenito. Look, you mustn't defend that primitive, irrational creature who doesn't know anything and who shouldn't be at the university."

"I don't want to talk about him; I want to finish this; you don't understand."

Naked, the Midget Turtle shone with the cream that she applied to her body; the clever fat female knelt down, letting the Almost Artist see her sex. She turned, offering herself to him.

"I don't want to tonight; I want to work, I tell you."

"You! When you want to! The truth is you can't do it anymore!"

"Don't start up again; there are other things to do. Anyway, you told me you were very tired. And I am too."

"But, why? You're at home all day scribbling."

"Thank you for your support. Is that what you think of what I'm trying to do? It's scribbling to you? But don't you realize that you live off of artists' scribbling?"

"I didn't say that."

"You didn't say it, that's what you think. You should have more respect for me. That's all I'm asking, respect for my work."

"But how can I? You've been working on that crazy thing for three years."

"That's how I work, it's my method of working."

"What you should do is have more respect for me for supporting the whole family."

"Shut up! Tomorrow I'll go and look for work. I'll forget about everything and work myself to death. That's what you want, for me to drop dead, to get lost."

"Leave, there's the door. Go, and see if you can survive without going running to your intellectual faggot friend who turned you into a charleton and a drunkard."

"Shut up!"

"You're the one who should shut up. I don't know how I've been able to stand it. And another thing, that professor that you defend so much is going to be kicked out; I'll do everything possible to get rid of him. Let him go to some high school in a Spanish-speaking neighborhood; he should work with those people and not in the university!"

"You're crazy; I pity you. You hate him because you're afraid of him. Actually, he has more of a right to be there than you. Go to bed, you make me sick!"

"And you, go make sketches for your stupid little pictures."

"Now look what you've done, the children have woken up."

"Well, go take care of them, that's all you're good for. I have to get to sleep because I have an eight o'clock class. So that you can eat!"

The furious mouth slammed the door against the wall whose scream joined those of the children.

The old man walked step by step until he got to the eucalyptus in front of the house. His hand kept his body from falling against the tree. It was hard for him to breath, his chest felt like a stone heaving forth the clot, a red trickle came from his mouth; he spit again.

"Damned cancer is killing me; that's what I have, cancer, but nobody knows it. I can't even talk, all I can do is think, that's how we end up, useless, but thinking."

The rag-like skeletal body shuffled over, exhausted, to sit down. The loud conversation between the man and the woman made him turn his damp face. . . . But why won't he let her go? She should go; she's a young girl; she wants to dance, enjoy the party. And she's worked hard for the clinic's success, she should participate in the celebration; there's nothing wrong with that. Pistol Man is very jealous; he thinks all the other men want to take her away from him. Of course he thinks that way because that's how he is. He should either accompany her or let her go by herself. That bastard is stupid, he's a bull with the mentality of a donkey. Poor Teresita. He should let you go because if he doesn't I'll stand up to him. Don't yell, I don't like it, don't yell in front of the children; they don't know anything. Shut your mouths or old Balibí, even though he can hardly get up, will go punish you, sinners, worldly sinners. Don't hurt my little children, don't harm my little angels. I'm going to get up and go let them have it for being shameless and scandalous. My legs, these legs don't want to do anything, they don't help me, come on, lazy legs, they're good for nothing, let's go, come on, there we go . . . His body was able to stand erect supporting itself . . . I feel so good that I'm going to see if I can get myself in the mood to go to the party, I have to go, it might be the last one in this life. . .

. . . Sometimes I think it's my last moment in this world. I'm tired. I have chest pains. Oh, thank God I have my wife, she's my salvation, I can escape all my troubles with her. Leti will help me physically and mentally, she knows how and she'll save me.

"Leticia, it's late, shall we go to bed?"

"First I have to feed the dog."

"I'll do it, don't worry, I'll take care of it."

"Thanks, I am terribly sleepy." . . . He's doing everything tonight. I know what he wants but I'm so sleepy. I know I'm going to say no. He's going to get mad, but I don't refuse him all the time; I love him but I just can't now, I don't want him to touch me, I want to go to sleep. He's going to get mad and he's going to make me feel guilty because I'm going to say no, I don't want to. How I wish he would understand what I feel. Poor thing, he's done everything to make things easy for me tonight, he cooked, washed the dishes, put the children to bed, he even fed the dog, he must be crazy to have me, but I just can't . . .

His arms let her go, his hand caressed her breasts, telling his loved one that he cared for her, that he needed her.

"Please, wait for me."

"I'm so sleepy, Eutemio."

"Don't fall asleep, please. It's early, go to bed but don't go to sleep."

The beloved felt her body sink into the mattress; she read the newspaper, the articles easily erased the desires of her husband who was locking the doors, making the house safe. Masculine desire arrived hard, at the bedroom; she was peacefully sleeping.

"Don't fall asleep, Leti, it's early, please, Leti, don't go to sleep."

His hands pulled down the covers and lifted the nightgown that covered her naked body. His lips kissed her legs, her buttocks, the soft back of the woman he desired.

"I don't want to, Eutemio, I'm very sleepy."

"But why, didn't you know that I wanted you tonight? I did almost everything so that we could go to bed early."

"It's not that I always refuse you, but that's all you want. Why don't you love me for myself and not for my body?"

"Leti, I love you for the woman that you are, the whole woman that you are, not just for your body. Please, Leti, let me put it in, you don't have to do anything, just let me come inside, please, Leti."

"I don't want to, I don't feel like it, I don't want you to touch me; it's not that I don't love you but I can't tonight; please understand, Eutemio, try to understand. And don't make me feel guilty as if it were my fault; come to bed, hold me in your arms, love me like this, tonight love me like this. Don't get angry."

"I'm not angry, why should I be? You have every right to say no to me."

"OK, then let's go to sleep."

"I don't want to sleep, you knew what I wanted and what I didn't want was to sleep, I'd rather go work in the living room."

"You always do that, you get mad and you go sleep in the living room. You're angry, aren't you?"

"No, I'm not."

"Yes, you are, Eutemio, don't lie to me."

"Yes, I am, I'm angry because I can never tell you no. I always depend on you. I practically beg you to give me what's yours, and yours only, and you can decide when you want to give it and when you don't. Don't you see that I'm your slave who can never say no to you, when you seduce me I can never refuse you, I can never say no, I can never say no, even when I'm sick I feel capable of sharing an orgasm with you, capable of doing my part for you. Don't you understand that I can never say no. Now when I want you and I know that you don't want to make love, what should I do? Go into the bathroom and masturbate? What should I do, hold on until you're receptive, until you allow it? I'm going to work in the living room; I have papers to grade, go to sleep, we'll see each other in the morning."

"But come sleep with me, Eutemio."

"Yes, I'll get into bed when I finish. You want me, you'll have me there. Just let me finish with these essays."

His frustration got out of bed and went into the living room to finish what he had to do. . . . Sometimes I hate my wife, there's nothing I can do except put up with it until she'll have me, damn it, sometimes I wish I had two wives, three, four if the others are sleepy, but I only love my Leti, and when she lets me, my Leti, I'm going to give it to you, in your mouth, in your vagina, I'll flip you over and give it to you from behind, I'm going to stick it in until you can't take it anymore, I'll rub your clitoris with my finger until you let me suck on your vagina, once you get there you let me do everything I want to, at that point you're completely mine, Leti, wait until then and you'll see how you give in to me. Leti, I love you, I love you and right now I hate you, I hate you right this minute!

"Eutemio, aren't you coming to bed?"

"Yes, I'm coming right now; I just have one more paper to finish."

The clock moved, showing through its glass facade Rodríguez's arrival at the preparations for the celebration. The clinic was a minimal scene set to achieve what was most necessary, but which would be used to the maximum. The police car arrived with three kegs of beer and Rodríguez who got out and went into the cement setting. Masculine and feminine bodies were preparing the room.

"Hi, Rodríguez, how are you doing?"

"Gabriel, how's it going?"

"Everything's set, I think the whole barrio will be here. How's the doctor?"

"Fine, Margarita told me he was getting better. He was very depressed but she said that he was better now."

"He's been working very hard, and the separation has affected him a great deal. Has he called his wife?"

"I don't know."

"Hey, Fernando, what about the gringos, what's Pistol Man going to do?"

"Nothing. I spoke to him and some others in the community and they told me they wouldn't do anything. It seems as if their attitude has changed. Now they agree that the clinic should go on. Pistol Man said that it was a good idea to have a clinic in the barrio and, according to him, it would lighten the work of the Anglo doctors."

"What work? If we go to them it's when it's already too late. And then the bastards send us home to die surrounded by our loved ones."

"That's what he told me."

"Don't trust him, don't trust anyone. Be careful about what they say."

"Well, I don't know, but maybe you're right."

"OK then, shall we have a beer?"

"No, thanks, I'll wait until tonight. I don't really feel like one. Everything's all right here, isn't it?"

"Yes, everything's fine, see you later."

The police car pulled away, it ate up the road, repeating the trivial nature of that subject, but it did what was necessary to arrive at the moveable place where bearded Logan was to be found, with his crooked cigar and stained farmer's overalls; the doctor greeted him and they stopped in the middle of the dust. The smile coming from beneath the doctor's hat communicated a change; he seemed happy, a smile planted itself on Rodríguez's lips as he drew up to the conquistador of germs.

"Michael, what's this? When did you buy it?"

"This morning I got up and Margarita told me that today was a day of rest, that no one was coming to work today, that the office was closed in order to open the new clinic. She gave me five hundred dollars and told me to go get a motorcycle. And me, the kid that I am, I took them and I bought this."

"You went to Corpus?"

"No, I bought it from the boy who works at Henly's gas station."

"He sold it to you?"

"Yes, I offered him four hundred dollars and he took them."

"Bah, it seems like they're changing. Maybe they're accepting you, gradually accepting you."

"How is everything going over there?"

"Fine, but don't go and help them. Let them make the preparations. They're doing it for you."

"Go ahead, Doctor, I'll follow you, I'll follow you to the ends of the earth. Go home and rest. Everything is ready and the party starts in two hours."

"Well, all right, let's go back to the office and we'll have a few beers."

"Ends of the earth, my foot, don't you realize what the young man is saying? Casimiro, wake up, he says that the compañeros on the other side are still sending weapons, but that the struggle is going to be concentrated in the South."

"We have to fight here, not in the South; don't be a fool, compadre, our land is here."

"But we can return well-armed with new men who can attract many more."

"How many days will it take us? . . . the roads are teeming with federal troops. It's impossible."

"There's nothing else we can do; our only salvation is to go south in order to get ourselves armed again. That's all, compadre. We've

208

lost everything, except the balls to start all over. If you don't go, Casimiro, I'm going alone."

"But where are you going?"

"To the South I told you."

"Where to?"

"To Atoyac de Alvarez."

"No, Marcelo! You're crazy, that place is a myth!"

"The boys say that's where he came from."

"No, Marcelo, that boy is the devil; he wants to trick you, it's all lies! Atoyac de Alvarez doesn't exist and it never has, it was invented by the government to justify its atrocities against the people of those regions. Don't let him fool you, Marcelo! It's the same thing that you saw on the hill when Manuel came. Marcelo, don't go! Don't follow him, Marcelo! Atoyac de Alvarez doesn't exist!"

The bus passed quickly through the open fields of the lost region that they wanted to reclaim as their own, it passed small trees, mesquites, stones, little streams and prickly pears that grew close to the highway. Faces change when you go from the city to the country — they look more rested, wrinkled by work and time, but less tense. They were all talking and looking out the window at their land. She saw the way in which the bodies adjusted to their surroundings as they climbed on the bus; they knew that there was a law that guaranteed the right to sit down wherever you wanted in a bus, nonetheless the driver told them where they were supposed to sit. At first she took no notice; she thought the driver was a gentleman showing her a seat. She remarked that the Chicanos sat on one side and the Anglos on the other. The doctor's feminine body suddenly got up and went to the Chicanos' side. The driver's eyes saw her in the overhead mirror and condemned her. The doctor had moved to a seat next to the window, in the other one there was a smiling old woman.

"It seems as if everyone knows their place except you."

"But I don't see why they have to segregate themselves."

"In these parts we, I mean people — Mexicans and gringos — haven't changed. It's the same bodies, the same faces, that have lived here for hundreds of years; the only things that've changed are material things, food, beer, that's gotten better, even the laws have changed to improve man's condition. But just look at this bus; everyone is in their place except you. Do you understand? There's still a lot of hatred around here, hatred that's been preserved for centuries, rancor that can't be easily eliminated."

"Does everyone live that way?"

"A lot of people live with an illusion, a dream, the very few that live the truth are men and women of action."

The young woman watched the road pass by, the crosses of a cemetery full of wooden crosses, flowers, brilliantly colored ribbons, happy and poor, entered the window. It was an isolated pantheon, decorated in a special, impressive way; it was not abandoned, people always brought flowers, there was someone in charge of cleaning the graves, of fixing their pictures of the Virgin, it was all earth, dust, and sand, no grass grew there, there was no water, it was brought in pails just to keep the faces of the dead moist. The old woman crossed herself and started to pray with her rosary.

"Señora, I've never seen a cemetery like that one."

"That's the Chicanos' cemetery, our cemetery. The gringos have a very pretty one with green grass, big tombstones, mausoleums, very pretty and expensive. Ours, however, is more human, the dead have someone to talk to. Doña Pachita cleans every day, she decorates the tombs. Our cemetery is a place where the dead continue living, where those who stayed can go and visit and remember those who have gone. I like it better than that cold thing that the gringos have."

"It's a very pretty place."

"But why do you say that? What do you know about those things, what do you know about death? You're too young to know about those things."

"No, I believe that death is with us at every moment, it's part of our lives; it's like two pretty girls who play together. They play with dolls, they're always trading them, they never tire of playing and the dolls always go from the girl of death to the girl of life, the two pretty children play through eternity."

"What you've said is true. Look, we're getting there."

"Where?"

"To Mathis."

"Oh yes, to Mathis."

The bus stopped in front of the post office, the only two-story building in town. The people walked down the inflexible streets that spurted with hot sand when the feet dug into their solid being. The disoriented doctor was hypnotized by what she had said and the tranquil weight of the old woman who was erased from her sight in the liquid air. Her intelligent eyes moved in a circle around the shadow of the fabulous snake-animal on whose head, on its trifurcated painted crest was depicted the birth of an egg without a yolk, laid by a rooster and incubated by a toad seated on a bed of manure. The three-tailed

210

creature with his shining eyes beneath the crown that decorated the mortal phenomena, could not be destroyed without a mirror to capture it while avoiding its glance. The doctor studied it, the malign inversion of the trinity that adorned the entrance to that building where the guardians of the treasures ruled the city. . . . What is that? What a strange thing . . . the head rooted to the anachronistic image moved back. Her body felt the chest of the surprised man who had been looking at the ground.

"Be careful, watch where you're going!"

"Excuse me, sir."

"Be more careful around here, watch yourself."

She crossed the street taking notice of the gas station. . . . I'll ask for Doctor Logan; there's a taxi parked there; maybe they'll take me to his house. Martínez didn't give me the address, he just told me to ask for the doctor, that everyone in town knew him. But what a strange thing to have that relief over the entrance to that building; how funny. Henly? I'll ask here. It seems to be closed, but it's just six o'clock . . .

The woman went to the window under the sign. A fat man was eating a sandwich. She felt hungry. The cup of coffee was emptied between the lips of the fat man whose hand furiously gestured her to go. The doctor tried to open the door that seemed to invite her to come in. . . . People are kind . . . As she entered he screamed so hard it made her drop the valise that almost toppled over.

"Get out, don't you know I don't like to be bothered between six and seven o'clock!"

"But . . ."

"Beat it. There's no gas, not now!"

"But I don't want gasoline!"

"You don't want gas? Then what do you want?"

"You have a taxi. I'm looking for Doctor Michael Logan. Where does he live?"

"Out there with the Chicanos."

"Can you please take me."

"I won't go there. I don't want anything to do with greasers."

"Can you take me there or not?"

"Not me. The boy will take you. And listen, do me a favor, don't come back here."

"Thank you."

The doctor put one buttock next to the other on the seat of the old and dirty taxi driven by a young man who said only one thing that the doctor's mind barely caught.

"The Chicanos are going to get drunk at a party tonight."

. . . I'm thirsty . . . I feel damp, dirty, I have to take a bath when I get there . . . I hope this is all worth it . . . Well, if it doesn't turn out, I can go back to the hospital . . . the people in this town are very strange, they all look like Germans, Henly, fat, red-faced, blond, ugly and that decadent, grotesque thing they have on the facade . . . it's an anachronism, this town is in ruins, it's practically deformed; the ancient creators of this disintegration create categories in the realm of the mind. Logan must know this, he knows history, he's not ignorant. Of course, one is aware of one's perspective, he realizes how rich life is. That's why, that's the reason he's here with these disgusting people. The houses that passed by the window were all the same, the Germans are evil, but they too had suffered a great deal earlier, but now they're the ones who have achieved power. That proves it, it's the system that's destroying us. My skirt is soaking, I'll have to change.

"Change the keg here in this corner. Look, here, man!"

"Gabriel, a woman is here looking for the doctor."

He went out, curious. He saw Henly's truck quickly leaving, then he saw the tall woman's dress, he noticed the drops of perspiration that ran down the two lines that led to her smiling mouth which was trying to hide her nervousness. From in between the suitcase and the medicine kit she held out her hand. Gabriel took it, realizing that she looked directly into his eyes.

"I'm Doctor Kastura."

"You're a doctor?"

"Yes, I'd like to speak to Doctor Logan."

"You want to speak to Doctor Logan?"

"Yes, that's what I said."

"Well the doctor isn't here now. He'll be here soon. If you'd like to wait. You've come at a good time. People are arriving for the celebration. Look, this is the new clinic. As a doctor this should interest you. Please come in."

"Thank you. I think I'll wait outside here."

"As you like, excuse me, they're calling me."

Her eyes had already noticed the four short paws that supported a piece of wood on top of themselves; she sat down long before finishing her conversation with the gentleman. The bodies arrived, they passed by her, sometimes they looked at her, sometimes they went by her without seeing her; the children were the only ones who noticed her, they turned their heads as they passed, they forgot her as they entered the decorated clinic. She was alone among all these people who were celebrating, celebrating a happy event: . . . Happiness is always celebrated; they killed their prey, they are going to eat meat, everyone would eat meat, it had been a week since they had eaten it. The naked men did not wait until they got to the cave. All the families gathered. The fire was lit, the barely cooked meat went to their stomachs; they celebrated with laughter, the children played, the men felt their stomachs grow excited; the women stretched out on their backs resting from the ingested meat. A man saw his friend's erection, he touched him. The other man laughed and told him to stroke it, and he began to move his hand quickly up and down the man's penis; everyone laughed, the children played and the women rested; another man came over to see why the two others were laughing; the one with the erection could stand no more, he did not know what to do with his desperation, the one who had come over lay down on his stomach next to him to get a closer look, the one who was rubbing the penis began to slap his buttocks, the one with the desperate erection did the same thing, now he was on top of the man who was lying down; he began to rub his erection, now his hands parted the other's buttocks. The hard penis entered the naked man; everyone laughed; the children were playing, the tranquil women were observing without any embarrassment; the other men were talking among themselves and looking at each other; now another had a hard penis; this man was near a female whom he had lie on her stomach and he entered her; the pain made her scream; she tried to escape but the other men and women were surrounding her; now the female was on her back, the penis was ready to burst; her legs opened and the man fell between them. Everyone laughed; the children were watching; the women opened their legs, the men fell upon them, one woman finished with a man and received another one, a man was with one woman and then he moved on to another one; everyone was laughing, everyone had eaten and played, happily they got up and walked to the cave . . . The women, the men, the children, were walking to the clinic, how happy they are, they are going to celebrate, they are going to celebrate their good fortune; everyone, all humanity was celebrating their good fortune . . .

A police car arrived raising the dust; everyone waved, shouted, called out, everyone surrounded the car; they took out the two men; they entered and the shouts of "Viva Logan!" awakened her to the reality that she saw as a dream.

. . . Logan, Logan is here . . .

"The Professor has now arrived."

"He's here? Well, tell him to step into the laboratory so that he can see that our literary criticism rests on a precise, proven, theoretical base. Tell him, tell him, that I'll wait for him in the laboratory. That way he'll be able to see the necessary implements with which to construct a book of literary criticism. Look, tell him to come here; he's going to be impressed and you'll see how easy it will be to convince him to come over to our side; you'll see how he'll want to learn to build books of criticism."

The Midget Turtle left the laboratory. She opened the mouth that she carried above her enormous breasts and, yawning, she entered the room where her gaping mouth was the first thing that one noticed about her.

"Oh, I'm so tired! Oh, hello, Professor, the Theoretical Roman is waiting for you in the room. Please come in."

"Thank you, Midget Turtle; why did you call me here?"

"You'll know in a minute."

He saw a little reading lamp in a corner casting a mysterious, erudite, dark, impressive light that intensified the atmosphere of a laboratory of historico-social context. The Theoretical Roman's hand pointed to the luxurious and comfortable sofa. The smiles of those from the betrayed, long nation were constant.

"How are you, Professor? I'm pleased that you have come."

"Yes, well, why did you ask me here?"

"Well, we want to discuss a plan that we have. We want to establish a program of Long Nation Studies; there are a number of people who are interested. Of course we, the Midget Turtle and I, can direct the study center. We will study everything about the Long Country and we'll publish a volume of essays every year. They'll be our own essays; this way we can help each other and bring more prestige to the department; this way we'll also be able to attract more individuals who are interested in this theme and we can even invite scholars and writers from the Long Country to come here to teach; this, of course, would bring a great deal of prestige to the department."

"Well, the idea seems very good; why don't you do it?"

"We want the department's official stamp of approval and we thought that if you were to declare yourself in favor of the idea at a meeting of the executive committee, everyone would vote for it."

"I don't know why you need my support; you have a lot of self-confidence, you should be able to convince the department easily. Furthermore, you don't need official permission from the department, do it on your own. There's no problem with that, anyway it's your duty as professors to create groups like that. And I'm very surprised that you've asked me to participate. Are you sure you want me to be part of such an erudite and all-knowing group?"

"You can learn about our methods; you could study how to construct books, how to assemble a scientific literary study."

"I don't want to learn how to assemble books."

"And when you're ready, we'll let you publish an article in our journal."

"And who's going to pay for this publication?"

"Well, we were thinking that because of the enormous prestige that would accrue to our journal, perhaps the department could pay half or even all the costs of its publication. If we had departmental permission it would become an official departmental project and I would be able to request the money."

"Oh, now I'm beginning to understand your motives. Look, I prefer to request funds for other things of more immediate importance, things that are directly related to the Chicano movement, for example. I see your train of thought, if I give my support you can say that a Chicano approves of it. That's how you'll try to calm down the Chicanos, and that way everything will be administratively legal. Why don't you think about establishing a center for Latin American Studies, or a center for Chicano Studies, or inviting some Mexican or Chicano scholars and writers?"

The Midget Turtle's smile turned into guffaws from her tobacco-stained mouth.

"Oh, don't make us laugh. We don't want to invite any more of those people. Look Professor, I respect them and all, but I still find them somewhat, how should I put it, a bit 'spontaneous,' 'instinctual,' rather 'primitive,' for us to want them, it's enough that there are a sufficient number here, we don't want any more, it's enough."

"Look, I'm going. I don't want anything to do with what you're planning; I also realize another thing; with the articles that you would publish in that journal you would be able to guarantee the Midget Turtle's tenure at the university. You should keep in mind that it's very difficult to turn a university into the Long Country; if you could you would bring everyone from the Long Country here. You're not really committed to anything; you just talk a lot about the Long Country. But the struggle isn't here, it's there, that's where you should salvage your culture. You are very similar to the Chicanos and that's what you refuse to accept. I understand it perfectly, you're afraid of losing your culture. That's why you should ally yourselves with the Chicano movement, there are many Latin Americans who sympathize with the Chicanos' situation, and they're still Latin Americans, but they're not intellectual snobs who are only committed to a national literature, they're not men and women who in the name of literature, of criticism, want to put themselves above the creators, or be more than literature itself, and that's the worst thing, that you believe you are superior to literature itself."

"We already know quite well what you think, if things don't go right for you, don't blame us. We wanted to help you, remember, we're your friends and we tried to help you."

"Yes, of course, thank you for your help; if it's like it was before I know what to expect. You've taught me one thing, and that is that you can't trust anybody in this world. Especially not you, people who really don't belong here. There are a lot of Latin Americans better trained than you and who have an awareness of what's happening in the Chicano world."

"All right, if you don't want to cooperate with us . . ."

"Think about a center for Latin American and Chicano studies and we'll see. Goodbye."

"You'll never have one here."

"Don't tell me that; look at what we've achieved."

"The doctor's right, we've all worked together, without your help, and now we have this clinic."

"Don't butt in, Rodríguez, this has nothing to do with you."

"What do you mean, I have a lot to do with what's happened."

"Oh yes, you're also involved in the rest of it."

"You know very well that I support everything that Logan does. You're the one who's opposed to all this."

"Listen, please calm down tonight. We have to celebrate, drink a few beers, and enjoy life. Please, Pistol Man, Fernando, a few beers."

"I don't oppose the clinic, what bothers me is the influence Logan has over people, especially over Teresa. That girl has become rebellious; she thinks about doing impossible things, things that she can't do. That business about wanting to be a nurse, now she even talks about becoming a doctor, these are impossible dreams, she can't do it, she's not capable of it. And it's your fault, Logan. You're to blame for her thinking that way. Watch out for yourself, Logan, watch out. And you too, Rodríguez."

"Look, Pistol Man, if you don't like what I'm doing now you can just fire me."

"No, continue with your work. I'm not going to bother you anymore. Have a good time!"

"Hello, Pistol Man. When did you get here? You came in very quietly. What a miracle!"

"I'm going now, Gabriel."

"Doctor Logan. Excuse me, but I forgot to tell you that a Miss Kostrura or Kastera, I don't know what her name is, she's here and she wants to talk to you. She says she's a doctor, but she doesn't look like one, she's very thin and tall."

"She's what?"

"She says she's a doctor?"

"A doctor!"

"I certainly remember that, old man, I remember how he shouted for joy, he shouted at everyone that now there was another doctor to help him, and that was before he saw her. Do you remember how he shouted 'Where is she?' 'Where is she?' Gabriel quickly introduced her and the doctor almost went crazy when he saw her and he couldn't believe that it was true. That's how it was, wasn't it old man? Yes, that's how it was, he met her with all that happy celebration going on, with lots of music playing: they were playing polkas, tex-mex style cumbias, music from the North, mariachis, everything. And the doctor was really dancing, and the lady doctor too, she mixed in easily with people, the doctor danced with Margarita, with Teresa, with all the ladies, the girls, he lifted up the little girls and boys and they danced the corridos together and he made them laugh; oh, what a good time the doctor had that night, didn't he, dear? He kept shouting that there was another doctor for the clinic, that he couldn't believe it, and he kept asking the lady doctor if she was joking and if she had really come to stay. He shouted this out from every part of the room, sometimes someone would be on the other side of the room and he would still shout it out to them. What a wonderful time people had that night, and how they all drank beer, and everyone ate, drank, everyone was in love, there wasn't even a single argument. It seemed as if the only one in a bad mood was Pistol Man; after he met the lady doctor he asked Teresa if she wanted to go and she said 'no,' because she wanted to talk to the lady doctor. Well, Pistol Man got furious and he stormed out like the devil. Don't you remember, dear? He got so red, that ugly old man, don't you remember, dear? No, well, the party went on until dawn; we had to go at about two, I really didn't want to, it was you who was falling asleep on your feet. But I talked to Doña Gertrudis, and she told me that the doctor got drunk and they had to take him home, practically carrying him. Who took him? Well,

Rodríguez, Margarita, Teresa, the lady doctor and old man Bilabí too. Don't fall asleep on me, dear, please, I haven't finished yet, don't go to sleep, it's just eight o'clock and you're already set for bed, come on, my dear. But Doña Gertrudis also told me that the doctor cried a lot that night, he was delirious, and everything he said was about his wife and children. He was calling for his wife and children, and he complained that they weren't with him. And he said ugly things about himself, he said that he was an egotist, a fool, a man who never should have been born and God knows what else. Doña Gertrudis told me that he vomited and got it all over everything, he was saying that he wanted to go back to his family, that he was afraid, and some other things. He fell asleep, crying. Oh, my old dear thing, I get so tired of you, you're like a mummy, sitting there nodding off. But what a party it was, I still have it clearly in my mind, I'll never forget it! It's as if it were yesterday. Don't you think my dear, don't you think so? As if it were yesterday."

The little black animal multiplied by eating and destroying the cells that kept the oxygen in the lungs; the tumor became a deeper purple and it grew bigger, producing a sharp pain in his chest. The living skeleton could hardly get up that morning, but his granddaughter's arms, his grandchildren's and Pistol Man's helped him into the police car. Logan and Kastura were waiting there to give him oxygen and drugs for the pain and the exhaustion. They wanted to stimulate his appetite but he no longer responded to any medication. Logan had suggested taking him to the hospital in Corpus but the old man Bilabí had violently refused. He wanted to die at home, with his family, it was natural. That morning before he got up he had spoken to all the children. He had explained to them that he was now very old and that the watch that he had in his chest had broken and that it could no longer be fixed. He told them that he had to go to a far away place, and that he would always want them to look for him in their dreams because he would be there, waiting to play with them. He also told them that every time they looked at the stars, that he would be there looking at them and making them think about him. He told them to be well-behaved and that he would always take care of them from where he would be. The children seemed to understand. He asked Teresa and Pistol Man for the impossible; he didn't make them promise anything, he just told them that he would be very happy if, before he went, he could see them married. Tears came to the old man's eyes; he was looking at them, he realized they made a lovely couple, and he realized that he loved Teresa very much, and that he had developed a

218

certain affection for Pistol Man. He never mistreated the children or Teresa, and since he had come to live with them he had never actually threatened them; he certainly had a foul mouth though, but when he had been young he also thought he was very macho. He was breathing the oxygen, looking at Doctor Logan, Doctor Kastura, Margarita, Rodríguez, Pistol Man, and at Teresa, dressed in white; he squeezed her hand, she patted his and she felt his pulse slowly fading away until it was gone. At eleven-thirty that morning old Bilabí was waiting for night to fall so that he could play in the children's dreams and walk among the stars making everyone think and remember.

"Look at the sky, Daddy, it looks like milk."

"Yes, it does. Can you count the stars? Start with that one."

"Eutemio, don't be like that, he'll get frustrated. Look how he is, trying to count the stars."

"Let him be, he believes that he can and that's what's important. Did you talk to Cody today? Did she tell you anything about Michael?"

"Well, he still hasn't written or called. She knows what's going on there from Kastura. She writes to her. It seems that Michael is lost in his work; she says they have a tremendous amount to do."

"Doesn't he send her any money, Leti?"

"The other woman, Margarita, sends her money every month for the family, the house."

"Maybe I'll go and see how he is. Of course, we could all go."

"Well, I don't know, we'll see. I still have a lot of work at the university. I also have some stories that I want to finish and send off to see if I can get them published. I want to publish an article or two so that the intellectual scholars don't complain."

"How are your classes going?"

"Fine, for me they're going very well. These two classes are very good, the students aren't just interested in taking up space and getting a grade; they want to learn and they're willing to work. Classes are going well, in general it seems as if things are calming down."

"Do you think they'll give you your promotion?"

"I've done everything I can, I just have to wait, but I don't think they'll change their minds."

"Daddy, Daddy, I counted them all!"

"How many stars are there? Tell me?"

"Oh, I forgot."

Pistol Man left the house very early. He went to the office. Fernando had already arrived. The door was open; his body entered carefully. He looked around, no one was there, there was no one in the back room.

"Fernando."

Pistol Man's body sat down, his hands pushed aside some papers, his back reclined in the chair.

"Why are you here so early?"

"I came because I need two boxes of ammunition."

"You've been practicing."

"A little bit."

"It seems like the clinic's doing well. All the Chicanos go there. And they have meetings at night too, don't they?"

"Yes, Logan and Kastura give talks. Doesn't Teresa tell you about it?"

"She doesn't say anything about what she does there."

"Why do you get mad at her? You shouldn't be so jealous."

"I'm not jealous, and don't you tell me that I am."

"OK, OK, don't get so angry."

"Listen, the people over here aren't very happy with those meetings that you've been having, especially with what's happening on the other side of the border. Things are getting worse there. And they say that someone from around here is trafficking in arms and that there's also drug dealing. People don't like those meetings; what's going to happen is that they're going to start asking to have the streets fixed, to have sidewalks put in and everything else. Don't start with that because it will go badly for you. That's what I tell you; things are going badly, and Logan is getting me more and more angry."

"He doesn't do anything to you, Pistol Man."

"He's involved in a lot of things; you don't know it but I do; I have information that you can't have!"

"He never leaves Mathis."

"Yes, but a lot of people come from far away to see him. And he's sending money to Corpus. That we know."

"Margarita sends it to his family. She doesn't send very much money."

"Yes, of course, but doctors make a lot of money."

"If you think they're making a lot of money, you're crazy, Pistol Man. It's jealousy that's driving you nuts."

"Don't start you bastard or I'll let you have it."

"I'm going, sometimes I think you're a hopeless case."

The old swollen calves smelled of alcohol; old Costa was snoring with the mask over his nose. He had entered the clinic in a wheelchair; his varicose veins had burst. The doctors had warned him, they had told him quite a while ago that he needed an operation. But the old man insisted that the medicines that Doña Gertrudis prepared for him were doing him good and that in time he would get better. Kastura was going to operate because Logan had never done the operation. The surgical gowns and white masks spread the odor throughout the room. The left calf awaited the scalpel that Teresa handed the doctor. Every vein went into the jar of water; when she finished five bloody tubes were sticking out of the red water.

"Michael, please talk to Doña Gertrudis and tell her she shouldn't let these people wait until the last minute to come and ask for help. This has happened a lot, not just with old people but with children, you have to talk to her and if you don't I certainly will. Margarita, you can talk to her, you know her better than everyone else."

"Yes, let me talk to her. Although I think she can be very helpful to us."

"We agree about that. But she shouldn't send them to us when they're practically dying. Please, explain it to her."

He had consulted three times with the department head; now he was waiting for the direct call from the dark-skinned people's president. He knew that the situation in the urban areas was getting worse day by day. No one could believe what was happening in that country; it seemed as if everything were controlled. The demonstrations in the workers' districts continued and more peasants arrived in the city every day. The urban guerrillas had organized the districts in a different way than before. They basically followed the established methods but what was new here was that they joined together the children who were abandoned with those who were not and then they incorporated everyone into a new family. Many of the districts were under the control of a guerrilla; the districts they organized first were those that had water wells and a supply of food. The districts were surrounded by barricades of automobiles, stones, mud, wood, anything that could be piled up to make protective barriers. From the airplane tourists saw the smoke from the bonfires that the people built to block the entrance of the army. When they landed the tourists would ask what was going on below. The officials said that they were destroying those neighborhoods in order to modernize the area. They all accepted this as something beneficial. The Mexican press did not report what was happening in these places; they wanted to keep the situation within the country. Nonetheless, some families had left and had reported what was happening to the newspapers of other countries.

The rumors started that Mexico was undergoing an explosive urban crisis. Evans knew it all; his observers brought detailed reports of the situation. Now Evans was expecting a call from the Presidente.

"Bob, the Mexican ambassador is here."

"Good. Tell him to come in."

"Good morning, Doctor Zertuche."

"Good morning, Mr. Evans. Shall we wait together?"

"Yes."

The two bodies, without exchanging a word, saw through the window the park where children were playing. Life passed by through this modern picture, clean, tranquil. The two hearts that were waiting did not feel that tranquility; they desired it but they would never be able to have it. These days the ambassador had been smoking a great deal, his throat hurt, his voice had become hoarse. Evans had lost weight and his face looked tired. They had both often thought of telling everyone to go to hell; but they never would. They were trapped in a system that allowed no exit. The light on the telephones went on. His hand indicated that Zertuche should pick up the other telephone.

"Good morning, Señor Presidente."

"Is Zertuche listening."

"Yes, the ambassador is here."

"Very good. Evans, you must know what is happening. Your government is not taking our situation seriously, Evans. They pay more attention to the conflicts in the Middle East and Africa. Casimiro's on his last legs in the North; the army has carried out my orders; nonetheless, there are reports that other guerrilla groups are forming in Casimiro's name. The situation is even more serious in the urban zones. In addition, North Americans have led attacks on our prisons. Lecumberri is the most recent example. You send us arms, but that can't destroy the incipient movement that's developing. Also, and what is the most critical, is that you have not been able to stop the contraband of weapons to the guerrillas. What is more, the international press is starting to write about the activities of these rebel groups. The time has come when you have to stop the contraband of arms to the Mexican guerrillas as soon as possible; you'll have to prevent the entrance of groups of North Americans willing to rescue North Americans who are prisoners in our jails and finally, what is most important is that your president take a new position in reference to what is going on in this country because certain economic changes will take place that profoundly affect international relations. Good, Ambassador. Zertuche has been brought up to date and he is waiting for a meeting with the North American president. That is all, Evans."

"No, that is not all, Doctor Logan, they have also mistreated my children in the schools; they try to abuse my daughters and they don't want to fix the streets."

"I want them to at least put lights up for the night to keep the robbers away."

"My daughter graduated as a teacher and they refused to give her a job. They said she didn't dress well and she spoke English badly."

"Why don't the firemen come to our neighborhood?"

"Why don't they fix our cemetery?"

"We want better jobs or for them to pay us the minimum wage."

"The police mistreat our sons."

"They always stop and search us; and they ask us for our papers."

"I was born here."

"We came here because we know that you can help us, Doctor. We know that at least you'll try to help us. The clinic has been in existence now for a year and a half. In that year and a half it's helped us a lot. Many, many people come from far away to be treated by you, a lot come with all their things, to stay, because they feel safe here, in this neighborhood. We have discussed our situation here and in many other places and we've realized that things are bad for us. We should have a better life, we have a right to it. We came here for you to help us."

Before them stood heavy, holy, leather boots decorated with powdered sugar, the tight pants with fine silver threads, a golden skirt on top, the white silk shirt shone in contrast to the heavy jacket of gold and black ornamented with iron crosses and sacred hearts. On top of the white neck rested the miraculous doctor's red beard; his red hair curled around his virulent eyes, his wide, straight nose of a face at peace. A halo of transparent gold framed the powerful saint. The immense white wings protected his entire body. His left hand lay over his heart; in his right hand he carried the holy spear with which he destroyed the legions of the established norm: . . . What do these people want? Who do they think I am? I'm just a doctor, nothing more, don't they know that? All I want to do is help them with medicine. What have I gotten myself into? What the hell am I going to do now? What more do they want from me? . . .

"Michael, Michael, say something to them."

"What do you want me to tell them, Kastura?"

"Well, then I will."

"Yes, you do it."

"Listen a moment, please. At this clinic we can and want to help. This is what we propose. First, we have to set up a citizens' council that will be responsible for communicating our grievances to the government of this town. Also, we should all speak to the rest of the community, explaining to them our organization and goals. We also think we should request legal assistance."

She had already put the children to bed, they were very tired and they fell asleep right away. She sat on the sofa, the living room was dark; the rays of sun fell on the potted plants. She felt tired, her body was limp, weak. She looked at the medical books and she felt a warm sadness in her breast. She touched her thighs, hips, waist, she moved her hands up her breasts, lowered them to her stomach, she lifted her feet to the edge of the sofa, she began to stroke herself, she felt like crying; she looked at the pictures of the children with their father, the wedding pictures, the picture of him. She got up and went to the children's room, they were quiet, safe, she covered them and went to the bedroom, she went into the closet and touched his clothing; she touched herself, she rubbed herself. She went to the bed, unbuttoned her blouse, took off her bra, trousers, panties. She saw herself naked in the mirror, she saw that she was beautiful, with a full body, lovable, desirable, she stretched, turned around, opened her legs, she bent over, she looked at her sex between her legs, her hand went up, she caressed herself with her palm, her fingers stroked her clitoris; she stood up, turned out the lights, went to the sofa in the living room, sat down, put her knees against her breasts, her hands ran up her calves stopping at the knees, slowly she separated her legs; two hands went to her moist sex, her fingers made love to her clitoris, three fingers penetrated the opening, the other hand caressed and stroked; she felt tense, good, ashamed, hot, more rigid, now four fingers sunk in, she didn't hear, she thought nothing, she felt, she just felt, she threw her head back, the hand buried, the finger concentrating on the clitoris made her raise her legs more, she felt, felt more, and more, and more, more, more, more, mmmorrre, ay love meee. . . . She stayed like that for ten minutes, she was afraid to move, after fifteen minutes she got up, looked outside, no one, she made sure that no one could have seen her. Her naked body walked to the kitchen, she opened the refrigerator, took out a beer, she went to the children's room, they slept, she went to the bedroom, she sat in front of her dresser, she turned on the soft light and began to comb her hair in front of a photograph of Michael.

"Oh, but you're beautiful, your soft dark shoulders, look at yourself, you're the most beautiful woman in the world. You're desirable, and I get jealous when other men see you; you're mine; tell me you are, tell me that you're mine, please say it."

She was combing her hair, seated, naked, in front of her dresser, she turned her head from one side to the other so that the naked man with the hard penis would kiss her neck. He kissed her shoulder, her arms, he knelt down to kiss her legs, he put his head to her stomach, he looked up and his tongue reached her breasts. She was combing her hair, he stood up to find her mouth with his lips, she stood up; she went to the window, she noticed that the lights were out at Cody's. She turned to embrace her man; she turned out the light, lifted up the covers and threw them on the floor, she got on the bed and Eutemio followed her.

The two men pursued him, one at each shoulder, their mouths spewing their complaints into the ear of the man who was rapidly walking to the last room off the corridor. The enraged men were almost ready to hit him for his lack of a response.

"Answer, Evans. What are you going to do about this?"

"We can't allow the son of a bitch to give us orders!"

"Who the hell does he think he is?"

"Calm down, gentlemen, we'll talk about this matter in the meeting. Please, I want you to remain calm."

The three suits went into the meeting room. The voices shouted out when they recognized Evans' brains. His hand pushed them into their seats, calming them down for a moment in which order was established.

"All right, one at a time."

"The consulate called me."

"A consul came to talk to me."

"I got a call. We all know that if the arms to Mexico aren't stopped, that bastard will hold up our payments."

"My company has two million invested there."

"We've got more; we can't lose that market."

"What are you going to do, Evans?"

"And do it soon!"

"All right, don't worry, we know who is responsible for smuggling arms into Mexico. We've been investigating the case for a long time and we are almost sure that it's a man who lived for a short period in Corpus. Now he lives in Mathis where he has a clinic. However, we know that he treated one of the smugglers that we apprehended. This man admitted that the doctor had given him assistance. Later, after certain treatments that were able to convert this man into one of us, he confessed that Logan was the one responsible for everything. Now the prisoner who works at the university has been sent to another school where he has a similar position and collaborates with us. We also have information directly from Mathis; I've maintained a constant dialogue with the police. Further, Logan is organizing the Chicano population; he's inciting them to riot. Taking into account all our information, we conclude that Logan is the leader who is in charge of the group that is sending arms to the South and that he is also politically dangerous because he's become a political leader of the barrio. Now, in order to be absolutely sure we went to the Department of Health Education where they are carrying out an investigation for a workers' clinic in that area. Here is Mr. Ratree Bussarekornserivit who will give us his report."

"It's quite simple: we've talked to all the doctors in the area, including those in Mathis. All of these doctors have said that Logan has caused a series of problems; they have all refused our offer to direct a medical center for migrant workers. The principal reason is that they don't want more Mexicans in the area because they cause damage and they affect the way of life in the town. They say that this has been proven by the radical activities that Logan has incited. In addition to this they've stated that a great number of Chicanos come from very far not just to consult with Doctor Logan but to stay and live in the Chicano neighborhood of Mathis. According to the doctors, Logan continues to provoke poor relations between the Anglos and the Chicanos. For this reason they have refused to establish a clinic. And to conclude, they said that it would not surprise them if Logan were trafficking in arms in the South because he knows a lot about arms. He is always shooting behind the clinic. That is all, thank you."

The recommendations of the businessmen, congressmen, government officials, were spontaneous and almost unanimous. Logan had to be convinced to leave Mathis and he must be forbidden, by any means necessary, to deal in armaments. Everyone was convinced that these future actions would be for the benefit of both countries. That is what they all declared.

"Ratree, no one accepted the offer about the clinic?"

"No one."

"OK, I want you to offer it to Doctor Logan. This order has come from above, so there won't be any questions or comments from anyone about it. Ratree, you'll prepare the forms, contracts, and checks. Make an offer with every possible advantage for the doctor, his clinic, and the town. I'll go to Mathis to get Logan's commitment. Gentlemen, you may rest assured that Mr. Logan will not cause us any further problems."

The decision had been made by calculated, cold, and rapid means. The bodies left, attached to their own paths, when they separated, no group existed; no one would say that the meeting had taken place. The decision had been made without it being known who had originated it. These men and women were limited extensions of the powerful. Evans, angry, annoyed by what had been decided, began an automatic performance of an irrevocable process, in an inhuman frame of mind. He went to his office, he asked his secretary for what he believed necessary and what had sentimental value; he knew that he would not return to this office; he picked up the telephone, dialed Pistol Man's number, and began to liquidate someone named Bob Evans.

"But they haven't disappeared; they exist and they love you, Michael, I'm going to confess what we've done, well, what Margarita has done practically since the time you and Cody separated. We've been sending money to Cody every month and a letter explaining how you are and what's happening here. Now I think that you should write or call her. Don't be a fool. Margarita will understand; she's told me from the beginning that she didn't want to separate you; she loves you but she also has a lot of respect for Cody. She won't be opposed to it. And Cody won't wait for you forever."

"Thanks, Kastura, but I still don't want to; I don't want to because I'm afraid that this will all end. It's very simple, I haven't finished here yet. To talk to her and the children would be the end; I know that I would have to go back to them. But I can't do it; I still haven't finished here."

The two doctors finished their coffee and entered the waiting room where fifty eyes were waiting for them. Ninety patients came through the office every day; and one of the doctors was always ready to go to a sick person's home. The community meetings, lead by Kastura, continued with increased attendance.

We have summoned you here, Professor, to tell you that we've noticed a positive change in your attitude. Even though you are not per-

227

fect, and perhaps you will never be perfect, as we are, we have decided that perhaps you will be able to continue here a while longer; of course, everything depends on your reaching academic perfection, the way the Theoretical Roman, the Midget Turtle, the Little Koala Bear, the Oneiric Cyclist, the Marxist Pinnacle, the Aristocrat and all the supreme masters of this scholarly institution have; I, Baldy Foureyes, tell you, as a friend, that the stories that you have published have received very good reviews. Nonetheless, we realize your limitations, but in spite of them, and even though you are not perfect, we are going to keep you here a little longer. The university believes that it should and so do we. So you see, we are your friends."

"You aren't doing me any favors; I deserve to be here and I should be here. I know what I have to do and you won't be able to stop me."

"I remember, he was a strange man, different, and at the same time not so strange. He came in a white car; he parked beneath that animal that decorates the big building. I remember that because when he got out of his car he was looking at that thing; he stood there until Pistol Man came up. He was dressed like a hippy, the way the doctor dressed. I don't know who he was or why he came; the only thing I know is that I saw him; I saw him once but I knew instantly that he was an official, at least he had the air of a very powerful man. He talked to Pistol Man for a few minutes and they went into the jail. Once they did that I realized that he was a policeman; we had had a lot of problems with the boys from our neighborhood and with the gringos too. They couldn't stand each other; Doctor Logan had treated several of them who had been stabbed; I wouldn't have helped them; damned kids cause more problems; let them kill themselves. Well, as I was saying, I was sure this gentleman was a policeman. I sat there for a long time, hours maybe; I had to rest because I had had an infection and Doctor Logan told me that I couldn't walk a lot; that's why I was resting. Well, as I was saying, I sat down to rest; I was there two hours; I tried to get up but I couldn't and when I fell I saw Pistol Man and that person leaving the office; the bastard saw me lying in the street and didn't do anything. Those gringo bastards can watch you dying and not do anything; that bastard even laughed; I remember, I remember very well that the son of a bitch laughed; he laughed at me, that's why I remember."

. . . It seems as if the doctor's done very well on his own; Pistol Man said that these people had done everything; it's very, very well done. I'll sit here, on this bench, the young lady thinks I'm another patient.

228

Let her think that, let's see what she says to me. It's almost six o'clock and there are still a lot of people waiting for him. These people look very poor; it would seem that they never wash; dark, ugly; all the little old men are smoking and coughing, their old bodies look like balls of clothing; some of the girls have babies, others don't, they're very young; I wonder what they're doing here? Why do these strong men come? That little boy is really crying, he doesn't want to come in ... that bearded fellow must be Logan ... oh, the puppy; the little boy wants his dog to come in with him; let him come in, don't be mean; if you don't the boy will keep on crying. My puppy, I had one like that too; but it left me, I never had another one. That woman must be Doctor Kastura. But what's she doing in this place? Everyone wants to be a revolutionary; a bunch of over-educated fools without any common sense. The dog's come in, how cute. Here comes Logan ...

"Doctor Logan, please, I've been waiting for an hour; leave the dog alone and listen to me."

"Señora Fernández, you have to be patient. Doctor Kastura will see you right away. Please wait just a little longer."

... Here comes the young woman ...

"Sir, this is your first visit, isn't it?"

"Yes."

"Could you please fill out these forms?"

"No. I'm not a patient. I've come to talk to Doctor Logan. It's an extremely important matter. I realize that Doctor Logan has a lot to do but I have to leave as soon as possible."

"What is your name?"

"Ralph Cramer. Tell him that I'm from the Dallas Department of Health and Education."

"Señorita Teresa, please tell Doctor Logan that I'm tired of waiting."

"Señora Fernández, Doctor Kastura will be with you in just a moment. Excuse me, Mr. Cramer."

... Aha, here comes Kastura. She's pretty; it is a soft, different kind of beauty, the beauty of an intelligent woman. Why did she let herself get stuck out here? I wonder what they're doing to that little boy. The poor thing is screaming now. No one is listening to him, no one is paying attention to what's happening, everyone is talking, they seem to be happy talking about their illnesses, that's all I hear; just illnesses. Everyone is sick. I've never been sick; I live a good life, a life free from impurities. Who's that woman? It's Margarita; Pistol Man talked about her; she's the one who runs the place. The diminutive suffix of her name is a lie. She's a gorgeous woman ...

"You're Mr. Cramer."

"I'm Margarita Avilés de Estrada. They told me that you wanted to talk to Doctor Logan."

"Yes, I want to talk to him."

"Come in to his office, please."

"Thank you."

. . . What an office, it looks as if he uses it as an examination room. The desk is a disaster; you can tell he's very messy. I hate that, you have to have at least some organization . . .

"Good afternoon, Doctor Michael Logan."

"Ralph Cramer."

"You wanted to talk to me?"

"Yes, it's about an extremely urgent matter. I'll be very frank with you; you are our last hope. I'm from the Department of Health and Education in Dallas. For about three months we have been trying to find a doctor who is interested in establishing a medical center for the migrant workers in the region. All the doctors we've talked to have rejected the idea for various reasons. Furthermore, let me repeat, I'll be very frank, we didn't come to speak to you sooner because the doctors that we've seen don't speak well of you and your clinic; they expressed reservations about your professional conduct."

"Oh, yes, how strange. I wouldn't have thought that."

"Well, personally I wasn't satisfied; that's why I came to see you and to observe your clinic. What I have found is a very well organized and efficient office. You have the perfect building for what we want to do. Well, I've come here to offer you a workers' clinic that everyone else has refused. The plan is very simple; the Department of Health and Education guarantees you these funds annually; all you have to do at the end of the year is prove that the money has been spent on patient services and the improvement of patient services. That's all; there's no catch. What do you think, Doctor?"

"I accept."

"You accept? Don't you have any questions?"

"No, if it's as you describe it; I can use the money to hire more doctors, to enlarge the building, to buy more drugs, equipment. We need the money and we'll put it to good use. You're offering me something that I've always wanted; I can't say no. The only thing I beg of you is that you send me the money as quickly as possible."

"Thank you very much, Doctor Logan; the formalities will take several weeks but you'll have it as soon as possible. Here are the forms that you have to sign. In the next few weeks we'll send you some more forms to fill out and sign. The person in charge of your grant is Mr. Ratree Bussarekornserivit; he'll be working directly with you. Thank you again. Now you can dedicate yourself totally to medicine."

"I always have, Mr. Cramer. Thank you very much."

"I'd like to clarify one thing, I'm in Dallas but from now on you'll be working with Mr. Bussarekornserivit."

"Yes, I understand, excuse me but they need me in the other room. Please leave all the papers with Margarita. Goodbye."

"Goodbye, Doctor Logan, thank you."

The white coat disappeared through the door; Margarita pointed to the waiting room. She received the papers. Evans stared at the shoulders, the breasts of the beautiful woman. She looked up at him, interrupting his daydream. Everything was in order. The man turned around, only four eyes were watching him from the empty benches. His feet quickly took him out, impelling him into the night where he vanished in the dust.

"Fernando, sweep the entrance, there's a lot of dust; please vacuum the rug too, Fernando, don't get mad."

"But you knew that everyone was coming today, everything is done at the last minute. Whenever we have company we're in a state of panic, cleaning, picking things up, it's always the same."

"Please don't be angry, I just want you to vacuum the rug."

"All right, but we're not even going to be staying here, we're going to a restaurant that's six miles from here. Michael is going to make an announcement and he wanted to get everyone together."

"What is it?"

"I think it's something about the money they gave him."

"It's about time. He's been sending in forms and talking on the telephone for six weeks."

"Well, that's because they have to be very careful; it's a lot of money you know."

"Francisca, when is Doña Gertrudis coming? I hope you told her to come an hour early because you know that she moves like a snail."

"Here I am you nasty thing; here listening to everything you're saying. I came in through the kitchen. Now, I'll take care of you, Fernando. You just wait and see."

"Oh, Doña Gertrudis, I was only joking."

"You lose respect for me and I'll get you, you scoundrel."

"Francisca, here they come. Come in everyone."

All the bodies came into the house, they exchanged signs of friendship and recognition. The world is a pretty place when you are with your friends. Their bellies were ready for the steak, the beer and the wine, the promised dinner.

"Hey, Michael, did they come through town?"

"Of course."

"Didn't the Anglos, the two-faced congressmen say anything to you? They're furious because you're getting the grant for the center."

"Well, they'll have to get used to it; people get used to everything with time. But now let's eat and drink and forget about the obstacles. I'll confess that I'm really feeling good, and I want to be with you tonight. And I'll confess something else, I think I'll be with Cody, Shane and Jason soon."

"Let's go then, that's really something to celebrate."

All of humanity that mattered to him in those happy moments was to be found in Fernando's police car. Night was falling when they went through town; the blue eyes, and the brown ones, recognized them as they passed, their hatred spit at them, they wanted to expel them but there were now a lot of them, there were a lot of people who had allied themselves with the doctor. He didn't know it, but Kastura had spoken about the matter, it seemed that they would be successful. Kastura mentioned how horrible the animal was that decorated the post office; Fernando, Francisca, Gabriel, Margarita looked past it; the animal saw Logan and did not let him out of its mind.

"Margarita, why didn't Teresa come?"

"Poor girl, it's really going badly for her with Pistol Man. I tell Michael to let her go. She's always fighting with him. And just because she works with us. It's her decision; I don't want to butt into her life."

The conversation continued the whole way. When they got to the restaurant, laughter broke out in the night's clear sky. They went through the doors; they sat down at the table, the sideward glances of the patrons began, the horrible, dangerous mixture of this group, the manager nodded affirmatively to the waiter, they were served beers, wine, and from time to time tequila, the marvelous meal was served with more wine, beer; the coffee came, the brandy came. The discussion rose, the joy raised his voice, he screamed, he declared victory over a feeling hundreds of years old; Logan ordered more wine, more brandy, more tequila. Hours had passed when Francisca and Fernando rose. They said goodbye with warnings about drunkenness, telling Logan not to drink a lot.

"Don't worry; if I'm with you, you'll take me home."

"Gabriel, are the guys coming for you?"

"Yes, Fernando, go ahead. Take care of him. Francisca, watch out for him."

"Good night, Michael, and thanks."

His hand lifted the glass of brandy, a laugh escaped from other mouths that paid no attention. The couple left without being noticed. More drinks came. The songs were shouted; the pointless discussions only inspired laughter, guffaws. Logan slowly got up and emerged on the outside shouting in his drunkenness, arguing with the stars about what was philosophical about his situation. He screamed that he thought he saw the purpose of his work, that for the first time in his life he had really achieved a valuable goal. Inside, the conversation continued; they talked about the possibilities of guaranteed money that Logan had announced that night. In a few days the money would be transferred to Logan in a bank in Corpus; the formalities had been completed, the money was certain, and Logan was celebrating outside, out of control, drunk, he raised his hand and began to shoot blanks at the sky; inside the laughter at the jokes continued, the wine was passed around again; the manager wanted to choke them, furious, he dialed the numbers.

"I don't care, he's good and drunk and he started shooting a pistol. Come and get the Mexican greaser-lover. Come soon or I'll kick them out myself; I shouldn't have let them in. I knew that this was going to happen; it always does with these bastards."

Logan, leaning against a car, tried to spit and white saliva stuck in his beard; his stomach pushed the sourness upward; he vomited on the car. Inside the voices shouted with anger, the manager made them leave, he did not want money from Mexicans, and they should never come back because he would kick them out. The women held back Gabriel who wanted to pound the man's red face. The police car wailed as it approached the absurd nebulousness of drunkenness. Outside they were yelling at the manager; they talked to Logan, they encouraged him to get up, they swore at their friends who had not come, they shouted curses at the manager; their eyes perceived the red lights of the screaming police car; their eyes were blinded by the strong white and yellow lights of the car that skidded, screeching, covering them with dust as it stopped, nearly hitting them. The police car's motor was running.

"Hey, Pistol Man, it's about time; that bastard threw us out, the bastard refused our money."

"Gabriel, against the car. And you two as well. You too, Michael. Right now."

His hand and arm grabbed the sick man and threw him against the car. He searched the men and women.

"OK, who's got it? Where is it Logan, where is it?"

"What? What? What? Takkke meee homme."

"He doesn't know anything, can't you see that he's really out of it? Leave him alone, Pistol Man, let him be."

"Don't you get into this, Gabriel!"

"What the fuck are you looking for?"

"The pistol."

"What pistol, bastard?"

"The manager called and said that Logan was shooting."

"He was outside here, he didn't shoot inside. Your damned pistol must be lying around here, you idiot, look for it."

"Where is it, Logan?"

"Takkke me homme . . ."

"Look, there it is, in front of your car."

"Thank you very much, Kastura."

The handcuffs appeared; he pushed, Logan fell face down on the ground; his arms were pulled behind his back, he cried out in pain, the handcuffs were put on him and another sharp cry was heard.

"Don't hurt him; the handcuffs are too tight."

"Get out of the way, Margarita."

He pushed her and then opened the door of the burning police car.

"Why are you taking him? He didn't do anything; don't be a bastard, Pistol Man, don't be like that."

"We'll take him home; leave him here."

"No, this idiot is going to pay me now. Look, here I have the pistol and for carrying it without a permit it's going to cost him a pretty penny. And the restaurant manager says he's willing to testify that Logan threatened him. Here's your damned hero; look at him drooling like a hopeless drunk; he doesn't even know what's going on."

"You bastard, I'm going to break you with my own hands."

The fist flew with confidence splitting Gabriel's lips; he found himself spitting blood on Margarita's dress as she tried to help him up. Pistol Man grabbed Logan by the arm and forced him into the back seat of the police car. As he got in, the doctor's head bumped against the door, breaking the skin on his forehead. The seated body fell, fainting, it slipped sideways. The burning police car left weaving in and out of the sandy earth that flew up to cover the three of them who were left there alone. In the car the two of them sped off at an alarming pace.

"Now, you were really there, Doctor. I told you from the beginning that you should leave, but no, you insisted on staying, on making trouble for everyone. You should have gone with your wife, you'd be better off there with your children. What would they say now? Look at the shape you're in, Doctor. You idiot, you've made a lot of problems for me, you stupid educated bastard, you think you know it all, you miserable bastard."

"Ohh, ooh, it hurtts, oh, Cody, Cody, Cooddyy, Sha . . . Sha . . ."

"You can't even talk, bastard, shut up, shut up your educated fool mouth."

. . . Blood, I'm swallowing blood . . . wrist, no wrist, blood . . . Cody, Codyy, at hoomme . . . aay my head's hurt . . . blooddd . . . forgiive, forgive me. . . .

"Pistooolll."

"Shut up, bastard, be quiet I said."

"Cody, I love Coddyy. Forgive, forgive me, Margarita. Where, wheree . . ."

"If you don't keep quiet, I'll break your mouth. Shut up!"

"Kasturaaa, I need, ooh, it hurtss."

"Shut up, shut up! Don't you hear me, you bastard, I'm yelling at you, shut your mouth! Be quiet!"

"Forgive me, ple . . . please, it hurts, Te Teresa. Aaayyyee!"

The groans joined with the screech of the police car's tires as it turned on the highway, the mind that saw the doctor mounted like a dog, penetrating the vagina and the anus of the innocent girl was no longer capable of making sense. He saw her turn her head, the feminine face was laughing at him; he saw the doctor's prick full of the feminine excrement of the girl he loved. He saw her lick his penis, eat the educated doctor's balls, he could imagine nothing else, his rage opened the door, he fell, grunting inhuman sounds; his hand reached the other door, the open, fuming police car made the doctor, who had come to his senses, afraid; the animal clawed him as it dragged him out, the fists exploded time after time, he heard constant blows in a place in his brain, the bleeding wrists, he wanted to save himself, constant screams were heard in another part of the brain; blackness, there was no light, he sat on his foot.

"I won't forgive you for this! Here, take that!"

"Oh! Oh! aaaahh!"

His body felt the sharp pain in his stomach, his feet fumbled trying to find the ground that slipped beneath them, he lost his right shoe, his body twisted, mouth up, his feet and legs pushed the loose earth, making his head move forward, distancing himself from Pistol Man, crazy, bloodied, wet.

"Don't go! Bastard, don't leave! I haven't finished with you!"

His feet and legs took on the strength of his battered body that went farther away from Pistol Man, who had the Magnum three fifty-seven in his hand; the stretched-out body's eye was paralyzed; he continued moving away from Pistol Man, his shuttered mouth could not articulate . . . nn . . . vaa, uaa, aaaa, nnnnnnnnn . . .

"Don't try to escape! Don't move or I'll shoot!"

Boom. Boom.

The sum was subtracted into an integer of secrecy.

III

He had arrived at the new office physically tired; he felt his spirit enlarged by a job well done; he always had to do it well because that was the way he was, everything neatly finished, perfect. The new secretary came in telling him the schedule for the new day; she finished her song with a note stating that the Mexican president would call in a few minutes. The executive got up, drew his body near the table where his cup was waiting, empty; he lifted up the coffee pot and filled the cup, he sat down again in front of the beautiful, elegant desk, to wait for the dark-skinned man's call. The instants, the seconds, and the minutes passed but in a coffin they are not counted. The buzz of the telephone announced the head of state.

"Listen, Evans, how are you? I just spoke to the President. It seems as if everything has been successfully resolved."

"Good morning, sir. You're right. I didn't expect it to turn out this way; however, as you said, sir, it has all turned out perfectly for everyone."

"We're here, the enigmas are being solved by themselves. The situation with Casimiro no longer exists. He was found dead in a canyon near his village. They told me he died of hunger, that he seemed to be trying to find his village. Strange, isn't it? A man like him not being able to find his own village; that's what hunger can do to you; it makes you lose all sense of direction. Now we're going to squash those urban guerrillas who insist on continuing to fight. We won't take long to find them; it will be easy with the new arms that you are sending us and the death of that fellow will put a stop or at least hold up the arms shipments to the rebels. Well done, Evans; you'll know very soon how grateful I am for jobs well done. Goodbye, my friend."

"Yes, goodbye, thank you."

He got up; he took the cup; he looked outside, the cloudy day made him return to where the coffee was. He called in the secretary, she came in and he took a good look at her. He was a perfectionist, he liked things to be well organized: . . . Organization, that's what these people need; but they don't have it, a demonstration is all they expect and then nothing. A few shouts and then silence, not even the newspapers, nothing, absolutely nothing. What a beautiful woman; she seems to be very smart . . .

"Look, Miss, I don't even know your name."

"Who are you? Identify yourself."

"Bastards, they don't even know us! You represent us and you don't even know who we are. You see, not even your damned elected representatives know you!"

"Calm down, Gabriel. Please, calm down!"

"I don't want to calm down, we've been calm and look what they've done."

"I'm Kastura and these people are friends of Doctor Logan's; they've come to protest the assassination."

"Let's burn the ugly damned building!"

"Yes, burn it!"

"Destroy it all!"

"No, stay calm; we want you to respond to our questions. We can agree on that, can't we?"

"Let Kastura speak."

"Don't mess it up, Fernando, we're fed up with dialogue and rhetoric. That's what they want to hear from us, violence, so they can suppress us more, squash us and put an end to our organization. Don't you see their plan?"

"Let Kastura speak; let her explain."

"First we want to express the fact that the people do not agree with the report issued by the police department. We believe that Logan did not attack Pistol Man and that Pistol Man did not act in self defense. There are several witnesses who have declared that the doctor was so inebriated that he could hardly stand up; he was incapable of attacking anyone. Furthermore, he didn't feel well; he had vomited. Also, why couldn't Pistol Man who is bigger and stronger than the doctor, why couldn't he subdue him? He could have done it easily when he took him from the restaurant, furthermore he had handcuffed him. And how do you explain that the doctor was brutally beaten? Haven't you seen his deformed face? It's evident that Pistol Man beat him before he killed him. And why haven't they let us see Pistol Man's police car? Why is he not to be found in town? And where is Pistol Man now? We know that he took Teresa and the whole family. Why isn't he in prison or at least why didn't they detain him here in Mathis until after the witnesses had been examined. The people insist that these questions be clarified immediately or they will be forced to take stronger and more direct action."

"Chicanos, listen to me, I'm de la Sorre, the representative that you have elected. I know; I am sorry about your loss and I promise you that justice will be done. But to achieve it we have to follow the processes established by the democratic system in which we all believe. You have to believe me; I promise you that justice will be done; and if there is a guilty party responsible for this terrible death, that individual will serve the appropriate sentence as dictated by the legal process."

"Pure bullshit!"

"Fuck you, you damned sellout!"

"Your mother will pay for it!"

"I beg you to be calm; I know that you're angry about what has happened. But look, if you start to burn buildings, the only thing you're going to achieve is a powerful reaction on the part of the government. They'll send the National Guard. We don't want that. Don't force us to do that! Please, listen to me! Please!"

"Please, Cody, Shane and Jason are with us; they're with Eutemio; he's taking care of them. Your parents will come soon; I talked to them. Cody, they know what has happened. Please get dressed, it's cold and you're going to get sick. For your children, Cody, please get dressed."

"No, I'm waiting for Michael; he told me that he was going to come back. I love him; he told me he loved me."

"Michael can't come back; he's no longer with us; he can no longer come. You have to realize what has happened. The children know now; we know, your parents; we've cried a lot. You should cry. Why don't you cry, Cody? Cody, cry, please cry and then you can get dressed. Cody, cry! Cry, Cody!"

"No, I'm waiting for Michael! He told me that he was coming back!"

"I remember the wake very well. They came from all over to see him, to pray for him. Oh, may God keep him in heaven. I remember when they brought the coffin; I was there, a plain coffin, we thought that that was what he would have wanted. He was a very simple man. The whole neighborhood was there, they came to say goodbye to the doctor. I remember, I remember that they loved him a lot; I brought him Margarita and Felipe and he loved them, he loved her and the boy too; I remember that I loved him a lot; but it's difficult to remember his face now; sometimes I see him; sometimes I make a great effort to see his bearded face; I just have a blurry image of his face; that's the worst thing; the worst, not being able to remember. But how they had beaten him; they had dressed him very well; with his blue pinstripe suit; but even with makeup they couldn't hide the black and blue marks on his face. Everyone came except his family, his wife and children; yes, it's better for them to remember their daddy the way he was, when they used to play with him. Yes, it's better that way. I don't know why Pistol Man beat him so badly. He left; he took Teresa and the children and he left; they don't know where he is. The officials said that he was waiting for the legal process. That he had made his declaration and that was all, and he left. Oh, the poor children the doctor left! The young wife! Pretty, very pretty, she's alone! Why do we do these things to each other, just to make our hearts heavier? Why didn't they kill me? Kill old Gertrudis! I don't want to witness these things! Oh, I remember, yes, I remember that I loved him."

One afternoon, outside the house, Eutemio watched the children shouting, laughing, and running happily. Shane's beautiful face suddenly turned and she stared softly at him; suddenly her eyes were sad. Her little brother's call made her run to his side and she forgot again. Eutemio kept watching them. . . . That's how children are, my children. It's painful for me to know that they are going to hurt me; they'll make me laugh, loving them as much as I do fills me with happiness. And we make them cry . . . Michael, you'll never see your children grown; let them become good people, let them be great people for you, because you were a great person. And I had promised to go and see you. You were better than everyone, Michael; better than the doctors who condemned you; better than the wisemen of the university who do nothing and think they are so superior. You were a man of action, you learned how to know life and to live it. You won't see your children grow up. I love them Michael, because I loved you and I never went to see you. Why did they do this to you? Why did they separate us? And I never had time to go and see you. I never had time!. . .

It was drizzling on the earth and on the crowd that was taking the doctor to his final home. They went through the muddy streets of the barrio, through the center of Mathis walking toward the cemetery. Hales, Martínez, Rodríguez, Margarita, Gabriel, and Kastura carried the coffin to the cemetery . . . What an idealist, what an idealist, look how you ended up . . .

. . . If you had come to work with us you'd be sitting pretty, Michael, why didn't you understand that? Why didn't you understand?. . .

. . . I'll be the sheriff now; we'll insist on it; and some day Pistol Man will pay for it. You'll see, Michael, some day, some day. Why can't we be ourselves? Really, Michael, why can't we be ourselves?

. . . I've lost you, I've lost you, I've lost you, I've lost you, Michael. Why did I lose you?

. . . The bastards always fuck us; they always win, they win all the time, they're always right, I'm tired of it, I don't know what I'm going to do. Forgive me, Michael, forgive me. It was my fault! Forgive me!

. . . Michael, you're not so heavy, you're not so heavy. Your work will go on; I promise you that; your work will go on . . .

Hundreds upon hundreds arrived and followed him to his new home. Young Doctor Logan was the first Anglo to ever be buried in the Chicano cemetery of Mathis, Texas.

. . . It's incredible; today it was stated that Pistol Man acted in self-defense. Nonetheless, due to the circumstances they asked for Pistol Man's resignation. And then the bastard Anglos and the sellouts on the City Council voted unanimously to change the name of Mathis's main street to Michael Logan Avenue. And is that all? Are we satisfied with that?. . .

The children were asleep. Leti was with Cody. The professor lay down on the sofa, he crossed his hands; he pretended to be dead, because that was how Michael was at that moment, at that instant. He felt hatred, great hatred, a rage that he knew he had to control: . . . Is that all? Is that all that Michael Logan's life is worth? Are they going to keep us quiet with that? Shit! We're so stupid! In a month no one will know anything about it. They killed and nothing will be done about it. It can't be allowed. I'm not going to forget him; I'm not going to allow it . . .

He got up, and walked around the room with his fists clenched, he walked in a circle, trying to calm himself down; he went to the table where the typewriter was. He became calmer; he sat down; his fingers' alphabet hardly felt the keys, one struck one letter, then another, another and Professor Morenito began to write: *Death of an Anglo*.